FORBIDDEN ROAD

CONNIE J. JASPERSON

TOWER OF BONES II

Copyright © 2015 Connie J. Jasperson
All rights reserved. Except as permitted under the U.S. Copyright Act of 1976, no part of this publication may be reproduced, distributed or transmitted in any form or by any means, or stored in a database or retrieval system without the prior written permission of the author or publisher.

This is a work of fiction. Names, characters, places and incidents are products of the author's imagination or are used fictitiously and are not to be construed as real. Any resemblance to actual events, locales, organizations, or persons, living or deceased, is entirely coincidental.

ISBN-13: **9781680630152**
ISBN-10: **168063015**

First Edition August 2013
Second Edition May 2015

Graphics © Connie J. Jasperson
Fantasy Ruins 2 © Unholyvault | Dreamstime.com
Map of Neveyah © Connie J. Jasperson

Special thanks to Eagle Eye Editors
www.eagleeyeeditors.me

Published by Bard Books
In association with
Myrddin Publishing Group
Contact us at - www.myrddinpublishing.com

A SUBSIDIARY OF MYRDDIN PUBLISHING GROUP

DEDICATION

This book is dedicated to the memory of my parents who would have been so proud to see my work published. Mom, you had faith in my scribbles and encouraged me to pursue writing even when times were hard and I could see no way before me. Dad, your endless supply of tall tales, your music, and your ferocious love of life despite the difficulties inspired me more than I ever admitted. I was fortunate to grow up in an eccentric family!

This book has been through several incarnations, and wouldn't exist without the tireless efforts of Carlie M.A. Cullen, Maria V. A. Johnson, Irene Roth Luvaul, Sherrie Degraw, Leah Reindl, Daniel Riffero, Margaret Clear, Greg Jasperson, and Alison DeLuca.

BOOKS BY CONNIE J. JASPERSON

WORLD OF NEVEYAH
Tower of Bones (Tower of Bones series book I)
Forbidden Road (Tower of Bones series book II)
Mountains of the Moon (forthcoming July 2015)

HUW THE BARD

TALES FROM THE DREAMTIME

Chapter 1 ~ Mage-Duel

Edwin entered the practice yard, still clutching the note from Father Rall instructing him to attend. He never worked out during his healing shifts. He was uncomfortable displaying his battle-mage abilities but couldn't ignore the instructions to clear his calendar. The big question was why. Still, he buried his annoyance under a polite smile as he passed through the viewing area to the dressing room.

What's Father Rall up to? His stomach churned. *He knows I don't indulge in the endless, stupid dueling for position in the Temple everyone seems to adore. I don't have anything to prove. I am a healer, for the love of Aeos. Everyone knows healers don't duel.* Edwin obeyed the Holy Father's wishes, despite his irritation with the situation. *I hope he's not betting on me.* It was apparent Father Rall was planning a mage-duel, but it didn't make sense. Edwin never participated in duels. His skills as a healer-adept were all he cared to display.

Rall Ivarsson had occupied the Holy Seat for nearly twenty years. A gentle, kindly, giant of a man, Rall had once been the Temple Armsmaster and was well known for his love of wagering on the outcome of mage-duels. *I'm sure he's betting on one of us.* Edwin tried not to feel bitter about the situation.

Friedr Freysson, a fire-mage, was instructing a class of second-year novice healers in defending themselves with the staff and appeared to be about done with his class. Edwin noted Friedr wore his red leathers instead of the brown ones he normally wore for teaching, although he was still wearing his general-purpose brown-lacquered armor. *Friedr must be my opponent. He knows what we're doing today, and he didn't warn me.*

Edwin saw the humor in the situation—usually he knew everything first, but not this time. Now he felt more resigned than irritated, and his temporary storm of angst passed. With some chagrin, he realized he had been manipulated by the master of all manipulators—kindly, formidable Father Rall. The only reason Edwin could fathom for this display was Father Rall must have had another true-dream and this was necessary for some greater purpose.

Zan Christophson was geared up and waiting for his turn to receive abuse from Friedr. He waved at Edwin, who smiled and waved back.

Edwin was the only air-mage in the Temple, and as such, he was a most accomplished battle-mage. Unlike other healers, Edwin was a master swordsman, although few people were aware of it. The common teachings of the Temple decreed the two magics, healing-magic and battle-magic, could not exist with equal strength in one person because they were opposites. Yet they did coexist with equivalent potency in Edwin, creating a never-before-seen aspect, newly named air-magic. Air-magic combined all four of the elements with healing empathy, making Edwin the most formidable battle-mage in the Temple when it came to spells and swords.

He pulled his hair back and plaited it into a thick braid, fastening the end with a leather thong. It felt unnatural to reveal his tattoos or *augmentations* as they were known in the Temple. He wasn't ashamed of them. Very little ever embarrassed Edwin. He concealed them because they did not belong exclusively to a healer. It unnerved his patients to see the marks of an assassin on him, so he only wore his hair back to spar with Friedr. When he'd first arrived in Aeoven as a young journeyman, Friedr took him to be fitted for his first armor, which he was now wearing. Even though he'd not been fully augmented at the time it was commissioned for him, the smith-mages were surprised by his conflicting augmentations.

Edwin was the only battle-mage whose individually bespelled armor was such a deep midnight blue that at first glance it was nearly black. Black was the color of the assassins' guild's special stealth armor, which they never wore in public. Even more unusually, his armor sported random placements of lacquered green leaves outlined in gold. No other battle-mage had ever been given green on their armor. Green was the healer's color, and only they wore green armor, in shades that varied individually.

From the sounds outside the men's dressing room, an audience was gathering. The tiers of benches surrounding the practice yard were filling up. He tied his bandanna around his forehead so sweat wouldn't blind him, though he rarely worked up a sweat anymore. Knowing he had an audience put him off balance and, trying to settle his stomach, he grounded and centered himself. *Father Rall must have a reason. He does nothing without good reason.* The thought reassured him somewhat but didn't take the edge off his nerves.

When Edwin opened the door from the men's dressing room into the viewing area, he nearly turned back. The overwhelming sense of too many people crammed into the tiers made him wish for nothing more than to lock the door against them. *Firm up your barriers, idiot! You know better than this.* Composing himself, Edwin passed through the gathering crowd, pretending not to see the astonishment on many faces, answering surprised greetings as he wove his way through the crowd.

He was absolutely the last person they expected to see enter the practice yard in full battle-dress. The comments rippled through the tiers as they continued filling. "There are green leaves on his armor. Look, that battle-mage has green on his armor! Do you see his augmentations?" Also, "Edwin. It's Edwin Farmer! I thought he was a healer." or "Who is that? I don't recognize him."

What's the entire abbacy doing here? Is that Elis, come all the way from Bannoc? Edwin suddenly remembered it was the winter conclave so of course the abbacy was all in attendance, but he also realized this match had been planned weeks ago, and it worried him. He comprehended that his reaction to the element of surprise was part of the Holy Father's devious plan, and now he wondered what else was in store for him.

He entered the shielded practice yard through the gate, closed it behind him, checking the ties and strength of the shield as was his habit, making sure no magic would rebound out of the area. He'd set it himself so it was maintained by the natural chi from the packed earth of the practice yard.

Friedr waited with Zander Christophson. Edwin knew Zan socially, of course. He was their friend Christoph Berryman's adopted son. Still, Edwin had never worked with him, as Zan was a very young journeyman battle-mage and had only recently returned from his first posting.

The two had apparently just finished a brief tutorial, and the younger mage was obviously tired and winded, though Friedr hadn't even broken a sweat. Physically, Zan was like his cousin Dane, who was Christoph's bonded life-partner. He was tall, dark-haired, dark-eyed, and mercurial, but while Dane was a healer, Zan's main strength was lightning, as demonstrated by his augmentations. However, they also proclaimed his ability in all of the other elements.

"Hello, Edwin, do you know Zander?" Friedr's innocent smile immediately put Edwin on his guard. "He's the son of Christoph Berryman and Dane Bransson."

Smiling broadly, Edwin shook Zan's hand. "Oh my. A formal introduction for the crowd. This little workout must be something serious," Edwin remarked as he also clasped Friedr's shoulder. "I know him rather well actually." His forced cheeriness was not too noticeable, at least not to anyone in the crowd. He said in low tones, "This is turning into a circus. What's going on that I don't know about?"

"I don't know. I was just told to be here," Zan returned Edwin's clasp and smile. "I put in my bid to join you on your quest. I've been using every trick in the book to get them to choose me." His smile was warm and sincere, but he was obviously taken aback by the stealth runes that rode just behind Edwin's earlobes, and his eyes betrayed his uncertainty.

"You've not been practicing. If you're chosen, you'll be practicing daily with Edwin, Christoph, and me. Every member of this team must be most proficient with his weapon, or I'll want to know why." Friedr's words made Zan flinch, although he tried not to show it.

Seeing Zan's embarrassment, Edwin admitted, "I suffer daily at Friedr's hands." Edwin cast spells for healing on the suffering young mage, drawing the surprised attention of the healers among the throng gathering in the tiers. Dressed as he was and with his augmentations bared, many of them did not recognize he was Edwin Farmer, who worked with them daily. "Most of my battle strength is in air-magic and fetching. It'd be good to have a strong lightning-mage to round us out. Our Friedr is lethal with his fire spells."

"Ah, thank you for the healing. I'd heard you were also a battle-mage, but I didn't realize it until now. I know nothing of air-magic or this 'fetching.' I've never heard of it." Zan, whose frank gaze took in all of Edwin's visible augmentations, knew full well what they implied, but not what he should make of them. "Your prodigious healing skills are what most people mention about you, that and the esoteric theories in shielding that upset the older clergy. But my father, Christoph, quested with you. Why didn't I ever hear of this?"

"As far as I know, I'm the only one in the Temple who's an air-mage. I prefer to work as a healer. But why *would* you know this? You've been in the novice barracks and then away on your journeyman posting," Edwin reminded him, secretly casting a calming spell to ease his confusion. "You've not been around much, and most lightning-mages don't notice a lot going on around them anyway."

"That's true. I'm terribly self-centered," Zander admitted wryly. "If I didn't hear my own name mentioned, I probably didn't notice it."

At last, Friedr was fully geared up in his red-lacquered armor, his bandanna tied about his forehead. He spoke quietly to Edwin. "About your theory regarding the way shielding is taught—the abbacy will be believers after today. Father Rall has decreed we're to demonstrate a few of our special moves. I've asked Zan to stay and watch us so he can get an idea of what we do before he finally commits to this mad quest. If he decides to continue, we'll give him a private session on shielding after we're done."

"A good idea," Edwin replied heartily, sensing Friedr had something ugly planned. He mentally sighed, saying aloud for the benefit of the audience as well as for Zan, "Well then, Friedr, have you regained your strength from dancing swords with Zan?" He healed Friedr, casting the spells to make him fully rested so Edwin had no unfair advantage in their upcoming sparing match.

Friedr gazed at him with the flat look he had perfected. "That was an unnecessary waste of your chi, Edwin Farmer. I was perfectly well rested. Everyone knows that." A snicker rippled through the throng at his expense, and he glared at them.

"Hmm, right. So, you're planning to make my wife a widow and leave my son fatherless today." Edwin's wry grin lit up his candid, blue eyes as he added, "I'll just tighten my gear a wee bit better. Can't have anything flying off, since you're obviously out to teach me a lesson in humility." Zan's face betrayed surprise and curiosity at this exchange.

Friedr snorted again, saying loudly, "So tighten your gear, farm boy, for all the good it'll do you. We're done playing games—*this* time, I'm going to kick your backside around the yard."

Edwin's trademark smile illuminated his face as he replied, "That's what you always say, barbarian." His retort was also said for the benefit of the crowd. "Don't worry. I'll heal your poor, bruised butt afterward." He patted Friedr's shoulder and crossed the yard to take his place, calling over his shoulder, "I'll try not to hurt you too badly."

Friedr shuddered inwardly, dreading the damage his reputation was about to receive. Edwin was already smiling that obscenely cheerful smirk, which meant he suspected what Friedr had planned and was prepared with some devastating new trick. He squared his shoulders and began the lesson Father Rall had asked him to give to the Temple at large today.

The growing crowd was hushed, expectant. People were still squeezing into the viewing area.

Friedr turned to the journeyman, speaking for the audience's ears. "Zander Christophson, you'll stand over here out of the way but where you'll be handy."

Friedr directed him to where he wanted him positioned. "We'll now begin your lesson in shielding. Raise your shields, Zan," Friedr called loudly, "You have been taught the traditional method, and you're considered to have the most excellent shielding ability of all the journeymen currently in the Temple. Use the basic shield and the standard elemental battle shield you were so carefully taught to the best of your ability. Do *not* under any circumstances drop them. Keep raising them, and if they fail, get out of the way immediately." Warily, Zander raised his basic shield and primed his elemental shields for use as needed, wondering what they were about to do.

Friedr's voice rang, "Remember what I told you. At some point, you'll be asked to do something you'll consider strange. You're to do exactly as you're asked when you're asked to do it, no matter how strange the request seems." Zan nodded his head but clearly did not understand.

Bowing to the audience and then to each other, Friedr and Edwin began by sparring with weapons only and gradually increased the tempo as they ran through the warmup exercises. The crowd buzzed as their practice swords flashed in a display of skill that left Zan breathless. By the time they were fully warmed up, both Edwin and Friedr had forgotten about the audience.

After a few minutes, Friedr suddenly fired off a devastating combo of fire and water, his best steam attack, and immediately followed up with the physical attack. The audience groaned. Many were sure Edwin was already defeated and were wondering why they had been summoned to the conclave a week early. Some had traveled for more than a week to witness this mage-duel, at Father Rall's orders.

Edwin allowed the fire to roll off his shields and then sent the boiling water back to Friedr with a bit of earth mixed in to form a boiling mud attack, bleeding enough water off so it was not quite strong enough to break his shields. Friedr's shields bowed under the super-heated mud. He was temporarily blinded, but his shields held and the boiling mud slid off. The onlookers gasped, and many now cried out in fear for Friedr's life, but Friedr plowed through it, parrying Edwin's physical assault. Still sparring in between spells with their swords, they lobbed spells back and forth and did it all without missing a step.

The onlookers were awed by the strength and infallibility of Edwin's shields, amazed they were not crushed and destroyed in the first volley. No matter what Friedr threw at him, his shields never buckled or even bowed, standing rock solid before the most intense combos Friedr was famous for. Even more disturbing to the experienced battle-mages, Edwin seized the magic Friedr threw at him and returned it in concentrated assaults, keeping Friedr dancing. While Friedr's shields held and did not break, they were obviously not quite as firm as Edwin's. Edwin's return volleys were carefully calculated and just shy of breaking Friedr's shields. Most of the magic's strength he quickly bled off before sending it back, causing the crowd to gasp again.

Many tenured seniors commented on the way the two combatants, and most particularly Edwin, had retained such vast reserves of chi despite the magic flying and rebounding all over the practice ground. None of them had ever seen the use and reuse of magic in the ways they were seeing it now. Some spells bounced back and forth several times before being allowed to dissipate. Each time an element came back to him, Edwin reshaped it and returned it in a different form, whereas Friedr did not reshape it but did return it with as much force as he could muster. Edwin's ability to quickly concentrate and reshape the rebounding magic and redirect it efficiently back at Friedr was mentioned by several people, "Did you see that? How did he do it?"

Zan saw Friedr redirect the magic back to Edwin, and though it was unfocused compared to Edwin's reflected magic, it was still deadly. He frantically raised shield after shield, wondering, *How are they doing this? This is madness!*

It was a rare thing to see a full-on mage-duel, especially when one as skilled as Friedr was so hard-pressed in a battle. Usually, duelers were limited to the element of water. Many battle-mages were shaken by Edwin's ferocity and skill with the sword, and many were simply aghast at his speed. Predictably, the knot of senior healers did not appear at all surprised as they had worked with him since he came to Neveyah, though the journeymen all stared at him, stunned.

Edwin and Friedr battled back and forth. The sheer aggressive power of their physical attacks and the use of their shields to turn their opponent's magic back on each other was a radical departure from the normal sparring match between professionals in the Temple hierarchy. Only now were most of the stunned senior clergy in the crowd beginning to understand Edwin Farmer's radical theories on shielding were in fact the most important thing to happen to battle-magic in a thousand years. The tiers were full of mages who felt chagrin at their own inflexibility. "We mocked him and didn't give his suggestions any credence," murmured an older mage from Braden. "I fear I owe him an apology."

The combatants separated and circled, each looking for an opening. They launched vicious combos at each other, pressing forward with their weapons, neither one ready to give up, though Friedr was sweating heavily. They continued in this fashion until it gradually dawned on Edwin that Friedr was not going to send him any lightning. Most particularly, he did not return any of the lightning Edwin fired off at him, simply letting it crackle off his shields.

Zan's eyes popped as Edwin casually fired off a lightning spell known as a thunder-fist. *Why did he say they need a lightning-mage? He has as much strength in that element as I do, maybe more.*

Others had noticed Friedr had not used any lightning, and they knew he had some strength in it. "They have Zan stationed there for some reason, but for what I can't imagine." The mutters ran through the crowd.

Friedr had deliberately worked his way around so his back was to Zan. He concentrated on dancing over Edwin's earth attacks and then pressing his own physical attack. Zan switched his elemental shields extremely quickly but not fast enough to keep up with the spells flying back and forth, and it had not gone unnoticed by the senior clergy. Zan's mentor, Father Rall's son Kalen, remarked dryly that Zander had always had the best ability with shields in his group until today.

His wife, a fire-mage adept named Gayla, replied, "But really, Kalen, who of us could keep up with those two madmen firing round after round and combos like that? I surely can't, and I'm far better at shielding than you or your journeyman. But of course, they have fought D'Mal himself and are here to tell about it."

From the corner of his eye, Edwin could see Zander standing amazed at the intensity of this exchange, and tossing up elemental shields as fast as he could, and not really keeping up with the rapid exchange of elemental magic. Edwin layered a full shield over him, tied it off, and began looking for an opportunity to bring Zan into the fight. Friedr nodded at him when he saw Edwin shielding Zan. *He wants me to get Zan into this to see if he'll be frightened off.*

Zan's eyes widened as he felt Edwin shielding him and immediately began examining it.

Friedr was beginning to look a little winded, relying more and more on magic. *Time to step it up,* Edwin said to himself, dodging and then pressing forward. Using his wind-magic to speak to Zan while returning Friedr's fiery volley took a little concentration, but he was well able to do it. *"Zan! Hit me with a cat-zapper,"* Edwin whispered on the wind for Zan's ears alone. *"Just do it!"*

Zander started and looked around him to see who had said it. Surprised, he looked at Edwin with one eyebrow raised. Clearly, he was not sure he had heard him correctly. Edwin nodded encouragingly, and Zan looked at Edwin, eyes wide open in surprise. *"Do it!"* Edwin winked at him, smiling, and not missing a beat, easily returning Friedr's assaults. *"I just need a little cat-zapper. Aren't you curious?"*

Shrugging his doubt about Edwin's sanity and completely afire with curiosity, he muttered, "All right, but it's your funeral. Hope your shields are up to facing off against two mages firing at once against you." Zan had always been taught a mage couldn't fight two mages at one time and shield himself properly because shields could not be changed fast enough to keep up with the different elements.

Zan fired off the low-level bolt known in the trade as a cat-zapper at Edwin, clearly wondering if he was about to get fried for stepping into the battle solely on the perceived whisper of one of the combatants. A cat zapper was a small enough spell and took little chi for the average mage.

Friedr had just released another fire-spell, and his look of dismay was comical.

Edwin snatched the lightning Zan cast at him and bled off half its strength, concentrating it. Instantly wrapping the fire Friedr just cast around his lightning in a dizzying spiral, Edwin formed it into a needle and fired it at the base of Friedr's shields faster than anything Zan had ever seen in his life. The crowd gasped as one.

Diving out of the way as his shields went down amid a spectacular, blazing shower of sparks and a cloud of dust, Friedr rolled and then sat up. Dead silence reigned as he shouted, "You dog! I hate it when you do that." He leaned back on his hands, but his glare was ruined by his proud, paternal smile.

The crowd erupted into thunderous cheers and applause, taking Edwin, Zan, and Friedr by surprise. Edwin's stomach lurched as he saw many of his patients in the crowd. *Oh dear Goddess, I'm ruined now. My career as a healer is over.*

Chapter 2 ~ **Enlightening the Abbacy**

Edwin dropped his shields and lowered his sword. Numbly following the etiquette of the arena, he bowed to the cheering throng of enthusiastic onlookers. On rising, he saw his father in the crowd talking to Abbott Garran, who wore his old-style fringed red leathers, having obviously just arrived in Aeoven. Edwin's father was dressed similarly, but in ancient turquoise leathers. The unique sword Edwin had heard about but never seen was belted to his side. He waved a greeting to Edwin and gestured for him to continue with his teaching exercise. *"See you later, Dad."* He sent the whisper to his father, who gave him a stunned look but nodded.

Edwin walked over to Friedr, offering his hand to help him up, to the cheers of the onlookers. "Aw...you wouldn't have withheld your lightning if you hadn't wanted me to get Zan involved. You and the powers-that-be set this up for that purpose." He smiled at Friedr's sweaty red face, knowing he was right.

Friedr nodded his head, grinning. "I knew you'd figure it out when I didn't send you any lightning." He dusted off his leathers, still trying to get his breath back. "The College of Warcraft has never seen anything like that, I'll bet."

"Probably not." Edwin's healing-senses quickly checked Friedr over to make sure he was not seriously injured, healing his bruises and contusions, to the applause of the healers in the crowd. A wide-eyed young healer named Rena, who was Edwin's current upper-level novice assistant, then cast heal on Edwin, though he did not need it. He bowed to her and smiled his thanks, wondering how he would explain this display to her.

Edwin and Friedr turned to see a completely dumbstruck Zander warily observing this exchange. His fire shields were up, and his weapon was ready, but the look on his face was comical. "Please don't hurt me, Friedr!" He clearly expected Friedr to dismember him. "I'm sorry, but you did tell me to do what I was asked." Edwin had to place a damper on his urge to laugh at Zan, and his grin betrayed his amusement.

"Oh, stop it. Lower your weapon and relax, you idiot." Friedr's remark was not comforting. "I told you to do what you were asked, no matter how strange, and you did it well." Zan lowered his sword but left his fire shield up. Friedr rolled his eyes. "I promise not to hurt you. I'm a big boy now, and I'm quite used to finding myself face down in the dirt, thanks to Edwin Farmer. I do it every day, just not usually in front of everyone." As if reluctantly, Zander's fire shield faded.

"Edwin, if you did that with only a cat-zapper, what damage could you inflict with a really massive charge?" Zan's voice was shocked and horrified. "You bled half of it off before you did it, and it still shattered his shields."

"You don't ever want to find yourself on the receiving end of that, Zan. Trust me, I've seen the results and it's not pretty." Friedr dusted off his leathers one more time and looked over at Zan, chuckling. "So, Zan. Do you still want in on this little vacation?"

Edwin laughed at Friedr's jest. "Let's hope it *is* a vacation, compared to last time.'

Still slightly dazed, Zander nodded his head. "You couldn't keep me away now unless you kill me and tie my corpse to a post to keep me from following you." He dropped his shield fully. "Where in all the Hells of the Eleven Worlds did you two learn those tricks?"

Edwin, despite his worried blue eyes, looked like he had been out for a brisk walk in the park, a little exhilarated and by no means winded.

Look at him, not even sweating. He's beginning to realize what he just did. He won't like what I'm about to do next, but Father Rall insists it must be done. Friedr's thoughts were well hidden behind his professional smile. *I'm sorry, Edwin.*

"Well, don't look at me, Zan. Edwin is the master, and I am the merest of students." Friedr was still speaking to the crowd of onlookers as much as to Zan. "I've learned everything I know about shields and rebounding magic from him. I'll tell you this—I can't beat him, not with my sword or my magic. He kicks my backside every time. Edwin could have brought down my shields with a water/earth spike or simply one of his finely focused fire spears long before you tossed him the lightning. He chose not to because he loves sparring, and he's a healer. He would never hurt me intentionally.

"This demonstration was partly to see if you could work with him, and you did well. All Edwin needs are two elements in a usable form, and he can take down any shield ever made. He brought down Stefyn D'Mal's shield with the massive lightning bolt D'Mal himself cast at him and used the fire I tossed to him to make the lightning needle you just saw, only on such a huge scale the unfortunate minotaur who was acting as the vector for D'Mal's mind-magic literally exploded. Edwin's earth/water magic could shake a house down if he chose it to. He can call water out of the mist or the clouds. His many uses of air-magic are very esoteric, and you're not ready to hear the rest of the skills he has."

"Friedr, for the love of Aeos, don't talk so loud! Don't say these things." Edwin's eyes were anxious. "I've patients over there who're terrified of me now. This is going to ruin me professionally. I've worked hard to stay in the background as a battle-mage for the sake of my practice as a healer." The healers in the crowd nodded sympathetically. "Healing is my life!"

Zan was torn between sincere sympathy for Edwin's plight and unholy glee at the thought he might have the opportunity to learn from the man who was now proven the strongest battle-mage in the Temple.

Friedr hated that he had been the one to air Edwin's secrets to the Temple at large. "I'm sorry, my brother, more sorry than you'll ever know, but Father Rall has decreed the entire Temple will accord you the respect you're due. I will see that honor accorded to you here and now," Friedr replied, placing one hand on Edwin's shoulder in commiseration. "My self-image has suffered today. All who were watching know I was working as hard as I could to delay the inevitable trouncing you publicly administered today. Friedr Freysson is no longer undefeated, and this was a very visible fall from my pedestal." His words clearly did not ease Edwin's fears for his practice as a healer. Friedr patted his shoulder again, shaking his head. "We'll both be facing much questioning after this and none of it pleasant, I fear."

Friedr continued, "If you intend to go on this journey with us, Zan, you'll be working very closely with Edwin and learning many things you thought were impossible. First of all, today we'll begin work on shielding. You're considered most adept at shielding, which is why you've been selected from the group of applicants for today's demonstration."

Zan nodded, unsure of where Friedr was going, and fearing he was in trouble. He was right.

"Edwin could take your pathetic shields down without your even knowing he'd done it until it was too late. He doesn't need to use a bolt of magic to do it, because no one knows shields better than Edwin Farmer." Friedr looked out the corner of his eye and saw Edwin's face growing more disturbed by the minute.

"Another thing you should know from the beginning is when Edwin stands with his weapon at the ready and smiles his ridiculously goofy smile, you're going to need a healer, although he's usually gracious enough to heal you after he beats you black and blue. You'll have to set aside your notions of how things work, and you'll have to do many things that won't make sense at the time. Are you adaptable?" Friedr looked at Zan expectantly.

"As I said before, you'll have to kill me to keep me away now. I'm considered a fairly good lightning-mage, but you're something else entirely," he said candidly to Edwin. "You weren't at all truthful when you claimed weakness in some magics. No one would ever suspect what lurks under that far-too-pretty face."

"That's what everyone says." Friedr clapped Zan on the shoulder. He looked slyly at Edwin and then he said in a low voice, "Just wait until you see what happens when we take Pretty-Boy to the common room at the first inn we come to on the road."

Few things could embarrass Edwin, but Friedr knew exactly how to get under his skin. Edwin's irresistibility to the free women and friendly-girls who hung on him in the common rooms was the one thing that did embarrass him, more than he had words to express. He turned bright red. "But I am a bonded man. They won't…. Friedr, that couldn't happen anymore. Surely it won't be a problem now?" Edwin had a mortified expression on his face, confusion and embarrassment giving him a hunted and slightly wild look.

"I don't understand," Zander said, looking from Edwin to Friedr.

"Don't worry, Zan, you'll understand when we get there," Friedr laughed wickedly at Edwin's distress. "Now raise your best all-purpose shield. Pretty-Boy here is going to give you a lesson." Immediately, Zander's basic shield snapped into place, firm and rock solid.

"Shut up and raise your own shields, barbarian," Edwin muttered to Friedr, red-faced. "We won't have time for hanging about in the common rooms. This'll be a working expedition." Calming and centering himself, Edwin turned to a completely mystified Zan and began the lesson, speaking once again for the onlookers as well as for Zander. He showed no hint of his own inner turmoil. He was now the instructor in charge of the lesson.

"We'll begin with the way shields are traditionally built and thrown up for each individual spell that's cast.

I'm sorry if I misled you, but I didn't actually say I was weak in some magics. I said I was strong in air-magic. Air-magic requires equal strength in all four of the elements and great strength in healing. Those two strengths combined with the stealth rune augmentation are the marks of the air-mage."

Edwin casually untied the knots that held Zander's basic shield tied, and his shield melted away, to his shock and dismay. The observing crowd gasped. Murmurs rippled through the tiers. The members of the abbacy sat in stunned disbelief as Father Rall's assertions were proven true before their eyes.

"Whoa! What did you just do?" Zander had found himself shocked and surprised far too often for his own comfort during the morning's exercise.

"I warned you he could do that, didn't I?" Friedr smiled at Zan's consternation, speaking low. "This is the first step to developing a true battle-magic shield that'll save your life while we are sneaking around in Mal Evol." Zan looked up at the mention of the shadowed valley. "Yes," Friedr smiled grimly. "We must be prepared for any eventuality in that place. The creatures that roam wild in the badlands are deadly to those unprepared travelers upon whom they regularly dine. I choose to be no creature's easy meal."

Edwin continued his lesson. "As you saw, the style of shielding you've been taught is not nearly as effective as a layered shield. Can you call all the elements?" Edwin knew he could but asked for the purpose of the onlookers, as some lightning-mages could not easily call water. Zan nodded, and Edwin said, "Good. Now call just enough water to fill your palm with a scant amount." Curious as to what they were going to do with that element, Zan did so, and Edwin then told him to use that water to form the lightest, finest water-shield possible for him to maintain.

"What we do differently making our shields so unlike traditional shields is this: using a fine, light novice water-shield as the base, we layer the individual elemental shields so they create one all-purpose shield. We do this instead of throwing the standard shield up for each spell cast at you. If you maintain this layered shield at all times, you'll be a lot less vulnerable to attack."

Zan had erected a shield and was waiting for further instruction. "Good," said Edwin, speaking to the audience. "Now, earth is also usually readily available as an element for quick use. Call some earth to add just the finest layer. Look at Friedr, see how he's done what I'm asking?"

"But this is wrong—the elements fight each other. They can't work that way!" Zan's face made Edwin laugh. The younger mage's shields would not stick together and kept repelling each other.

"Friedr said almost exactly the same thing when I first showed him." Edwin watched Zan's face as he attempted to do what Edwin had asked of him, satisfied that Zan would try to do whatever he was asked.

"Not so heavy," Friedr told Zan. "Make the lightest, finest shield you can out of earth." Zan bled off half of the density of his shield. "If you try to use the heavy battle-shields you were taught to toss up for every spell thrown at you, then, yes, they'll fail. They'll fight each other, and disintegrate. Make it the lightest, finest shield in each element you can manage, and then the elements will cling to each other and form a shield nearly impossible for a normal mage to break." Friedr saw the disbelief on Zan's face warring with the knowledge of what he had just witnessed in the duel. "Not only do they work incredibly well, but with practice, you can layer every element you have the ability to use. When you tie them off with another of Edwin's little tricks, they'll maintain themselves with only minimal chi drain from you. That means you can save your chi and your attention for something important."

Finally, Zan was able to layer earth over the water, and his look of astonishment was echoed in the faces of the crowd who watched the lesson. After he had learned that first trick well, he was able to add all of the other elements with ease, as if he had been doing it that way all along.

"Excellent! You are a quick study, Zan. But now, the next thing you need to learn is how to properly tie off a shield. Think of it as if it were a ward," Edwin said. "Healers make wards, which most battle-mages cannot make. But even battle-mages can use those sorts of ties because they're not specific to the magic. They are just ties and are common to both magics." A ripple of comments ran through the onlookers at hearing that pronouncement. "We'll take the knot and add this little twist. This is the key to tying off your shield."

At the end of the exercise, Zan had the ability to erect, carry, and maintain a fairly creditable shield, with minimal drain on his chi. Should he be the one chosen to complete the team, he would be working closely with Friedr, Edwin, and Christoph from that day forward. Both Friedr and Edwin were confident that Zan would be selected as their fourth member, or Father Rall would not have chosen him as the third mage in the day's lesson to the Temple at large.

Chapter 3 ~ Dane's Kitchen

Late that afternoon, Zan sat at his parents' kitchen table discussing with Dane the events of the day, watching him as he prepared dinner. "I've never seen anything like Edwin. He's the best-kept secret in the Temple. Why is it no one knows anything about him other than he's a healer who also espouses bizarre theories on shielding?"

"Well, have you actually looked at his augmentations?" Dane was already more than a little tired of talking about the quest, but he knew he would have to endure it at least until the preparations were actually underway. "He's been augmented with as many runes for stealth and luck as he has with ones for strength, empathy, and wisdom, and those are just the ones we can see. And I know they'll be augmenting all four of the questers rather extensively, so be prepared. I think they'll be announcing the fourth quester today or tomorrow. I've been told to clear my calendar on Frosday so I can help the four cope with augmentation reaction. They *never* do that for senior mages unless the omens speak of a seriously large augmentation for each of them."

"I can't imagine I'll be getting too many more, but we know the magic chooses what's needed. That's assuming I'm chosen for this. But I *must* be selected! My head will be spinning like a top until I know for sure." Zander slipped into the emotional rollercoaster Dane knew so well. "A quest like this could make my career. But what if they don't want me after all?"

Casting a spell for calm on his highly strung cousin, Dane was able to get on with his preparations for the evening meal. *I had to do that. He'll burst something the way he's going,* he told himself, justifying a slightly improper use of his healing skills. "Don't worry so much, Zan. Father Rall and the abbess wouldn't have set that little show up for you if they did not have two things in mind." Dane felt sure of what the high clergy had planned now.

"What do you mean?" Zander was able to think clearly again. "What am I not seeing here?"

"Well, for one thing, the abbess wanted to see if you could work with them, which you did extremely well. Also, they're going to force a change in the curriculum for battle-shields, and the senior staff has just been put on notice. They've deliberately kept Edwin's unique abilities quiet for a long time out of respect for Edwin's personal wishes. Because of that, most of the higher clergy think he's a bit of a crackpot." Dane scooped vegetables into a pot, which he then set on his stove over the fire-box.

After adding a few more pieces of wood to the fire-box and closing the grate, Dane continued with his observations. "Today, they saw he's not only correct about the theory and application of layered shielding, but he's more than capable of taking all of them to pieces using only his shields as a weapon. Most of them have forgotten he's the only mage ever to be a healer-adept, a battle-mage, and a mage-assassin, if they ever even knew it in the first place. They've not considered the true power he so carefully hides under that mild-mannered but scrumptious-looking exterior."

"I saw what they saw today, but I don't see what you're getting at." Zan thought that nothing was ever what it seemed with Edwin Farmer. "Yes, today he proved himself a mighty battle-mage, and all know him as one of the great healers, but...."

"Zander, listen to me. *Three* disciplines combine equally in him. Because of his circumstances, Edwin has been forced to develop skills you can't imagine, several of which weren't on display today and will never be revealed to an audience. Think about this—how did he convey to you he wanted you to send him your little cat-zapper?"

"I heard him whisper to me." Zander's eyes widened as he realized what had truly happened on the practice ground. "It was like he was next to me, speaking in my ear." He shook his head slowly. "Holy.... How does he keep such a secret?"

"That's not even the half of it. I'll tell you what happened in Mal Evol before the battle with D'Mal, just as Marya told it to me. You were in the novice barracks at the time, so you wouldn't have known about this." Dane gave Zan the full tale of the quest that brought Edwin Farmer to Neveyah. He ended with Edwin locked in a true-dream and, using his control of what he referred to as fetching, trans-locating a knife from his own chest, lodging it in the right eye of the mad priest, Stefyn D'Mal. "And all of this was verified and placed in the Temple records, should anyone choose to find it, that is. Although I suspect many of the old codgers are doing just that this afternoon."

"How does someone have the willpower to do something like that? But I suppose if anyone could, it would be him. No wonder the senior clergy fear him,"

Zan mumbled in astonishment. "They're scared he'll make them look like a lot of obsolete jackasses who're more concerned with hanging onto their dignity than winning the war. This is exactly what he did today with that demonstration. And he didn't even know he was being set up, any more than I did."

"He came to Neveyah not knowing anything about magic or weaponry. During the quest to rescue Marya, he was developing and refining skills never seen before." Dane stirred the pot of soup and left it to simmer while he tidied up his kitchen. "He's continued refining these skills out of the spotlight for the last few years because he had no reason to let his ability become generally known. It was hoped the senior battle-mages would see the sense of his teachings and embrace them without having to go through the display today.

"Of the tenured adept battle-mages, only Father Rall, Abbess Halee, Abbott Garran, Moran, Piers, Elis, Friedr, Aeolyn, and, of course, Marya, now she has lost her healing empathy and has only her water-magic, have taken to fully using the new techniques. But all the healers have done so. Edwin himself teaches barriers to the novice healers. They must pass his class and don't advance until they do. Edwin hopes there will be no healers with fragile barriers ever again. Even your father has reliable barriers now, and his were the most fragile of all. Christoph will tell you that himself if you ask him.

"The true scope of Edwin's abilities would frighten some people, especially those who don't realize he's the most decent and ethical man in three worlds." Dane paused, trying to gauge Zan's reaction to his tale. "He has the strength of character to stay in the background, giving the glory and accolades to the other mages. Everyone underestimates him—that's a huge mistake on their part. I suspect he's the only living being the mad priest fears."

Zan snorted scornfully. "Well, they'll be lining up to take his classes on shielding now. Every senior instructor not teaching was stalking me and sneakily poking and prodding at my shields all afternoon. I was uncomfortable walking the halls. Everyone wanted to corner me about Edwin and then prod my shields." He rolled his eyes. "Well, in all honesty, even I had a hard time believing him until he and Friedr got mine set up. I still have trouble with the new ties, but I'm not going anywhere without them. I suspect his are up all the time, but I can't sense them. I couldn't even out on the practice yard. Yet I know they were there because everything Friedr threw at him sheeted off or rebounded in the form of a weapon."

"The reason you can't sense his shields is because his healer's barrier is woven into them, which is impervious too." Dane smiled grimly. "The battle-mages should take notice now, though. Today's demonstration must've shown them what Friedr's been trying to get them to see. We begged them to listen to Edwin, to no avail, ever since...well, you know what happened."

They were silent as both of them thought about the recent death of a young fire-mage who became lost in her magic. The incident was still fresh in everyone's mind, though only the healers ever mentioned it.

After a moment of watching Dane expertly slicing apples and cheese, Zan said morosely, "I'm such a child to think I'm anywhere near the class of mage they are.

What an idiot I am, begging to be allowed to go on this quest—I'm not fit to polish their boots!" He leaned his head on his hands, wallowing in a fit of insecurity.

Dane rolled his eyes. "Oh dear Goddess, help me. I can see it's going to be hell until they announce the fourth hero. Zander, you idiot, pull yourself together. I'm not wasting any more chi on you. Here," he said, handing Zan some carrots and the peeler. "Peel these for the salad and do something useful. Your father will be home from work soon, and I want him to relax, not worry about you. Busy hands, Zan. Busy hands."

Chapter 4 ~ Edwin's Kitchen

Edwin enjoyed a quiet dinner with his family, pleased his father had returned to Aeoven permanently. Although his father had been urged to return many times, he had always refused. Edwin was curious as to why he had changed his mind. During their meal, John held Edwin's small son, Jonny, as he napped, unwilling to put him down even to eat. "I've done this before," he said to Marya, with his eyes twinkling. "I missed him after you two returned here when you last visited me."

Marya laughed and said, "I knew you'd miss him. I hoped missing him would encourage you to come home to Aeoven.'

John's story had a familiar ring to it. "It turns out the Goddess Aeos has decided it's time for John Farmer to return to Neveyah," he said with a faint smile. "She apparently sent Garran a true-dream well over a month ago, telling him to meet me at the portal instead of the usual place. I knew something was happening when a sheep went missing. That seems to be the signal Aeos uses to call us to the portal. So I closed up the house and put a simple water shield on it that is keyed only to you, Edwin, or to me.

"The neighbors just sort of forget the house is there, so it stays safe. It's the kind of simple magic mages here in Neveyah know, but isn't known in Markett. I gave the livestock to young Josiah Legg and told him that I'm off to live with you two. I did say we'd be back one day. He sends you his regards. They named their baby Meri, by the way, and she's as cute as a button!"

Edwin smiled and nodded. His childhood friend now had three daughters.

John grinned. "Then I dug out my old leathers and packed my kit and armor. Lastly, I strapped on my sword and left to 'look for the sheep.' That's how my dad did it too when he came back here to live when I was a novice," he told Edwin. "Sometimes, the farm in Markett stands empty for long years at a time. But we always go home eventually. It's the only true home we have. The farm is our retreat when things become unbearable here. The Almighty Father keeps our home safe for us." He paused, wondering if he was ready to live in Aeoven after all these years. "To my surprise, Garran was waiting at the portal when I fell through it."

***

"I wish I'd asked you to come back with us when we visited you after Jonny was born," Edwin told his father later as they washed the dishes. "I've hated the thought of you being by yourself. It's bad, being alone so much."

John was silent, as always considering his words before he replied. "I wasn't ready to return to this place permanently, until now. I needed to wallow in my misery and grieve for Andia, and I couldn't do that while I was raising you, son. I've finally come to terms with it now though."

He looked out the window over the sink at the evening sky. "This time, after the three of you left and I was alone again, I realized I've come to terms with many things. I'll be here to help Marya with Jonny while you boys are off saving Neveyah. I have a plan to create a position as an animal healer, putting my knowledge to good use. I'll be happier doing that than if I had to teach water-magic to bored children who'd really prefer to be flashy lightning-mages instead."

John carefully did not tell Edwin the truth about the crippling wound his magic had suffered so many years before, or about the day he couldn't even bear to think about. "This way, I can do something useful and be a part of your life too."

The Temple was so short of battle-mages, Edwin doubted Father Rall would allow John to let his magic languish for too long but said nothing. "Well, I'll feel better knowing you're here when I'm gone. I just hope we can get this done fairly quickly. We aren't planning to confront D'Mal. We're just going to free the land itself from the Dark God's poison so the native plants that belong there can bloom again, and the thorns will draw back to the land they came from." Edwin set the plates on the shelf.

"How in hell do you plan to do something like that?" John's normally impassive face showed his surprise at the magnitude of the quest.

"I know, it sounds mad." Edwin laughed at his own temerity in agreeing to such a quest. "When we were there before, we discovered Tauron's will was imposed on the land through some means, and then shielded. We're guessing it was done through the Throne of Stone and Bone since it controls all of the land of Mal Evol. If I can figure out the way the shield is tied off, I can take it down. Once D'Mal's shield is down, our plan is for Christoph to use his healing ability to cleanse the soil. Then I will reset the shield so D'Mal can't sense it, hopefully without his noticing anything has happened. We'll do this the same way he took the land in the first place. We'll work our way into Mal Evol, one hectare at a time, building cells like a honeycomb."

"Son, do you really think he'll let you do this without a fight?" John looked at him closely. "I see. You know there'll be a fight, but you hope that either it won't happen, or it'll happen late enough that you'll have gotten most of your work done, and then you'll have won. That's why you've been training harder than you ever let on. You flat out kicked Friedr's butt all over the practice yard today, and you didn't even work up a sweat. You were seriously pulling your punches with your practice sword." John smiled at Edwin's discomfort. "Poor Zan. That skinny lightning-mage doesn't stand a chance once you start training him seriously."

"I don't want to teach weapons or offensive magic. Friedr is the genius there. As far as battle-magics go, I enjoy teaching healer's barriers and battle-shields, though I've had a lot of trouble getting students to come to me for training in shields. I have too radical an approach for most of the senior battle-magic staff's taste." Edwin still found it strange that so few could open their minds to a new view of an old problem. "The healers on the other hand have developed a curriculum that totally embraces my concept of barriers woven into a water shield. They're much more flexible than the battle-mages are."

"You'll find everything has changed when you go into work tomorrow." His father's eyes twinkled. "I saw a lot of cranky old men and women standing around loudly swearing they'd always known you were on the right track."

Edwin laughed and said, "On the right track! Completely daft is what they've all declared at one time or another. When I applied to teach shielding three years ago, Zylda even went so far as to say my extreme augmentations had affected my reason."

"Zylda has always been full of herself, so I wouldn't worry about anything she has to say. Besides, today they saw you dismantle the Temple Armsmaster without even blinking an eye. Even those old duffers could see you didn't pull any of your really fancy combos out of your bag of tricks. You simply matched Friedr and made him work hard while the two of you were beating on each other with your swords. But what you did to his shield was astonishing. I admit I was proud of you, son." John squeezed his son's shoulder. "I think you may be better than my dad was, and he was better than Father Rall."

Edwin looked at his dad in surprise. "Aw, thanks, Dad, but I know my limitations and so does Friedr. He kicks my bottom regularly."

"Don't think you can fool me. He may be better at other forms of combat but not with swords or magic. I know a thing or two about them, remember?" John looked his son in the eye and handed him a clean, wet pan to dry and put away. "I was pretty rusty at both swords and magic when I fell through the portal. Garran gave me no end of grief over it. I told him a sword is no use on the farm, where a bow does the job more efficiently. He told me then you're the best swordsman in Neveyah right now. He's right."

Edwin blushed and said, "Anyway, I plan on avoiding any fights once we're back in Mal Evol, and I've the means to do it. I'm going to use my air-and earth-magic to stay as silent and unseen as the assassin they all seem to think I am after today's little display." He sighed. "You saw the strange looks I got this morning. I'll be lucky if the elder mages let me in their front door, much less let me heal their creaky old bones, now they've seen the 'real' me." Edwin's laugh hid the fact that underneath it all, he was unsure of himself. "We won't be working out in public anymore, so maybe they'll forget about my 'evil' side."

His father was not fooled. "Son, I'm guessing you won't be working full-time as a healer much longer," John gently told his son. "You'll be developing new ways to turn the world on its head and teaching old dogs new tricks—as well as beating up on Dane and Christoph's boy."

"Well, I'm *not* going to quit healing until they make me," Edwin told his father firmly, with a spark in his eye and his chin set in the way John recognized as a copy of his own stubborn streak. The comparison made him smile. Unaware of his father's amusement, Edwin continued, "I enjoy healing more than anything, and I only do the battle-magic for fun and to keep my chi balanced. I love my work, even though this year was so hard, what with Rall's wife, Feia, dying, and Halee's husband, Bryson, passing away so young. I'm going to lose so many more people I love, unless they learn to put a buffer between themselves and the magic. It's so simple, but they won't listen! For me, healing is the real fight, Dad. And when we're done with this quest, it's what I'm going to do for the rest of my life."

"I know, son," His father's face was full of pride. "It's a battle that should be fought."

As they finished the dishes, Marya opened the kitchen door to say Christoph and Dane were in the sitting room. She'd been uncharacteristically quiet all afternoon, and Edwin knew he'd done something to upset her. It had happened before, when they were young and first bonded. He knew it was nothing to do with his father. When he reached out with his empathy, her anger felt all tied up with Friedr for some reason. He promised himself they would talk later. When Marya was unhappy, he was unhappy. The link between them was too strong.

"You two go on out there. I'll make some tea and bring it out." John bustled about the kitchen, happy to have a task. "And I see Marya still has some cookies left from your Holy Day feast. I'll bring out a plate of those with the tea."

As Edwin entered the sitting room, he laughed to see Jonny had a grip on Christoph's nose and was pulling on it with all his might, while Chris mock-wailed, "Ow! Ow! My poor nose!" Jonny crowed with delight, kicking his little feet and batting at Chris's face with his tiny hand in an effort to grab his nose again. Snuggling the baby close, Christoph looked over at Dane and said, "Our Zander is officially on the team. He passed Friedr's test with flying colors." He was bursting with pride, and so was Dane.

Dane said with a smile, "Frankly, I'm thrilled. I couldn't have stood another day of trying to keep him from going to pieces over this. He was anxious before, but after today, he was completely obsessed. He's down at the common room in the Weavers' Quarter celebrating with his friends."

"Edwin—you've shaken up many a person's view of the world," Christoph added with his wicked grin. "Old Henley was completely aghast that we've been sending a Temple assassin to heal his gout so regularly."

Edwin groaned. "I knew it! I'm sure my healing practice is ruined. I never should've let them put me out on display like that."

"Yes, he was aghast but still demanding you be on time tomorrow." Dane's grin grew sly as he quoted Henley, "'And tell him from me not to bother trying to hide his true colors! I don't fear him one bit!'" They all laughed at his perfect mimicry of the querulous old fire-mage. "You're in high demand for healing, Edwin! Beryl and Abbess Halee have decided that until everyone has had a chance to be healed by 'that healer who throws fire' you'll be so busy you may need to have an extra journeyman assigned to assist you."

***

That night, in the darkness of their room, Marya was unable to sleep for worrying over something. Her fretfulness kept Edwin awake, but she refused to talk about it. Finally, he lowered most of his empathic barriers as if he were going to perform a healing on her so all of his senses could feel what she was feeling, even though he knew it was an invasion of her privacy. *She was forced to endure D'Mal's casual rummaging through her thoughts and feelings, and I'd never do that. I only want to know what she's worrying about. It's unfair she lost most of her empathic abilities and can't return the favor.*

He lay there with his senses wide open, allowing her emotions to touch him, then raised his barriers again and rolled onto his side facing her. Leaning on his elbow, Edwin looked down at Marya, waiting for her to open her eyes and look at him.

"That's unfair, Edwin," she said, looking up at him with anger sparking her brown eyes. "I just need to sleep, and I'll get over it."

"I know," he said, but he still continued to look at her.

"Just go to sleep, please." Marya was not upset over something he had not done or said. Now Edwin sensed it was a mixture of anger, hurt, and guilt she was feeling.

"I will when you've explained to me what the problem is so I can think about how to make it up to you." Edwin carefully refrained from smoothing her hair, though the habit was strongly ingrained in him. "If I know what I've done, I can be sure never to do it again, right?"

Her silence was hot and angry. Tears formed in her eyes, and it took all the strength he could muster not to reach out to comfort her. *I have to allow her space to work through this.* This was the hardest part for Edwin. His all-consuming love for his wife drove him to distraction at times, but with her traumatic past, this was a place where he knew he had to tread carefully. *Do not apply pressure to her, do not do it.* He willed himself to stay on his own side of the bed.

Suddenly, she sat up, plumping the pillow behind her, and glared at him. "All right, if you really want to hear it, but it just makes me look more pathetic than I already am." She leaned back against the headboard, looking down at him.

"What do you mean?" He was honestly mystified now but looking up at her, he caught himself admiring her profile in the moonlight. Her perfection distracted him as it always did. Abruptly, he called his vagrant mind to order.

Completely unaware of her husband's distraction, she spoke reluctantly. "Today you took Friedr down in front of everyone." Marya's lip quivered. She was so angry she was crying. "You bested him without even trying, and everyone saw it. You weren't even tired, and the battle-mages were all raving about how you hadn't used very much chi."

Edwin nodded in agreement, waiting for the rest. She was not angry on Friedr's behalf. It was something else, something too complex for him to figure out without asking her.

"Afterwards, everyone hounded me, asking how I could've kept something so amazing as your battle-skills a secret for all these years," She looked down at him, and he nodded at her, meeting her eyes.

"I never knew." The three words each dropped like lead into the silence of their bedroom. "I didn't know you've developed into a better warrior than Aeolyn or Friedr or even Abbott Garran. You are suddenly acclaimed by everyone as the finest warrior of our generation, and I never knew." She gave a sob that was much like a hiccup. "What else don't I know about you? What else have I let slip by because I've been so busy and involved with Jonny and my work that I've neglected you?"

Understanding dawned in Edwin's eyes. "You aren't mad at me. You're angry with yourself, fearing you've not paid attention to me and we're growing apart. But it's not true. I've been working out with Friedr every afternoon for all these years, and I've gradually honed my skills. Maybe the only one who knew besides Friedr was Christoph, and that's only because he spars with us occasionally. It didn't seem particularly important to me and still doesn't."

He held her hand to his cheek, and then he asked, "May I open my mind to you? Will you look and see what I haven't told you?" She looked at him, mystified. "Yes, Marya, everything—even the fears I haven't told to anyone."

"I wish I could, but you know I can't read you." Her face was carefully blank when she spoke of the loss of most of her healing abilities. "Besides, a man must have some secrets. Friedr says so!" Her teary attempt at a smile failed.

"But I can do this, if you'll let me. I'll bring you into my mind," he told her. Laying his head on her lap, he centered himself and placed her palms on either side of his forehead. Carefully building the bridge between them, he laid bare his mind. One by one, his barriers fell, and he allowed her presence to fill his mind. All his hopes and dreams were there for her to see and every one of his failings and fears too.

Feeling her pulling away mentally, he sat up, automatically raising his barriers. Pulling his hair back from his face, he laid down next to her with his head on his pillow.

"Oh, Edwin," Marya's voice caught. "I love you so much. I never realized how much you love me. I mean I knew it, but now I *know* it. You honestly love me." She slid back down next to him, wrapping her arms around him. "I didn't realize how much you dread the common rooms. I just thought it was funny the way friendly-girls behave around you. I was a healer, so I know they can't help themselves. They just glare daggers at me when I'm with you. But don't worry! You'll be fine when you get to the next common room on the road." She kissed him. "You won't act on any of your impulses. You never have and never will. If it'll make you feel better, Friedr will just have to protect my interests. I'll get Aeolyn to tell him."

Edwin smiled in the dark, knowing exactly how Friedr would react to that. *Oh, Goddess. Friedr is going to kick my sorry butt all the way from here to Mal Evol.* His arms tightened around her, and his lips sought hers. "I love you, Marya. You were always the only one for me, even before I knew who you were, and always will be."

"I know, Edwin," Her whisper was soft, and her lips brushed his neck and his shoulder. "I know."

***

Aeolyn and Friedr had just put Rynne in her little bed, hopefully for the night. Christoph and Dane had stopped by earlier to tell them Zan had passed the test and had been added to the team, to their son Freylin's eternal delight. He adored the stories and songs Christoph always had time to tell him. Tonight, Freylin went quietly to bed with no tears because Uncle Chris had a special story just for him, about Aelfrid Firesword and the dragon. Freylin's great hero was Aelfrid Firesword.

Now the house was quiet, the children were sleeping, and the two tired parents were making ready for bed. "I knew Edwin was improving, but he's really made some advances, especially with his sword techniques," Aeolyn said quietly as she slipped into bed. "He could mop the floor with both of us together, couldn't he? I'm almost afraid to spar with him when I go back to it. According to the midwife today, I should be able to return in two weeks or so."

"Well, he doesn't beat me up every time, but most of the time, yes. The strange thing is, he still doesn't seem to realize he is better than me." Friedr's voice was low, so as not to wake Rynne, who slept in a cradle near their bed. "And he wouldn't strain or push you if you do work out with him. He'll stay at your level. He's still a healer first, and he knows you're still a nursing mother. Edwin is the gentlest warrior we've ever had."

"What's it like, having a student like him?" Aeolyn toyed with her husband's long, red curls that were loose and tumbling over his bare chest, well past his waist. Her own fall of dark hair mingled with his. "These days, he's more of a friend, not someone I work with. When he first came to Neveyah, he was so eager to learn and willing to work hard. Is he still the same man he was then?"

"Yes, although I'm the student now in all except bare-handed combat. He's gaining on me there, but being the heavier man works in my favor." Friedr yawned and pulled his wife closer. "I'm in desperate need of a hug. The world now knows what a sham I am, though it had to be done. If they don't change the way they teach shielding, the Temple will lose more than Mal Evol. We'll lose the war, and any survivors will be reduced to slaves for the children of the Bull God."

"You're so silly. No one should have the reputation of invincibility. Too many young hotshots want to try their luck at being the one to kick your backside! Edwin had no wish to do so. You could see the resignation in his eyes when he entered the practice yard, and he'll never let them parade his skills again. Besides, he loves you like a brother and wouldn't be who he is without the instruction and guidance he's received from you. He didn't ask the Goddess to curse him with this threefold magic. And everyone knows he's your star pupil now. You can add it to your resume!"

Aeolyn rolled on top of Friedr, her dark hair falling all around him as she gazed down at his surprised face. "Is it only a hug you're wanting, dear one? Did I mention I saw the midwife today? She told me I'm well healed from Rynne's birth." Aeolyn's lips and hands consoled her husband in the best way she knew how.

Friedr quickly forgot to feel insecure, exactly as Aeolyn had intended.

Chapter 5 ~ A Tempest in the Temple

The next morning found Edwin back on his rounds and making house calls on his elderly patients. Edwin sent his healer's senses delving the body of the elderly lightning-mage he was treating for symptoms related to cancer, which was unfortunately a rather common ailment for mages whose careers involved long and excessive work with the element of lightning. Speaking through the mental link to Rena, who made notes of his comments, Edwin said, *The cancer is advancing through her system, but she still has time. Her nausea is caused by dehydration, which in turn, causes nausea...a common problem for lightning-mages... this will help with the pain...*

He placed a dampening field over her and cast a spell for soothing, layered with a pain-relief spell, and tied it off. He bolstered the spells with some mild herbal pain remedies. *She doesn't yet need the poppy for pain, but I think we'll have to bring Marya in to work with her soon.* Withdrawing his senses and automatically raising his full barrier/shield combination, he tied them off as was his habit. His empathy was such that he would be incapacitated by his patients if he were to go without barriers.

"I've heard you're a fire-mage or an assassin of some sort, but it seems so odd, with you being a healer and all." Gerde spoke in a quavering, elderly voice. Only a year before she had still been able to teach, but the disease was taking a heavy toll on her. "I can see you are indeed a battle-mage, but you're good to me and that's all that matters."

"Yes, the Goddess has blessed me heavily, but I'm not a fire-mage. My battle skills lie more in air-magic." Edwin forced a smile and pulled his hair back for yet one more elderly patient to see his radical assortment of tattoos. "You need to drink more water, Gerde. You're becoming dehydrated, and this is making you feel weak and ill. I'll make you some with citrus and honey and a pinch of salt. These three things will help, but you must drink eight cups a day, every day. Remember the things you yourself have taught young lightning-mages about the curse of not keeping the elements balanced!"

"It upsets my stomach to drink water, so I've not drunk as much as I know I should." She sighed. "It's the cancer. It's too hard to fight it some days, but most days I still love my life. You've helped so much with the pain."

Edwin spoke gently to her, "You know we can't cure this illness, but we can keep you from suffering. Don't give up, you've still so much knowledge about the elements to offer us younger mages. I'll mix this for you, and you tell me if it tastes good. Once your fluids are re-balanced, you'll feel much better, I promise."

Gerde drank the water he prepared for her and gave him a faint smile, "Yes, you're right. This tastes good, and I think it'll stay down." She looked at him shrewdly, and her gnarled finger lightly touched the rune for stealth that rode just behind his left ear. Her old voice was filled with compassion for him. "I suspect these augmentations are not as much a blessing as they are a curse, Edwin. I hear you're going off on another quest. I'll miss you. You're a good healer and I've been lucky to have you." She tried to send him all the sympathy she could muster, despite her illness and lack of healing ability, and he couldn't help but smile as he felt her encouragement of him.

"Thank you, Gerde, for trying to heal the healer," Edwin's open, sincere smile charmed her, much as his grandfather's smile always had. "You've no idea how much that means to me. I've really enjoyed working with you. You're an amazing person, and I've learned a lot from you. Anyway, I'll be here for a while yet, as we still have preparations to make. I'm sure you remember how that is from your own quests." He checked her pulse and looked carefully at her nails and the skin on her hands. Patting her hand and sending her soothing, supportive emotions, he said, "I'll show your daughter how to make the water for you, and I'll be back on Lunaday."

His whole morning had been much the same, to varying degrees, with all his patients. Even old Henley had been more concerned about Edwin going, as he put it, "haring off on some silly quest with that barbarian, Friedr" than he was about Edwin being augmented as a Temple assassin. "No one understands what happens to old fire-mages like you do. They think gout is from eating wrong, but it's our occupational hazard." Henley looked sharply at him and then said, "I saw you take my favorite protégé apart like he was a novice yesterday. It did him good. Now he knows how I felt when he did much the same to me." He chuckled wickedly, and added, "I rather enjoyed watching it!"

Edwin shook his head ruefully and replied, "Friedr is my mentor. I learn from him daily. I have to stretch to beat him. I'm better in some areas, such as shielding and use of rebounding magic, but he doesn't accept less than my best when we work out."

"I would hope not. I trained him better than that! Well, I just wish you weren't going to waste your time in Mal Evol," Henley muttered. "It's a shame the best healer I've ever had also has the misfortune of being the finest battle-mage of the century, and now I have to try to break in a new healer. Whoever they send won't be as good, I guarantee you. But I made my share of fruitless quests as a younger man, another occupational hazard in our profession!"

As Edwin worked his way through the morning, he began to believe he would still have a practice to return to when he finished the quest in Mal Evol.

After meeting Marya and having a quick lunch with her and Jonny in the Temple garden near the nursery, he went up to his tiny study high in the College of Warcraft to plan when he could submit his thesis for review.

He greeted his secretary, Meryle, whose desk was placed in the hall outside his door, much like a messenger's desk. Meryle was a fifteen-year-old, upper-level novice water-mage who would undoubtedly be testing for her journeyman's pin soon. She was diligent in her work and had become very good with her shielding. She was a settled and reliable young mage.

Edwin was the only instructor who didn't qualify for a journeyman secretary or a proper reception area. His study was actually an old converted storeroom. Still, he did have a window, though he had to keep it open year round for air. The room had just enough space for his small desk, an extra chair, and his full bookshelves.

Edwin had barely gotten his window open and had just sat down at his desk when Meryle knocked on the door, telling him a senior instructor was in the hall and would like to see him if it was convenient. The most senior water-mage, Cayne, wished to schedule a private tutoring in shielding, whenever Edwin could squeeze him in. As the afternoon progressed, in between his two classes on healer's barriers, he had visits from nearly every tenured adept battle-magic instructor, all requesting the same thing.

His last visitor of the afternoon was Abbess Halee. She'd been watching to see who climbed the four flights of stairs to Edwin's little closet of a study, and after looking at his list of requests, she decided he would have to offer two advanced classes in shielding, and all the senior staff would be required to take the course, as would each of the journeymen. "I'll inform them myself so no one gets their nose out of joint over not being given the preferential treatment their status allows them. You won't have time for private lessons. You only have about six months to train for your quest. Even though most of the senior staff never goes questing, they all know what being in service to the Goddess means. So you and Friedr will have to share the shielding course between you."

Her voice hardened, and her blue eyes were like slate, "But they'll *all* take the course and pass it, or they'll not be teaching here any longer. The time for foolishness and ego-stroking of these old fools is long past. This is the way shielding will be taught from now on in all of Neveyah. Father Rall has decreed it, and it will be so."

"Abbess Halee, I need to submit my thesis to the assembly, if I may?" Edwin's humble request both surprised and pleased the Abbess. "I know they're accepting them for consideration at the winter Conclave of the Abbacies."

The long, winter conclave was in progress, and as far as the Abbess could see, Edwin would have his official appointment to tenured adept battle-mage status at that meeting, thesis or no thesis, but she did not tell him that. "If you have it ready, go ahead and send it to my assistant and I will submit it for you," she replied with a determined glint in her eye. "We're moving you to a much larger study with a proper outer reception room. You will also need to hold your classes in one of the larger classrooms. Jules Brendsson is moving to the position of archivist, so you're now in charge of the entire program."

"I thought he liked his job." The elderly mage had often said he would never quit working in some capacity, and he had several tasks he did for the Temple.

"He did like it, but the archivist's position opened up and it's exactly what he wants to do. He'll still be available to stand in for the Holy Father when Rall is traveling, and he'll also be able to help me out when my assistant leaves on his quest with you."

Edwin nodded. "That will relieve Christoph. He was worried about you not being able to find an assistant who understands what your research entails."

Halee grinned. "I know. Anyway, you'll share this with Friedr, who will assist you in instructing, and you will each have journeymen to support you, one of whom you already know. I am giving you Zander Christophson since you will be questing together, and Zan must be able to work with you seamlessly. Father Rall's true-dreams are clear on that. Meryle will stay with you as your secretary since she understands the program and is good at scheduling around your healing duties. She's due to test for her journeyman's pin soon anyway, which will be perfect since the senior staff just walks all over novices."

"Abbess, I do appreciate the honor, but what about my patients? It will be months before we leave, and they need me. I need them," Edwin would refuse to give up healing if asked to do so, although he was pleased that shielding was finally being given a proper place in the College of Warcraft and Magic. "My true calling is that of a healer. It's how I'll spend the rest of my life after this quest, Aeos willing."

"That is why you and Friedr will share the course. We need him to continue with weapons training until we have our replacement for him, and we must keep you healing. Old Henley is adamant about that!" Halee admired the determined old fire-mage and his tenacity. "I can't deny Henley anything he really wants, not after the sacrifices he has made for Aeos. He wants you as his healer for as long as you are still here."

Later that same day after classes were done, Friedr and Edwin had stripped down to just loose linen trousers as they worked on the formal discipline of the Three-fold Way of fighting, a form of grappling that involved throwing the enemy to the ground. This more ritualized discipline of the Temple Assassin was kept as hidden as any other Temple secret. The arcane discipline of the Assassin's Guild was never discussed outside of the Temple. The guild was really a support group for those mages who had been chosen by the Goddess to do specific secret tasks, often dark in nature.

As Friedr and Edwin washed up in the men's dressing room, they discussed what the Abbess had planned for them, trying to figure out how to include Zan and Chris in the evening workouts.

"We'll have to make the evening workout a foursome since much of what we'll be doing will require us all to work together. Of course, Christoph is woefully out of practice."

"We need to work with Zan and Chris on overlapping layered shields at some point too." Edwin's voice was somewhat muffled by his towel as he dried his hair. "It was what made all the difference for us when we went up against Brec and his boys at the farm once D'Mal stepped in and possessed Brec."

"I agree. We can incorporate it into our nightly workouts. However, we *have* to do something about Christoph. I want Chris to learn the Three-fold Way of fighting, at least the first forty forms, because it'd be good for him to have some ability to fight without his staff. But will he do it? He's still good with his staff-work, but lately it's been hard getting him to spar with us." Friedr pulled his comb through his damp hair, wincing as it hit a knot. Then he began plaiting it into his usual, long braid.

"It's probably because he's a healer more than anything," Edwin replied, running his comb through his own damp hair, which he left loose. "He's not a fighter at all. He can barely call enough water to build a proper layered barrier, and his empathy is much stronger than that of other healers, which causes him no end of problems. I've never seen him kill anything when we skirmish, though he's excellent at tripping and disarming them for us to kill. He doesn't even argue well. You know that. He always gives in instead of holding firm to his convictions, and then feels bad about it all night."

"All the more reason for him to learn some defensive skills. Dane's as good as you are with the staff, and he makes me work for it nowadays too. I know for a fact he's been nagging Chris to spar more often. He told me so yesterday," Friedr said. "As you've repeatedly reminded Chris, we won't always be there to save his sorry backside, but still he keeps dodging my suggestions to learn this." He stuffed his dirty workout clothes into the Temple laundry hamper. The linen trousers were Temple property and would reappear on the shelves in the men's dressing room in the morning.

"Get the Abbess to order him to do it." Edwin knew the only person who Christoph couldn't evade was Abbess Halee, whom he respected more than anyone else in the Temple.

"That's a good idea. Sneaky, but good. That brings us to my other problem." Friedr's flint-blue eyes glinted in total contrast to his angelic face. "Zander will be useful on this trip when it comes to fighting. He has one wicked trick, which tripped up Herris today in my advanced weapons class. He looks like his left side is open, but it's a ruse and Herris went for it," he chuckled. "The arrogant git went down like a sack of potatoes. The only trouble will be teaching Zan not to rely on one trick. He's just like most lightning-mages—brilliant, erratic, and inherently slothful. That's my problem." Friedr rolled his eyes. "Just like all young journeymen seem to do on their first posting, he let himself get lazy and now has very little stamina. Will you take him in hand and daily beat some sense into him with your sword? He needs private tutoring." Friedr looked at Edwin questioningly. "Can you add this to your schedule?"

"Yes, if he's willing to work with me in the morning before I go to the infirmary," Edwin's mornings were always his best time. "Otherwise, we'll have to find time later in the day. I want to leave the evenings free for our families as much as possible. I'm not going to give up my Sunnaday afternoons or my Restdays—they're the only time I really get to spend with Jonny right now. I get called to healing emergencies often enough as it is. And Freylin really needs his dad, don't you think? He's full of mischief."

"If it isn't one thing, it's another with that son of mine." Friedr couldn't quite disguise his pride in Freylin's somewhat legendary creativity. "It's bad enough having this hanging over our heads without letting it rule our lives. The last quest wasn't so bad because Aeolyn was leading it, and we had clear omens, which we don't seem to have this time. It worries me. Also, we didn't have children or other responsibilities. It was the only thing on our minds." The big man He stood and stamped his feet down into his boots, then sighed, his morose expression at odds with his cherubic face. "Frankly, I'm not excited about getting more augmentations tomorrow morning. I don't want to end my days as an assassin like you!"

"Well, we can't plan what we'll do until the augmentations have been made, and we know what Aeos wishes for us." Edwin laughed, hiding his own nervousness. "I just wonder where they're going to put mine. Probably on my calves. There's still some room there although not very much. Or you'll have to go easy when you kick my backside for a day or two!"

"Hah! Dream on. You hope I'll go easy on you." Friedr laughed too. "You do have a point. though. You're pretty much covered already, so I can't imagine yours will be too extensive this time."

***

Edwin peered through the flashing spots that interfered with his vision, trying to see himself in the mirror of colorist Janae's treatment room. He was stark naked, but he wasn't body shy. Janae had seen him before, as had her assistant, so that didn't worry him. What did worry him were the new brown vines with brown and green leaves winding up both legs from toe to ankle to hip in close spirals, almost like layers. The new vines now entwined with the ones that had already graced his thigh and twined up to his buttocks.

Very little unaugmented skin now showed on his legs and buttocks. The vines rose over his hips, intricately crossing over his buttocks, joining the leafy vines and thorns that already trailed across his back. Together, they covered his back, with tendrils rising over his shoulders. Many new runes for wisdom and strength were closely woven into them.

A new, large crescent moon now rode just below his navel, cupping it. Green stars were sprinkled up both inner thighs and on his belly, crossing his chest. The moon and stars were healers' augmentations, and the brown vines signified earth-magic.

"I'd hoped Aeos had finished with you, Edwin." Janae's voice sounded strange. She was seriously overextended, but Edwin couldn't think clearly enough to help her, though he knew he should try. "I saved yours for last, thinking it would be least, but…."

"Rest. You should rest." Edwin's voice was thick, and the words were hard to form. "You need a healer. You need…." He held a loose linen robe in his hands, not sure why he had it. "Your journeyman, Elner, where is he?"

The heat was rising in Edwin's veins, and he worked hard to control it. Surges roared through his brain, a torrent of chi.

The last time he'd been augmented so greatly, it had taken all of Christoph's attention to help him control the surges of chi gathering in his system, and this augmentation had been much more extensive.

Edwin stood staring at the mirror and did not see Janae fall unconscious, lying next to Elner's unconscious form. He'd forgotten her, forgotten everything but the all-consuming fire in his veins.

Edwin tried to focus on building his barriers with a good buffer next to his skin. If only he could concentrate….

Concentrate? What was he going to do? A roaring sounded in his ears, and his blood felt ablaze. All he could see was an ocean of red. He was an empty vessel yet was filled to overflowing with sensations demanding to be set free, though some distant part of him still refused, sensing it would be very bad to do so.

Clutching something in his hand, he walked blindly toward the anteroom. He paused in the doorway, no longer sure of where he was or why he was there.

Christoph and Zan looked up, seeing Edwin standing naked and clutching his still-folded robe in front of him. His eyes were wild. He was shaking and sweating, and obviously out of his mind.

Seeing the magnitude of Edwin's new augmentation, Christoph pulled himself together and said, "Oh dear Goddess, not again. Zan, Friedr, help me get him into his robe." They were all three fighting surges, but with Friedr's help, Chris got Edwin partly covered so they could lead him out into the specially shielded garden set aside for just that purpose. Due to his own extensive augmentation, Christoph was having problems with his own barriers and couldn't seem to get one over Edwin. "At least I was able to layer dampening fields over you two before my own augmentation was done."

Edwin tried to pull away from them, and Christoph grabbed his arm. "Edwin, can you hear me? You have to smooth the flows. Edwin, concentrate!" Christoph's voice had the sound of panic in it. "Edwin, you have to help me here." Something was building under Christoph's feet. "No, no don't do that…bleed the chi off, don't use it!" Chris's thoughts skittered all over, and he couldn't get a grip on them. "Earth…I can feel earth…." He could sense a massive earth spell building and had absolutely no idea how to counter it. "Edwin, don't do that! Bleed it off!"

Friedr and Zan both looked as frightened as Christoph felt. Friedr tried to raise a basic earth-shield and couldn't focus enough to do it. The ground began to rumble beneath their feet, as Zan's effort at shielding failed too.

"Bleed it off, Edwin!" Friedr yelled at him. Their terror grew with every rumble in the garden.

"He can't hear you." Zan's voice seemed to get Edwin's attention. At least he looked at Zan with unfocused eyes. "Bleed it off!"

The ground under the shielded garden rumbled ominously just as Dane entered from the healers' entrance, and the water in the koi pond shot up as if it were a fountain. Dane immediately layered a heavy dampening field over Edwin, cutting the others off from him, striding across the lawn, casting and layering spells as he went. Shielding everyone from the torrential outpouring of unfocused chi that cascaded from Edwin, Dane shunted it away from him to bleed off harmlessly and then layered a buffering shield over him, with a semi-permanent shunt venting the excess chi away.

He then turned to the others, who had each been heavily altered also. Of the three, Zan was most changed. "Good, it looks like Chris got a field up over you two before you could do any damage, but Christoph, you need some help." Dane layered a dampening field over Christoph, who was then better able to concentrate on smoothing his own flows.

Looking about the garden, Dane saw an older journeyman healer, Denis, and called to him to go to Janae. "She and Elner must both be in a bad way. She would never have let them out on their own if she had use of her senses. Then come back here and help me with these four, please." He suspected she must be in serious trouble after he saw the extent of the augmentations she had been called to make on the four of them.

"Janae...," Edwin's eyes were focusing again now that Dane had bled off the chi gathering in his new augmentations. "Too much." He began struggling to go back to the colorist's studio. "It was too much for them."

"Don't worry about them. We have them well taken care of, I promise. Let's just work on smoothing the flows for you, Edwin," Dane said. "Let's walk over here for a moment, and we'll level these currents a bit."

No matter what spell Dane cast to calm him, Edwin couldn't seem to stop fretting about Janae. Dane kept the dampening field layered on him, bleeding off the chi as it built up and forcefully keeping him diverted from the two colorists' plight. Finally, he said, "I don't want to have to put you to sleep, but you've *got* to stop being a healer long enough to be healed yourself!"

At last, four healers carried Janae on one stretcher and Elner on another through the corner of the garden to the healers' entrance. "See, there she goes. They've taken her to the infirmary where she'll be just fine." On seeing that, Edwin calmed down. Soon, Denis returned to work with Zan, Friedr, and Christoph, rebuilding their slipping dampening fields and helping to smooth Zan's flows. Zan was shaking and sweating as much as Edwin and fighting to control the surges.

Soon after, a semi-retired healer-adept, Rayne, entered the garden. "Don't worry, Dane, I'm here to help." She took Christoph and Friedr, who were still shaken, leaving Denis free to concentrate on Zan. "We'll have this under control in no time."

They walked in circles in the small garden, bleeding excess chi off from Edwin and Zan. After an hour, the healers deemed Edwin and Zan could handle bleeding off their own chi and returned to work, leaving

Dane to finish the day in the way originally scheduled for the five of them.

***

Christoph, Friedr, Zan, and Edwin sat at a table in the shielded garden, discussing what their augmentations might mean. Edwin alternated sitting on a soft cushion and lying on his stomach or standing. Both sides of him were tender. The only places not augmented were either very private or on the soles of his feet.

Dane had cast special healing and pain relief spells all morning on the four of them. The healing could not be done too quickly, or the mage would have more trouble adjusting to the augmentations. They would be healed over by the afternoon but their newly colored skin would be tender for several days, as getting used to storing the excess magic would take a while. The four mages were used to the feel of new augmentations, but in much smaller increments. Of them all, only Edwin had ever before received large augmentations and never as large as this.

Dane applied soothing ointments, and made them drink an herbal tea with willow for pain and special nutrients to help with the severe augmentation reaction.

Edwin was unable to get comfortable. "At least if this goes the way my last big one did, I should be nearly back to normal by the day after tomorrow. But I'll still have to make house calls tomorrow morning." He groaned. "I never thought I'd be begging you to heal my butt!"

"And I never thought I'd have to heal that part of your anatomy," Dane replied, trying not to chuckle at Edwin's plight.

Christoph had been given the augmentations representing earth and water. Brown, leafy vines twined with the green, leafy ones he already had. Blue flowers now bloomed on the green vines. He kept shaking his head with wonder. "I can sense the soil now, Edwin. It has a strange texture. And I can easily find water, which I was only able to call when I really concentrated. This is going to make plant healing so much easier. For me, earth does not feel like a weapon. It's more like a warm, nurturing cocoon. But I could really sense when you were shaking the Temple down. It was terrifying."

Edwin said, "Even *I* can't shake down the Temple, not with the way I've shielded this garden. No one else felt it, I guarantee you." He agreed with Christoph about the texture of earth.

After more discussion, they finally decided Edwin's augmentations were for the same purpose as his original ones, though what the magnitude of his augmentations signified was still a mystery. "Why would anyone ever need the amount of chi you'll have access to?" Zan's question was echoed in all their faces.

"I'll worry about that when the time comes," Edwin told them. "Marya might be a bit upset at first, but she'll get used to my colorful self. The magic knows what it needs. I suppose it's too late to change it back." The others nodded.

Of them all, only Chris was happy with his new tattoos. Friedr and Zan were not as philosophical as Edwin about their augmentations. Both men had the look of men who were faced with a lifetime of horror.

"I don't know how Aeolyn is going to take being married to me now." Friedr's voice was uncharacteristically quiet. "She married a warrior, not a gentle healer." He'd been subdued all morning, since he first looked into the mirror and saw the crescent moon on his brow and the healer's stars on his right cheek, falling in a trail down his neck to his chest and belly, along with the blue lightning bolt on his left cheek in front of his ear.

Runes for empathy had been woven throughout his other augmentations, and a green, leafy, blue-flowering vine woven with runes for empathy trailed from just below his left ear, crossing his chest and also twined about his thighs, winding around the dragons that had been augmented there over the previous year. Beneath his right ear was a tiny crescent moon. "I won't have time for healing in the infirmary. I have a full schedule now." He fidgeted nervously, stricken with insecurity such as he'd never felt.

Dane realized what was happening to Friedr, explaining how his new empathic ability was beginning to assert itself. "Friedr, watch what I'm doing for you." Dane layered a healer's barrier over Friedr. "Before you and Zan go home tonight, you'll both have to know how to build and maintain your own healer's barriers."

He had already shown Zan how to do it. "You already know how to tie them off. It's the same as for Edwin's new shields. Once you're able to make shields again, lace your barrier into your shields and you'll find it'll stay up."

As the barrier took hold, Friedr calmed down and could think clearly again. "This is going to take some getting used to." He shook his head. "Aeolyn doesn't like weak men."

"You'll soon find out healers are the strongest men and women you'll ever know." Dane glared at him.

"You've been unable to see the true reality of life until now, barbarian. This'll truly make a man out of you."

"You misunderstand me, Dane. *I* am terrified. I fear I won't be able to handle it," Friedr confessed, his blue eyes full of dread and worry. "I don't consider healers weak! On the contrary, I think you're the bravest people I know and have always thought so. I can't bear the thought of allowing someone to be as close to me as a healer must do with a patient. *I* am weak."

"I know exactly how you feel, Friedr." Zan's dark eyes were full of concern and apprehension for his own future. "This is just so wrong. How could this have happened to me?"

Friedr looked at Zan's transformation for the first time and realized with a surge of pity that his own could have been much worse. He murmured consolingly, "We'll get through this somehow, Zan. If Edwin can do it, then so can we."

Zander nodded, trying not to wallow in his bout of misery.

Christoph was so wrapped up in his own transformation that he wasn't really listening. He could see the others were worried, but for some reason he couldn't sympathize with them. He was just so darned happy! He thought about another time Friedr had been full of self-doubt. "Friedr, remember the time Edwin accidentally burned off your beard because you didn't shield yourself well enough, even though he warned you to?" His eyes sparkled wickedly. "You were sure Aeolyn would never share your bed again. She quite obviously did!" He doubled over laughing at the memory. "You kept moaning, 'My luck was in my beard!' all night!"

Zan looked in horror at Christoph. "Oh Christoph Berryman, how could you say that to his face? *No one* mentions the beard to Friedr, ever."

Friedr turned bright red, and his eyes looked like they were going to pop out of his head. He suddenly radiated anger.

"Firm your barriers, Friedr," murmured Edwin, trying not to snicker.

Zan glared at Christoph, who was now cackling uncontrollably. "Friedr—please don't kill my father! He's gone mad with augmentation reaction!" Zander's brown eyes suddenly took in Friedr's innocent, teen-aged face. "Wait a minute—I never knew Edwin did that to you. But everyone says D'Mal burned off your beard in the big battle you had with him."

"Yeah, it's what they *say* all right." Christoph's mood was contagious. "I wonder who started that rumor, Friedr. Who would do such a thing?"

Edwin couldn't help it. His guffaws became howls bordering on hysteria. Zan looked at him nervously. He finally calmed down enough to gasp, "It was hilarious, with you almost cutting your own throat trying to shave off the rest with your sword." Edwin's sides hurt. The joke was stupid, but it just seemed so funny. "Chris, what was it he yelled at me?"

Friedr fumed.

"He kept yelling, 'A warrior whose beard has been violated shaves with his sword!'" Christoph stabbed the air with an imaginary sword. Zan burst out laughing at the mental picture Christoph had just presented, completely forgetting Friedr had a terrible lack of humor regarding the incident of the beard.

Once again hooting maniacally, Edwin pounded on the table.

"What are you so happy about, farm boy?" Friedr's outrage was marred by his own tendency to giggle. "My reputation has suffered terribly thanks to your inconsiderate behavior. No one takes me seriously anymore. They all call me 'Cutie Pie' behind my back, just like when I was a novice! One stupid minotaur even called me a 'cute little boy with a toy sword,' right before I gutted him."

"But you *were* so cute,' Edwin gasped. "You're still just so awfully cute." Zan and Christoph could hardly breathe at this point.

"You have no room to talk, pretty-boy," Friedr said, stifling his chuckles. "You're the lonely barmaid's dream come true." He turned to Zan. "When Edwin walks into the common room, the poor things swarm him. I swear you can't pry them off without a crowbar! Just try to get one to serve you a drink with him at the table—there won't be one girl who'll pay any attention to you all the way to Mal Evol. He attracts women and beasts in equal quantities. Your sword will be busy, Zander, but nothing else!"

"Oh, a low blow, barbarian. I would trade you my burden any time." Edwin's attempts to calm himself failed. He blurted out, "Marya swears she'll require you to protect her interests, Friedr. And now that you're a healer, you can't kick my poor wounded butt for it." That set them all off again, and Edwin stood up to gasp for breath. "I can't believe I've been augmented on my backside. Oh, Goddess, it hurts to sit down, but it hurts to stand up too."

"It was probably the only place available." Friedr said, once he got his breath back. "The soles of your feet are the only patch of bare skin left."

"Sad but true," Edwin agreed, also attempting to speak more soberly. "Remind me not to swear to any more quests, no matter how good it sounds at the time."

Dane made a note in his file that they had now entered the silly phase of augmentation reaction and smiled, satisfied with their progress.

Despite the hilarity Zan had remained fairly quiet. His augmentation was less radical than Edwin's but was nonetheless extensive, and he too had been under a heavy dampening field all day. He was still in shock over his transformation. He was strong in all the elements, but his main strength had always been in lightning. Zan's augmentations up to that morning had been well-balanced for a battle-mage. They were still well-balanced, but now he had many more of them, far more than any normal mage would ever need.

The rune for wisdom over Zan's right eye was new, as was the luck rune on his left cheek. The green, leafy vine with blue flowers climbing his left arm from wrist to neck was new also, as were the runes for empathy and wisdom closely woven into it.

His back was adorned with his original yellow lightning bolt crossing from upper right shoulder to his waist, but it now had the addition of healer's stars and the green vine with blue flowers twining it and trailing to his left hip. Strength and stealth runes twined and wove through it. A crescent moon rode the web between his thumb and forefinger on his right hand, and green stars were placed on each knuckle of both hands. Healer's stars were sprinkled down both legs to his knees. A brown, thorny vine with small blue flowers wound among the stars. All the elements were balanced with equal strength.

Worst of all—at least to Zan—he now bore the crescent moons of the healer-adept. Now he had the marks indicating he had been given a full and equal gift for healing, along with one other, shocking addition— the stealth rune. A large rune for stealth was placed under his left arm, and another large one was centered under his right ear. Many smaller stealth runes were hidden elsewhere. *What does it mean? Why did this happen to me?* His mind ran in circles, but he hid his confusion and uncertainty, laughing and joking with the others.

Zan was now fully aware that, with the exception of Christoph, the others were all as confused and uncertain as he was and worried about their own futures. The knowledge didn't comfort him. The fact he could feel their thoughts without their voicing them horrified him. It was as if a window had opened in his mind, making him privy to the thoughts and feelings of everyone around him.

As the afternoon wore on, they passed through the silly stage and entered the sleepy stage. They napped fitfully on the cushioned lounges, and Zan periodically woke, feeling overwhelmed with emotions he knew were not his. *I was so much happier before I knew how other people felt.* Checking, he realized he had let his healer's barrier slip again, and he carefully rebuilt it and layered it into his shields as Dane and Edwin had taught him, tying it off. *I just never saw myself as a healer.*

I'm far too selfish and self-centered. What a mess. Maybe I'm an assassin. Oh, Goddess.... He opened his eyes to see Edwin lying on his stomach and looking at him.

"You're not an assassin, any more than I am, Zan. You'll get used to it, but I don't think we're assassins. You're a lot like me now. Maybe not as strong, but I think you'll find you're an air-mage." Edwin's eyes closed and he drifted off.

Edwin lay dozing on his stomach. Periodically, he woke and wondered how he was going to make it through the next few weeks, trying to work without letting the world know he had been augmented extensively again.

Christoph lay with his arm over his eyes, looking as if he was sleeping. He was wide awake, thinking furiously about his next paper on the theory and application of earth-magic from the perspective of a healer. Water-magic would be the subject of paper that followed.

Friedr dealt with his appalling alteration the way he always dealt with difficulties—he slept, dead to the world.

As the afternoon passed, they woke, then discussed the changes they were going through and what it might mean for them on a personal level.

Dane told Friedr, "Your ability is such we'll have to fully train you, or you'll run into some problems. You have the strength to be, at the very least, a fine journeyman healer. The Temple needs you desperately. You have no idea. You may end up as an adept. I can't really tell at this juncture, but you do have the strength of an adept if you can allow yourself to do it. Your augmentations say you have the ability, but only your willingness to completely submit to Aeos's plan for you will allow you to fully realize it.

"There've always been battle-mages like Rall and Halee who have over time gained a small ability to heal," he reminded Friedr and Zan. "We don't try to make them into healers here in the infirmary since they really are only able to tend to small injuries and such, but their skills as field medics are critical in their posts with the Temple Militia. We do keep an eye on them because of the problems the empathy causes when they first use their elemental-magic." His serious tones had their attention. "You two will require the proper intensive training healers must have for you to properly use your gifts. You have been chosen as healers just as Edwin has." Dane's voice took on a grim note. "But there is a problem lurking for all three of you, and for Christoph most especially, I fear.

"Battle-mages with minor healing empathy are thought most likely to lose themselves in the magic and die an ugly, needless death, just as healers with no ability whatsoever to call water are the most likely to suffer empathic shutdown. When you begin calling elemental-magic all three of you absolutely *must* be vigilant in maintaining your healer's barriers woven into your battle shields with a buffer next to your skin. Edwin will help you.

"Zan, you're in a different position from Friedr. You've been given the stealth runes. To my healing-sense, you feel much more like Edwin than you do any other sort of mage." Dane looked sharply at Zan who, for once, was paying attention. "It may be you'll be an air-mage too. Time will tell. I do know this: in order to keep your chi balanced, you and Friedr are both going to have to divide your time between the two disciplines as Edwin does."

"That would be good!" Edwin agreed, his eyes lighting up. "It's been hard being the only one. And I'm glad you've been blessed with the stealth rune, Zan. Now I won't stand out so much."

"I see why you always wear your hair down, though. I was a fair lightning-mage, but what will I do now?" Zan felt overwhelmed, confused. "I had a plan for my life. Now though, I don't know."

"Don't worry, my brother," Edwin said, placing his hand on Zan's shoulder. "We'll work it out and you'll be much better off, you'll see. I've always found the greatest joy in my life as a healer."

Zan nodded. He was touched Edwin had called him brother, sensing he meant it and feeling grateful for Edwin's calm serenity in the face of his own radical augmentations.

Dane once again spoke firmly to Christoph, Friedr, and Zan about the necessity of maintaining their barriers at all times. His professional voice hid his concern. When he first saw Christoph's transformation, he had been stricken with the terrible dread that Christoph would not be able to maintain the proper barrier/shield combination. He buried his fear and refused to acknowledge it.

As the College of Warcraft and Magic closed down for the day, they were deemed able to go home. Zan would have to stay the night with Dane and Christoph, as they both felt he should not return to his bachelor apartment alone just yet.

Privately, Zan was happy to stay at his parents' house for the night, as he was terribly confused by the changes that had occurred so abruptly in his life. *I'm an idiot, needing Mommy and Daddy to comfort me,* he thought as he settled into his old room for the night. *When am I going to grow up and leave home? I spend more time here than I do in my own place. Tonight I'll stay here, but starting tomorrow I'll be adult and live in my own home. Dane needs the time we have left to spend with Chris, and they don't need me hanging around. Gah! How could I have not noticed that before?*

***

The colorist, Janae, was also the older sister of Abbess Halee. She had been treated in the infirmary, where she was receiving the best of care. She would be there for longer than just the one night, as would her journeyman, Elner. Father Rall and Abbess Halee sat in her darkened room, quietly discussing the radical augmentations she had been called upon to make that day.

"We must keep this from spreading around the college. The healers won't talk about it, and the fuss was confined to the colorist's garden, which was shielded by Edwin Farmer himself, using John's technique, so we should be able to keep it quiet." Halee's voice was rough from worry. "What a mess." Her eyes filled with tears as she said, "My sister is all I have left, you know. Aaugh, Goddess! I miss my husband. Bryson was so good with this sort of thing."

"His death has been hard on you. It's only been two months, Halee, not long enough for you to get past the initial pain of his loss. Believe me, I do understand. I'll never be completely over losing Feia." For the sake of the Temple, Rall needed to keep her pulled together. "You aren't to blame for this. The auguries weren't clear as to the extent of the augmentations. They only indicated they would be more extensive than usual. It's only hindsight that makes it apparent now. But the omens were very clear in this—all were to receive augmentations on this day before noon." His voice was low so as not to disturb Janae. "The magic chooses what will be required. Janae had no choice. Once she entered the trance, it was too late. A journeyman alone couldn't have performed any of these augmentations, and there are no other adepts in Aeoven right now. Colorists are simply too rare. We've never had enough."

"I know, Rall. But this is a bad omen. We should have read the signs better and called for Jamson to assist her. This needed two adepts and possibly two journeymen. When I look at the signs now, I can see we didn't read them and that's my fault. I failed my sister!" Her voice caught as she adjusted the blanket that covered Janae's sleeping form. Janae's face was pale, but she was recovering and wouldn't lose her abilities. Rall patted Halee's hand. Her and Bryson's only child, a son, died soon after birth, and they never had any other children. With his death, she felt truly alone, although everyone tried to keep her spirits buoyed up.

She was exhausted, but wouldn't leave her sister's bedside. "Nearly losing Janae and having a mage of Edwin's caliber going mad with augmentation reaction are bad omens. This quest has had a bad one for every good one since it was called. Now I fear greatly for

Edwin's safety. The prophecies speak of 'the beloved hero' falling to darkness, and it has not yet happened."

Halee recited the prophecy, though Rall knew it as well as she, "The Dark God laments his betrothed, she chooses him not. The hordes of the broken lands despoil verdant Mal Evol. Now send the heroes four into the land ruled by the Throne of Stone and Bone. Should the treasured one be lost to darkness, those left to walk in the light must flee down the Forbidden Road. Treasured and Beloved, beware the voice of reason. Long days of darkness shadow the realm. The poisoned land flowers, but death walks amidst poison and thorn. When blooms the land again, the day of redemption is at hand. Four heroes journey to bring forth the spring, but balanced on the edge of reason is the outcome."

Rall nodded. "That's a troubling prophecy."

She agreed. "We know the land of Mal Evol cannot be saved until the Beloved Hero falls and at least one generation has passed, or perhaps even two. I believe if Edwin falls to darkness, we will have a dreadful, terrible enemy on our hands. His new augmentations indicate he will be the strongest earth-mage in the Temple, and his strength of water is now equal to his father's. With Edwin's command of air-magic, D'Mal would have an invincible ally." Her eyes were red and ringed with dark circles. "And what do you think John would do if such a thing were to occur? He'd go mad."

"It won't be Edwin who falls to the blandishments of the Bull God," Father Rall replied, patting her hand gently. "I've foreseen Edwin's future. Perhaps the one who is to fall has fallen already." He knew more than he was saying but was unwilling to voice his true knowledge when Halee had so much to worry about.

Instead, Rall told her enough of what he knew that she would be somewhat mollified. "Two quests have failed in the last year. Four questers, *all* of whom are most beloved, have gone missing and are presumed dead, my grandson, Ivar, among them. Don't worry about Edwin. He will preserve Neveyah, just as his father before him did. I have foreseen it. Those four will save us all."

Rall's eyes were moist at the thought of his grandson, a promising, young fire-mage. Still, he had two other grandchildren and his son, Kalen, and Kalen's wife, Gayla. Gayla was his oldest friend's daughter, and that meant he was bound to Jules Brendsson more closely than blood could ever bind them. The two men had shared Ivar's loss and found strength in their unity. He reminded himself, *My life is rich because I still have family.*

Chapter 6 ~ Love is All There Is

The early winter days passed, turning into weeks, during which the questers managed to fall into a routine that allowed them to have the most time with their families. Marya quickly discovered that kissing the new crescent moon on Edwin's belly to "make it all better" led to some interesting moments. Aeolyn also greatly appreciated the way Friedr looked now, with all the healer's stars and took every opportunity to let him know it.

The two women did quite a bit of whispering and giggling, a fact their husbands noticed but wisely chose to not mention.

Daily, Zan accompanied Edwin on healing rounds and then assisted with teaching barriers and shielding classes. Edwin was the only mage who had the skills to teach Zan to use his air-magic. They worked well together, and soon developed a close friendship, Edwin feeling very much like he had found a younger brother.

Zan was quick to learn and willing to try anything regarding battle-magic. Initially reluctant as a healer, once he got past his anxiety, he proved kind and gentle with their patients. Not surprisingly, Zan was interested in taking up the task of healing emotional trauma.

Having two healers for parents and also having been terribly injured as a child, he understood well what was involved. "Now that I have this ability, I can perhaps repay you for everything you've done for me," he said, when Beryl, the Dean of Healers, asked him what area of healing he thought he would want to focus on. "I can think of no greater calling than to follow in you and Christoph's footsteps as a mind-healer."

Zan also immediately began developing his skills as an air-mage. While he fervently hoped never to have to will a knife from his chest, he was good at moving paper and wood from place to place. The hard thing for him was learning to whisper on the wind the way Edwin did. He was not as yet very good at it, his range much narrower than Edwin's. "I wasn't very good to begin with either," Edwin said. Zan could eavesdrop well and at a great distance. He had to work much harder at calling water from the mist than he did at whispering on the wind, perhaps because of his affinity for lightning, although he persevered and improved each day.

John Farmer had begun attending the class for the retired mages, where he had reconnected with many of his old friends. He intended to present his plan to teach veterinary skill to the conclave before the annual long-session ended, but needed Halee to submit his proposal to them. "Every animal healer with an ounce of healing ability has long ago left Aeoven to help the farmers in the rural areas. I can resolve that." He handed her the sheaf of papers that was his carefully crafted curriculum, with all the costs and benefits clearly laid out.

After reading it, Halee agreed to support him but was disturbed that he refused to teach water-magic. After a long discussion, she accepted that he felt unfit to teach magic. She was able to get his request on their agenda on the last day of the conclave.

Healers were in terribly short supply, and John's veterinary school gave Father Rall the incentive to start a special college for herb doctors and animal healers. "Even though they aren't gifted with magic, they will be bound to serve Neveyah the same way all Temple healers are. No one will lack for good medical care nor will they fear abuse at the hands of a fraud."

Having received the Temple's blessing, John immediately began training several promising children and young adults to handle most common ailments, despite the fact they demonstrated little healing abilities and no affinity for magic. They wanted to heal animals, which was all that was necessary.

***

Zander and Friedr were astonished when, on the day after they were augmented, Edwin asked if they too could see the elemental-magic with their healing-sight, though Christoph was not surprised. Opening their healing-sight, they watched him calling water, and they could clearly see the rope-like energy of the magic. "Now I understand why you learned so quickly when you came here." Friedr's amazement was echoed in Zan's face. "I knew you thought you could see magic, but now I know you *do* see it."

"This is a huge advantage," agreed Zan. "I knew lightning felt very different from water, but now that I see why, it's amazing." Like a child with a new toy, he could not resist looking at the magic at every opportunity.

Surprisingly, Christoph had also developed the skill of calling water from the mist, proving the ability was connected to having strong healing-magic combined with a strong water affinity. He was sure Friedr could call water from the mist too if he tried and pushed him until he too developed the skill. Christoph's waking moments were now consumed with his research into how the magics worked and what their differences actually were.

"It's strange how I can call water from a cloud now, when before I could barely get it from a well with a bucket." Christoph's remark made Abbess Halee smile. She sensed he was trying to write a library of new theory, because he wrote at least one paper a week and often wrote two or more.

Christoph would never again work as a healer in the infirmary, though his skills as a mind-healer with emotionally damaged patients were sorely missed. His new abilities with water-and-earth-magic had turned his healing ability to plants and soil healing. Abbess Halee insisted Christoph now concentrate on his study of magic theory and application and develop his plan for healing the soil of Mal Evol. He approached this with a true appreciation for both sides of magic, diving headlong into learning every aspect and nuance of uses and applications for his earth-and-water-magic skills.

***

Edwin, Friedr, and Zan had each visited the blade-smith to have new blades created especially for them. It was the first time in two generations the Temple smiths had been asked to make even one special magically enhanced blade, and now they were making three. A staff would be created and bespelled for Christoph, and while his was the first, the master smith-mage had been sent a true-dream that told him all healers would have a staff bespelled for them from this time forward. Christoph's staff would be the great masterwork of the smith-mage whose task it was to create it.

They also went for the final fitting of their new armor, which was as secret and arcane a ritual as that for the blade, but was done much more frequently. Nearly every mage and healer out on Temple business had special armor bespelled just for them two or three times in their life, depending on the needs of their quest, so that wasn't too unusual.

A fire-mage adept named Dario, whom Friedr had regularly trounced in mage-duels when they were young journeymen, ribbed him. "Those new healer's stars mean you're a gelded pony now. Everyone knows healers can't use swords or battle-magic." He'd been out of Aeoven on Temple business during Friedr's mage-duel with Edwin and simply couldn't believe the rumors he had heard. The resulting duel was quick and ended with predictable bloodshed, and bruises on Dario's part.

Friedr magnanimously healed him and offered to give him the chance to try to best him again, no matter how many tries it took. "I can do this as often as it takes," he said in his friendliest manner. "I have all day and more than enough chi. If I'm too gentle for you, Edwin Farmer should be done with his class soon. He's a gelded pony too, you know. Perhaps he'd be able to offer you some sport. He certainly kicks *my* butt on a daily basis!"

Dario wasn't about to test that theory. He refused the offer, apologizing profusely. "No, no, thank you anyway. You've handed me my ass in a hat as always, and I accept it. Now I owe you an ale at the Mages Rest—bless you for healing me so we can enjoy it!"

Friedr was actually disappointed Dario had quit so soon. "I wonder how many times I could heal him and then wipe the floor with his sorry backside before I run out of chi?" he asked Edwin as they walked home that evening. "Has that ever been done? I'd like to do it just to see if it could be done."

Edwin just smiled and shook his head in mock despair. "Thank the Goddess you're still the consummate barbarian, Friedr. We were beginning to worry you'd turned into a civilized man!"

"Why, thank you, Edwin. Coming from you that means a great deal." Friedr couldn't keep from grinning happily all night just thinking about it. Aeolyn just rolled her eyes when he mentioned he would have liked the chance to test his limits.

***

A deep, personal understanding of the pitfalls of using and misusing the combined healing-and-battle-magics was brought home to Christoph.

He was enthralled with using his new abilities, but his barrier/shield was fragile and often dissipated while he was immersed in the magic. Sometimes he could bring himself back when he had sent his senses out searching the earth or the waters, but not all the time, and someone always had to bring him out of the trance.

One problem was that when he sent his spirit out sailing under the earth or riding the water his body forgot to keep itself warm. During the warm weather, it would not be an issue, but during the winter, this could cause the mage to die from hypothermia. This was a very recent discovery. Only Edwin Farmer had ever been able to do this, and until Edwin suffered from it, no one knew it could even be a problem.

Another problem was a well-known dilemma that had plagued mages since the beginning of time and was one of the reasons the Temple created the College of Warcraft and Magic in the first place. An inexperienced mage could inadvertently enter the element, at which point the element consumed him. It happened most often with fire- or lightning-mages and was rare with earth- or water-mages yet well-documented reports existed in the archives of it happening to young mages of those elements.

Cayne, the new instructor of water-magic, tutored him in the basics the day after the augmentations. He had seen the mage duel as a signal that experimenting with new forms of magic was the new norm. However, he didn't believe what he'd heard about healing empathy causing trouble for battle mages, and didn't understand that Christoph, being a healer by nature, could become lost in sensations of the elements, and wouldn't be able to bring himself back.

Upset with Cayne's lack of perception and worried about his father, Zan approached John Farmer, offering to work with him in repairing on the failing sewers out at the husbandry complex if he would tutor Chris in the process.

Frankly, John needed the help. Still unable to fully use his magic due to battle trauma, but too ashamed to admit it even to Edwin, he was back at the stage of a young journeyman, and he was likely to not get the drains repaired by the day he had promised to have it done by.

Teaching Chris the basics helped John regain his strength and rebuild his visualization skills. He was able to show him many ways to use the elements of earth and water for creating irrigation and drainage systems, but even he was unable to convince Chris of his peril when it came to the sensuality of the magic.

No matter who chided him, Christoph always let his buffer slip, and Zan wasn't sure if he was doing it on purpose of not.

Edwin caught Christoph using his magic when no one was around to bring him back. Livid, he reminded him of the dangers of leaving his body for prolonged lengths of time. "What will happen to this quest if you die before we even get to Mal Evol? You know what you need to do there, and I will make sure you do it, but you have to be alive when we get there, or your dream of making the land bloom again is over before it can even begin."

Chris promised to take more care, but the sensuality of the magic was a temptation he couldn't walk away from, despite the danger.

Dane argued with Chris several times for not properly buffering himself and thereby allowing himself to get lost in the magic, when he, of all people, knew better. "I can't believe you're behaving like a novice with your abilities. Don't make me set restrictions on you." The threat of restrictions got his attention, and Christoph promised to work harder building his barrier/shield. He faithfully promised to only use his magic when someone was there to bring him back, swearing to Dane he would be responsible in the use of his new magic abilities.

Despite his promise, Christoph allowed himself to get lost in the magic again and again, and Dane's fear and anger at Christoph's failing erupted in a series of quarrels.

***

Two weeks after his radical augmentation, Christoph did not arrive home at his usual time and did not send a messenger saying he would be late. Knowing in his heart what had happened and fearing the worst, Dane sent a messenger for Zan to come quickly. He immediately responded, joining Dane to search the gardens.

It was only the third week of the New Year, and winter had arrived in force, along with wind and rain. Together they searched everywhere they could think of in the rain and dark, frantic, and fearful that if they got the Temple Watch involved in searching for Christoph, he would be barred from going on the quest, which would break his heart.

Finally, just as they were about to get Edwin and Friedr to help, they found Chris sitting on the damp earth in an out-of-the-way corner of the freshly spaded garden behind the chicken barn, lost in the magic. It was obvious he had simply sat down with the intent of taking a brief look at the newly turned soil but was alone when he had done so, and once in the trance had been unable to resist the sensual lure of the magic.

Unfortunately, only the day before, he'd sworn to Dane he would never again do such a thing until he could reliably buffer himself from the magic and bring himself out of the trance. His promise to Dane had obviously been forgotten.

Terrified they were too late to save him, Zander shook him from his trance, finally bringing him back to confused awareness, while Dane wrapped a cloak around him, casting healing and strengthening spells. Christoph shivered uncontrollably, weak and incoherent when he tried to speak. "His pulse is too slow." Dane's voice was sharp with worry. Wrapped in Dane's cloak, they carried Chris home.

Fortunately, their house was not too far. The skin on his face and hands was blue with cold, and Dane cast more healing spells to keep frostbite from setting in. Dane labored for an hour, trying to heal him. Linked, Zan followed along with his sight, supporting him and in the process learning more than he ever wanted to know about treating hypothermia.

Christoph had recovered enough to be terribly embarrassed. Of course, he attempted to apologize, but even he was aware of just how lame his excuses sounded. In his usual way, he was fully aware of the trouble he had caused, but tried to play it down.

"I'm sorry. I didn't mean for this to happen. I was just looking at the soil, and I forgot what time it was. I swear, I promise I'll buffer myself better. I really didn't intend to go so far. I just didn't realize so much time had passed, that's all. I wasn't paying attention. I can pull myself out of the magic whenever I want to. It won't happen again, I promise."

His hollow excuses and pathetic apologies didn't ring true, even to him. Christoph knew that subconsciously or not, he did *not* buffer himself properly, and therefore he was solely to blame for his near-death experience.

Kneeling in front of Christoph and casting a healing spell one more time, Zan was unable to find the words to express himself. Confusion, fear, and anger warred in his heart. His voice, rough with emotion, was harsh as he said, "I love you, Chris. You're the father I always wanted. But you're risking your life if you insist on working alone, because you're not, for whatever reason, able to maintain a buffer next to your skin, and the magic always gets the better of you. Be honest about this. Lying to yourself can kill you, when it comes to your magic. Lying to us is not going to change the fact that you can't handle the magic without someone to bring you back."

Christoph's face sagged. He dropped his eyes, and his shoulders slumped.

Zan didn't care. "You *must* let Edwin and me work with you before you go and kill yourself. You're too stubborn for your own good!" His voice was loud, and sharp. "You *knew* when you sat down in the corner that you might not be able to bring yourself back. Yet you did it, knowing full well you'd *promised* you wouldn't do it again." He forced his father to look him in the eye. "We're not going to allow you to die because you can't remember your promise when you're out of your body. We'll set a truth geas on you if we have to."

Zan didn't see Christoph wince as he rose and slung his cloak on over his shoulders to leave. After embracing Dane and squeezing his shoulder supportively, he quietly let himself out the front door, leaving Dane standing in the bedroom, angry and silent. Christoph sat on the bed, sick to his stomach with regret and fear.

While listening to Christoph's lame excuses, Dane had become more and more livid, clenching his mouth shut to keep from screaming. As the door closed behind Zan, Dane reached his breaking point. The stark realization he had been a fool, regularly enabling Chris's self-indulgent behavior, burned away all his barriers, exposing the hard core of raw pain accumulated in small amounts over the length of their relationship. Trivial hurts, casually inflicted wounds had slowly formed a small core of despair in his heart

This hard stone of misery lay dormant, deeply buried under his resolve to make the best of every day. Dane himself had been unaware of its existence until this moment. Now that it was unleashed, the pain of his knowledge overwhelmed him.

Abruptly shouting, "I don't *care* about your apologies! I don't *want* to hear your excuses!" he paced back and forth in their bedroom, too upset to remain still. His rage, long kept under control, exploded with the violence of a storm crashing down upon their home. For the first time in their long bonding, Dane told Chris exactly what he thought. His black eyes snapped as he hissed, "You *lied* to me, and I forgave you just like I always do, believing you really meant what you said. Your refusal to admit you know deep down in your heart that you're not able to break out of the magic is just a form of lying. It's a lie when you make those easy promises to me, and you know it." Dane's face had gone dusky with his wrath.

White-faced, Christoph opened his mouth to apologize, but Dane cut him off, brushing away his words with a wave of his hand. His voice broke as he shouted, "You swore to me yesterday you'd only use the magic when someone was there to bring you back. Now, only one day later, you're found like this, nearly dead of your own stupidity." Tears of rage stung his eyes, and he turned away, hands clenching and unclenching as he fought the urge to strike at Christoph with his fists.

Christoph shrank back from Dane's wrath, unsure of what would happen next. The moment passed, and speaking more calmly, Dane faced Christoph, forcing him to hear his words.

"Before we were bonded, it was other men, which was bad enough. Then it became small lies of convenience, promises made to keep me happy so you could do whatever you wanted."

Hearing the truth so bluntly laid bare, Christoph looked away, unable to meet Dane's condemning eyes.

"I've forgiven you over and over for those small lies. I don't even expect you to honor them anymore. But now…now your risk-taking is deadly. You risk your life with this madness. I can't believe anything you say anymore, no matter how many promises you make about shielding yourself properly." Dane's voice rose with every word he said, his features harsh with condemnation.

The anguish in Christoph's face was heartrending, but Dane was beyond caring by that point. "Your promises are nothing but lies! They're the most hurtful kind because they're *always* what I want to hear, but they're still nothing but lies in the end." Now he was overcome with the need to get away from Chris, away from the situation.

In a cold fury, Dane crossed to the closet and began tossing his clothes into his pack. "I can't live with you anymore, knowing you're courting death like a lover and planning to leave me alone and crying at your grave. I have to leave I have to get out of here right now if this is how you want to die. I'm going to stay with Zan."

Shaken, Christoph begged him to reconsider. "No, no, Dane, you're just hurt because I've done it again. Please don't do this. Please don't leave." He clutched his arm, but Dane shook him off. Tears streaked both of their faces. "We can solve this!"

Dane was halfway to the door, but he turned back. "I'm a tenured senior healer, remember? I have a duty to the Temple that supersedes my loyalty to you. Hear me now, Christoph Berryman. If you don't set your shields up so they buffer you from the magic and are tied off properly, I'll restrict you the way a young novice is restricted." Dane's voice dripped acid. Christoph's eyes widened, hurt Dane would consider such a thing.

Novices had unique barriers imposed on them so they could only use their magic under supervision, and Dane was an expert in imposing those sorts of barriers. "If I were to tell the abbess about this gross stupidity, what do you think she'd do? She'd set the restrictions on you herself, and she'd demote me back to journeyman for not bringing this to her attention sooner. You simply cannot risk yourself in this fashion."

Christoph looked at the floor, unable to even look at Dane. "I know, Dane. You're right, and my behavior is inexcusable. I don't know what else to say."

Dane set his pack down and placed both hands on Chris's shoulders. "How embarrassing it would be for you to have as an epitaph 'Here lies what few remains they could find of Christoph Berryman, the man who preached what he couldn't practice. He died proving he was right all along.'"

Dane picked up his pack, turned, and opened the door.

Christoph clung desperately to his arm, begging him to stay. "No, Dane! I said I was sorry. I swear it won't happen again." Frantic to keep his bonding together, he choked out, "I promise! I swear by everything I hold holy."

"Aaugh, Goddess what am I supposed to do now? This is what you promised only yesterday, you damned fool." Dane was torn, and angry at himself for being so. "I love you, Christoph. I always have. No matter what cruel thing you do, I love you. But I won't stand by and watch you court death the way you seem so compelled to do. I'm sorry, but I have to get away from this tragedy in the making. I just can't take it." Pulling free of Christoph's grasp, he walked out the door and began down the path to the street. "Goodbye, Christoph."

Christoph broke down, sobbing. "Dane, please—come back." The absolute truth of his love for Dane took Christoph by surprise. Stricken by the knowledge of what he was losing, that Dane could actually walk away from him, he was utterly broken. He knew without a doubt his life would be worth nothing without Dane. "Dane! Don't leave me, please, though I know I deserve it so many times over." He leaned against the door jamb, tears running down his face, sobbing as Dane turned and looked back. "I've never deserved you, but I've always loved you. Always."

He couldn't watch Dane leave. Covering his eyes as his legs gave out, he slid down the door frame, sitting and sobbing, not caring if the neighbors could see him or not. "No one has ever meant anything to me, except for you. You and Zan are the one good thing in my life, and I never deserved you. I did treat you dreadfully when I was young, so badly I don't know why you still loved me. I admit it, to my eternal shame. But since we bonded, there's never been anyone but you. Truth-read me if you don't believe me, please! I beg you to. I swear it on my vows to Aeos—I'll do whatever I must to regain your faith and I won't let you down. I swear it on my vows to the Goddess."

Sighing at his own stupidity, Dane turned back. "It's always a drama of some kind or other with you. Why can't I just walk away? I deserve better than this. I'm an idiot."

"You *do* deserve better than this," Christoph's voice was thick with self-loathing, and he was unable to look up, but he forced himself to say it. "I'll set you free, if that is truly your wish. But I'll never love anyone the way I love you. I beg of you, please give me another chance to prove it to you." His shoulders shook, and he was exhausted from the agony he had caused. "Please?"

Dane looked at him and then walked back into the house, setting his pack down. His face was set and hard with fury, as much at himself as at Chris. A feeling in the pit of his stomach told him he had just made a terrible mistake. He couldn't stop himself listening to Christoph, although he knew he was a fool. "Why should I believe this will be any different than any of your other promises? And if you don't have something besides lame apologies to offer, I'll pick up my pack and I won't look back!" Dane's anger made his voice too loud, but he was also past caring what the neighbors thought.

After a long, hard evening of frank discussion, they managed to put aside the pain. Awake in the silent darkness of their room, Christoph experienced a moment of absolute clarity. He realized the power of the magic paled in comparison to the power of love.

Love is all there is, love is the only thing worth fighting for. Thank you, Aeos, for giving me one last chance with Dane, he thought. *Now I have to prove to him I'm worthy of his decision to stay. Somehow, I have to make him glad he didn't leave me, and I know what I have to do to ensure that.* Tears rolled down his cheeks until at last, just as the sun was rising, he drifted into an exhausted sleep, still holding Dane, unwilling to let go of him.

Waking only a few hours later, he sent a messenger to both Edwin and Zan, asking them to meet him and help him with his barriers, despite it being Sunnaday.

As soon as he was free from his woodcutting crew, Edwin was curious but happy to help. He'd been worried about Christoph's problems with shielding and barriers and knew Christoph would never ask him to give up his Sunnaday afternoon without a very good reason. On leaving the mages' quarter for the wood lot well before dawn, Edwin noticed a lamp still burning in Chris's home, which struck him as odd.

Zan arrived at his parents' home ahead of Edwin. Christoph began by apologizing to him for the events of the previous evening. "Thank you, Zan, for being there to save my sorry ass. I beg you to forgive me and allow me to make it right with you."

"Christoph, you're still the man I always wished was my birth father. You made me who I am today. I know you didn't plan to do that last night, but you scared me to death. I can't lose any more family." He hugged Christoph in a rough hug, hiding the tears that stung his eyes. "You and Dane are all I have!"

His words struck home with Christoph, who struggled to keep his emotions under control. "I've always wanted to be worthy of your respect, and right now, I don't believe I am. This is the part of the conversation where I usually try to make it look better with a little lie. I'm not going to this time."

"No, no, don't do this to yourself," Zan replied. "No one is perfect. I wanted *you* for my father, not some ideal father from a storybook."

Christoph mutely hugged Zan. At that moment, Edwin arrived, and after sitting him down, Christoph confessed to Edwin that he had nearly broken his and Dane's bonding over this problem.

Edwin was silent, sad but unsurprised by this turn of events, and then said, "This has always been the difference between you and me, Christoph." He sighed, shaking his head. "I have a terror of losing control, and you don't. In many ways, you enjoy the feeling of having survived a dangerous experience, and so you push the boundaries a little further each time. You did the right thing to come to us with this problem, brother. We'll not fail you."

Chapter 7 ~ Marking Time

Zan had undergone a fundamental change that at first worried Dane but now pleased him. Before the augmentations, Zan was the image of the classic lightning-mage, mercurial, brilliant, flashy, and just a bit lazy. He'd never been able to settle down with one girl, flitting from relationship to relationship. The most recent of his former lovers, a pretty water-mage named Dyenne, had been exceedingly angry with him when, prior to the augmentations, they parted. She'd been rather public in the voicing of her displeasure.

One of the peculiarities of the social system within the Temple clergy was the custom of breakfasting, which was a result of their having no kitchens in the bachelor quarters. Thus, if two unattached journeymen of the opposite sex were seen breakfasting alone together in the dining room on Restday morning, it was assumed they had an informal understanding, and the other journeymen would not poach on their territory. The gossip mill in Aeoven was rife with news of who was breakfasting with whom, and rumors traveled through the clergy faster than lightning.

This frequently led to a somewhat public dissolving of understandings that had gone badly and since leaving the novice barracks, Zan had been the center of the storm in several unfortunate displays of jealous angst. His most recent misfortune occurred on his return from Einar, when he nonchalantly took his place at Dyenne's table as he had regularly done before his posting, attempting to take up where he'd left off as if nothing had happened.

Unfortunately, rumors of Zan's transgressions with the friendly-girls in Einar had filtered back to Aeoven, making him somewhat of a hero to the older boys who couldn't wait to become journeymen and emulate him, and a pariah to one lady in particular.

The morning of his return from Einar he'd come up behind her, kissed her cheek, sat down and said, "Hello, love. Did you miss me?" His eyes sparkled, sure she would forgive him.

Dyenne stood up. "Zander Christophson, I'm not one of your friendly-girls!" She then emptied her pitcher of water over his head and left the dining room in tears, while he sat shivering and wet, wondering where he went wrong. Though he repeatedly tried to appease her in the weeks before Holy Day, she was unyielding, refusing his every overture. At last, he gave up and left her in peace, though he was sure his heart was broken forever.

After the augmentations, Zan became much less of an extrovert, not putting himself in the spotlight at every opportunity as he was known to do before. He still frequently had too many thoughts to articulate at once, as lightning-mages often did. Also, he still had some rather erratic changes of direction conversationally, but they were not nearly as pronounced. Zan actually made good sense when he expressed himself now. With each day, he settled more and more into an even temperament. His extreme highs and lows leveled out to a reliable, generally positive attitude.

Daily, Zan assisted Edwin on his healing rounds, finding to his great surprise he was overwhelmed by the affection and responsibility he felt for his patients. He often thought about them and was concerned about their welfare when he was not working in the infirmary.

Gerde had been pleased to see Zan with Edwin, as he had been in the last group of young novices she had taught. "It's good the Goddess is making battle-mages into healers now, Zander. Maybe you'll avoid the cancer, with those fancy shields everyone is talking about."

The enjoyment Zan found in healing had opened his eyes to his other problem. By his own fault he was lonely, and now he was leaving on a long quest. He knew it wouldn't be fair to court anyone even if he could find a girl interested in being courted by him. The changes in him had so far gone unnoticed by his peers, other than his strange augmentations.

Zan hid his loneliness by presenting the image of a man who hadn't noticed he was alone in life. *No sense whining. Folks don't want to hear it. Besides, I have to leave one day soon, and no woman will get involved with me before I get back.* He had begun spending many of his evenings down at the pub so as not to wear out his welcome with Dane and Chris or Edwin and Marya. He often sat in the corner by the fire reading a book. The friendly-girls had given up on him though he had long been one of their favorites, and his behavior confused them. They often sat in the corner with him while he read poetry aloud to them, but now that he was a healer, he could never be more than a friend to them. He couldn't bear to just casually use them, when he now understood their motives and feelings.

He would much rather have been with his friends or his parents than at the pub. John Farmer often went with him, but only to the one in the Temple District, although he wouldn't say why. Zan just assumed he didn't want to stray too far away from home. It never occurred to him that friendly-girls weren't welcome there.

***

John Farmer had been inundated with invitations to duel since his return to Neveyah, but he had made it clear he would only engage in a contest if the city of Aeoven would benefit from the magic he expended. He was seen as being an eccentric prima donna, but he didn't care.

The truth that lay behind his refusal was a deep secret, his shame and his punishment—and something he couldn't bear to think about.

He was crippled magically. John could raise shields, he could water a garden, he could do anything that was a domestic form of magic except one thing— he couldn't sense fire at all, couldn't even light a candle. Right after the war, the day he realized he had lost most of his gifts, he had been convinced it was punishment for his arrogance and for a crime he'd committed in the panic and rage of the moment. The incident that had caused his disability deeply affected his relationship with Garran and to a lesser extent also stood between him and Halee.

All three felt solely responsible for what had happened, and they couldn't talk about it, not even to each other.

Since the last days of the war nearly thirty years before, John had been unable to sense his magic if he even thought about casting it as a weapon. He had hidden his disability well, being as creative with what he still could use, but he was unable to fight with it.

Garran was unaware that he was crippled and thought he was just being a stubborn ass. He had his own guilt to deal with in regard to the same incident.

Even though John was the head of veterinary-healing he was not considered a healer and was held to the same rules as other battle-mages who were heading departments. Therefore he was required to regularly prove his skills to the weapons master by dueling.

That presented a problem but he was a wily strategist. Turning that rule to his favor had required creativity on his part. He simply said he had dueled all he ever wanted to and refused to use his gifts just to entertain bored mages. Instead, he agreed to fight with swords to prove his weaponry skills, but refused to use his magic unless it was to rebuild walls, or irrigation systems, saying the quality of the work should determine the winner, and the people of Neveyah should benefit, not his ego.

Rall agreed to John's quirky requirement, because getting most senior mages to do that sort of work in their free time was terribly difficult, and the Temple didn't have enough novices to handle those tasks anymore. But, despite having accepted John's eccentricity, Rall felt he was hiding something, although he couldn't imagine what that could be.

With that simple stroke of genius John managed to find a way to satisfy the requirement that he duel without confessing his disability. Turning each duel into a competition of domestic magic, he and the other senior mages repaired a large part of the city's crumbling infrastructure.

John Farmer had always been eccentric. His refusal to duel the traditional way surprised no one, and impressed some of those who had known him before, causing them to reconsider the value of how they used their magic.

The morning after winning a contest with Zylda, a senior lightning mage, in which they had repaired the sewers in the market district, John received a message from Father Rall instructing him to see the colorist. He was a bit dumbfounded, as he hadn't had any new augmentations in over thirty years. Though he was somewhat concerned as to what an old mage like him could possibly be getting in the way of new augmentations, he dutifully appeared in the colorist's study as he was supposed to.

When Janae and Elner were finished, John Farmer was the first mage ever in the history of the Temple to have been given healer's symbols in blue. Two blue stars now rode on his forehead above his right eye, and three more were tattooed on each of his wrists, just below the dragons he had borne for more than thirty years. A blue crescent was placed on the web between his right thumb and forefinger, and one crossed the palm of his left hand. On his thighs, tiny blue stars and runes for empathy, wisdom, and healing were sprinkled within the thorny vines he'd been given at the age of seventeen.

He examined his new augmentations in the mirror, as did Janae. "Just when I think I've seen everything, along comes something new." John's comical expression made Janae laugh, seeing him caught somewhere between dismay and laughter. "From the augmentations I've been doing lately on your family, strange is normal. I think Aeos has just announced she approves of your chosen craft and considers veterinary healing an essential part of the College of Warcraft and Magic. I'll be curious to see what these stars enable you to do. You may even be able to link with other healers. This will be interesting."

***

As the crocuses began to poke their heads through the occasional snow, the four questers wanted nothing more than to get on the road and complete the quest. But it was too soon. Once spring arrived, they would take Zan and Friedr, and begin practicing for their quest by healing and shielding the west of Neveyah.

Father Rall told Halee that all he knew about their departure was they absolutely *had* to be in Mal Evol when the moon was dark in the month of Scorpius. "In the first month of the Harvest season, the dark of the moon falls on the fourth day. They must be there at all cost on that day."

Chapter 8 ~ Spring

Once Zan and Friedr completed their final anatomy tests, they would make their required away-posting as healers. They would have opportunities for healing as they went about the task of shielding the land and the people. For this reason, they would stop at every farm and village they came to before they finally took the long, dark road into Mal Evol.

Two weeks after Friedr finished training in surgery with Darlen, head of surgery, the four questers traveled by horse-drawn cart to the far west of Neveyah. They had yet to find a way of working together, and the area would be a good place to practice furthest away from the poison that slowly crept out of Mal Evol. They drove the trade road to the portal that led to Ariend, the world Edwin had grown up in.

It was a four-day trip in the wagon, although it had taken Aeolyn and Edwin two weeks to make the journey on foot.

Once at the portal, they briefly looked in at Edwin's old, family home. He was surprised to feel a pang that his home was, for all intents and purposes, abandoned.

"But it's not abandoned, Edwin," Zan told him as he looked around the empty sheep corral. "It's waiting. Can't you feel it waiting for you or your son to come home? I can feel the shield protecting this place. When you return, it'll be just like it is today, no matter how long you're gone."

Although the others were glad they'd finally seen the farm where Edwin had grown up, he almost wished he hadn't paid the old place the visit. However, he said nothing of his disquiet. *Someone once said you can't go home again,* he thought. *Now I know what they meant.*

They returned to the portal and went back to the spot simply known as the Meeting Place, where they camped for the night. "This is as far west as we can go. Let's sense the soil here and see if anything needs repairing," Edwin suggested. "I don't expect we'll find anything terribly wrong, but Friedr can link with us and see what we'll be doing. Then we'll set the widest shield-cell we're able to."

"Good idea," replied Christoph. "There're always small things we can improve, and we can set the first shield, covering this area back to the portal." He turned to Friedr, who looked faintly nervous. In truth, Friedr had been dreading the moment but was determined to endure it as manfully as he could. Unaware of Friedr's concern, Christoph said, "When Zan and Edwin link with me, I can sense the soil for more leagues than I can walk in a day. With you joined with us, we'll be even better."

After giving it some thought, Friedr replied, "I *am* curious. I want to do this more than you know, but I've found giving up control of my healing-gift and magic difficult, though I trust you like a brother. Linking is difficult for me. I came to healing too late to just leap into it as you three do. I tend to work alone, healing small injuries and performing minor surgeries. Darlen understands. He's a lot like me in that way." Friedr eyes were worried, but he smiled a self-deprecating, little smile. "I'll do it, of course. I've done it before just to prove I could and for the testing during the first few weeks of my training."

Chuckling, Christoph replied, "We know. It's why they set you up with Darlen in the first place. Not every healer is comfortable in the link, which is why many talented healers don't rise past the journeyman level. But without them, where would we be? Those journeymen are the core of the healers. Knowing your trepidation, Beryl wanted to ease you into it. You came into this so much later than anyone else, and we can all see how much it bothers you. We understand you're a very private person."

Zan debated saying anything, but finally decided to just say it. "I know how you feel, Friedr. I had trouble opening myself fully to this when we first began, but after the first few days, I understood Chris doesn't read *me*. He's using my gift to enhance *his* ability to read the soil. You'll see. It'll be easier each time you do it." Zan's reassurance did somewhat ease Friedr's fears. "I was terribly uncomfortable giving my father access to my gift, and I didn't want him to read my mind. But I had nothing to worry about. I still have all my secrets." His cheeky wink made Friedr chuckle.

Edwin centered himself and began reaching out to Christoph, who reciprocated. Then Zan joined with them, and finally they felt Friedr lightly join with them. At last, Friedr fully relaxed, drew closer to them, and opened himself to Christoph.

Sailing under the earth, Christoph expanded his healing senses, tasting the soil and feeling the general health of all the myriad things and creatures in it. Finding that the soil was mostly healthy, he guided Zan and Edwin in eliminating a fungus assailing a grove of trees. Then they redistributed leaf-litter evenly over the general area. After they had taken care of the soil and plant life, Edwin took over, and they built the shield by combining their elemental strengths as they had practiced. Christoph provided earth, Edwin contributed water, Zan added lightning, and Friedr offered up his fire. Using his air-magic, Edwin wove the elements together and guided each of the others in weaving the spirit barriers into the elemental shield. He then linked the barrier/shield to the chi of the soil and anchored it to the earth, tying it off. Altogether, they spent nearly an hour healing the soil and building the first cell of the western shield.

As they withdrew from the link, Friedr was quiet. Finally he remarked, "This will always be healthy land and will be protected forever. I'm proud I was a part of this. No unwelcome creatures from other worlds will want to nest here. That alone will greatly decrease Tauron's ability to influence our lives."

"And the beauty of it is no one else can take the shield down," Edwin assured him. "It is keyed to all of us. Only the four of us working together can take this shield down or alter it. The land will be healthy and productive long after we're gone."

Christoph was elated. "Friedr, it was so much easier with you adding your gift and spirit. We'll only have to do this once a day from now on because the four of us working together can actually build the shield around us farther than we can drive the wagon in a day." His jubilation faded as he said, "In Mal Evol, we'll be walking, so we won't be traveling nearly as far. Besides, a healing journey is always done on foot."

"Smaller cells will be stronger anyway. Besides, it's the only way we can meet the people and help the ones who need us." Friedr shrugged. "I always enjoy the journey more when walking."

"We just get so much more done this way," replied Christoph. His laugh was hesitant as he said, "I guess I have this nervous fear we won't get it all done once we embark on the eastern shield."

"No need to borrow trouble, my brother. We'll do what we need to do and still be home by the middle of Harvest," replied Friedr. "I don't intend to miss my daughter's first birthday!"

They spent the next fourteen days building the cells of the western shield and returned to Aeoven with a much better idea of how to heal the land and shield the heart of Neveyah. Gradually, as Zan had predicted, Friedr became used to linking, and it became less of a problem for him.

Chapter 9 ~ The Children's Garden

On a bright Sunnaday morning in the middle of spring, several days after they returned from shielding the west, Edwin walked around the sitting room of his home, bent over in that peculiar waddle parents teaching a child to walk have assumed since the beginning of time. Laughing and giggling, Jonny held tightly to his father's fingers as his little feet took their first halting steps. Edwin, along with John, Zan, and Friedr, had been up since well before dawn to go out to the woodlot with their respective work crews to cut and split firewood for their contribution to the Temple stores. They returned home to care for the children so Marya and Aeolyn could leave for their work group.

"The boy will be walking on his own before you know it," Edwin's father commented. He squatted opposite them, holding his arms out to Jonny. Jonny stopped with one foot up and seemed to want to let go of Edwin's fingers and run to his granddad, but he couldn't figure out how to do it yet.

"Come on, son, let's go to Granddad." Laughing, Edwin and Jonny walked over to John, who received a big hug from his grandson.

"I can't believe he'll be a year old in two months," Edwin said as he sat opposite his dad. Jonny sat, bouncing in his grandfather's lap and playing with his favorite toy, one that Edwin had made for him. It was a small wooden duck on wheels and could be pulled by a string. He couldn't pull it by himself yet, but he loved to play with the wheels and often chewed on the poor duck's bill. "He's coming along well with his walking. I hope I get to see him take his first solo steps."

"Just enjoy each day you can, son," his father told him. "Time flies by too quickly when you have a little one. They grow up and leave home to save the world before you know it." His smile was unforced and relaxed, very different from when he had first returned to Neveyah.

A knock sounded on the front door. Edwin opened it and found Friedr standing there. Baby Rynne, wearing a rainbow-colored sweater and matching socks, was in the baby pack strapped to his chest, facing forward. Her bright blue eyes and bright red curls were shaded by a white sunbonnet that sat askew. The girl's little legs kicked happily as she gnawed furiously on the end of her father's long braid. Freylin proudly wore his new straw hat and his father firmly gripped his hand. Dancing with excitement, the boy held the toy horse Edwin had made for him in his other hand.

"We thought maybe you'd like to go to the children's garden with us," Friedr said. "Since Aeolyn and Marya are off at their quilting group, I thought we should do something fun too. Besides, Freylin is in need of burning off some of his energy. He was apparently jumping on his bed and ran afoul of his mother while we were out cutting wood this morning."

"I tol' Mama sorry, Dad." Freylin gazed at his father with a serious look on his little face. "Din't mean t' break my bed. But you can fisk it, Dad, right? Was a accident, sorry."

"I know, son," Friedr said, rolling his eyes, "I know. I think it'll be a day or two before I can find a better wooden slat to fix it with. In the meantime,

Freylin must sleep on the floor tonight because that's where his bed is now."

Edwin choked down a laugh, and looking at John whose eyes were also twinkling, he said, "I dimly remember doing something similar. I too slept on the floor for a night or two."

Soon they were all meandering down the street to the children's garden, walking at Freylin's pace, talking and joking. It was one of those rare spring days, sunny and warm, that indicated summer was just around the corner. They sat at one of the tables near the sandbox, and Freylin headed there to play with his little carved, wooden horse. His red curls bounced under his hat as his chubby legs trotted over to it.

Rynne was fascinated with her father's hair and kept putting the end of his long braid in her mouth. He took it away from her, but somehow she found it, and it always went straight back into her mouth. "She's as determined as her mother," Edwin told Friedr. "You're in for a fun time with those two!"

"Well, it won't be boring, that's for sure," Friedr agreed, and then he was silent for a while, as they watched Freylin, who chattered at his toy horse and played in the sand. At last, he said, "We're going to miss a lot of their lives, even if we're only gone for a season."

"Whoa, son!" Edwin caught Jonny, who lunged at Rynne, trying to touch her and nearly leapt from his father's arms. "We'll do what we have to, no matter what. I've seen what Tauron has to offer, and there's no way I'll let him have Neveyah. I'm not going to let our children become slaves of the Bull God."

John nodded, with a rather proud smile on his face. "It's why we do what we do, right, grandson?" Jonny paid no attention to his grandfather. He was busy squirming in Edwin's lap, trying to get Rynne's attention.

"Come and sit with Uncle Friedr and Rynne, Jonny." Friedr lifted Rynne out of the pack and held her on his right knee, making room for Jonny on his left. "I agree. It's why I swore to this quest all those years ago. But we didn't have children then, and it's just hard to think of leaving them."

"Dad was always there for me. I've no memory of him ever being away," Edwin replied. He turned to his dad. "I think I must've been about Freylin's age when you returned from the second quest, am I right?"

"Yes. Andia told me you missed me quite a bit at first," John replied. "At least my father was there with you. It helped a lot."

"It's why I am glad you're here now," Edwin answered, as he played with Rynne's little hands, trying to distract her from chewing on her father's hair. Jonny sucked his thumb, watching Rynne with serious, blue eyes.

"And I'll be a good uncle to Freylin and Rynne, I promise. We're only a few doors away from you," John told Friedr.

Friedr, relieved that John would be looking out for his family, said as he flipped his braid back over his shoulder, "I appreciate that more than you'll ever know Rynne doggedly began looking for the braid again, her little hands rooting around her father's side, searching for her quarry. "My father died right after my little brother was born. Aeolyn's parents are gone too. With you around, at least they'll have a grandfather's wisdom, which is important in the village where I grew up."

Rynne gave up looking for her father's braid. She'd found John's instead.

Friedr and Edwin both looked forward to finally receiving the swords that were being made for them, wondering how the blades would express their unique magic.

For the most part, John was silent, while the two men talked, unaware his untidy braid was getting rather slobbery. The mention of swords disturbed him, and he fought to hide it. Finally he said, "My father told me about the bespelled sword, named Scorpion, that my grandfather had. Granddad was a great battle-mage by all accounts and was fairly strong in all the elements but was a water-mage more than anything else. Scorpion could rebound spells at the caster. No one else could use his sword. It was keyed to him."

"Well, we can do that with our shields, so it'll be interesting to see what the magic thinks we need on this quest," Friedr said. "Aeos has a plan, and I'm curious to see how it unfolds. Terrified but intrigued." They all chuckled knowingly.

"Well, you always told me those involved in Aeos's plans lead fascinating lives," Edwin reminded Friedr. "And we do. But your sword is rather special too, Dad, or so I've been told." Edwin wondered what his father would say—he never mentioned his sword. "Grandfather made it for you, so Father Rall told me."

"Riverbinder. It *is* unique, but it was never the magic sword of legend I needed it to be." The set look on his father's face made Edwin regret he'd mentioned it. "When we were fighting in Mal Evol I needed a sword like Aelfrid Firesword had, and if Riverbinder was that sword, I never figured out how to make it work." He grinned at his son by way of apology. "But I was able to draw chi through it, and it did enable me to cast much larger spells than I could without it. It did make me seem far more powerful than I was, which was not really a good thing, because the others began to rely too much on me and my imaginary skills."

He fell silent, watching Freylin, and then his eyes turned back to Edwin. "The edge never dulls. It's one of the most beautiful weapons you'll ever see, and no other sword fits my hand as well. My father was a true master smith." He laughed, but the tightness around his eyes betrayed his inner disturbance.

Soon Rynne began fussing. After squirming a bit, she dropped John's soggy braid to chew on her hand. Jonny took his thumb out of his mouth and offered it to her. She looked at the wet thumb curiously, tears in her stormy eyes, and then patted his hand. They all laughed as they collected Freylin and started to walk back to Edwin's place for lunch.

"I'm going to have to watch her around him if he turns out like his father." Friedr glanced at Edwin slyly. "Until I saw it happen to you too, John, I thought Edwin's problem was a fluke. Now I realize it's a family curse. I'll never go to the pub with you two again."

"Well, as long as we stay in the Temple District, we don't cause trouble because the friendly-girls don't bother coming down to this area," John laughed. "I knew it was a mistake to go out of the neighborhood. It was a curse to my father too, right up to the end of his life. But he was a lightning-mage, and he died young, the way they often do. The blood cancer got him."

"That's one of the things I'm hoping to change," Edwin said as he once again put the sunhat on Jonny. John reached for Jonny and carried him home while Edwin carried Freylin on his shoulders. The boy was wild with delight, riding on Uncle Edwin's shoulders and thrilled to be as tall as his father. "I believe with proper buffering next to their skin lightning-mages won't get cancer so often, fire-mages won't develop gout, earth-mages won't be stricken with congestive heart failure, and water-mages won't suffer kidney failure." Freylin bounced on Edwin's shoulders. "Frey! You'll fall if you don't settle down a bit." Edwin got a better grip on Freylin's legs, and the boy calmed down, still giggling as he clung to Edwin's head, blocking his vision somewhat. Edwin grinned but just let the boy enjoy himself.

"Well, we'll be the ones testing your theory," Friedr replied. "I certainly take your instruction to heart."

"Henley looks a lot better since he took the seniors' shielding class with me," John added. "He's walking better and talking about working out again. He isn't much older than me, maybe ten years or so, but I quit using the magic before I suffered any damage, I hope."

Edwin looked at his father with his healing sight, seeing he was healthy and young for his age, and told him so. "You'll be around for a long time, Dad. You're the healthiest grandparent in the Temple."

"All the friendly-girls at the Weaver's Rest Common Room think so too," Friedr said wickedly. "Oh, how they think so."

John rolled his eyes as he opened the front door.
***

Dane sat at his kitchen table, eating a small lunch of bread and cheese, feeling completely out of sorts. Christoph was off at his tailoring group, but Dane hadn't felt well enough to go to his own soap-making group. He'd not slept well, waking up from a nightmare and being unable to get back to sleep until nearly dawn. The dream had been horrible, so vivid and frightening, a dream of Zan in a dark, dank cave with tears running down his haunted, dirty face.

Dane's rational mind told him he'd dreamt of such a thing because underneath it all, he didn't want them to go off on the mad quest they had sworn to. *It's difficult for us, both being healers. Everything I think must be kept buried and is starting to come out in my dreams. If only I had someone to talk to about this. I can't let Chris know I'm worried, or he won't be able to do what he must. I can't ask Marya for a sleeping potion because she'll ask me why I don't just have Chris cast sleep on me. Then she'll worry too.* After thinking about it for long enough to worsen his headache, he went to lie down for a while, thinking, *Maybe I'll fall back to sleep.*

He lay there, too upset to sleep, when someone knocked on the door. Dane got up and answered it despite his wish to ignore it, fearing one of his patients was having a crisis and needed him. Zander stood there, his smile quickly changing to concern.

"I'm not feeling very well right now, Zan. I just need to lie down for a while."

Zan could feel how tired and upset he was. "I'm sorry. Let me help you for a change," Zan replied as he pushed Dane back to bed. "I was just looking for some company, but I'll heal you so you can rest. Then I'll leave." He waited until Dane was settled before casting a pain-relieving spell for his headache. "You've cared for me all of my ungrateful life, so let me care for you now." He cast the spells as lightly as he could and layered them so Dane would sleep for at least three hours. "Sleep well, Dane. I sense you're disturbed about something. I'm here to listen if you decide to talk about it, but I won't press you. Sleep now."

"It's only bad dreams troubling my sleep. I just need to get over it on my own," Dane murmured. "Your spells were gently done. You've been paying attention to Edwin." Zan smiled at the praise as Dane drifted off into a peaceful sleep.

Quietly letting himself out the front door, Zan debated going to the pub. Instead, he turned and walked to Edwin's house. He was looking for companionship, but now he was worried about Dane. *He's a bundle of misery, but what can I do about it? Who do I know that can help him?* Dane had buried all his emotions too well, so Zan was unable to pick out exactly what had his cousin tied up in knots, but he did have a shrewd guess. *He's upset about Christoph going off with us on this quest. But we have to go, they were sworn to do it before the Goddess years ago, and now I've sworn to it too.*

He looked up at the bright blue sky, enjoying the sunshine after the long, dark winter. *I can't tell Christoph because Dane would kill me if I shared his true feelings about whatever this is with Chris. Besides, it wouldn't help anyone. We'd still have to go, but Chris would be loaded down with guilt and wouldn't be able to do his work as well.*

Edwin opened the door, happy as always to see Zan, welcoming him into his cheerful home. Zan could hear Friedr and all the children in the kitchen with John. Quickly deciding this was not the time to bring Dane's worry up, he followed Edwin to the kitchen and joined the party.

Jonny's eyes lit up on seeing him, and he held his arms up for Zander to pick him up. "San! San!" Jonny jabbered at him happily.

"He knows my name." Zan was completely surprised and sincerely touched as he picked Jonny up, bouncing him and tweaking his nose. Jonny giggled and tried to grab Zan's nose. Somehow, the right time to talk to Edwin about Dane never came.

***

Early one morning, a few days before summer solstice, Edwin came downstairs to find breakfast prepared and a strange man who resembled his father sitting at the table sipping tea and reading. "What the…Dad? You…you cut your hair. You look…way different. It's like I don't even know you." Edwin tried not to gape. "What made you decide to cut it so short? You look like a soldier now."

"Apparently, I've become an unkempt mess. It's a lot easier to keep tidy this way." John ran his hand over his scalp, enjoying the bristly feel. "Despite my wishes to the contrary, I've been forced into dueling again, and will have to duel until I have reached my top rank. The hair sort of gets in my way." He shrugged. "I've tried stuffing it down my backplate like you do but it pulls at my neck. I don't like the feeling."

"You've always been an unkempt mess. But that little tail behind your ear might get in the way then." Edwin's grumpy expression made his father grin even wider. "Why did you leave that part long?"

"It's there to remind me that I let stupid pride ruin my life and destroy my closest friendships. I'll find out if it will bother me or not this morning. You just don't like change, son. You never have."

Edwin tried to absorb the difference the haircut made in his father's appearance. His whole bearing was different—as if he'd faced a crisis of some kind and come out on top. "Why is Rall making you duel now, after all this time? Didn't you manage to convince him that putting your magic on display is a waste of chi unless it's being used for the good of the community?"

There was no way John could explain to his son the details of what had happened the night before, how the Goddess had used Halee to break through his block, forcing him to use his offensive magic instinctively, nearly breaking him in the process. And then, what had happened between them after…his secrets were his to keep.

But he'd been expecting that question and was prepared. He handed Edwin a crumpled note. "Rall scheduled me to duel with Halee last evening, despite the fact I wasn't ready. Not that I wanted to—I didn't. But I do what Rall tells me to."

Edwin raised his eyes from the note. "This is ridiculous. You aren't working as a battle-mage. You're a veterinarian. Healers don't have to duel, so why should you?"

"Well, I'm a battle-mage and not a true healer, so I guess it's expected. I may be forced into teaching novice water-mages in visualization, whether I want to or not. There are problems in that department, and I may have to help out for a while."

"I know about the problems there, but…." Edwin looked sharply at his father, sensing truth but also prevarication. "What happened last night? You were still gone when we went to bed."

"Nothing." His father actually blushed. "I told you. I was scheduled to duel and I did."

Finally grasping that his father was not going to discuss it, Edwin said nothing further. The realization that his father had secrets was disconcerting, but he let it drop. Soon the two of them walked to the Temple, just as they always did, and the subject was not mentioned.

He did have something he wanted to talk to his father about, though. "Dad, you mentioned the novice water-mages. I've noticed something about them in my shielding classes that could be a problem. They're undisciplined, and they're the slowest learners because of it. Is that normal for them?"

John shook his head. "No. It might just be this group. Not all young mages arrive with the ability to discipline themselves, and then they don't really do as well as the others."

"Something about Cayne makes me wonder. I think he's avoiding me." Edwin glanced at his father, seeing an unreadable expression. "Something about him bothers me."

"That *is* odd." John couldn't hide his concern, but all he said was, "Cayne has changed. We were friends when we were novices, but we were sent to different places after we became journeymen, so I don't know what happened to change him. You might want to talk to Kalen. He was Cayne's commander during the war."

***

On the last day of the month, the four were called to the armory to collect their armor. They were all surprised upon seeing it. They'd each been given armor of a deep shade of brown. It was lacquered in the same type of light-absorbing finish that characterized stealth-armor, which was matte black. Their new armor was bespelled to protect them from the poisoned earth of Mal Evol and would deter the scorpions and snakes from getting too close to them.

"This is a type of stealth-armor, although it's certainly not what we normally make," the armor-smith told them. "It's the most interesting armor I personally have ever been involved in making. The spells woven into it allow you to blend in with the scenery, go silently and with less chance of injury in the thorn forest. Tauron's earth magic won't affect you, and your own earth-magic will be stronger." Their new leathers were the same deep, warm brown. From a distance, they looked very nearly like standard-issue armor and leathers. Only upon close examination were the differences were visible.

Friedr's armor had stylized flames and stars embossed at random points with small crescent-moons, leaves, lightning bolts and water drops, but they were all simply raised designs with no color to them. "These aren't so pretty to look at," Friedr stated as they carried their new armor and leathers to the men's dressing room at the practice yard. "We'll bore D'Mal to death in these."

"Well, if they work as they're supposed to, we'll survive to return and you can wear your pretty red clothes again," Christoph asserted wickedly. "You're such a clotheshorse, Friedr."

"I'm just glad *you* mentioned it, Friedr," Zan laughed, "because I was sure thinking it." They all laughed. "I too have a love of fine clothes."

"Well, these are for the journey. I don't think we need to wear them during business hours before we leave Aeoven if we don't want to." Edwin looked at Friedr for confirmation, and he nodded his head. "We must try them out though. Christoph, you can send us some earthquakes to see how well they work, right?" His armor was much like Zan's, with a crescent moon over the heart.

Christoph's eyes showed his unhappiness at being asked to use his gift as a weapon, even to test the armor. Although he understood the sense in doing so, his stomach clenched at the thought. "Yes, I can do that, and maybe I should dump a river on you while I'm at it," he replied.

The others all looked at him, startled. Christoph realized how he sounded and immediately apologized. "Oh, I'm sorry. I don't mean to sound so awful about it. It makes me feel sick to even think of using my magic that way."

"If it'll make you happier, Christoph," Edwin offered, "I'll test you three, and Zan or Friedr can test my armor. It's not that important." Zan just looked from Edwin to Christoph and nodded his head. Friedr's eyes had assumed the flat, narrow look they always did when he was displeased, but he nodded his head.

The armor, not surprisingly, worked exactly as it was designed to, and no earth magic touched them. Later after their workout, as they walked home together, Friedr chided Edwin for letting Christoph off the hook so easily about using his magic as a weapon. "How's he going to learn to use it properly if all he does is sail under the earth or ride the water?"

"Friedr, he's using it to the best of his abilities and keeping his chi balanced," Edwin said. "We're not going to turn him into a warrior. He can't use his magic in the way you want him to. He's been given this gift to do one thing and one thing only – purify the water and heal the soil."

"But it just seems so wrong to waste his gift like this," Friedr said. "Are you sure he can do what you can't in healing the soil?"

"Friedr, this isn't like you. What's really wrong here?" Edwin stopped walking and waited for Friedr to answer.

"I don't know. I can't explain it. Maybe it feels like a weakness to me," Friedr replied, shrugging. "I'm concerned it could make the team vulnerable."

"I understand how you feel, but he's still the same person he's always been," Edwin reminded him. "If he couldn't kill with his staff before these new augmentations, how can he kill now with his magic? He's not going to change fundamentally just because he's been given a new skill. Nothing is different, Friedr. He has a task to do, and we're going to help and protect him while he does it."

"You're right, as always. It's only…I'm not sure what to make of the changes in any of us, except for you," Friedr said, unable to fully explain why he was worried. "Perhaps I thought he'd eventually be able to defend himself at some point. But you're right. He's no different than he was before, except now he's as stubborn as any other earth-mage. We've always had to watch out for him and defend him against the rats and other villains."

"What he brings to this is his healing ability, which is unlike anything the rest of us have. He sees into the soil, Friedr." Edwin explained as best as he could, "I'm only able to do some of what he can do in cleansing and healing it."

"All right, I believe you. I'm sorry I've been pushing Christoph so hard. I'll let him work out in the way he feels most comfortable from now on. We three will have to put together some moves that will let him work with us the way he did with Aeolyn on the last trip." They were nearly at Edwin's doorstep now. Friedr clasped Edwin's shoulder and said, "I'm glad you're coming along on this trip. Sometimes I don't know who I am anymore. I'd be lost without you, my brother." He briefly looked Edwin in the eye and then looked away. "I just wish I knew why Aeos felt I should become a healer. She must have a reason, but why will we need four full healers? A couple of stars would've given us enough empathy to enable the shield with you and Chris to pull us into the link."

"Sometimes I wonder about it too, Friedr. This is not the simple, straightforward quest we had last time." Edwin's blue eyes were dark with fatigue and worry. "Tauron's thorns are poised to overtake Neveyah and must be stopped. We have to do it, or there'll be no future for our grandchildren. And I won't waste what time we have left here worrying about something we can't change. You're coming along well as a healer, Friedr. Whatever waits for us, you'll be able to meet it, no matter what. Are you sorry you've been diverted down this path?"

Friedr saw his own worries reflected in Edwin's face. "I don't regret it, Edwin, but I've had a hard time getting used to the augmentations over the last six months. Becoming a healer was difficult for me. You'll never know the fear and anxiety I felt in the first month. It was far too intimate for me to cope with at first, and I nearly went mad with dread before going to work each morning. Only my vows to Aeos kept me going to the infirmary and doing what I was supposed to. But now, I'm dealing with accidents and injuries in the infirmary and it's much easier. It's much less personal than the healing I assisted you with those few times." He smiled self-consciously. "I'm not the man I always thought I was, Edwin."

"You're a stronger man than you ever knew you were, Friedr. You did it and never let on how it bothered you. But the many different kinds of healing work we'll be doing on your healing journey will require you to link with us in the way you don't feel comfortable. We may have some serious injuries or even births to attend. Can you lower your barriers enough to do this?"

Edwin's question caught Friedr by surprise. "Well, yes, of course, if I have to. I'll do whatever it takes." Friedr shrugged. "This is why I have trouble understanding Chris sometimes. We think so differently."

"It'll be fine. You won't have to open your mind to us—you know it's not like that. We'll simply link our healing sight, and you will ride with me or Christoph and lend your strength to the mix, observing what we're doing, and then you'll be doing what you've only been reading about until now." They stood on Edwin's doorstep. "But right now, you and Zan have to write those essays on your studies that will earn you your journeyman pins. Then we can get started on your healing journey and begin our great task. Both tasks should take about four months all together, and then we'll be home, hopefully in time for Rynne's birthday." Edwin's comment elicited an answering smile from Friedr, who nodded and turned to walk on down to his own door.

"I just want to get it done and over with," Edwin called after Friedr.

"I know what you mean, my brother." Friedr replied over his shoulder. "I know *exactly* what you mean."

Chapter 10 ~ Under the Solstice Moon

On the day of the summer solstice, Jonny took his first solo steps. Marya was walking along with him when he suddenly let go of her fingers and decided to walk to his father, a big smile on his face. He took four toddling steps all by himself and then lunged into his father's arms to the sounds of his parents' laughter and cheers.

That afternoon, they walked to the Temple for the big solstice celebration with Aeolyn and Friedr's family. They met up with many of their friends along the way. All the street performers were out and at their best. The children were agog at the displays of sleight-of-hand and tumbling, and the jugglers were very popular among both children and adults.

The Temple gardens were beautiful, and the tables were all set for the special communal meal they would share under the stars on the shortest night of the year. Everyone had contributed to the preparation in some way. Father Rall led them in a prayer of thanksgiving, and then the party began. Children ran and played all night long, and their parents watched them with a lenient eye.

At last, the musicians started playing, and the dancing began, which was what Marya and Edwin had been waiting for. They loved to dance and were very good at it, knowing all of the traditional dances and many country dances too. They, along with Friedr and Aeolyn were the center of attention that evening in the dancing square, their skillful dancing drawing applause from the throng.

John took his turns in the dancing square, dancing most of the evening with Halee. They too received a great deal of applause. "I'd forgotten how much fun you are to dance with, John," Halee said, her eyes bright and her cheeks red from dancing. "Remember that solstice in Fleetside? We taught them all how to dance, you and I."

"I'd forgotten how much I enjoy dancing," he replied, his arm about her waist and his blue eyes sparkling with a challenge. "I hear another one we know…c'mon girl, let's show them how to do it right," and holding hands, they ran back into the square, both laughing. Soon they were the center of an enthusiastic audience, all clapping and urging them on.

Christoph and Dane were also eagerly sought after as partners, and soon the dancing square was filled with music and happy people, all wearing their festive best. It was a colorful, happy, riot.

Unfortunately, Zander had suddenly wilted when he saw Dyenne dancing with Kiel. She looked so completely happy, as she had never done in his company. Suddenly, he realized he had not *loved* her, as much as he had wished to *win* her, as if it were a game. *But I'm different now, much more settled. I'm an air-mage now, and it's changed me. I can never again be light with women. They're not counters in a game.* He felt his loneliness rather keenly and sat quietly watching Freylin playing with his young friends and rocking Rynne or Jonny to sleep, depending on which parents were dancing. He was no longer sure of himself where girls were concerned.

Finally, Dane and Chris decided to take matters into their own hands. "I can't stand to see Zan like this when he should be having fun," Christoph told Dane. "I think he should be pushed a bit, don't you?" They led several shy, young ladies who were journeyman healers over to ask him to dance, and he enjoyed the evening much more than he thought he would.

One young lady in particular, Anna Potter, had been admiring Zan from afar. She had gained her journeyman's pin just before the Feast of Aeos. When she began working in the infirmary, she often saw Zan with Edwin Farmer in the corridors and admired his darkly handsome countenance. She was a pretty girl who had just turned seventeen, with dark, curling hair and deep blue eyes. Her wicked sense of humor was sharp and her conversation intelligent and witty. Zan found himself enjoying her company very much indeed. Chris and Dane watched them dancing, smiling indulgently as their boy perked up in her company and his old spark returned.

At the midpoint of the evening when the bards took a well-deserved break, Christoph stepped up to the stage with his harp. With Dane singing harmony, the two proceeded to entertain the group with some of Christoph's favorite love ballads, the first of which was the touching and beautiful *Song of the Lovers' Tree*. Dane's voice complemented Christoph's beautifully. It was obvious they often sang together. Soon the bards returned to the stage, and the dancing began again. With all the adults trading the babies, the music and dancing continued until the small hours before dawn.

Later in the evening, Edwin came across his father and Halee seated on a secluded, trysting bench, holding hands, deep in earnest conversation. Then they paused and leaned toward each other, gently kissing in the moonlight.

Joy washed over Edwin, and smiling widely, he tiptoed away, thinking, *This is what they both need, Aeos—they need each other. They each know what the other has lost and are both so lonely. They'd be very good for each other. Please Aeos, Goddess of Hearth and Home, bless them with happiness. They give so much to you and Neveyah.* His heart lifted and he felt Aeos had heard his prayer.

Edwin smiled widely when he caught up to Marya, his relief and happiness lighting up the party with his trademark smile. He whispered in her ear, and she threw her arms around his neck, joy written across her face. Then, hand in hand, they ran back to the dancing square while Dane contentedly rocked Jonny. With a smile of bliss on his face, Christoph held Rynne and he marveled at her small hands and perfect face while she slept. Freylin slept on a blanket next to Christoph's feet.

Anna brought her mothers, Lianne and Rea, over to meet Dane and Christoph, and soon the four were talking animatedly in low tones so as not to wake the sleeping children. As they talked, they watched Anna and Zan with indulgent smiles.

When at last tired parents carried sleeping children home, every face wore a smile. If some people woke feeling a little under the weather, it was only to be expected after an event as lavish as the summer solstice party at the Temple in Aeoven.

No classes were held the next day, but everyone stopped by the gardens to help clean up. Edwin and Marya couldn't help but notice John and Halee working together, deep in conversation and laughing often.

***

The next working day, Edwin, Friedr, and Zan went to the armory to receive their special swords, and Chris went to receive the special staff created just for him. Each felt more than honored to receive the finest blades ever to come from the Temple armory. The blade-smiths were pleased to see their masterworks going to the hands they were created for. The master smith took them to the armory barn behind the smithy, where everyone was gathered.

The swords lay in their scabbards on a workbench cleared for the occasion. The scabbards were bespelled to enable the wearer to heal more quickly. Though plain from a distance, as with the questors' armor, the scabbards were intricate and beautiful up close. The blades were as yet unnamed, for when a bespelled weapon was made, the name was given to the mind of the master smith at the moment he bestowed it upon the recipient. The Goddess herself named her swords in accordance with her purposes.

The blades were razor sharp and would never dull, and each was a thing of beauty and elegance.

First, the master smith bowed before Christoph and ceremoniously presented him with his new staff. It was beautiful, made of a single heart-oak limb bound with intricate and delicately wrought, steel vines inset into the wood of the staff. The bottom was capped with a steel cup, and the top was capped with a wrought-steel star, the center of which held a clear, pure crystal the size of a child's fist. The staff was a true work of art.

The master smith declared, "The Goddess Aeos has named this staff Earthbinder. It will empower your earth-magic. Do you swear to wield it only in the service of the Goddess Aeos and the people of Neveyah?"

Humbled and awed, Christoph accepted the staff. A bell tolled, ringing through him, body and soul. Holding the staff over his head, Christoph offered it to the Goddess, making the vows with all his heart. The bell echoed through his very essence, ringing pure and sweet, sweeping through him with an unutterably exquisite joy that forever sealed him to the staff. From that moment on, for anyone else, Earthbinder was just a pretty staff, albeit a strong one. He stepped back, overwhelmed and stunned by the experience.

The ceremony was repeated twice more for Friedr and for Zan. Friedr's sword was named Dragonstorm and Zan's Stormbringer. Each man was sealed to his sword to the tolling of Aeos's bell in a moving and profound experience neither man would ever forget.

Edwin received his sword last. The master smith bowed and reverently buckled the brown-lacquered steel scabbard to him. Edwin unsheathed the sword, and as it rose in offering to the Goddess, the Master smith proclaimed the sword was named Leviathan. It was the greatest of the three swords, combining the powers of Dragonstorm, Earthbinder, and Stormbringer in one mighty weapon.

A ray of light shone on Edwin, and a bell tolled deep and clear, ringing through his bones, echoing to his very soul, sealing him, binding him. "I swear upon my vows to Aeos and all I hold holy to use this sword, Leviathan, only for good, to defend Aeos and the people of Neveyah. I swear it with my heart and soul." He heard himself speaking the vows, and they resonated in the air about him. Still the bell tolled; he was alive with the sound. The beauty of it was almost unbearable.

As every fiber of his being resonated, a voice proclaimed, "Now begins the quest in earnest. Send now the heroes four to the Shadowed Land. Beware! Beloved, the true task for which you were born begins. The storm rages, the door opens upon the field of battle, in grief recall the Forbidden Road. The Beloved Hero will rise on the day of redemption. Mist and shadows shroud the truth, but the Hero Foretold shall one day set them free."

Falling to his knees, Edwin's eyes were blinded by the radiance of the bell's tolling through his heart, mind, and soul. The knowledge that he was loved, overwhelming in its intensity, flooded his being.

He returned to awareness of his surroundings, tears coursing down his face. At last his vision cleared, and he saw Father Rall looking at him with a compassionate expression. Abbess Halee spoke urgently to the scribes. Edwin wasn't sure what had just happened, but he knew something unexpected had occurred. His father had an inscrutable look on his face.

The master smith knelt before Edwin, took his unresisting hand, touching it to his forehead. "The Goddess speaks through you, Edwin Farmer. Blessed are we to have witnessed her words!"

"The Goddess does indeed speak through you today, Edwin Farmer." Father Rall's kindly face tried to reassure him, as it dawned on Edwin that he'd had a foretelling. "This is your second foretelling, as she spoke through you once before, did she not?"

"Ah...it was not such a profound experience as this, as I recall. Aeolyn would be able to give you the text." Edwin was confused, and his hands were shaking. "I heard the prophecy, Father Rall, but I didn't know I was the speaker. Does this mean we are to leave soon?"

"Yes, I think it does," Father Rall beckoned to Abbess Halee. "The Abbess is the expert in interpreting foretellings."

"I didn't mean to do that." Edwin's face turned red with embarrassment. "I'm so sorry."

Zan rested his hand on Edwin's shoulder, while Chris patted his other shoulder. They knew how little he enjoyed being the center of attention.

"We never intend to do that," replied Father Rall with a wry smile. "Sometimes the Goddess has a sense of the dramatic." He chuckled, glancing at John, who shrugged. "Well, at least the scribes were here and got it all down. I believe we need to schedule a meeting of the clergy for the blessing of your departure, perhaps tomorrow evening."

"So when do we leave?" Friedr's question was echoed by all. Dane reached for Marya's hand, and Aeolyn put her arm around him. "I'd like to be home for a special girl's first birthday."

"I don't see why you can't leave a week from today. We will get your classes covered and make sure you have your supplies waiting, then you four can be on your way." Abbess Halee smiled widely. "The healers are already scheduling someone to cover your patients. And Friedr, just so you know, Garran has asked to return temporarily to teach your weapons classes. Moran will take care of Braden Temple in his absence. Garran has been instructing him to assume the post of abbott, at another temple, and this will give him the last bit of training he needs."

She regarded the ring of faces, seeing a range of emotions on all of them. "Don't fret. All will be well. In the meantime, spend this time with your families. Wind up things at the college tomorrow and turn your patients over to Rayne with a good heart."

That afternoon, they all gathered in Edwin and Marya's sitting room to plan their departure and go over their list of supplies. They would spend part of each day for the rest of the week working out and getting used to their new equipment, though they would do nothing else to take them away from their families.

Aeolyn personally requisitioned their supplies. She made maps of their route into Mal Evol, with two caches marked from which Edwin and Zander could fetch supplies. In that way, if the journey took longer than they hoped, they would not be forced to make the choice of abandoning the quest or eating and drinking from the soil of Mal Evol.

"What we don't have here, we must do without." Friedr's brow was furrowed as he pored over Aeolyn's list. "I think you've taken our every need into consideration and then some." The others agreed.

"Two months from now when you arrive in Braden at the end of your healing journey, all will be waiting for you. Once you have your supplies stashed properly, you can begin the main task." Aeolyn's fingers tapped the table as she considered all the possible things that could go wrong in caching the supplies.

As they walked home, Christoph and Dane were silent, each one caught up in his own thoughts. Arriving at their steps, Dane stopped and picked some lettuce and pulled a few carrots and a few other vegetables from the narrow plot that bordered their walk. "I'll get dinner going, omelets and a salad maybe. I'll let you know when it's ready. It's warm this afternoon, so let's eat in the garden since I'm cooking out there."

"That'd be wonderful. I'll just pull some weeds and get these borders straightened up while you're busy." Christoph was suddenly overwhelmed with the realization he was leaving his home behind, his heart uncharacteristically heavy. *Dane is my home and my life. How I wish he could come with us.* Saying nothing of his gloomy thoughts, he said "I'll do the back garden tomorrow. I want to make sure everything is right for you before I have to go." He swallowed and looked away, bending down to pull an errant weed.

"I know, love." Seeing his own feelings reflected in Christoph's eyes was more gratifying than mere words could ever be. *He's having a terrible time with this too. He really does love me. He shows it every day in small ways.* Smiling, Dane said, "I'll break out a bottle of wine to celebrate the amazing things that happened today." He went out back to the garden-kitchen to prepare a romantic dinner for two.

***

As they left Edwin and Marya's pleasant home, Aeolyn and Friedr also found little to say. Rynne slept on Friedr's shoulder while Freylin ran in circles around his parents. "I think I'll repaint the shutters and get them hung back up tomorrow. I'll make sure they're securely latched back. Then you won't have to worry about them when Harvest comes." Friedr's voice was unusually quiet. "The bad weather comes in from the east side of the house, and the laundry porch gets chilly in Saggitus."

"Good idea. If you could fix the loose board on the back steps too, that'd be helpful," Aeolyn replied. "If you take care of the children, I'll fix dinner in the garden."

"Sounds good. As for my household tasks, I'll feel better knowing they're done." Friedr paused, opening their front door. "I wish you were going with us on this journey. That's what made the other quest fun."

"Sadly, the children wouldn't cope well with the journey." Aeolyn laughed at her husband's gloomy expression and hugged him, careful not to disturb their daughter. "You'll smell just like your armor for who knows how long." She thought for a moment and then smiled wickedly at him. "I'll miss that smell, that and sneaking off with you on 'scouting' expeditions."

"As will I, my dear one." Friedr's eyes gleamed. "We should do some 'scouting' tonight!"

***

As the others left Edwin's house, Zander stood up to leave, feeling odd with no one special to spend his last week with and unwilling to intrude on his friends' time with their loved ones. While he had seen Anna several times since the Solstice party, he knew it was wrong to court her, because he would be leaving so soon. It hadn't occurred to Zan to talk to her about his situation. He didn't want to pressure her the way he was wont to do in the past, for fear he would drive her away.

"Zan, will you stay and have dinner with us?" Marya's eyes were warm and concerned for him. "We have more than enough if you don't mind vegetable soup. Today was a momentous day for us all." She smiled encouragingly and added, "I made blackberry jam for the biscuits."

"I like vegetable soup, thank you, and your blackberry jam is to die for. I'd be happy to stay for dinner." Though he smiled, he looked to Edwin for reassurance that he was welcome.

"You must celebrate with us, brother. We airmages must stick together," Edwin told him, with his usual frank grin. "Don't worry, Zan. We can play a game of stones after dinner. Besides, Halee will be here tonight too." He grinned at his father's sudden smile.

"Zan, you can help me put Jonny to bed while they get dinner on the table," added John, feeling absurdly happy at the thought of Halee visiting for dinner—their secret romance occupied most of his thoughts. "I got the boy fed while you were all busy doing hero stuff." He reached for his grandson. "Let's get him cleaned up and into his nightclothes." Jonny held his arms up to his grandfather, his little jam-smeared face tired and ready for bed. "Just a quick wash, grandson, and then into bed you go."

"Ah dah," agreed Jonny, sleepily, as his father and mother kissed him. "Nigh-nigh, Ahmah. Nigh Da." Once they put Jonny into his bed, he immediately fell asleep. Now that he was walking, he only sucked his thumb when he was tired, since he needed his hands for exploring the world. Nevertheless, as now, he still slept with his thumb in his mouth.

John looked at Zan out the corner of his eye, and as they entered the kitchen, he asked him, "Is something on your mind, son?"

Taken by surprise, Zan said, "Oh, nothing important. It's just the usual fluff, nothing to worry my friends about." Zan did not look John in the eye. "We've had some major changes in our lives since we started preparing for this quest, haven't we? I've certainly changed. I was beginning to think we were never going to actually leave. Now here we are, packing up to go. With Christoph going on this quest, Dane is being left behind. He'll be alone, and I'm worried."

John recognized the diversionary tactic, and knew what the real problem likely was. "It'll all come together for you, Zan. It did for me and it will for you," John replied reassuringly. "Don't worry about Dane. We'll take care of him, I promise."

"Thank you. You don't know what that means to me." Zander didn't know what to say. "He's all I have left of our blood. He raised me from the time I was five until I went to the Temple. In fact I don't really remember much before that, just a few glimpses, really. My mother died when I was five, and I've very few memories of her. She was seriously ill for most of my early childhood, and Dane's parents raised me mostly until the fire. Then Dane became my mother-figure, sacrificing everything for me, until I was taken to the Temple." He realized he was prattling again. "I'm sorry. I just babble at times."

"I'm interested. You had two very young fathers raising you. That's remarkable in itself." John encouraged Zan to talk. "We Farmers haven't gone to the Temple as young novices since my grandfather. Markett was on the Neveyah side of the veil when he was young." They sat in the pleasant kitchen, listening to Edwin and Marya laughing in the garden as they set the table for dinner. "The Goddess called me to the Temple at fifteen, so I had one year as a novice. I think

I held Edwin back because I wasn't ready to lose him. I realize that now."

Zan thought about his childhood. "When I was eight, Chris started visiting. When he was around, we were happy, and more than anything, I wanted him to be part of our family. Even after I went to live in novice quarters, I had most of my weekends and holidays with Dane. I was so happy when Dane and Christoph were officially bonded and adopted me as their son. Though he's only eight years older than me, Christoph has always been more like a father to me than a brother. He cares for me like any parent cares for a child. He gives me the sort of advice and encouragement I see you giving Edwin. Dane is the mother in our house. Nothing would get done without him chivvying us along."

"I can see Dane that way," said John, smiling at the image and thinking of how true it was.

"I know our family is different, but it's a loving family and it's all I've ever known. Dane and I were born in Nola. My mother passed away right after my aunt and uncle died in a house fire. Mum was never able to care for me, so Auntie cared for us, making sure I was fed, clothed, and educated. I don't have real memories—not even the fire—I only get occasional glimpses. Somehow I got out, but my aunt and uncle didn't."

John was suspicious of Zan's lack of memory of that terrible event. *He must've been in a seriously distressed state. The healers have special techniques for severely traumatized children to enable them to live normally. Christoph is a master in that art.* "That's often the way it is for small children," John agreed.

"I have a dim memory of being picked up and pushed out of the little window of my attic room, sliding down the thatch and falling to the ground, but it's not clear. It's like a story I was told. I know they must've saved me because I'm here, right? My arm was broken." His brow furrowed as he tried to remember. "My poor mum's lungs were so bad she couldn't climb stairs, so she always slept in the sitting room. She somehow stumbled outside and was lying out on the grass. She never really woke up and later died in the infirmary.

"Dane was a journeyman, and I lived here in Aeoven with him after that. It must have been hard for him, but I was loved and well cared for, and I knew I always would be. I do realize I've been relatively sheltered though." Zan chuckled wryly at his own spoiled self. "Chris has always been determined I would never suffer or want as he did as a child. Even when he still lived in his bachelor apartment, he embellished all of my clothes and saw to it our weekends and holidays were fun and family oriented. I've been terribly spoilt, as Dane frequently reminds me. Dane keeps me grounded."

"You're lucky to have them as parents," John told him. "They do love you. They fret and worry about you like two hens with one egg in a nest."

Zan laughed at the image, saying, "I couldn't agree with you more. It's exactly the way they are!"

***

Zan climbed the stairs to his bachelor apartment, wishing a cheery goodnight to Aiden Kalensson, the novice lightning-mage on messenger duty. It was still warm, and his sitting room was cloaked in shadows.

Lighting a candle, he looked around him as he often did upon returning to his rooms. Though they were his, the rooms weren't really homey. He'd done nothing to make them more cheerful, and they somehow felt cold and empty to him, despite being hot and stuffy. Granted, he spent more time in his rooms since becoming an air-mage than ever before, but even so, they didn't feel like home to him.

His new sensitivity to the moods and emotions of others made him aware his parents actually were still young and wanted to have time alone together. He'd become fairly good at knowing when it was time to leave and hadn't stayed in his old room since the night of his augmentations. *I'm not a lightning-mage anymore*, he thought. *I notice things I never would have before.*

He threw open the windows and stood for a moment, looking out on the gardens, letting the fresh air in, and placing the screens in the windows to keep the bugs out.

Watching the lovers who strolled hand in hand in the warm darkness, he shook his head. *I'll be glad to leave. There's nothing here for me other than a few books.* Sitting at the table, he looked at the candle flame, unable to stop feeling depressed. *I wonder if Anna will still be interested in me when I get back. I certainly won't find anyone to compare with her in Mal Evol or anywhere else in this world. I'm still young, but Friedr was bonded at my age. Will I ever have a warm, comfortable home like my parents have? Gah! Why am I doing this to myself?*

Zan was startled by a knock on his door. Opening it, he found Anna standing there, looking slightly nervous, and his heart raced. His smile was warm and honestly surprised. "Hello, Anna. What brings you up to my little attic space?" *I'm an idiot! Why did I say such a stupid, banal thing?*

"I heard you're leaving in a few days." Anna's blue eyes looked up at him, full of humor at Zan's surprise. "I'd like to spend time with you before you go. Would you like to walk with me for a while tonight? I know it's late, but tomorrow is Sunnaday, and I don't have to get up too early."

"A good idea." Zan felt almost giddy. "It's a perfect night for a walk."

Anna took his hand, and they walked down to the gardens for a stroll in the warm evening air.

Dawn found them on one of the secluded trysting benches, arms wrapped around each other, with Anna's head resting on his chest. Both slept with faint smiles on their faces.

The week that once seemed to stretch ahead of Zan, long and lonely, now flew by all too quickly. For the two young lovers, the day of his departure came all too soon.

***

The morning before they were to embark upon the quest, the four companions gathered in Abbess Halee's study, receiving their final instructions. "You will heal as needed at each place you pass. Friedr, Zan, as you know, this is your required away-posting as journeyman healers, just as Edwin's first quest was for him. Believe me, you will be learning a great deal about healing on this first part of your quest." She smiled and looked at her notes. "Since you have two senior healers guiding you, you will be carrying a full medical kit and perform surgeries as needed. Besides being one of the finest practitioners of the internal healing arts, Edwin is an adept in general surgery, and Christoph is an adept in pain-relief- and sedation-magic. You will learn a lot from them on this journey.

"We ask all battle-mages and healers out in the field to reach out with their senses, testing for mage-talented children and budding empaths, at every farm they pass and in every hamlet. I would ask you to please do the same.

"And another thing…please, all of you, wear your old armor until you get to Braden because it is flashy and the children will be drawn to how impressive you are." Friedr and Zan looked at each other, beaming, which made Edwin and Christoph grin in response. "I'll send your new armor to Braden so it will be waiting for you there. If you visit each town and farm on the way and heal as necessary while building the shield here in the heart of Neveyah, you will be on the road for two months. You should have seen nearly every sort of healing emergency at least once by the time you arrive. That's a good healing journey by any standard." The warmth and encouragement the abbess embodied underscored her strength of purpose.

She continued, "We need your abilities in information gathering, Edwin and Zan. Eavesdrop everywhere. Someone is subtly encouraging people in southeastern Neveyah to hide their mage-gifted children from the Temple, and we know Mal Evol is the source. Something is afoot in Mal Evol, but we don't yet know what it is. We need you to whisper the word that the mage-gifted belong in the Temple for their safety and the safety of everyone around them. The people need to understand that Tauron sees their children as a threat and will prevent them from being properly trained. You know how to do this, Edwin, and Zan will learn by watching you." The two men nodded.

"Now, we come to the final point I want to make. Once you leave Braden, you must remain hidden to accomplish your mission. Your new armor tells us this, as much as the auguries. If you are forced into the open, abandon the quest and return as quickly as possible. Seal off the lands of Neveyah first and then build outward into Mal Evol from the Braden Gap. That way, we will lose nothing if you must abandon the quest, and you will have a safe route to return by."

Chapter 11 ~ The Road East

In the early hours before dawn, the companions walked out of town through the still, deserted streets, leaving via the eastern gate, and took the Eastern Trade Road. They carried full packs, their unique weapons, and also led a pair of pack ponies laden with medicines for the town of Arlen. From Arlen, the medicines would be distributed to the rural areas along the Escarpment at the base of the Mountains of the Moon.

As they walked, Edwin looked over at Christoph with a mischievous grin and asked, "Did you bring them? I brought mine." Reaching into his vest and withdrawing something, Edwin began juggling three brightly colored balls. Zan's look of astonishment made Friedr laugh.

Christoph grinned, reached into his vest and pulled out three of the same. He too began juggling them, and to Zan's utter amazement, he and Edwin began an incredible show as they walked along. They tossed the colored balls back and forth in a dizzying display, laughing and looking like they were street performers in a solstice parade.

"How come I didn't know they could do this? I mean, of course, I knew Chris could juggle but not Edwin. I must learn how to do this," Zan told Friedr. "I had no idea they were so talented." Zander's love of new toys was well known.

"Well, I thought you'd say that, so I brought you something to train with." Friedr chuckled wickedly as he handed Zan three round rocks he and Freylin painted just for this purpose.

Zan looked at the rocks and smiled wryly back at Friedr, who grinned challengingly, holding three brightly colored rocks of his own. "This is what Chris taught Edwin to juggle with, and though he had many lumps on his head for the first few days, it seemed to work, so I thought we should learn the same way. We'll either become proficient or unconscious." Zan laughed and began bouncing his rocks from hand to hand, looking at Christoph and trying to emulate him.

As the morning progressed, Friedr and Zan both began to get the hang of juggling, and the sounds of the forest were interspersed with occasional yelps of pain and much laughter as they traveled the trade road.

"Use your air-magic, Zan. You'll find your control improves immensely," Edwin suggested. "Friedr, try to use your combined senses to help you control the rocks. It'll help you develop other useful skills."

Zan nodded, and immediately his control improved.

Friedr looked at him, clearly not understanding what Edwin was getting at. "Friedr, just extend your senses as you do when you're fighting. You use all your senses when you fight, don't you?"

"Yes, but how did you know that?" Friedr looked at Edwin, dumbfounded. "That was my secret weapon. You never let on you knew the reason I'd improved. You just let me think I was being sneaky."

Edwin laughed as he replied, "Of course I know what you're doing, though no one else does. The way you fight has completely changed. You fight like I do now, using all your skills because it gives you an edge." Edwin reminded him, "I'm a healer too, Friedr. I know when someone is using his senses to gauge my moves.

We have an edge, and Aeolyn says every edge we have is to be used to our advantage. Use it now, and you'll benefit."

They stopped at every farm and cluster of houses to see if anyone was in need of healing, to simply check on the welfare of the inhabitants, and to sense for young mages. As they did so, they met many old friends from Edwin's first journeys and healed several people of minor illnesses. Friedr and Zan alternated putting into practice all the skills they had been learning at the infirmary. Edwin and Christoph observed but did not interfere, as their journeymen were doing well.

Each day was the same. They walked great distances and then walked some more. This part of the north was mostly uninhabited and was seldom traveled, as it was the long road to Braden. It was nearly twice as long a route as the Southern Trade Road. This road was used mainly by merchants and the Temple mail coaches that served the rural population, all of whom were heavily guarded. Lush forests of firs and evergreens, watered by chill brooks that flowed into swift-running rivers, comprised the landscape from Aeoven to Arlen. This wild beauty was broken by tiny clusters of farming villages, the largest of which had fewer than fifty families. Towering over it all and appearing to grow ever larger with each day was the awesome escarpment of the fabled Mountains of the Moon. On a clear day, they dominated the eastern horizon.

Toward evening of the second day, they were attacked by a pack of beasts, the so-called feral rats or rat-people. They were not actually rats, being half the height of an average human, but their faces were rat-like, and they had long, sharp claws they used as weapons. They were vicious, mindless, and easily dispatched with the companions' new weapons without even calling magic. Edwin hated having no solution to dealing with them other than to kill or be killed.

As they scouted, they hunted for small game to fill the cooking pot. They made camp and drew straws to determine the rotation for cooking, and soon Zan was roasting two hares. "I hope you've learned something about cooking from Dane," Friedr asserted. "Chris's cooking is not such a pleasure, as I recall." Zan snickered and agreed with him.

"I heard that, barbarian," Christoph called from over his shoulder. "Of course it's true, but you don't have to remind me."

"But your cooking has improved, Chris. That toast you made the other day was reasonably delicious," Zan told him wickedly. Christoph just laughed. He didn't look forward to eating his own cooking either.

At midmorning of the third day, they entered the village of Sevya, little more than a wide spot in the road with a small general store, several farm houses, and a grist mill, all surrounded by a wooden palisade. Their arrival was heralded with great joy and relief by the inhabitants, as the miller had been seriously injured. His arm had been mangled in his machinery. "His sleeve got caught when he was oiling it," his frantic wife told them. "It just happened this morning, and I've done everything I know how to do. I'm afraid he'll lose his arm, and then what'll we do? How will we work the mill and feed the children if he has only one arm?" Devi Miller was in terrible pain and had slipped into shock, compounding the problem.

Edwin would lead in healing the miller, and Friedr would assist him in the surgery. He had to gain experience in healing battle wounds, and this was as serious as any battle wound might be. Christoph and Zander would handle the sedation and pain management, while Edwin and Friedr handled the delicate work. Sari, Devi's wife, was awed to have two senior adepts to work on her husband, and the fact they had journeymen with them comforted her. "I can only thank Aeos for sending you to us. I had no way to call for a healer since I couldn't leave him like this and he can't travel. The traveling healer was through here last week, and I don't think she'll return until next week. But she's only a journeyman. I don't know if she could handle this."

Christoph silently agreed with her. This injury was well beyond a journeyman's skills. Nonetheless, he told Sari, "I know Bekki, your traveling healer, very well. Both Edwin and I have had the pleasure of instructing her. She is capable and would do the best she could."

Edwin immediately placed Devi under pain-dampening spells and tied them off, while Christoph placed a small forgetting on the man so the memory of the trauma was no longer so sharp. This immediately eased his shock. Then they prepared to sedate and hold him in a deep-sleep so Edwin and Friedr could do the delicate work of rebuilding his muscle and bone.

"This is like nothing I've seen before in my short career as a healer," Friedr murmured to Edwin, his face white as he unpacked the medical kit and prepared to boil the instruments. "This'll be a true test of my courage. I'm a terrible coward." He was echoing Zander's thoughts completely, judging by the look on

Zan's face. Christoph carefully removed the bloody bandages, exposing the mangled arm for Edwin to examine while he cleaned it.

Edwin delved Devi's body, strengthening him so he would not slip back into shock when they began the healing process. While the instruments were being sterilized, he spoke to Friedr and Zan, soothing their fears, unconsciously falling into his role of leader, speaking as an instructor.

"This is why you must make your away-posting as a healer. You can't get this sort of experience in Aeoven. Your first traumatic injury and surgery are always the hardest. Fortunately for me, I grew up on a farm. I was well acquainted with veterinary medicine since my father and I couldn't afford to hire an animal healer when one of our flock was injured or sick. We handled all the births and minor surgeries ourselves, so the transition was much easier for me." Edwin spoke calmly, his matter-of-fact tone easing their jitters. "I'd already seen some of the more serious injuries, only not in people. My father taught me all he knew, and I learned a great deal from our neighbors too.

"However, in Aeoven, we see very few traumatic injuries, so you haven't had the opportunity to develop this aspect of healing. The surgeries you have assisted with, until today, were very minor and weren't as emotionally difficult for the victim and his loved ones as this injury is, though they did provide you with some training in using your healing-gift. This surgery will provide you with both technical knowledge and practice.

"This is certainly not the worst injury I've seen, although it's very serious. Observe Christoph and see the way he's inserted a small forgetting into Devi's mind. This is Christoph's specialty, and you'd do well to learn this skill. I've used it successfully in treating seriously traumatized patients. Casting a small forgetting allows the calming and pain-relief spells to take hold more efficiently."

The instruments were finally ready, and the four of them gathered around Devi, preparing to link. The work they'd done with the shield had helped Friedr to get past his dislike of this process.

Christoph was doubtful they could save the man's arm. It had been years since he had done any actual healing of a grievously injured person. He buried his doubts so no trace of his fear was evident to Zan or Friedr. "Remain linked with me, Zan. Follow me as I delve him to gauge the strength of his heart and the health of his lungs. This sedative aspect is as important as the actual surgery and just as dangerous. Without us supporting him, Edwin would have to divide his attention, and he wouldn't be able to heal this arm as well. We'll constantly strengthen Devi and monitor his heart and breathing, as these deep-sleep spells sometimes cause the patient to forget to breathe. Edwin and Friedr will work to reassemble the muscle and bone."

Zan had turned pale but firmed his barriers and focused on Christoph. Soon, they were in a light trance.

Edwin noted Friedr's white face and told him, "Barriers, Friedr. Firm your barriers and separate yourself from the patient's pain and fear. You must maintain separation or you won't be able to work. Focus on me. This is a puzzle we are going to reassemble. We four will save his arm. You'll see."

Edwin's confidence encouraged the other three, and soon Friedr was able to concentrate.

"Think of this as a battle wound because it's the sort of thing you might see from a mêlée that's gone badly. First, we must stop the bleeding and make sure his fingers have blood flowing to them."

Edwin entered the teaching/healing trance, and soon Friedr found himself completely absorbed, as did Chris and Zan. "As you remember from your anatomy classes, the blood must flow through both arteries and veins, or the limb will die. This is good…there's still some blood flowing to his extremities, and even the smallest blood vessels here can be reconnected, so we're fortunate."

Using the surgical instruments to manipulate the bones and tissues, Edwin and Friedr used their gifts to make the delicate connections and grow the bone together. Zan followed with his senses as the mutilated arm was made whole again.

Their patient would be in a great deal of pain for a while. Tissue and bone regrowth was always accompanied by a certain amount of discomfort as the nerves made their new pathways. Devi would be relatively pain free within two weeks but would still be required to rest his arm in a sling for many weeks so the new bones could fully harden.

At last, Edwin finished the delicate work and emerged from the healing trance, as did the others. The procedure had taken just over three hours, but Edwin was pleased with the results of their efforts.

That evening, the miller's wife begged them to stay in their home as guests and couldn't do enough for them, insisting on doing their laundry. "Please make use of the bathhouse. You'll rest so much easier. Whatever you need, just ask and it's yours." As if they were at the infirmary, Friedr and Zan alternated a watch over Devi all night, maintaining the pain-dampening spells.

The next day, still in a teaching frame of mind, Christoph instructed Friedr and Zan in compounding potions for pain relief from local ingredients, which put Devi to sleep but were good at easing his pain. When they left Sevya, there would be a good stock of medicines, and Sari would have some idea of how to use them.

Edwin and Christoph were pleased their two journeymen's first emergency surgery went so well and were confident the two would be able to work well in serious situations.

Both Friedr and Zander were secretly proud to have found they had the courage to actually do the work needed. In fact, Friedr now began to feel surgery was his calling, which didn't surprise Christoph. Privately, he was pleased with Friedr's predilection for surgery.

"When it comes to your interests, you're a passionate person, Friedr, and a good surgeon must have passion," Christoph told him. "You'll do well if you choose to continue in this field. I've heard you did well with your anatomy lessons, and I know you aren't afraid to work hard. It's a difficult field to gain expertise in, but I believe you can do it. Surgery is the one area where a dedicated journeyman surgeon is often as effective as an adept. The skills and abilities required aren't as much about the magic as they are about knowledge and proficiency. You have the ability to gain those."

"Thank you, Christoph," Friedr replied, rather surprised by how important Christoph's high opinion was to him. "Your words mean a lot to me!"

The companions stayed two days longer to make sure the miller's arm was healing well. He was able to move his fingers by the time they left, but Devi understood he should not work for at least two months, to give his bones a chance to fully heal. Though they had been reassembled and mended with the healing-magic, they could only regain their strength with time.

"It's better for you to go without now than to ruin all our work and lose the use of your hand anyway," Edwin cautioned. "Give this note to the Temple mail coach when it comes through here next and you'll receive food and anything else you may need while you're healing. You may find your neighbors value you and will help since you've helped them for all these years."

When they were told what he needed, the man's neighbors were more than glad to help. The miller's wife was terribly grateful to the healers, sending them off with fresh bread and cheese for their journey.

As they left Sevya, Edwin thought about how few healers the Temple had and how many more were needed. It depressed him none of the young people of Sevya showed any sign of talent for magic or empathy, but on the positive side, the young daughter of Devi's foreman said she wanted to go to Aeoven and be trained as an herb doctor. Devi agreed to make the arrangements to have her sent to Aeoven in the hope she would come back to Sevya as a permanent healer.

Zan and Friedr alternated assisting Edwin at major surgeries when required. Unfortunately, they were required more often than they'd expected. The rural people of Neveyah felt the shortage of healers mostly keenly even though most Temple healers spent half of their time posted away on healing journeys.

The weather remained nice as they traveled, and at first, they were rarely bothered by the rats, though as they approached the Cascadia Escarpment, the attacks occurred more frequently.

Each day, they built a cell in the shield to keep the thornbushes from encroaching on the heart of Neveyah. "Once you three kill all the rat-people infesting the area, they shouldn't return. The shield should repel them." Christoph's confidence uplifted them as they refined their skills. "At least we have the chance to practice working on the scale we'll need to work at when we get into Mal Evol."

They passed many farms and went through several villages too small to have inns, though they had common rooms where the locals could gather. Edwin always managed to avoid those places, which tickled Friedr no end, and he mercilessly teased Edwin, who just shrugged and smiled sheepishly. Zan was mystified at their exchanges, but no one enlightened him. "You'll see, Zan," Friedr told him, grinning. "I won't spoil it by telling you."

In each place they came to, they secretly tested for young mage-talented children among the nine- and ten-year-olds and looked for empaths among the older children and young adults.

After twelve days on the road, the companions approached Arlen, the town of the mercenaries. As they walked toward the town and the Thieves Nest Inn, Edwin thought of the first time he'd visited five years before, thinking of the changes he'd heard Jaxon had wrought in the city. "I wonder if Jaxon's in town," he said to Friedr. "He's a good source of information about what's going on in this part of Neveyah."

"If he's in town, he'll come and find you," Friedr replied. "He has an unhealthy interest in your affairs, Edwin. He always asks about you when I travel through here. And he's so flowery when he talks, it's hard to listen to him." Though he appreciated the help Jaxon always freely offered them, Friedr did not really like the thin man who was so much more than a mercenary. His foreign mannerisms grated on Friedr's nerves. "I know he's your kinsman and all, but I don't feel comfortable discussing your life in detail with him. He does usually have useful information to share, though."

"Like me, he keenly feels the lack of family. He's my second cousin and is the only family left on my mother's side. We're the only blood he would claim in this world other than his children, so you can't blame him for being interested in me and my father." Edwin's face became tense as he added, "You know why we have to keep our kinship a secret. I don't dare draw attention to him in any way, so we'll have to act as though it's business as usual. We'll have to go to the common room tonight. If he's not away on business, he'll look for us there." He looked uncomfortable, and Friedr laughed at his obvious uneasiness.

"Don't worry. I'll stand over you with my sword drawn and keep the lustful ladies of Arlen from throwing themselves into your bed." Friedr's sly laugh got Christoph's attention.

"Are you picking on Edwin again? He can't help it." Christoph's smile was as impish as Friedr's.

"Maybe you should tie your hair back. Perhaps your augmentations will scare them away."

Friedr tossed Edwin a leather thong. "You should keep it tied back anyway. You don't look like a warrior. You look like a friendly-girl, wearing your hair all loose like that."

"I know. My father points that out to me regularly," Edwin replied morosely. "I just—ahhh, forget it." He stopped and pulled his hair back, braided it, and wrapped it with the thong Friedr gave him. "Zan knows what the problem is. The stealth runes like to be hidden. He wears his hair down and long now too, if you haven't noticed. So does Moran."

"Actually, I hadn't noticed Zan's hair until you just mentioned it." Christoph looked at Zander, whose dark hair had grown down over his shoulders. "How could I have missed that?"

"You've been busy, Chris," Zan reminded him. "I don't feel comfortable with the rune exposed."

"They're stealth runes. It's their nature," Friedr said. "But you *should* wear your hair tied back while we're on this quest, Zan. We won't have time to stop and put out any accidental fires in your lovely, dark locks once we leave this town. The feral rats are quite a problem out here, and they often have their sorts of mages traveling with them, although they're really not too adept with the elements, as crazed as they seem to be."

"Why, Friedr, I never knew you liked my 'lovely dark locks,'" Zan replied with a sly grin, but Friedr didn't rise to the bait. Edwin had caught him with that line before, so he was not disposed to fall for Zan's disrespectful mockery.

Disappointed he had not managed to needle Friedr, Zan said, "I'll braid it back now if it'll make you happy." He quickly braided it and tucked it down the back-plate of his armor. "Better?"

"Much better," Friedr said. "Now at least I don't feel like I'm questing with ugly, badly dressed friendly-girls."

Friedr was about to make another snide remark at Zan's expense when Edwin said sharply, "Fire-mage! On the right!" A ball of fire sailed out of the brush, splashing off Edwin's shields, followed by the slashing claws and fangs of the rat-like creatures. Instantly, they were fighting once more. Friedr dispatched the mage with a fire-spell of his own, and the other rats were quickly dispatched.

"I just realized something—they *do* seek Edwin out first." Zander's amazement showed in his voice. "I wonder why?"

Friedr just shrugged. Then he took a good look at Edwin, saying happily, "Well now—Edwin is bleeding. It's a battle wound and my turn to practice. Christoph, watch me and tell me how I'm doing." Edwin eyebrows rose at Friedr's elation, but he submitted to his tender ministrations, thanking him afterward.

"You're getting quite good, Friedr," Christoph told him, grinning at his enthusiasm. "But it really is bad form to act so happy about it, you barbarian."

***

They entered the northwest gate of Arlen and walked toward the Thieves' Nest Inn. "How're the baths here?" Zander asked. He was looking forward to a hot bath and a good meal.

"Not as good as the inn in Wister but fairly good. They have an attendant in each side to keep the place clean and the hot water coming and good deep tubs. The brew they serve here is good, and the food is better than most inns along this road," Edwin replied. "They also have a tub we can use to do our laundry and a line in our rooms to hang them on. Washing clothes and bathing in that stream three days ago were okay, but I'm down to one set of clean clothes again. And I don't mind saying I like hot water for bathing, though we'll see little enough of that on this trip."

Zan agreed with him wholeheartedly.

The new walls of Arlen were built right into the base of the Cascadia Escarpment, where the sheer walls of the western slopes plummeted down to the rolling plains of Neveyah. The city, which had been bursting at the seams six years before, now straddled the Fleet River and still felt full to bursting. Most of the town had the feeling of newness, as if it had only recently been built.

Every town in Neveyah was walled and fortified, but to Friedr's experienced eyes, Arlen had become an exceptionally well-planned stronghold. The ten-meter-tall walls had a deep moat around the outside and a manned parapet along the top. They were built from locally quarried stone. Mail-clad guards walked the parapets and watched the gates.

Inside the walls, the narrow, cobbled streets were lined with equally narrow two- and-three-story dwellings painted a riot of colors. Ornate, heavily carved woodwork decorated every shop and home. The people spoke with a strange accent and seemed very foreign to Zander. They were all polite and friendly, pretending not to scrutinize Edwin and Zan.

Zan found their clothing quite different too. The men wore silken shirts tucked into tight-fitting breeches, with polished, knee-high boots. The women wore elaborate dresses for everyday tasks. In Aeoven, no woman could afford to dress like the ladies of Arlen did. Zan wasn't sure what to think—everyone looked like it was a feast-day. *It's like being in a foreign country,* he decided. *They all talk and talk but say nothing I can understand.*

The effusive innkeeper put them in two of the four rooms he kept set aside for Temple business. "Forgive me, mages. There are only two rooms for you. The new healer and her guards may return tonight, and they must have the other two."

Edwin told him not to worry. They were just happy to have clean beds.

"It's as you say, sir mage. The beds here are both clean and comfortable, I assure you." The good innkeeper studiously ignored Edwin's unusual augmentations, though he had missed nothing and well knew the significance of the stealth runes. Immediately after leaving them to settle into their rooms, he secretly sent a stableboy off with a message.

"He just sent a message to Jaxon," Edwin told Friedr as he returned to his body. "He's in town, so I'm sure we'll have a visit from him tonight."

"This town has really grown since I was here last," Friedr observed. "This place is easily twice as large as it was."

"I sometimes wondered at my mother's accent, but I knew Dad had married her in a foreign land," Edwin told him. "She was from the old city of Mal Evol. She lived there until she was eleven and then went to the Temple for training as a healer." He always felt a strange sadness when he thought of how close his father and his companions had come to abandoning their quest in a failed attempt to rescue his mother's family. That detour to Mal Evol City had cost the life of one they had loved and could ill afford to lose. With Pauli's death, they had lost their chance to fully complete their quest.

Down in the common room, a local boy played simple, but lively songs on a fiddle. Friedr, suffering from a minor digestive ailment, had to step outside to the men's privy for a moment, leaving Edwin on his own. The moment Friedr left, the friendly-girls moved in. Wearing his hair tied back and baring his augmentations did not appear to deter the barmaids and the friendly-girls in the least.

Zan came down the stairs to find Edwin surrounded. Every one of the free women in the room hovered around Edwin. They watched his every move, resting their hands on his shoulders and toying with his long braid, telling him how intriguing they found his augmentations. One bold girl stood behind him and put her arms about his neck. "I like a man with tattoos. I find yours fascinating. I'd like to see all of them." She touched the vines on his neck, sending shivers down his spine. "Are you tattooed everywhere?"

Fortunately, the barmaid appeared with his ale and shoved her aside. She then leaned over him, suggestively pressing her very ample bosom against his back to serve him his ale. His face grew redder with each moment. "Can I get you anything else?" she asked in a whisper, her breath tickling his ear.

Undeterred, the bold girl the barmaid had nudged aside sat next to him, squeezing in as closely as she could, and said, "I've never seen a mage look as fine in Temple leathers as you do in those. They show off your manly arse perfectly." She stroked his thigh possessively. "I like your arse. Are you tattooed there too?" She pointed at a very private place. "Let's see all of them." All the girls agreed and offered to help him out of his shirt so they could see his tattoos more clearly.

"Please, don't," Edwin said, moving the bold girl's hand. "I'm bonded, and I love my wife. Please leave me alone." His eyes were slightly wild, and he blushed furiously. "Please, go away."

Zan sat shocked by the friendly-girls' behavior, unsure of what to do in such a situation. That Edwin needed help was clear, but Zan had no idea how.

The bold girl and her friend elbowed the barmaid out of the way, and each taking a hand, they urged him to dance with them. Edwin's polite refusals, being taken for encouragement, fell on deaf ears. His refusals began to have a touch of desperation to them. "*No*, thank you," he told them again and again. "I don't want to dance, thank you. I'm bonded. I'm bonded!" The look in his eyes was that of a hunted man. Zan watched in amazement as they tried to drag Edwin to the dance floor. Edwin pulled away and firmly sat down.

Christoph came down the stairs just as the drama really began to heat up. Zan looked at Christoph, mutely asking him what to do. Christoph cast 'calm', though it had no effect. Unfortunately Christoph's love of drama interfered with his desire to defuse the situation.

Finally, Zan stood up and told them firmly, "Please! He said he's not interested. Leave him in peace." They glared at Zan and then ignored him, but they did let go of Edwin. Still, they stood right beside him, refusing to move on. "He's told you he's bonded. Let him be!" Zander said sharply. The friendly-girls glared at Zan as if he were trying to steal Edwin for himself. "Oh, good grief, ladies, please give him some space. He's bonded. He loves his wife!"

At that moment, Friedr returned to the table and rescued Edwin, telling the women, "Go away. He's a bonded man and not interested. Shoo! You're neglecting your friends." He took them by the arm and pushed them back to the bar. "Now stay here—see? Your friends are lonely."

The friendly-girls stood leaning against the bar, looking longingly at Edwin and completely ignoring their regular friends. Their hot, sultry eyes followed his every move. The barmaid tended to her customers, giving them scant and surly service while watching him with a dreamy-eyed expression, praying his cup would run dry and she could soon refill it. She was so desperate to have a legitimate reason to approach the table that she eagerly waited on Chris, Zan, and Friedr.

"I've never seen anything like that," Zander said with awe. "It's truly amazing."

"You should see what happens when his father is along for the evening," Friedr smirked. "The poor girls nearly split themselves trying to decide which one they want more." He cast a wary glance at the bar. "I must say though, these ladies are very stubborn. There is something markedly different about the women in this town. They are much bolder than friendly-girls elsewhere. I admit I've never seen them behave like this."

"That must be why John never goes out of the Temple district." Zan had wondered, but never asked. "The friendly-girls don't come down there, and the barmaid is married to the innkeeper."

"I *never* want to go through that again!" Edwin said with his face still somewhat red. "It's the worst it's ever been. There must be a way to avoid it and still get a glass of ale and a bowl of soup."

"I agree. I don't know what causes it, but women do love to look at you, though most are not so aggressive," Christoph said, trying manfully not to laugh and finally giving in, howling at Edwin's discomfort. At last he got his breath back and said, "Friendly-girls have been known to leap across tables to get to you, but I've also seen some very respectable women completely lose their train of thought when you walk into a room. It's the Goddess' way of insuring your bloodline. Marya certainly didn't put up a fight, as I recall."

"I don't know what it is, but I could do without it." Edwin glanced uneasily at the ladies lined up at the bar, watching his every move. "You won't let them get at me again, right? Friedr? Friedr?"

Friedr watched him but did not answer, his face nearly split with a grin.

"Aw, Friedr, these women are crazy. They said…they offered…. Don't laugh. This isn't funny at all." Edwin's face was bright red. "Gah! Listen to me. I'm reduced to begging for your protection."

"Yes, Uncle Friedr will protect you from the big bad friendly-girls," Friedr mocked him, since Edwin had finally said what he wanted to hear. "Besides, your wife will beat me black and blue with her staff if I don't protect her interests. She's already told me so!" He shrugged.

Edwin rolled his eyes. "Mock me all you want. I can easily endure that. Just don't let them near me." He shivered involuntarily. "I'm not made of stone, Friedr, and I love my wife. There's only so much a man can stand, but I can't leave this room. I have to stay here until Jaxon finds us."

Shocked at this admission, Friedr laughed uproariously. "I knew it—you're human after all!" He laughed until he was gasping for breath. "Oh, Edwin, of course I'll guard you." Edwin just looked at the table, his expression carefully blank, not seeing a lot of humor in his situation.

"I don't think it's funny, Friedr," Zan said, looking at the ladies nervously. "He shouldn't have to put up with their behavior. He's not a pleasure-boy, existing only for their gratification. But it's all they can think of when they look at him. Even the bonded ladies are thinking about it. The combined weight of it is crushing his barriers." Edwin and Christoph looked at Zan sharply, and Edwin firmed his barriers.

Friedr looked at Zan and then blushed himself. "I'm sorry, Edwin. I owe you an apology. If I'd looked at you with my healing sight, I'd have seen how badly this affects you. We've always joked about it, but it really isn't very funny, is it? I promise not to let it get out of hand, my brother. From now on, I'll help you deal with this problem. Am I forgiven?"

"Of course. I can't seem to deal with it myself as they don't take any notice of what I say, and...well, now you know...." Edwin shifted uneasily in his chair. "I'm a weak man."

"The fact you're a weak man like the rest of us comforts me, Edwin. Well, let's have some food and more ale. That'll help."

After dinner, they played a game of stones to pass the time. Just as they were finishing a lively game, two men in grey leathers and wearing chain mail entered the common room. After a brief look around, one opened the door to the street, and they stationed themselves on each side of the door as a small, thin man with lank, dark hair approached their table. He wore clean, but well-worn grey leathers cut in an unusual style and walked with a wary grace and sure confidence in his own ability.

His face was prematurely lined and careworn, and although he was only Edwin's age he looked much older. The guards remained at the door, watching both the common room and the street, hard eyes missing nothing and no one. A third guard stood at the foot of the stairs.

"It's my kinsman, Edwin Farmer," he said, smiling and clasping Edwin's hand, and nodded to Friedr and Christoph, taking in their recent augmentations. "There've been many changes in your lives, sir mages, some harder than others I'd wager. The Goddess has blessed you all quite heavily...." He glanced briefly at Zan and missed nothing in that fleeting glance. "Are you taking apprentices in the assassins' guild then, cousin?" Smiling sardonically, he held his hand out to

Zan and introduced himself. "I am Jaxon Sellsword. You're welcome in my little town, apprentice."

"Zander Christophson." Zan shook his hand, taken aback and not too happy at being referred to as apprentice. *He acts like he's the lord of this place or something.* He decided he didn't much care for the arrogant mercenary. Still, he treated him with every courtesy as his parents had taught him. *Friedr doesn't much care for him either. But Christoph and Edwin both seem to like him.*

Jaxon looked at Christoph and then back to Zan, one eyebrow raised. "A fine son you have, healer. I'd heard you had a son with the mage-talent. He'll bring honor to your name."

"He does already," replied Christoph, his eyes lit up. "We've great pride in his accomplishments." Jaxon nodded as if he expected no less.

To Zander's surprise, Edwin was genuinely pleased to see the man, smiling his trademark charming smile. "My father has returned to Neveyah and sends you his regards." Jaxon's eyes widened marginally, and he nodded. "He's pleased to know you're well and still in the family business, if in a less public position than your grandfather once held. Also, the Holy Father, Rall, wished me to remind you my mother's family long served yours, and we continue to serve you, though we too serve in a different capacity. He also wishes you to know your efforts will mean all the difference when the time comes, though *we* may not see the results."

So briefly did the emotions vie on Jaxon's face, Zan thought he might have imagined it. *Edwin has deliberately said something significant, but what? He said several things, I think.*

"Please convey my thanks and my understanding to His Holiness." Jaxon spoke with no trace of his usual flowery evasions. "I'd hoped…but it's of no consequence. Our sons or grandsons will surely see that day, yes?" After a moment, he sighed. "It's good to know John Farmer has returned to Neveyah. Sadly, 'the family business,' as you so tactfully put it, has been quite hectic lately, as you might imagine."

The sardonic smile was now firmly back in place. "We are spread too thinly to make any appreciable difference in the local population of the displaced rat-people. But the booming business is supplying our needs in my little kingdom here and helping us to provide such medicine and food as we're able to divert to the shadowed lands. The main problem now is getting it into the city and distributed without drawing unwelcome attention. The penalty for getting caught is a trip to the Shadow Castle and a slow, painful introduction to the Dark God."

Friedr's eyebrows rose, and he leaned forward, interested in hearing whatever Jaxon might have to say. He said, "When business is good in Arlen, there's trouble elsewhere in Neveyah."

Zan was truly mystified now, looking from Friedr, to Jaxon, and then to Edwin, trying to understand what was going on at their table.

"The Temple should know." Jaxon spoke quietly, his eyes roaming around the inn, seeing everything and everyone. "Business is too good—we're unable to keep up with the demand. More of my people find their way to Arlen each year, so many that we're soon to have a Temple of our own. However, we can supply only three guards to any merchant at this time. You won't see many travelers as you head south along the Escarpment."

This is troubling. He's asking for help from the Temple, Edwin thought. Casually, he agreed, saying, "We've seen few travelers on our way here and only those from our own Temple traveling on foot. Is anything interesting happening in the homeland other than the gradual relocation of our people?" Edwin's gesture took in the community both inside and outside the common room.

Jaxon leaned back with surprise. "Ah. So is this another mission of stealth and retrieval then? You're too late. No one remains of those whose missions failed last year. They've gone to the dread god who rules there now." His voice was sad but sure as he leaned forward, lowering his voice so only the others could hear. "I can tell you this—the mad priest no longer resides in the Shadow Castle. He's been permanently recalled to his adopted homeland. Apparently, the civil war among his people is still a thorn in his side, more so with each passing year. He has appointed an exceedingly high priest, Dalgek, to handle administrative details such as collecting taxes and enforcing laws, making him Patriarch of Mal Evol— this places Dalgek on their high ruling council. He is utterly devoted to the mad priest.

"The baron still rules Mal Evol, issuing orders through his right hand at the keep of Mal Evol, a warrior-priest known as Lork, using him in the same fashion he once used a minotaur-priest named Brec. Lork is not the warrior Brec was and not as clever. Lork has enemies within his own walls." His companions nodded. "Some think he's been promoted above his ability. But so far, he has eaten the heart of each who'd take his place. Sooner or later, though, a stronger, smarter minotaur will dine on Lork's heart, and a new warrior-priest will rise to his position. The baron doesn't care for any of his minions, save they do his bidding. It's the way in their society."

Jaxon quickly looked around the room, and then in a near whisper, he said, "It's rumored that Baron D'Mal has attained the power to create a portal, though it burns him out. He doesn't do such a working lightly. He sends his guards directly from his adopted land into the keep when it's necessary to send replacements. It's not known if he can place the portal anywhere he wants or if it must be located in a certain place, but it appears he cannot walk through it himself. When he comes to the Shadow Castle, he must ride in his black carriage, taking the long road from Serende."

The companions looked at each other with surprise and consternation upon their faces.

Jaxon continued. "Another thing disturbing me is the news that lately he's sane more often than not. While he's not capricious and cruel, he's reasoned and harsh. Still, it's easier for my people to survive under his yoke while he remains sane, though we're less able to come and go as freely."

"That's interesting news indeed," replied Edwin thoughtfully. "It's too early to know how we'll be affected by this in accomplishing our little task, but it's useful information."

Jaxon smiled, thinking for a moment before saying, "Perhaps you go to rid us of the new scourge? One which will soon be unleashed upon my poor land."

"We go to rid that land of a scourge." Friedr leaned forward, intent on Jaxon. "But we'd welcome more information. Some scourges are more recent than others."

"Indeed, Sir Fire-mage," Jaxon said with a tight smile. "I'll illuminate you. I've been informed a certain unwanted tenant who has usurped an old castle of mine is once again breeding dogs. You know what this means, I'm sure."

"This is troubling news indeed." Friedr sat back, shock on his face. "How long has the Baron had this hobby?" He shuddered, his mind racing. He could almost feel the hot breath of the Bear Dog as its razor-sharp fangs barely missed goring his face. "I had some experience with his pets, the last time I visited his home."

"I see you understand my dilemma," Jaxon replied, his usually smiling face serious. "I was told today the pair he received less than half a year ago has bred most prolifically, having produced two litters of eight or nine pups each. There are now nearly twenty of the beasts, half of whom are approaching breeding age. My understanding is when the numbers reach one hundred they will be released into the wild to provide sport for the legions languishing in the haunted castle."

"If watching your fellows being mauled and torn to shreds by monstrous, savage beasts taller than me, with eight-inch, razor-sharp fangs can be called a sport." Christoph's wry comment elicited an answering smile from the mercenary.

Jaxon agreed. "Here lies the crux of the matter—it's rumored the legions sometimes coat their blades with the saliva of these creatures. I'd thought to visit the Temple in Aeoven for guidance, but your arrival has saved me the trouble."

Again, they looked at each other with dismay.

Jaxon changed the subject, signifying his business had been satisfactorily conducted and was now concluded. "I've purchased a harp for this establishment, Christoph Berryman, hoping you and others who were trained like you might pass through here on occasion. We see very few bards." His eyes twinkled as he said, "To ensure our continued obscurity, we prefer our small town doesn't rate highly on the bardic circuit. Would you consider entertaining us this evening?"

Christoph's face lit up. "I'd be honored, Jaxon. I'm rusty as I had to leave my harp in Aeoven, but I do miss it."

"Your tales are legend here in Arlen," Jaxon assured him. "All who tell the epic tale of *The Fall of Ariend* are measured against you, and all fall short of the mark. The tale is dear to my heart, as you know." He beckoned to the innkeeper who brought the harp case, bowed, and returned to his post at the bar.

Christoph blushed and replied he hoped he would live up to Jaxon's expectations. "This is a very fine instrument, Jaxon Sellsword," Christoph said, stroking the beautiful harp. "It's an honor to be allowed to play this harp. It's a masterpiece."

Jaxon rose from the table, and his men closed in around him. The townsfolk began filling the common room as if by a signal. They were enthusiastic in their praise for Christoph's songs and stories, hanging on his every word. His love ballads brought tears to the hardest eye. His comic songs had them rolling on the floor with laughter. He enchanted the audience with the traditional epic quest-tales, the harp providing the backdrop. When he told his tales, his listeners lived the stories with him. He was gratified by their applause and cheers and humbled by their praise.

At first, while Christoph was warming up with a silly song called "The Giant and His Wife," Zan was a little disturbed. He finally whispered to Edwin, "I love Christoph's tales as much as anyone, but why are we hanging about down here? We should be upstairs discussing what we've heard."

"No, Zan. Jaxon's price for the information was for Christoph to perform as only he can. See how these people have packed into this place? They really do see very few bards here, being this close to the haunted mountains, though they've talented musicians of their own. Jaxon cares deeply for his people's welfare and happiness. Tomorrow, we'll visit the sick, and also we'll test for mage-talented children. We'll also look for empaths among the young people. We benefit from this far more than he does," Edwin told him. "If we find just one with mage-talent or one empath, we have more than justified dallying here."

"He seems awfully friendly toward you," Zan muttered darkly. "Why does he share his information so freely? He's a mercenary, isn't he? Why doesn't he ask for gold?"

"He has a reason. Trust me. He understands the value of what he shares. Jaxon is much more than simply a mercenary, Zan, so much more. He's my kinsman and my friend. I trust him as much as I trust you," Edwin replied, smiling at Zan's wary mistrust of the mercenary. "The Temple owes him much we can never repay. Without him, I might not have been able to free Marya. I'll tell you the story of Jaxon Sellsword because you should know it, though I must caution you, it's a Temple secret. His handshake indicated his wish you should know. But right now, we should listen to Christoph entertain these people. He's in rare form tonight."

Chapter 12 ~ Arlen, Nola and the South

During their stay in Arlen, Edwin and Jaxon spent some time visiting families Jaxon suspected might have mage-talented children, and they did find two girls. One had healing potential, and the other was a potential water-mage. During their walk about town, guarded as always by Jaxon's bodyguards, the two men had a chance to discuss the ties that bound them together.

Later, they dined in Jaxon's pleasant, modest apartments above his wife's hat shop. While Eleia bustled around getting the two older children to bed, they played with Jaxon's twin baby daughters, Delena and Delora, then rocking them to sleep in the tiny courtyard garden behind the shop.

"It's strange to think the mad priest is my cousin too," replied Edwin, awed as always by the links that bound him and Jaxon to their common destiny.

"Although we must hide the truth from the world, it doesn't change the facts. He's so much a creature of the Mad God, he's beyond redemption, but he's of our blood, and we have to accept it. We don't have to like it." Jaxon felt a familiar sense of loss when his thoughts turned to his murdered father's half-brother. "The prophecies say you, your son, or your son's son will kill him. It's a nasty job that must be done for the good of our world."

"It always comes back to the secret that lives within the Shadow Castle, doesn't it? I don't like killing anything, as you know. Still, I *would* try to kill him if I had the opportunity." A sense of certainty filled

Edwin's heart as he added, "But I know it won't be me who ends his life."

"I can't tell you how much I look forward to that day," replied Jaxon, thinking about the people he had not yet managed to save. "I pray I'll live to see it. I fear we're in the end-times of which the prophecies speak. Many who steadfastly remain children of Aeos still live hidden in plain sight throughout the valley. I must still try to save those who live in the general population of the eastern valley and in the haunted city. The prophecies regarding my direct line are as specific as those regarding you."

Edwin nodded.

Jaxon continued. "The prophecy I'm thinking of says this: 'Keeper, you must save the remnant of my children, for when the end-times are upon you, you shall be barred from the valley of poison and beauty. The wall shall stretch from Horn to Horn and shall be the sign that none from the valley of shadows can enter the golden land. The eternal youth, the Lost One, will take the City of Gloom and those of my children left behind will suffer unto the third generation. He stands on the wall and gazes on the golden land, unable to enter.'

"I'm sure the 'City of Gloom' refers to the City of Mal Evol, for what can be gloomier than that forlorn collection of huts? I'm also convinced my eternally young uncle is the one referred to as the Lost One. His dread God keeps him locked forever in a state of youth we all wish we could remain at." Jaxon shrugged. "The valley is bad, but it's not really poisonous, though it's harsh. It's certainly not beautiful. No wall stretches from the Southern Escarpment to the Horn of Misery yet, so we have some time. Such an undertaking couldn't be accomplished quickly, as I'm finding out with my own walls here."

"I'd never heard this prophecy," Edwin said, as he mentally sifted through the ones he did know, hoping to offer Jaxon some comfort. "I'd like to have a copy of the prophecies you have, and I'll make sure you have everything I have. It's not my area of study, but Friedr will most definitely have much to tell you. I'll see to it you're fully informed of those prophecies we have witnessed." Edwin shifted uncomfortably. Hearing the prophecy about the valley bothered him for some reason he couldn't identify. He laid his discomfort down to his conscience, thinking, *Jaxon knows I can't tell him my purpose for going to Mal Evol. He understands, so I've no reason to feel so guilty about not being honest with him. But I must give him some sort of hope if I can find it.*

Unaware of Edwin's crisis of conscience, Jaxon explained, "The great martyr, Devyn D'Mal, the last abbott of Mal Evol Temple, was sent that vision the day the young man, Stefyn D'Mal, known then as Stefyn Black, arrived at the Keep of Mal Evol to tutor my father, who was a boy of fourteen. No one realized the significance of it then," said Jaxon. Bitterness crept into his tone as he said, "Who'd have believed only ten years later it would come to pass. To think a child of our blood would slaughter the entire family, lay waste to our country, and then give to the Bull God the one precious object that was the holy duty of our blood to shield and protect from harm! It's hard to wrap my head around it sometimes."

"Abbott Devyn was the first of the priesthood of Aeos offered up to Tauron in the great massacre, wasn't he?" Edwin had read the history of the fall of Mal Evol with great interest because of the part his father had played in it. "He refused to abandon the holy Temple to the legions."

"He was the first of one hundred and four of the clergy of Aeos whose broken remains burned in the purple fires of Tauron's dread altars during those black days. He fell to the legions of Tauron while defending the altar of the Great Cathedral. When they broke through his defenses, they cut him down and dragged him, still living, out to the great steps, where they hastily erected an altar to Tauron. Delirious with glee at having snared Aeos's highest priest in Mal Evol, the mad priest himself performed the drawn-out, gruesome sacrifice, thus killing his last, living, full-blood relative other than me. To this day, he believes he's the only living person who can use the Throne of Stone and Bone. That drama unfolded even as your father carried me to safety down the long, dark road under the earth. It was my great-uncle's sacrifice that kept the mad priest's attention away from your father and his companions, enabling them to rescue me."

Jaxon's gloomy features grew even more pensive as he told the sad tale. "The diaries of the two survivors of the carnage in the Temple are very clear, saying the abbott most certainly knew what he had to do and what his end would be. He did it anyway, crafting a plan that would give your father the most time possible." He shook his head as he pondered the enormity of the lives sacrificed so he might live. "I've tried to live my life as well as I can, to honor the abbott's sacrifice and to prove myself worthy of the sacrifices made by your father, his companions, and so many others, that I might live to work Aeos's will."

"Jaxon, your efforts to save the remnant of Aeos's children still in Mal Evol will live forever as one of the great works of your bloodline. Though it must remain unspoken outside of these walls, your work will be the foundation of a great dynasty." Edwin decided to tell Jaxon something he'd only spoken of with Father Rall. "Two years ago, I dreamt a true-dream I don't know the meaning of, but I'll tell you anyway. It concerns you, Friedr, and Zan, as well as me. I've only spoken to the Holy Father of this. The others don't know I've had this dream."

Laying his hand on his heart, Jaxon nodded. "It's a Temple secret."

"You and I stood before a door. This door was built into the hillside of a valley I'm all too familiar with. It's the same Green Valley where I once fought Stefyn D'Mal. The door in the hillside was open. We camped before the door, waiting for news. Somehow I knew it was the Forbidden Road, the road that leads under the earth to the Shadow Castle. We were old men but still strong. Friedr and Zan waited with us, and they too were strong, old men. Friedr was lamed but it was an old injury. He wore a brace and walked with the help of his staff." He looked at Jaxon, feeling love for his cousin, whose struggles to save the people of Mal Evol were by necessity unknown and unrewarded. "Your grandson will live and reign in Mal Evol."

Jaxon sat silently, thinking about what Edwin had said. Finally, he said, "I thank Aeos you've been allowed to come into my life. You give me the strength to continue when I'm so tired." A sardonic smile crossed his face. "At least we'll see the day that we nonetheless work so desperately to stave off." His chronic exhaustion made him look even frailer than usual. His infant daughters slept peacefully in their pram, completely oblivious to the poignant turn the conversation had taken.

Despite his worry for his cousin's health, Edwin laughed at the jest. "Yes, we do seem to be doing that, but what else can we do?" Touching his cousin's cheek, Edwin delved him, finding nothing wrong that simple rest would not cure. Still, he cast a healing spell, strengthening him and making him feel rested. "Cousin, you *must* sleep more than four hours a night. For the sake of all Neveyah's people, you must try to sleep for at least eight hours each night. When you sleep, you rebuild your vitality. Believe me, my brother, those extra four hours a day will save your life. When you're exhausted, you accomplish little of value."

At Jaxon's stubborn look, Edwin laughed, "Please listen to me. I'm considered a fairly decent healer by some." Jaxon smiled despite his irritation. "You risk dying young because of the stress you place on your body. Your heart is strong right now, but I can feel it will not always be so unless you change your habits now." His voice took on a note of urgency. "You are our only hope of preserving the culture of Mal Evol."

Jaxon was surprised and at first a little disturbed Edwin had delved him without permission. Then he realized that Edwin was behaving toward him the way he would his father or any other beloved family member, and a wave of affection for his cousin swept through him. "Your words show you truly consider me your brother. I'll try. I give you my word."

***

After three days, the four questors left the town of Arlen, turning south along the Fleet River and heading to the rural valleys of south eastern Neveyah. They walked past the new Temple of Aeos, where the masons were already hard at work in the early light of day, and out of the Widge Gate. Arlen Temple was one of the first new ones to be built in three generations. Fleetside was getting the other new Temple. The new Temples would both be sent an abbott and some healers and teachers. In both villages, people were pleased to have a Temple in their community.

They continued walking the trade road south toward Braden, following the Fleet River as it wound south along the base of the Cascadia Escarpment. As they had done every day while on the road, they built another cell in the shield.

Turning off the trade road, they once again headed west, taking the long valley trail through the small villages of Drin and Nola. Nola boasted an inn of dubious quality, but they stayed as guests at the small Temple.

Nola was the village where Zan was born, but it wasn't familiar at all to him. At the Temple in Nola, along with their usual letters home, they sent a letter to Father Rall detailing what they'd discovered in Arlen about the dogs and also described their progress. They wouldn't receive any mail of their own until they reached Braden.

To Zan's disappointment, he could find no sign of the house he was born in. The ruins of the home where

Zan spent his early childhood were gone, replaced by a weedy, overgrown lot between two run-down houses. Nothing remained where his home had burned to the ground. Even the foundation and chimney stones had been taken away and reused, yet Zan was driven to look, to poke around and see if even one small thing could have been left behind. He stood for a long time looking at the empty lot. Finally, he spoke aloud to Christoph, "How could there be no sign it ever happened?"

Concerned for Zan's state of mind, Christoph carefully watched his adopted son's face for signs of distress. He was about to cast ease when Edwin placed his hand on Christoph's shoulder, pulling him away so as to leave Zander in peace. "Walk with me, brother. He has to grieve, Chris. It's normal. Let him feel it. You can't protect him forever. You and Dane did so much to help him when he was a child, but now he must truly heal. It'll come out at some point. Let it be now when he has us to support him." He walked with Christoph to the far side of the muddy street.

Christoph reluctantly nodded, his worry plainly written on his grim face. "Treating the emotionally crippled boy he was then is how I originally came to know Dane. I was a new-made journeyman of sixteen, assisting Beryl with her practice. I hadn't selected an area of study, and she felt it would help me heal from my own traumatic childhood to work with her in helping others. She was right. Helping others helped me more than I understood at the time.

"You know what my life was like as an apprentice bard. I needed to help others, and in the process, I was healed of wounds I didn't realize I still suffered from.

Zan was one of the first children I worked with who was *not* a rape victim. Beryl and I worked long and hard, helping him to get past his grief and terror. His lungs and burns had been healed by the great adept healer, Soren Torsson, who was the greatest healer in that area of practice, though he'd partially retired at the time."

"Soren still consults on the serious cases, and I was fortunate to work with him on a bad case three years ago," said Edwin. "He can't completely walk away from healing, though he is over a hundred now."

Christoph decided to just tell Edwin Zan's story. "One terrible night, Zan woke to find the house engulfed in flames. He, his aunt, and his uncle were trapped on the second floor by the flames. During the chaos of trying to escape, Dane's father, Bran, pushed Zan out of the second story window to save him. As Bran threw Zander out the window, the floor collapsed underneath him. Clinging to the window sill, Zan witnessed it.

"Zan's face, back, and arms were burned, but he suffered most from inhaling the hot smoke. He'd also broken his arm in the fall from the roof to the yard below, where his mother lay in the grass. The Temple here in Nola had two healers who did what they could for him and his mother, getting them stabilized, but their injuries required special care. Zan and his mother were immediately loaded into the Temple mail coach with the two healers and taken to Aeoven's infirmary.

"His mother later died from the smoke damage to her already compromised lungs. Her case was sad. She'd been addicted to daze-spice when she found herself with child, and the drug had destroyed her lungs. The smoke worsened her condition."

"That's terrible," Edwin agreed, thinking of the many friendly-girls and pleasure-boys he treated on his healing journeys during his early career as a journeyman healer. Those young people whose lives had been ruined by the addiction touched his heart. "Daze-spice is insidious and evil, but at least it didn't affect Zan. It's a miracle he was born healthy. So many of those babies are stillborn, and some who live are born deformed."

"That's true. He is lucky. After he was healed of his burns and lung damage, Zan was terrified of being left alone. His trundle bed was in Dane's room for the first four years he lived with him." Chris looked at Zan, watching as he and Friedr poked about in the brush, searching for some sign of his past.

"When I first met them, Zan was barely eight and still tormented by the memory. He couldn't bear to be away from Dane, which had become a Temple problem. He was beginning to show all the signs of being a lightning-mage."

Edwin grinned. "I've heard they're both hilarious and a little scary when the magic first shows itself."

Chris smiled wryly at the memory. "Their neighbor, old Lenex, the fire-mage, had a little dog who would bark whenever Zan approached the wall between their yards. One day, he was startled by the dog's sudden bark while playing with his ball in the garden and inadvertently zapped the poor animal. The dog survived, but even though Dane placed restraints on Zan, he had to go into novice training, and they called me in to see if my skills could be useful in enabling him live in the novice barracks.

"He did well enough in the Temple school during the day while Dane worked at the infirmary but would become hysterical if Dane wasn't there every evening. Zan's guilt ate at him like a poison. He had the unreasonable conviction it was somehow his fault his uncle had died. Beryl and I worked with him, bringing forward only good memories and making the old terrors dim and fuzzy. When he finally went to the novice barracks, he was a happy, sunny child with very little memory of his life prior to living with Dane. We worked with him for several years, reinforcing the suggestion-loops until he was a mid-level novice."

Falling silent, Christoph watched Zan, who wandered around looking at the vacant lot with a confused expression on his face, while Friedr followed him around, trying to help him sort it out. "I don't know if he can go through it again."

"Chris, my brother, listen to me. You're too close to this. Zan's no longer a traumatized child. He's a grown man. I can tell the loops you placed then are still holding." Christoph looked relieved. Edwin continued, "He needs to grieve properly, which he couldn't do before. You helped him and enabled him to live a normal life, but now you *have* to allow him to feel this. You can't shelter him forever." Edwin's hand on his shoulder emphasized his conviction. "You love him and don't want him to feel pain, but pain is part of life. If it surfaces, let him deal with it in his own way. He'll be stronger for it. If he needs us, we're here."

"I'll be guided by you, my brother," Christoph finally replied, his eyes worried. "I know you're right.

He's my son now. I can't be dispassionate where he's concerned and never have been. Even before I formally adopted him, I couldn't be detached because of my love for Dane. They became my family despite my own problems." He smiled wryly at Edwin and said, "Maybe I need this too."

That evening, Zander was much quieter than usual. When Friedr asked if he was okay, he simply said "Yes, thanks. I'm fine. I just have things on my mind."

Later after they'd eaten a pleasant dinner with Abbess Dela, her staff, and their families, Chris, Edwin, and Friedr played a game of stones, but Zander was withdrawn. When they were about to retire for the night, Christoph finally asked Zan if he was feeling well.

Zan turned to Chris, asking, "How could a home so full of love and happiness just burn down and there be no sign it ever existed? Auntie Jenna and Uncle Bran... they really *are* gone. I must've thought they'd be here waiting somehow, although I know it's impossible."

"No, it's normal, Zan. You were very young, and children find ways of dealing with things," Chris replied. "How're you feeling now?"

"Well, I'm fine, I think.... Dane and you are my parents, and I've always felt loved even when it was just Dane and me. Maybe it's just because there's only the three of us. It'd be nice to have a large family." Zan spoke wistfully.

"We do have a large family," Chris reassured him. "We have Edwin and Marya, and Friedr and Aeolyn, and their families. We have John Farmer, and Freylin, Rynne and Jonny. We have family. They love us."

"You're right. John said the same thing before we left Aeoven. We're fortunate, aren't we?" Zan's old smile was back, his spirits lifted. "I've always had the good fortune of being loved." A world of gratitude was in his eyes as he looked at Chris. "I know what you did for me when they took me to you for counseling, and I'm grateful. And thank you for letting me deal with this today without 'helping' me. I needed to feel it, so I can put it behind me now."

"Thank you for wanting me for your father despite my youth and failings. You'll never know what it means to me," Chris replied, gratitude filling his own heart. "Now you should try to sleep. Will you be able?"

"Yes. Actually, I do feel tired," Zan yawned. "See you in the morning." Once he was in bed, he dropped right off, slipping into a dreamless slumber.

***

From Nola, they made side trips to South Derry, Winne, and Moxy before they doubled back up the main trade road to Widge. After they left Widge, they detoured to the towns of Bannoc, Borgat, and Fleetside. Then they planned to go south to Morton before they finally ended the first half of their journey in Braden.

The side trips allowed them to construct the cells in the shield of Neveyah that they would expand upon in Mal Evol. All of Neveyah would be covered with the honeycomb shield right to the entrance to the valley of Mal Evol, and the soil would be protected from the influence of the poison that affected Mal Evol, should they be unable to complete their quest. This would be the longest part of their journey, but it was vital for them to heal and shield most of Neveyah before they could even think of entering Mal Evol.

Over the weeks as they journeyed through the rural valleys, all the people they met spoke of their worry that so few healers and mages were being found each year. Despite this, they found people were fearful of the Temple, and many would hide their children, having heard vague and unspecified rumors of rampant immorality and child abuse.

These rumors had no apparent source, but Friedr and Edwin agreed they could possibly be originating with traveling merchants from Mal Evol who'd been subverted by Tauron. The closer they got to Braden and the entrance to the Valley of Mal Evol, the more often they heard those tales.

Edwin and Zan spent a certain amount of chi, whispering counter-rumors as they passed each village and hamlet. They did their utmost to insert the idea that only Tauron benefited if their mage-gifted children died from lack of training. In each rural village, they visited the common rooms and stopped and chatted with everyone. At every farm, they helped in any way they were able, even helping one farmer get his hay in before the rains came. Their most important task was to show the people that the Temple of Aeos served them. They stayed at each local temple they visited and left behind fellow clergy who felt better about what they were doing and who felt more able to do the tasks set before them.

"This should be done more often," Friedr remarked as they left the town of Maundy, "But it's a dangerous journey. We're the only healers who're able to defend ourselves. The others must each travel with a squad of soldiers, which is part of what frightens the populace.

Perhaps as time passes, more battle-mages will be made healers."

"All healers must have guards when they travel nowadays, or they could end up kidnapped like Marya was. Their rescue might be impossible," Christoph replied, agreeing with Friedr. "Having dual-skilled mages effectively doubles the mages we have, and both sorts are badly needed."

Friedr didn't consciously realize it, but just as Zan had assured him, he no longer even thought about linking, simply joining with less thought than for sheathing his sword. He happily spent his chi healing Edwin of his gashes, alternating with Zan. They performed many more surgeries as they passed through the most rural area in Neveyah, and he was as fascinated by it as he was by the battle-arts. Indeed, for him, surgery had become a battle he fought with the same intensity with which he swung his sword. Concern for those who suffered and needed his skills far outweighed his fear of intimacy in the healing context. Gradually, Friedr gained an assurance that inspired his patients with the confidence he would do all that was humanly possible to heal them.

Friedr's ability to seal and regrow flesh and bone with minimal scarring impressed both Edwin and Christoph, and with each patient he saw, Friedr's approach to healing became more sensible and matter-of-fact, exactly like his approach to fighting. He was compassionate and gentle, but when something unpleasant was necessary, he was able to decide quickly the best course of action and do it with no fuss, thereby minimizing the shock and distress of the patient.

When evaluating their journeyman's progress, Edwin and Christoph both felt Friedr was developing the potential to become a superior adept in the area of surgeries and privately wondered if he realized his days as a weapons instructor were over.

They were equally pleased with Zander's progress and not surprised at the maturity he had begun to demonstrate. Zan had begun to find himself fascinated by his work as a healer. He'd become adept at anesthetic magic, having an instinctive grasp of what was needed in each circumstance and was rapidly developing skills in treating the people who suffered from chronic pain.

He developed a suggestion-loop he inserted in the subconscious that blocked pain when it became untreatable by standard methods. He modeled it on techniques Edwin and Christoph taught him in dealing with rape and trauma patients. Word of his techniques spread, and healers in the Temple infirmaries were often waiting with a list of patients they wanted to consult with him about treating. For the many patients whose chronic pain had long been untreatable, Zan's intervention was heaven-sent.

All the while, as they traveled about the country, they searched for likely candidates to send to the Temple.

Chapter 13 ~ Merik

"We haven't found many mage-talented children," Friedr muttered as they marched toward another tiny village. "They aren't hiding them either. There simply haven't been any since the two girls in Arlen." He was tired of the dismal weather and worried by the lack of possible candidates, having looked in every hamlet in southern Neveyah.

Christoph said, "The one girl may end up being permanently inhibited and sent home once she is no longer a danger. It's too bad, because we just don't have enough healers and she has the potential to make a decent journeyman."

"Perhaps Dane will whip her into shape, if he's still in charge of the new novices," offered Edwin. "He has no patience with novices who're spoiled brats. He worked a miracle with Pel, the boy from Ragat, who thought he should be given preferential treatment because his father was the mayor. By his third barriers class, Pel was a pleasant, intelligent boy."

"That's true—Dane does have a way of deflating bloated egos." Zander laughed. "My own sense of self-importance suffered under his brisk, but efficient effort to make me into a responsible caring person."

Christoph laughed at Zander's rueful confession. "Well, we know not every talented person is cut out to be a healer or mage sealed to Aeos. It's been proven time and again. A willful person who refuses to learn discipline won't be acceptable to Aeos and won't be offered the opportunity. I hope all that's wrong with her is she's spoilt, because it can be cured. But if she truly has a cruel streak, they'll obstruct her empathy permanently. It'll be as if she had burned herself out, and then they'll send her home. It's irreversible, so there'll be no chance of her playing her nasty little tricks on anyone when she returns." Christoph sighed heavily, looking at Friedr and saying "Your last beginning novice healer's staff class was pretty small, wasn't it? I only counted five students."

"We go through times like this. The year I was taken to Aeoven was a lean year too, or so I was told. We'll simply keep looking as the abbess has requested." Friedr shrugged.

They always had healing to do in the tiny hamlets of the fertile valleys west of the Fleet River. They had become a tight, cohesive team, almost able to read each other's minds whether healing or fighting.

***

While they traveled, they worked on discovering the ways their blades would be most useful. In the same way that their armor increased their magical defenses, the bespelled weapons increased the potency of their magic. One facet was a marked increase in the range of their elemental magics, with a distinct boost in force and a definite increase in available chi to draw upon. They learned by accident that when they channeled the earth-healing magic through their weapons, their range was increased dramatically and their chi-draw decreased. They were able to increase the size of each cell in the shield, which helped in the southwestern hills and valleys.

Often as they trudged from one farm to the next, they discussed the swords, whose potential usefulness they had yet to test to the limits. After a great deal of experimenting, Friedr concluded that, unlike the legendary weapons of history, the abilities conferred by the blades was limited, and casting large spells without pausing to draw chi had the possibility of leaving them without any at all. "We'll have to be cautious if we are in the position of having to cast a long series of large spells. If we allow ourselves to be completely drained of chi, I don't think we'd have the ability to draw any chi at all. We'd be hung out to dry if a battle goes seriously wrong."

Edwin agreed. "It's true that these weapons give us the ability to extend our chi for a much longer period of time, but there must be a limit to how much we can draw. I sincerely hope we're never in the position of finding out what that limit is."

"I can't imagine any situation that would cause you to run out of chi, Edwin," Christoph told him. "You have larger augmentations than anyone, even more than Father Rall, and now you have Leviathan to help you draw chi from the natural world."

Friedr felt a shiver of prescience at Zan's words, but quashed it, laying it down to the knowledge they were soon embarking into the Valley of Mal Evol, and the possibility they would find trouble in that shadowed land. "Still, if you somehow became completely drained of chi, I don't think even you would be able to draw any."

Even used simply as a weapon, each sword was a thing of beauty and when facing an enemy, the blades were devastating in their hands, sharper and more like living steel than any other blade. Zan said, "I'm honored and grateful to have this, beautiful thing, but it's too bad about the limitations. I knew they weren't like Aelfrid's famous fire-sword, or your father's mighty blade. But I've heard so many stories about magic swords saving the day and winning the beautiful maiden for the farm boy turned hero...." He paused and looked back at Edwin, who walked along lost in his thoughts.

"Well now," said Friedr, who was equally intrigued by Zander's notion, "that story has a familiar ring to it. I wonder...could those tales have sprung up around the farm boy's ancestor's adventures?" His eyebrows rose as he considered the idea. "We know his line always breeds true. Look at his father...and at his son, who looks just like Edwin must have looked at that age."

Christoph also looked at Edwin speculatively. "You know, when I was training as a bard, I was taught that all the bardic tales have a grain of truth in them somewhere. All the stories began with a real event, though they're heavily embellished. I'd bet if his original grandsire was anything like our Edwin, then he must be the source of most of those farm-boy-turned-hero tales. And now here we are, living our own legend. Who would've thought that I, Christoph Berryman, would be traveling with three mighty heroes on another absurdly dangerous quest, when I'm so much better at telling stories than living them?"

"Well, at least this one isn't as absurdly dangerous as the last one," Friedr replied with a chuckle. "This hero isn't feeling so very mighty these days. My goal is to just get this done and get home to my wife and children. They never mention that part in the tales, do they?"

"No, they never do. I admit I'm longing for home too. But soon, Friedr! We only have to spend the next month caching supplies and finishing the shield along the border. Then we can just do what we need to in Mal Evol and get home." Chris had a faraway look in his eyes. "I'll bet you never thought you'd hear me say something like that, did you?"

"I knew when you told me you'd asked Dane to be your bondmate you were serious about building a life with him," Friedr told him, a grin crossing his face. "You grew up on our first quest, my brother. You went through changes, and though we loved you as you were, we were pleased. I knew your bonding would be successful because you told me you wouldn't bond until you knew you were truly ready to put him first in your life. I knew it was one promise you'd keep."

While they talked, Edwin had been looking off into the distance, his mind obviously elsewhere. Friedr asked, "What's on your mind, Edwin?"

"I want to get this job done, but I keep thinking about those dogs. We'll have to do something about them. When we get to Braden, Moran will want us to add the dogs to the quest, and we both know it." Edwin looked down the road, discontented.

Friedr started. "No, I hadn't been thinking about them. This is supposed to be an easy quest, no danger, nothing to worry about." After a moment of contemplation he sighed. "You're right, and there's no one else with the skills to do it. But the last place I want to find myself again is in that accursed castle. So much for our simple quest."

"We got in and out okay before, and we can do it again," replied Christoph, feeling oddly delighted at the notion. "Those dogs truly are a scourge, as Jaxon so rightly put it. They'll overrun not just Mal Evol but all of Neveyah in less than a decade. They have no natural enemies, only other bear-dogs."

"I meant to ask you, what's so terrible about these dogs," Zander ventured. "I heard what you said at the table when Jaxon told you about them. Are they really that dangerous?"

"Yes," Friedr assured Zan soberly. "I was barely able to kill the one I fought. Aeolyn bears a scar on her arm from an infected bite she received when we dealt with the first breeding pair D'Mal brought to Mal Evol from Serende. The gash was immediately healed and washed and healed again. Christoph and Edwin worked together over the next two weeks but still couldn't prevent it from scarring. Untreated, she could have died."

Christoph explained, "They average in height as tall as me, and often taller. They have razor-sharp fangs longer than Friedr's hand, and their saliva carries infection. At least it's infectious for humans." He shrugged, saying "My understanding is that minotaurs are poisoned by it too. Minotaurs were once men, not unlike us, until they were allowed to undergo the change to make them the elite legions. Only the best young warriors of Serende are selected to experience the transformation, and those men who survive the rite will rise to the top of their society."

"Hearing that the legions use the dog's saliva to poison their blades is bad news, especially for Jaxon, whose mercenaries must often travel without the benefit of a healer. It's difficult to isolate and eradicate the infection even with the healing talent." Edwin shook his head. "We *must* avoid this while we're in Mal Evol."

"Speaking of avoiding things, Friedr, have you ever tried to see if you can sense the area around you? I can, through the soil, so I was wondering if you could use your healing-senses to feel the area you're in." Christoph looked at Friedr expectantly. "I periodically send my healing sight through the soil when I'm standing watch just ensure that we aren't being stalked."

Friedr was surprised, not expecting so sensible a thing from Christoph. "Actually, no, I don't have the stealth rune or air-magic, so it never occurred to me to try." He stood still and tried to extend his senses into the surrounding area as he would a patient's body. "Huh…there's a rabbit under a shrub," he said as he pulled his senses back in. "I can sense out in a small radius around us. It could be useful if I need to see around a corner or something, but I don't have much range. I'll keep practicing when I'm standing watch." He paused, thinking about the skill, and then said, "I don't think it's farseeing like Edwin and Zan do or what you can do with the soil. I think it's just an extension of my healing-senses being boosted by my personal shields since the radius is the same as the limit of my widest shield ability. I would bet you can do it too, Christoph."

Christoph closed his eyes, trying it. "Yes…I see what you mean. It's good to know. I need to write this up for Moran when we get to Braden. I've a lot of writing to do when we get there. My notebook is nearly full."

"Well, we just need to heal in Morton, and then we'll be on the last leg of this journey to Braden,"

Edwin said. "Morton is just up ahead, and I've heard they have some excellent hot springs."

As the evening closed in, they made camp, with Edwin taking his turn cooking their supper of reconstituted dried soup mix. He'd snared an unwary rabbit, which made the soup much tastier.

***

When the group walked into Morton the next day, they could each feel the surges of unfocused chi. "There's a young mage here," Zander said. "Can you feel him?" His eyes were alight with anticipation.

"A fire-mage, I'd say." Friedr sent his senses out. "He's out of my range, hiding somewhere more toward the center of town, but I feel his element."

"You're right, Zan. It's a boy," Christoph said, with his senses extended.

"In the livery stable," Edwin asserted. "He's hiding behind the door of the last empty stall. He's afraid of us for some reason."

"I'll bring him out," Zander replied. Closing his eyes, he whispered on the wind to the child, telling him he was wanted at home. The boy emerged from the livery stable through the back door and ran home, thinking his father had called him. Still observing him from afar, they followed him to his home.

Knocking on the door, they found a nine-year-old boy, Merik, who was showing all the signs of a budding fire-mage, and they immediately talked to his parents.

Dix and Lyona had been trying to hide him, as they'd heard the city of Aeoven was rampant with immorality. The four companions sat down and graphically explained the serious trouble he could cause without even trying to hurt anyone. They explained that the small fires that happened when he became angry would escalate, and he could kill someone or even himself by getting lost in his magic.

"His unfocused chi will drive him mad, and he will bring misery and death wherever he goes." Friedr was specific, going into detail regarding the problems Merik would cause were he to remain in the village for much longer. He finished by telling them, "The first time he uses his magic to harm an innocent person, Tauron will claim him, and he will become a rogue mage."

Merik's parents were shocked and dismayed. They'd been worried because fires seemed to happen around him even when he was not angry, but they didn't know what to do.

Although they were concerned about sending him to the Temple, his parents reluctantly released him into their care. Moran would send him back to Aeoven with a mage-escort on the mail coach.

When they were asked what sorts of immorality they had heard about, the parents didn't know. They had just heard it was an immoral and wicked city. It was the same thing they had been hearing all over southern Neveyah.

"These tales are lies that benefit Tauron," Edwin told the worried parents. "If your son dies from not being properly trained, he's one less mage to fight against the legions of the Bull God. Soon there'd be no one to stand against him. Then what'll happen to the people of Neveyah? They'll be less than slaves, just like the people of Mal Evol."

While Edwin spoke, Christoph set the restraints on Merik and immediately began bleeding the excess chi away from him. The boy began to feel better but didn't know why.

Edwin explained to Merik's parents that they were more than welcome to move to Aeoven to be near him or to travel there at any time to visit. "You must come and see for yourself what sort of place your son will be living in. If you choose to remain in Aeoven, there are many jobs available and good homes waiting for families who relocate there with their children." Edwin's trademark smile charmed the parents as much as his words. "I'm from Markett, a village no one has heard of, way out in the far west. My mother passed away a long time ago, and my father has come to live with my wife and me. He now works as a veterinarian and loves it very much. Friedr's mother stayed in his village up north, but she raises goats the Temple originally bought for her. Mages work hard for very little pay, but their families are well rewarded.

Friedr said, "Apart from Zander, we all have children of our own and understand full well how much you value your child." He assured them that Braden Temple would be more than happy to help them travel to Aeoven, to see for themselves how well their son was being treated. "But you need to understand he must be carefully taught how to use this gift Aeos has given him. He can only get the training and nurturing he needs in Aeoven at the college."

Zan smiled. "Aeos is the Goddess of Hearth and Home. Family is more important to her Temple than anything," he promised. "And I can assure you, he'll love being a novice. I surely did. Those were the best years of my life! Of course, my parents lived in Aeoven, but even so, I loved living in the novice barracks. And because I was there under supervision, I was no longer in danger of inadvertently zapping the neighbor's yappy pooch whenever he startled me."

After a moment of shocked surprise, Merik's parents laughed weakly, and Dix said, "I can see there could've been trouble there. Well, we believe you. He must go with you, and we'll follow as soon as we can take care of things here. Have they any need for another laborer? There is scant work here, but we make do. I can do any work needed. Lyona is good with herbs. She can heal many things not serious enough to send to Braden for the Temple healer to tend to."

"You're both needed more than you can imagine," Friedr told him. "There's no shortage of work available in Aeoven. The college is seeking herbalists to train, and Lyona could eventually be an instructor. You'll be paid well, and there are good homes going untenanted right now. You'll want to go and see Seneschal Lyell when you get there and tell him Friedr Freysson sent you. I'll give you a note for him." He immediately set about writing it.

After further consultation, the decision was made to immediately continue on to Braden instead of remaining in Morton as they had planned. With a tearful goodbye on the part of Lyona, the companions left Morton, taking the trade road east.

It would take Merik one week to get from Braden to Aeoven on the mail coach, stopping only to change drivers, eat, and take care of personal needs. It had taken the companions nearly two months to get to Braden from Aeoven by walking through every valley, village, and hamlet in southern Neveyah. They had found only three novice candidates, and one that might not do as well as they would like. They had healed many injuries and illnesses, some more serious than others. Now they walked with the anticipation of arriving in Braden and beginning the true task to which Aeos had called them.

Merik nervously set out to walk to Braden with them, but as soon as he saw some of the magic they could do he gradually became excited. Soon Merik was looking forward to going to the Temple, and his lively chatter amused them. Making it seem like a game, Zander tested him in calling all the elements, and though the boy was as yet unable to actually call them, he found Merik had some ability in all the elements and strength in fire. At this point, it looked as if he had no empathy for healing. Merik was a thoughtful, considerate boy, but it was too early to tell.

"You must imagine what you want as clearly as you can, Merik. This is called visualization and is the basis of learning how to use your gift. Don't worry. I could feel you trying to call each element exactly as I told you to, and you do have strength in all of them," Zan told him when the boy was disappointed that he could not yet make his magic work when he wanted it to. "It will be many months before you can use your magic reliably when you want it. In the meantime, the instructors will maintain the restrictions so you can't accidentally use your magic in your sleep or when you're angry. It took me nearly a year before I was able to call water reliably, and water is the easiest element to call, even for most lightning-mages."

Edwin immediately began instructing Merik in the concepts of building his personal shield with the buffer.

Soon Merik was tired and nearly in tears from his frustrations.

Friedr took over then. "Merik, this is the hardest time of your life as a mage. You've been told you have this ability, but no matter how you try you're unable to use it." He spoke to the boy in low tones as they walked. "Now we're telling you it will be many long years before you can use it the way we use our magic. It nearly drove me mad when I first came to the Temple. Then I met other children my age who were having the same trouble. Suddenly, I didn't feel so bad about it." Friedr's kind way with children always won them over. "The first task they'll give you when you get to Aeoven is to learn to do what Zan told you to—visualize clearly what you wish to achieve. Now, if you'll be patient and work with us the way we ask you to, you'll be one step ahead of everyone else when you get there."

The first time the beasts attacked them, Merik was both terrified and impressed at their fighting abilities, cowering against Christoph, whose staff protected him well. He was awed by Friedr, Zan, and Edwin and thrilled he would learn to use a sword himself one day. As the journey progressed, Merik became eager to get to the College of Warcraft and Magic and become just like his new hero, Friedr Freysson.

Three days later, the companions arrived in the garden city of Braden at midmorning, tired, footsore, and in need of new boots and clothes. Merik was immediately handed over to Daff, a young lightning-mage and friend of Zan, who was traveling back to Aeoven on the mail coach from his first away-posting.

Moran was pleased with their finds despite hearing that one young healer would possibly not make the grade. "Still, you've found three. That's excellent progress. Between us, we've now sent five to the college this season: two water-mages, a fire-mage, and two healers. It's been good to have you four out scouring the countryside. Now, you need to get settled into your rooms and take the rest of the day off. Come and have dinner with me tonight, please? I usually cook far too much for one person to eat, you know. Without Daff and his youthful hunger, who'll eat it?"

Chapter 14 ~ Braden

They were assigned rooms in the guest quarters. Friedr and Edwin shared a set of rooms, as did Christoph and Zan. They were much like the bachelor quarters in Aeoven with two tiny bedrooms and a tiny sitting room. The only difference was the guest quarters had one large men's bath and a separate large women's bath for the common use of the guests instead of a bathroom in each set of rooms. Being built over the original hot springs, the baths were large enough so everyone could sit in the pools comfortably.

Soaking in the hot water was utter bliss. As each tired mage eased aching muscles, the stress of the journey fell away. Reluctantly, they left the pools and returned to their rooms. Once there, they began the task of sorting through the mail that awaited them. Fully rested and ready to get down to business, they spent the afternoon reading their letters and writing replies. Though they'd missed the mail coach that Merik had left on, their correspondence would go to Aeoven on the coach that was due to arrive the next day.

Freylin and Rynne had suffered several ailments common to children, as had Jonny, and news had arrived on the personal front for both Edwin and Friedr. They were both due to become fathers again. With her pregnancy, Marya had regained some of her empathic abilities, and Aeolyn now had three small healer's stars on her shoulder. She received some necessary training in buffering and healer's barriers, along with field medic training.

"I knew Marya was regaining her empathy before we left, but she refused to believe me," Edwin told Friedr as they sat at the table in the rooms they were sharing. "Actually, she says she can't really control it yet, rather like a novice. It's probably caused by the pregnancy—apparently she's nearly six months along. This child will be born sometime after Holy Day." He shook his head in winder. "I can't believe I didn't know—but her cycles have always been irregular and she's had no morning sickness this time. Her letter says she's never felt better."

"I remember that she was pretty sick with Jonny, before you even knew she was expecting. I'm still trying to absorb the fact I'm going to have another child," replied Friedr. "We'd thought two would be plenty, but apparently Aeos has her own plan for us."

"I'm glad Jonny will have a sibling. I always wished for one." Edwin felt a surge of giddiness that he quickly buried, attempting to appear calm and dignified when he really wanted to jump around. "My family has only had one child at a time for several generations. I'd love to have a daughter. I always dreamed of having a large family, and now it's coming true."

Although he had sent her a letter from each Temple they had stopped at, Zander was surprised and ecstatic to have eight letters from Anna waiting, along with several from Dane. Each letter from her was signed "Love, Anna." He immediately sat down to write a long reply, boldly signing it "Your loving wanderer, Zan." In the last paragraphs, he was brave enough to tell her how often he thought of her and how every day that passed he missed her conversation and her sense of humor more than he had ever thought he could.

Most amazing of all was Edwin's letter from John, mostly full of small talk until the final paragraphs.

"I hope Halee will soon accept my proposal, and there'll be a bonding when you return to Aeoven. I'll always love Andia. Your mother was the love of my life, and we had ten wonderful years together. Regret and sorrow no longer blight my love for her. Instead she shines in my memory, and I feel joy when I think of her.

"Just as Andia was my love, so Bryson was Halee's. They were blessed with twenty-six good years together. She tells me the time you spent with her at the end of his life meant more to her than you will ever know.

"I find great happiness and peace in Halee's company, and I believe she feels the same for me. We're still young, and have many years ahead of us, balanced by the long years of friendship behind us. I've felt Aeos's hand on my heart in regard to Halee for some time now, and have nothing but gratitude that Halee has felt the same hand guiding her to me.

"I know you saw us kissing under the Solstice Moon, and I felt your happiness, so I'm sure my inclination in this regard isn't really a surprise to you, my son."

Edwin couldn't help smiling at the thought of his father and Halee finding happiness together. "No two people could deserve it more," he later told Christoph, when they met in the staff sitting room. Chris and the others wholeheartedly agreed with Edwin.

"All of Aeoven will celebrate if that happens," Christoph replied, feeling rather subdued despite the good news. "Dane mentioned they're always in each other's company." He was disturbed by how overwrought he felt from reading Dane's letters and was nearly overwhelmed with his intense homesickness. After spending several moments practicing his calming and centering skills, he was able to hide his turmoil under a smile. "Everyone who knows them is pleased that John has been courting Halee, supporting and encouraging her when her days are long and trying."

Since the day they were bonded, Christoph hadn't been posted away from Aeoven, although Dane was frequently posted away for short periods of time. Now, he'd been away for two months and was likely to be gone at least two more. While the companions were busy on the healing journey, he'd been able to keep the terrible homesickness he endured mostly at bay, although he'd suffered from periodic bouts just as the others had. Now Dane's letters brought home all the things he so desperately missed. He could almost hear his voice in the commonplace gossip and details of his daily life. His letters sharply reminded Chris of how entertaining Dane's wit and personality were and how much his companionship added to his life. Dane's humorous comments and observations were full of the warm, homey things Christoph missed more than he ever dreamed he would.

He forced himself to cheer up, reminding himself they would be home soon, as they were now more than halfway through the work they were to do on their quest. *We'll be home long before winter solstice.* Like a mantra, the thought comforted him. *At least I have Zan with me. Poor Dane is alone and worried about both of us. But he writes that Anna visits him almost daily. She has hopes our boy will bond with her.* Christoph smiled widely, thinking about Zan and Anna. *I may have grandchildren after all someday."* With that happy thought, Christoph's mind cleared and he felt able to continue the journey he had agreed to so long ago.

They dined with Moran that evening. He was a slender, physically fit man perhaps ten years their senior. He was dark in coloring, with dark eyes and straight dark hair lightly sprinkled with silver that he wore loose about his shoulders. His unadorned white shirt was worn over loose, linen trousers. Somewhat shy and unassuming, he had a friendly manner and exuded a quiet strength. Similar to Edwin he preferred to remain in the background, though he was Garran's right hand. Garran frequently declared nothing would get done in Braden without him keeping things moving in his quiet way.

Moran kept the conversation light, saying there would be time enough to worry later, and then fed them a hearty meal that was simple but tasty. "Over the years, I've learned to cook well enough to get by," he told them as he bustled about in his kitchen. His home, being stark and utilitarian, and somewhat untidy with books and papers stacked on the tables and window-sills, reflected his recent bachelorhood. The signs were everywhere that Moran once had a bonded partner. A framed, charcoal-drawn portrait occupied pride of place over the mantle, a laughing man in dark leathers with merry eyes and loose, curling blond hair.

Piers. He died in Mal Evol, Edwin thought as he looked at the portrait. Edwin, Chris, and Friedr all remembered meeting and working with him in Braden years before, but Moran didn't mention it, and they all respected his privacy.

On the walk back to their guest rooms, Friedr told them Moran's long-time partner Piers, had disappeared on one of the failed quests at the end of the previous year. "It wasn't well known that Piers had even undertaken the quest. He and three others went in to rescue Ivar Kalensson, Father Rall's grandson, but it was too late—Ivar was already dead. Piers was the sole mage in the group. Garran told me of this just before we left Aeoven. This must be kept close." As one, the others placed their hands over their hearts. "What Moran won't speak about is this—Piers survived in the dungeon for more than a month, during which time he was ritually broken. He was then sacrificed to Tauron."

The group nearly stopped walking, looking at each other, shock and horror etched on their faces. Friedr didn't have the words to continue, and characteristically, he clamped his teeth shut.

Edwin said, "I was aware of that. Dad told me the abbacy believes the secrecy of Ivar's assignment was compromised—that a spy discovered Ivar's team's mission. It was too much of a coincidence that the legions knew exactly where to find them. That spy must have leaked the information about Piers." Edwin put his hand on Friedr's shoulder and said, "I'm sorry to hear of this, especially knowing as I do what that month must've been like for Piers." Friedr sighed heavily but said nothing.

They retired to their rooms early, well fed and exhausted, but the tale of what happened to Piers weighed heavily on their minds. Sleep was long in coming, and when at last they did fall asleep, it was not peaceful.

The next day, they sat in Moran's study, discussing what they'd learned on their travels. His windows showed a good view of the Temple gardens, and the early harvest sun was shining brightly. They had moved on to discussing the dogs, and although Moran had been informed of their existence, he wanted to hear what Jaxon had said regarding them.

"Jaxon is worried about the dogs," Edwin concluded. "He's hard-pressed to provide protection to his merchants when they must travel. I think he won't be so burdened once the shield has been up for a while, since the numbers of rats and other beasts should diminish. They should find our land unpleasant to them and will hopefully remain high in the mountains."

"Bear-dogs…. I've heard much about them and none of it pleasant." Moran said, rubbing his clean-shaven chin, considering the situation. "You know this news has altered all the plans. Father Rall wants you to go and eliminate the dogs. This task must now take precedence over anything else. The beasts *must* be eradicated. I'd normally sneak in and do this." He pulled his hair back and showed Edwin and Zan the stealth runes just behind his earlobes. "But with Garran in Aeoven, I can't leave Braden right now."

The others all nodded. They already knew he had been augmented with the rune.

"Besides," Moran looked at Edwin with a wry smile, "you've a greater knowledge of the interior of the Shadow Castle than anyone. You and Aeolyn made the maps I've used, and three of you've been inside it. This is one task you must add to your list."

"Yes, but it was years ago," Friedr reminded him. "Much can change in six years. Still, we rather thought this would be added to our task. We'll somehow accomplish this."

"It hasn't changed." The tight voice and grim look on Moran's face suggested he had gone in looking for something, only to find what he went for was no longer there. "The maps are still correct—at least the dungeon and conservatory are still as they were mapped. I suspect nothing else has been altered. D'Mal doesn't like change."

No one said anything. They knew what he had gone in looking for.

"D'Mal is only rarely in Mal Evol these days, as he must keep a firm grip on his warlords in Serende. Whenever he returns to Mal Evol, they use the opportunity to mount raids on their neighbors. They chafe under his restrictions, and he's hard-pressed to keep them working their farms and the mines. They don't dispute they've prospered under his leadership, but they're Tauron's children and not good at living in peace with each other."

Moran smiled wickedly as he added, "Tauron created them as warriors, and now he wants to turn them into farmers and merchants. The average minotaur despises those who sell wares or work the land—in their eyes, the lesser people exist only to provide sport for the legions. Anyone who hasn't undergone the transformation is less than dirt to them. Yet their dread God now wishes them to farm, and so they do, albeit discontentedly. The lands east of Mal Evol City are dotted with pathetic patches of barren land worked by slaves. The wondrous change Tauron has wrought upon the land isn't beneficial to his farmers."

"We hope to change this," Edwin told him. "If we're successful with the rest of our task, the whole of the valley all the way to the eastern escarpment, the Serende Wall, will be turned back to the fertile lands they once were."

"We're to go directly to the Shadow Castle?" Christoph's eyes were alight with the thought. "This is a turn of events we can benefit from. We can use the throne to change the land back while we're there, so we won't have to spend all this time healing the land and setting the shield. We could heal the throne, and then all we'd have to do is set the shields on our way out of Mal Evol. We could be done with this and on our way home."

"No!" Moran, Edwin, and Friedr all objected at the same time. Christoph looked surprised and sat back, knowing more would follow. Zan just looked from face to face, wondering what would happen next.

"You can't jeopardize your quest by drawing attention to your presence," Moran admonished him. "D'Mal may not be in the haunted castle, but he knows everything that happens there. Trust me on this. He's attuned to the throne and will know the moment you touch it, which even *you* would have to do in order to heal it. His minion, Lork, is there, and Lork is his vector. D'Mal sees through his eyes and hears through his ears. When anything arises that requires D'Mal's personal touch, Lork is the means by which he handles it. Lork is immediate and effective, even when he has sole tenancy in his own body. It would be far too dangerous."

Moran sat for a moment, keeping his face carefully impassive despite his mixed emotions. He thought about what he had to say, and then he looked at Christoph, seeing mute rebellion in his eyes.

"Christoph, I'm going to tell you this not to make you ill, but because I want you to understand what you're going up against. D'Mal daily takes over Lork, and wearing Lork's body, he performs the sacrificial rituals that are…unholy…in the eyes of Aeos. You've been there and seen the remains of his offerings interrupted in progress before the ritual was completed."

He leaned forward to emphasize his words. "I know this for a fact—Lork is literally not there when D'Mal, wearing Lork's body, performs every aspect of the torture, rape, and dehumanization of his prisoners. It's Stefyn D'Mal, acting as the dread god's highest priest and using Lork's physical body, who offers the wretched remains of his 'guests' to Tauron in his ghastly sacrificial rituals."

"It makes sense he would have found another vessel," said Edwin, unable to shake the feeling of horror the memory of the dungeon roused in him.

"He does this daily in order to be in two places at one time. I know this because I've witnessed it." Moran's normally impassive face was marked with the grief of his deeply personal loss. "I've observed the change in Lork's demeanor when D'Mal shoves him aside and invades his body. It was by the grace of Aeos my hiding place wasn't discovered, for I'd have been offered up on that unholy altar."

The others sat silent as they absorbed the conviction of Moran's words and the immediacy of his pain, though their healer's barriers protected them from the rawness of his sorrow. Unable to stop himself, Friedr cast a spell for ease upon his friend, eliciting a faint smile from Moran. "Thank you, Friedr. I expect I'll get used to you being a healer—eventually. I…appreciate your concern, but I…I have to grieve my own way."

"Forgive me, Moran. I didn't mean to be such an idiot." Christoph's face had grown red with chagrin. "I'd no intention of being so cruel in the face of your grief. Please forgive me."

"I must learn to live with it, Chris. I know you spoke without thinking," Moran told him. "I was fortunate to have Piers in my life for as long as I did. I console myself with memories of good and happy times. Piers gave his life in service to the Goddess Aeos. Any one of us could be called upon to do the same at any time. I know we'd do whatever was required of us despite the cost. We all took the vows binding us to her service willingly and with all our hearts."

They spent the rest of the morning planning how to accomplish their task. They decided they would enter simultaneously from four sides and take out the guards with sleep spells. Then they would meet near the kennels. Once the dogs were taken care of, they would depart as silently and quietly as possible, recasting sleep as needed on the way out.

"We can kill this batch of dogs, but what's to stop him from bringing in more and starting over again?"

Zander asked the question they were all asking themselves.

"What we need is to find something we can use to make the very soil of Mal Evol poisonous to bear-dogs," Christoph said, pursing his lips. "I may have an idea. I know if a dog eats salmon from anywhere in southern Neveyah, and especially the valley of Mal Evol, he's likely to die."

Everyone looked at him, curious to know where he was going with it. "If a healer examines the salmon the dog ate, he'll see it's infected with a parasite deadly to dogs. Not every salmon has it, but salmon in Mal Evol always had a high likelihood of being infected. Thus, to this day, we who once lived in the valley make sure our dogs never eat salmon. I think we can use this to make the soil poisonous to dogs. The trick will be making it lethal to bear-dogs specifically and raising the mortality rate from ninety percent to one hundred percent. If we can't make it specific to bear-dogs, no canines of any sort will ever live in Mal Evol again."

Moran asked, "How can you adapt a fish parasite to live in the soil *and* poison it against the dogs?"

"The magic we're using to heal the soil can easily be adapted to this purpose," Christoph replied, warming to his subject. "Edwin and I have been altering parasites all over eastern and southern Neveyah, making them beneficial to the soil and harmless to plants." His enthusiasm lit up his face. "This one in particular starts its life in the guts of certain snails and then is excreted into the waters of the creeks and streams of Mal Evol. That'll make it easy to adapt because in times of drought, it lies dormant in the dry riverbeds just waiting for the rains. We'll try to isolate this and see if we can magnify it, changing its life cycle so it lives and reproduces itself in the soil as harmless to humans—and hopefully other canines—and perhaps will have a beneficial presence."

Edwin found himself completely caught up in the idea. "But we must hurry because summer is ending and the season is turning to harvest now. This is the time the salmon born in the creeks and rivers of Mal Evol are entering their breeding season. They're returning to where they were born to breed their own young. There'll be fish lying on the banks and dying. They always die after they have spawned, and most of the dead will be carriers." Edwin saw Moran's skepticism clearly painted on his dark face. "We'll figure out a way to do this while we're on the road, caching our supplies. We're actually becoming quite good at altering parasites so they become beneficial. We can easily do this."

He fell silent, letting Moran mull over their plans.

"Now you've both explained it, I see this is a logical idea," Moran said, after a few minutes of silent contemplation. "It should be the first priority for your journey into Mal Evol. Figure out the way to make the soil poisonous to the bear-dogs, so D'Mal can never be successful breeding them in Neveyah. Who knows how many there are now? We've no time to waste. Once the dogs are taken care of, you must immediately return here. If everything remains calm and there's no serious influx of legions into Mal Evol, you can go back and begin healing the land and continue building the shield into the valley." He checked his notes. "You've completed the shield to the northern, southern, and western walls of Braden. All you need to finish is the east wall of the city and the Braden Gap, which is the entrance to the valley of Mal Evol."

"If the fish breeding time is starting now, we need to wind up our business here and get going, or we'll lose our window of opportunity," Friedr said. "We need to change our plans so we waste no more time. Can you spare a couple of people to travel with us while we make the caches of rations and medical supplies? They can return with the ponies, and we can get on with sneaking into the Shadow Castle, which should save us two weeks. If we follow the old trail running along the river Morte to where it meets the river Lian, it should only take about twelve days to reach the hills above the keep. We'll need two or three more days to get into the castle and kill the dogs. Then it will be another ten or twelve days to return. This task will take us about a month."

"Yes, actually I can divert some people to help you." Moran laughed. "I've two armsmen who are just languishing here. They can go with you along the Morte River to make your caches. Their unit ran afoul of a herd of thunder-cows and left two soldiers behind to recover from injuries. Now they're healthy, very bored, and causing no end of trouble in town. They're recovering in the constable's holding cell as we speak. If you leave the day after tomorrow, they'll be back here at about the same time their unit is scheduled to return, so everyone will be happy, especially the constable."

That afternoon, they requisitioned clothes from Temple stores and also got new boots. Then they visited the armory and turned in their personal armor for refurbishing. They also collected the stealth-armor that, along with their other supplies, had been shipped to Braden to await them.

As they donned their brown armor, the armor-mage carefully checked the fit to ensure nothing had changed too much since it was originally made for them. Zander's armor needed adjusting in the shoulders, as he had filled out since he left Aeoven.

The armor-mage, a fire-mage named Jase who had been the master smith in Braden for two years, knew them all rather well, having been a novice with Friedr and Christoph. Fire-mages often became smiths, a trade neither Friedr nor Aeolyn had any desire to pursue.

"Your boy's growing into a man," Jase told Christoph as he measured Zan. "His armor will need to be checked again when you come back through. I don't think he's done filling out yet. He's what, eighteen years old? Has he done his first away-posting then?"

"He was posted in Einar for all of last year, assisting Abbess Jalaya." Christoph couldn't hide his pride. "He's nearly nineteen, Jase, and has proven himself a man on this trip." He received a wry smile from Jase as he added, "I'm trying not act like his father on this trip. For this, I'm just one of his companions, and he carries his own weight well. I think you know Friedr would have it no other way."

"I suspect he has proven himself many times over." Jase continued adjusting the shoulders of Zander's breast plate and back plate. "You're on the way to becoming as big as our barbarian, once you get your full growth, Zan. Of course, your cousin, Dane, is a big man, so it stands to reason." The armor-mage winked and added, "Christoph, you'll be hard-pressed keeping him in fancy shirts until he stops filling out." They all laughed, since Zan was the only one of them whose regular work shirts were usually embellished with tiny white-on-white embroideries.

"Christoph is very generous with his talents, and I am rather a dandy," he admitted sheepishly. "But I've noticed lately everything is getting pretty tight across the shoulders. I thought it might be from all the swordwork we've been doing."

"Well, no one in Mal Evol we're likely to meet will care you're not dressed in the height of fashion," Friedr told him, trying to disguise his own lack of appreciation for their bland garb. "You'll just have to suffer as I do." He looked at his armor with obvious distaste.

"Friedr Freysson, you're such a man of fashion." Jase laughed at him. "You always were. I think, though, you'll find this armor is much better suited to the tasks on your quest. It may not be gaudy enough for your taste, but this is the finest armor I've ever seen. There are spells for stealth and secrecy woven here not found even in the finest assassin's armor. I heard you have bespelled-swords too. Would you allow me to ease my professional curiosity and let me have a look at them?"

Carefully, Jase examined each sword and scabbard, pronouncing them master works. "You are the lucky ones to have been given these." Jase's cheerful countenance turned grim. "But it makes me wonder what lies in store for you in Mal Evol that you will need this armor. It worries me you might need this level of stealth." He thought of recent losses. "It's been a hard year for Braden Temple."

Forcing a cheerful smile, Jase continued, "And as for your staff, Christoph, I've never seen anything like it. You've a true work of art there. You four will never lack for chi as long as you have enough left to use to draw through your weapons. If you wait too long to draw your extra chi, though, nothing will help you. You must remember to draw as you go so you never lack for chi. In Mal Evol, you won't get a second chance, but you probably know better than anyone, right?" The armor-mage shrugged. "So, can you all come to have dinner with me and Lenna tonight? I've invited Moran already. She hasn't seen any of you since Zan was made a journeyman. She'll kill me if I don't get you over to our house before you leave Braden. She's fixing enough food to feed the whole town."

"Of course, we'd be happy to. We really can't take Edwin to the common rooms, you know. He just causes no end of trouble." Friedr smirked at Edwin, who looked surprised Friedr would say such a thing. Everyone else laughed at Edwin's discomfort, and he finally managed a weak grin.

"Is that still a problem? I'd have thought now he was bonded it would've changed for the better." Jase looked at Edwin, who just shrugged, slightly red-faced.

"Well, it's been entertaining," Christoph asserted, with a smile. "The more he tells them no, the more they seem to want him."

That evening, they enjoyed a wonderful meal and the hospitality of Jase and Lenna's home. Something about the homey domesticity overwhelmed the four companions with homesickness, and as they walked back to the guest quarters, they were quiet.

Finally, Christoph broke the silence. "I guess I'll just come out and say it. I'm really missing Dane and my own home right now." He grinned sheepishly. "I just want to finish this quest and go home. Then I'm never leaving ever again."

"I know just how you feel," Friedr told him. "But now we're halfway done. We've sealed the heart of Neveyah off from the poison. Even with taking care of the dogs, we should be home before Holy Day."

Everyone took heart at the sentiment, though each wondered privately what might arise next to change things around again.

Chapter 15 ~ The Valley of Sorrows

The morning dawned gray and chill, with early morning mists so common in that part of the land. The companions walked out the east gate of Braden, waving at the young earth-mage on gate duty. Immediately upon walking through the gate, it was apparent they were walking out of Neveyah, and into a foreign land.

With the closing of the gate behind them and their first steps down the rutted, long-unused road, Zan realized he was now walking into something dangerous and unknown. The sudden realization that this was not going to be as fun and noble a quest as he'd naively thought it would be left him at a loss for words.

Rough, low brush soon became straggly scrub and thorns as high as, and often higher than, Friedr's head. Strange birds voiced calls that sounded like taunts and were answered by even stranger cries. Snakes lurked in the undergrowth, but their armor and leg guards protected them from the bites of the startled reptiles.

"Why does the land change so radically here?" Zan finally asked Edwin. "This is the worst road I've ever seen!"

"Tauron's poison is nearly at the door," replied Edwin, wondering what was bothering Zan. "I thought you understood. We'll be in Tauron's Mal Evol in three days."

"I knew it on one level, but I guess I didn't understand what it meant," replied Zan, temporarily dismayed by the grim reality of the landscape. "I guess I was thinking of the adventure, not the reality. I was thinking it'd be like Aelfrid Firesword, all fun and adventure with no worry."

"Actually, Aelfrid Firesword's life must've been terribly difficult," said Edwin, walking next to Zan. "Think about it. He was forced to kill his closest friend who'd become a rogue-mage and gone over to Tauron. Can you imagine how you'd feel if, say, I went over to Tauron? How would you protect the people of Neveyah from me? What would you do?"

"I never thought about that aspect of the story," Zan admitted. "Making those sorts of decisions, having to kill someone you love in order to protect others you love, I can't imagine what that was like for Aelfrid." He sighed. "But I'd do it if I was forced to. I think it'd kill me though."

"I know." Edwin clasped Zan's shoulder. "Daryk was the most famous of the dark-mages, but most people don't know he fought desperately *against* Tauron's minions at Aelfrid's side when the two of them first came into their powers. He worshipped Aeos and loved Neveyah with all his heart. It never occurred to either Aelfrid or Daryk he would ever fall to Tauron, but there was no Temple and no vows to protect him from Tauron's blandishments.

"They had no college to teach young mages how to use their magic, so they had to learn how to control the buildup of chi and avoid the madness by gaining apprenticeships to older mages. Daryk was lured away from their kind master by a mindbender who was under Tauron's spell.

"It was because of Aelfrid's grief over the loss of the man who'd been closer than a brother, and his struggle to save the other mages still loyal to Aeos, that

Aeoven and the Temple exist today. Without Aelfrid, we wouldn't have the augmentations allowing us access to greater chi reserves, nor would we bind ourselves to the Goddess with the vows. It must've been a terribly hard time to live through."

"I see what you mean," admitted Zan. "As a kid, I read all the stories and just thought it was all good-against-evil, romance, and happy endings. But maybe it's just the way the bards tell it."

Edwin laughed. "It wouldn't be a good story if it was all dirt, bug bites, and poor sanitary conditions now, would it?"

Zan laughed and agreed with him. "I just realized something else I knew but didn't think about." Zan looked at Edwin with something close to sympathy. "Aelfrid was your many-greats grandfather, wasn't he?"

"Yes, apparently he was, so Father Rall tells me," Edwin replied, "but I too think of him as a character in an adventure tale."

The group led a string of four heavily laden pack-ponies, and traveled along with two bleary-eyed, hung-over soldiers named Benn and Div. The ponies each carried two large, sealed trunks tightly packed with supplies, eight trunks in total. As the morning wore on, the two soldiers began to feel better, and soon they were back to normal and were actually jolly companions.

"I'm glad we're on the road again. I don't do well in town," Div admitted to Zander as they walked along. "I always get into trouble when I go to the common room." Their armor was the standard brown with the leathers all soldiers wore. The armor was woven with spells to offer some general protection from elemental creatures. The Temple soldiers greatly appreciated the virtues of their armor.

The two knew they were traveling into Mal Evol with a group of healers, which was very odd. Usually, a squad was assigned to protect each healer, and they never went farther east than Braden. The strange color of their armor and their augmentations confused the two men. "We know a lot of healers," said Div wryly, "and I do mean a *lot* of them. But I've never seen one with lightning bolts or wearing anything but green armor!"

"We're always meeting new healers. Div can't walk away from a glass of ale or a fight," Benn quipped. "And every time he wakes up in the pokey, I wake up there next to him."

"It's cuz Benn can't just walk away and let me get killed, though many times he should've," Div said morosely. "When I don't go near the ale, I do pretty well. Every time we get a furlough or a pass, I always think, 'This time I won't drink any ale. This time I won't wake up in need of a healer.' I always mean to behave. And if I don't touch the ale, I do just fine. But the friendly-girls are the problem. You always have to buy them ale, and they always want you to drink with them." He sighed unhappily. "I can't drink just one glass of ale. I never have any memory of the evening after the first couple of glasses, and though Benn here does his best to keep me on the right path, somehow I always land us in the pokey."

"My father can make it so that you have the strength to refuse to drink wine or ale. It's one of his areas of healing," Zan told him. "Think about it, and if you decide it's what you want, ask him. He'll help you."

Div nodded slowly, thinking about the possibility.

An hour into the morning's journey, they were targeted by a pack of rats once again. Edwin and Friedr dispatched the attackers before Benn and Div even had their swords out.

"Been a while since we were posted with a mage," Benn said, hiding his surprise behind a professional grin. "I forgot healers attract them. You're pretty quick at killing them though."

"We've had a lot of practice," Friedr muttered, as he cleaned his sword. "We need to overlap shields, so the ponies and Benn and Div are protected if we run into a rat mage." They decided to have Edwin lead and Zander take up the rear, with Friedr and Christoph in the center, so their shields covered everyone well. "Since the rats always go for Edwin first, he needs to walk in front where they can see him easier." Friedr snickered as he needled Edwin.

"Thanks, Friedr. Now I'm bait. I'd be hurt if it wasn't so true." He laughed as he looked the ponies over to make sure they were not injured. "Well, the ponies made it through their first fight unscathed. I don't think they liked it though." Edwin built a layered spell, casting calm and soothe on each pony, and tying the spells off so the pony's own chi maintained the spells. "This should help them stay calm no matter what sort of beasts we face."

"We never traveled with a group of mages before. Never heard of healers using swords," Div cautiously told Edwin. His eyes were rather wide and wary as he peered through the dim and misty morning. "You're scary with that thing, smiling when you go for them. Pardon me, but it just seems unnatural."

"Many things about Edwin are a wee bit unnatural," Friedr commented. "You get used to it," he added, winking at Edwin, who just shrugged and continued checking the ponies, flashing his trademark smile.

Benn and Div received another surprise when they stopped for the night. Edwin, Zan, and Friedr worked out while Christoph roasted the pair of pheasants Benn caught earlier, along with some tasty root vegetables Christoph had found along the way. He was always looking for herbs and vegetables to go along with the game since their normal diet did not usually consist of much meat. Friedr was the only one of them who did not really enjoy vegetables, being raised in the far north where farming vegetables was limited to a short summer season.

In a stroke of good fortune, Friedr stumbled on a new trick when making a fire. There would be few campfires in Mal Evol, but thanks to his new spell, they would instead be able to read or talk by the light of a tiny ball of flame. Friedr found a way to place it on a flat rock. He discovered the trick while using an adaptation of Edwin's shields and a novice spell that used little chi and emitted no smoke.

The two soldiers behaved as if it were no big thing, accepting it as a given—Friedr possessed fabulous abilities no other healer of their acquaintance had, so miracles could be expected. But privately, Friedr was pleased with himself. "Now, we can have heat and light and won't have to worry about a campfire giving us away." When they were in Mal Evol six years before, they'd had no fire whatsoever. Friedr's new skill was a welcome addition to their evenings.

Edwin and Zan immediately learned the trick. The little flame would last about three hours. "This light is wonderful as long as we keep it shielded so no glimmer gives us away. There is no smoke, and it doesn't flicker. This is a great skill to have, Friedr." Zan immediately began calling it "Friedr-fire." "Think about how surprised Dario will be when you just casually light a room with your little ball of Friedr-fire. He's already suffering from a serious case of insecurity where you're concerned."

"But don't call it Friedr-fire. That's a clumsy name if ever I heard one," Friedr told Zan. "I don't know what to call it. Let's just call it a mage-lamp." Edwin agreed, and reluctantly so did Zan.

They sat around the campfire after they had eaten, and Div told them they should mount their guard in pairs from there on, unless they knew for a fact the area was clear. "This close to the Lian River, you're right up against the haunted mountains. Rats pop up out of nowhere and swarm you before you even know you're in trouble."

"We're still on the Neveyah side of the river, but the rats don't know or care," Benn asserted. "It's all the same to them."

"I've always wondered about them." Edwin polished his boots as they sat by the fire. "It makes me sad to have to slaughter them the way we do. It seems so wrong somehow. But they attack you and won't stop until you kill them."

"I've heard they're the lost children of the god, Ariend," Christoph replied. "I don't know how true it is, but they often look as if they were civilized folk only days ago. I don't know though, because I only know the bardic tales regarding Ariend."

Benn and Div looked at each other and then at Christoph. "We hear stories from the woodsmen who dwell near the haunted mountains in the north of Neveyah. Apparently, the rat people live high in the Mountains of the Moon, much higher than our people can go and not get the lung-fever. From what we've been told, there are whole rat villages run by the women of their sort. The men develop this madness once they get to a certain age. Their womenfolk drive them out of their towns to protect the children." Div looked at Benn for confirmation, and Benn nodded earnestly in agreement.

"The locals say when the rat's god is freed from his prison, the rats will be cured of the madness," Benn told them. "I never heard who their god is, or who put him in prison."

Christoph stared into the fire. "I wonder. It seems to corroborate the bardic tales in some ways. Only, the bards tell how the god Ariend was murdered by Tauron...."

Still thinking about Benn's story, Christoph remembered a passage from the Book of Life, an allegory detailing the war of the gods. He muttered, "Ariend, God of the Mountain World Cascadia...Mountains of the Moon...." His eyes widened, and he paused, thinking furiously. "Oh my.... Could it be? This could change everything!" He was quiet for the rest of the evening, thinking about the legends of Ariend and lost in his own thoughts.

That night, Christoph dreamed he stood before a living pillar of amethyst crystal. Inside the crystal was the skeleton of a giant of a man, the god, Ariend. The god was in great pain. In the dream, Chris knew the crystal had once been white but had been turned to amethyst by poison. When he woke for his turn at watch, he couldn't get the dream out of his mind, but what it meant he couldn't determine.

***

They crossed the great shield John Farmer, Abbot Garran, and Abbess Halee had built at the end of the Great War in an act born of desperation and which marked the actual border between the soil of Neveyah and Mal Evol.

Arriving at the border, they were forty leagues due east of the Green Valley and the abandoned farm where Edwin, Christoph, and Friedr spent a month when they fought D'Mal on their first quest to rescue Marya. It was there they made the first cache. Linked, Edwin and Zan would be able to reach that cache from anywhere in southern Mal Evol. Together, they could summon their supplies to wherever they were camped. Nothing made of metal was in the supplies since only Edwin could move metal, and it prostrated him to do so.

Just as he had while on his healing journey, Friedr carried the surgical instruments in his kit. Everything in the trunks was wrapped in packets made of beeswax-coated cloth, and the packets were then wrapped in oilcloth before they were packed and sealed in the cedar trunks. These trunks would be buried at each cache spot.

Each cache of four trunks contained two months' worth of supplies. The sealed trunks would remain safe from decay and insects for many years, though most likely, they wouldn't be left there more than two or three months at the longest. Each trunk was tightly packed with medical kits containing bandages, wooden splints, ointments, and potions. They also contained a variety of dry rations so the questers would have some diversity in their diet, along with two tightly rolled spare shirts, and two sets of underwear tightly rolled around two pairs of socks for each of them. Half of the supplies would be cached where they were now, due east of the Green Valley, and the rest would be cached four days further northeast above the banks of a creek south of the Shadow Castle. When they were linked Edwin and Zan could reach the caches from the farthest place east they planned to travel to, near Mal Evol City.

Most of the trails the Legions once used had grown over, so they now stayed on the old trade road, which was much quicker, although the bridges that crossed the streams had washed away in the periodic gully-washers that sometimes followed the rare, but intense rains. The streams were shallow, and the travelers forded them relatively easily. The old road itself had become little more than a wide trail.

Edwin and Zander's scouting with their air-magic helped immensely. They had seen no sign of any legions in the whole of southern Mal Evol since entering it.

Finally, they came to the place where they would make the last cache. On the last evening Benn and Div were with them, Div sought Christoph out for "some advice of a personal nature," and they went off for a private conversation. When they came back, Div had the look of a man at peace with himself. Benn said nothing, but he also had a much happier look about him.

Zan was relieved too, glad to think they wouldn't find themselves waking up in the next gaol they come to. He had developed a friendship with the two soldiers. He was going to miss them, thinking fondly of them as a pair of happy wanderers.

Each day they had traveled together, Benn and Div developed greater respect for the four questers, and when they finally came to the place where they would make the second cache, it was with some sorrow the two soldiers had to return to Braden without those whom they considered "their" mages. Before they left, Edwin checked the ponies over one last time, patting and reassuring each one and making sure their shields were tied off.

"I hope the shields will last until you get them back to Braden, but now you've no healers with you, maybe you'll go unmolested," Edwin told Div.

"We sure are going to miss you. No one will believe us when we tell them about our healers throwing fire and killing rats with swords. They'll think we've slipped it, for sure." Div shook hands all around, and Benn clasped everyone's shoulders. Then they turned and headed back to Braden, leading the now-unencumbered ponies. Soon Benn, Div, and the ponies disappeared into the thorn forest, leaving the four companions alone in the wilderness once more.

"It seems sort of quiet without them, doesn't it," Zan commented to Edwin. "I hope they'll be all right without us. They will, won't they?" He gazed in the direction they had disappeared, a wistful expression on his face.

"They should be fine. They're used to traveling here. It's why they were chosen for this task. But if you want to, you can still scout the air and whisper warnings to them. Maybe you should for as long as they're in your range," Edwin replied, "It'll be good practice. And it'll make you feel better."

Zan gave Edwin a slightly guilty look and nodded, temporarily robbed of words. Finally he said, "Who'd have thought I'd turn out this way, actually concerned about others?" He shrugged, a self-deprecating smile on his slightly red face.

"It's the price for having gained healing empathy. The longer you work with your empathy, the more it changes the way you view the people around you." Edwin clasped his shoulder.

Nodding to hide his confused feelings, Zan closed his eyes to ride the air, scouting the area.

After caching their supplies on the high ground well above the riverbed, they remained camped near the banks of the River Morte on the far west side of the huge valley of Mal Evol, bathing and doing their laundry. The cache was actually due east of Arlen, although the dangerous and impassable Cascadia Mountain range with its sheer cliffs and often thousand-foot drops stood between them and the strange town. They were four days due west of the Shadow Castle. Now, they took the time to finalize their plans for sneaking in and killing the dogs.

Crouching on the riverbank, Christoph and Edwin worked on isolating the parasite they intended to magnify and spread over the soil of Mal Evol, while Friedr and Zan linked and used Zander's air-magic to scout the area thoroughly. This was the first time the two had done so, and Friedr was surprised at the range they had when they worked together.

Christoph instructed Edwin as they knelt on the bank over the carcass of a dead salmon. "We know this little organism spends part of its life in the soil when the creeks dry up, so it should be easy enough to alter some of them so they spend their whole life in the soil. It'll be easy to make them so deadly no dog is immune to the infection. The hard part will be mutating them so they only affect the bear-dogs.

"The problem is we can't do it until we get there and actually see the dogs. Once we know how different their metabolism is we can make it specific only to them. Then Zan and Friedr can enter the link, and we'll spread them as far around the general area of the Shadow Castle as we can, in the same way as we've done so often with the leaf litter and other beneficial soil amendments. The now beneficial parasites should then spread themselves even further until the whole land is poisonous to bear-dogs. But if we can't do it quickly, we'll just have to make it so no dogs of any sort can live in Mal Evol ever again."

Edwin agreed with him. "Either that or face the possibility D'Mal will eventually succeed in introducing bear-dogs to Mal Evol."

"I'm sorry, Edwin, but I won't be able to actually kill the dogs when we get there." Christoph paled. "I can create and change the parasite, but...."

"Don't worry, Christoph. I rather doubted you could. First, I'll cast sleep on them and whoever is guarding them, before we're even close to them. When they're all asleep and we can approach them, I'll stop their hearts. They won't feel anything, I promise you."

Christoph mutely nodded.

They spent the afternoon studying the entire life cycle of the parasite, and when finished, they'd formed a good plan to eradicate the bear-dog menace once and for all.

Friedr and Zan returned from scouting. "All we need now are the dogs." Edwin gazed at the evening sky. "Chris and I have it figured out pretty well. Now what we have to do is plan entry into the Shadow Castle. Moran's plan is for us to make liberal use of the sleep-spell. Aeos has blessed us all as healers, and I think this is the reason why. She knew we'd have need of special tricks. We enter from four sides, casting sleep and converge on the barracks and the kennels, putting everyone we come across to sleep. We want to keep our presence inside the castle limited.

"The way we'll gain entry is this—Zan and I will scout the Shadow Castle. Linked, we'll have much greater strength and he'll see what I see. We'll try to use our air-magic to unlatch windows or doors on each of the four sides so we have easy entry. If it doesn't work, we'll have to put the old man and woman to sleep and then go in through the kitchen.

"Once inside, we must use our stealth armor to the fullest to go as quietly as possible, with our senses extended both ahead and behind us. Once every guard is asleep, we'll go to the kennels, casting sleep on the dogs once we get there. When we're all at the kennels, I'll stop the dogs' hearts. Then Chris will delve the dogs to see if he can tailor the parasite so it'll seek out bear-dogs and only bear-dogs. Hopefully he can, or we'll have to "use a bigger hammer" as my dad would say, and even foxes will likely be casualties of the parasite."

"We need to get in and get the job done and then get out as quickly as we can." Friedr dropped down beside Edwin, wearing a discontented expression. "I don't like splitting up, but I can see it's the only way we can get it done in the time allowed by the sleep spells. But if even one of us gets caught, we're all in the soup."

"Then we mustn't get caught. There's too much riding on this." Zander said what they were all thinking. "I just want to remove the dogs and return to Braden. Then we can finish our task and go home." His eyes turned to the west, and he smiled wistfully as he added, "There's a girl waiting for me, and I plan to ask her to bond with me when I get back. I've had enough adventure for a while!"

Christoph smiled, thinking, *I'll have a grandbaby yet. Dane and I will be the best grandparents a child ever had.* He fell asleep thinking of all the tiny clothes he'd made for other people's babies, and of all the wonderful things he would make for a grandchild.

Just as had happened nearly every night since entering Mal Evol, once he had fallen into a deep sleep, his dream was filled with the throne hidden deep beneath the Shadow Castle, hearing the god trapped within it cry out to him, begging him to ease his suffering.

Once again, Chris tried desperately to heal the throne but could not find the cause of the poison.

Chapter 16 ~ Poised on the Edge

For the next four days, they crawled through the thorn forest. Few paths were visible anymore. In the six years since the legions had left Mal Evol, few people had used the roads, and no one kept the trails open. Even the formerly-wide trade road was rutted and overgrown.

On the fourth night inside Mal Evol, Christoph spent his watch with his senses extended under the soil and was able to read the earth nearly to the soil under the haunted keep. Every night, his sleep had been disturbed and far from restful. His vivid dreams were haunted by the throne and the god he was sure still lived within it. For some reason, he didn't feel comfortable talking about his dreams to the others, and so he remained silent.

I don't know anything for a fact, he thought, trying to justify his need to keep his vague plans secret. All Christoph had to go on were dreams and fantasies. No one would take him seriously if he told them he wanted to heal a god who might not still be alive. *Tomorrow, I'll be close enough to search the keep myself.* He promised himself that once he knew if his dreams were correct, he would talk to them about it. His musings were interrupted by something that caught his attention. *But what's this? A barren ring around the keep. What could have caused this?*

Edwin woke for his watch. He and Christoph linked and sent their combined senses to the barren ring, a swath of grass nearly half a league wide. It was bizarre. The thorn forest simply stopped abruptly. The

Shadow Castle sat in the middle of the barren ring like the hole in the center of a fried sweet-cake. For a space of nearly half a league, thorns surrounded the walls of the castle just as they always had done, and then the wide-open swath encircled the keep.

"It doesn't make sense," Friedr said when he woke up to stand his watch and they told him what they had seen. With Friedr linked to them, they could tell the swath had been deliberately burned into the thorn forest some months before, and it was regularly burned to remain vegetation-free.

"Why didn't they burn everything right up to the castle walls? Once we cross the bare area, we'll be perfectly hidden again. And we can easily cross it after dark once the moon sets. With this armor, no one will notice us." Friedr withdrew from the link, thinking about what they had seen. "This doesn't make sense. I don't like it," he repeated, sitting on his heels and regarding the gradually lightening sky. "There must be a purpose to this. D'Mal does nothing without purpose."

"I agree, Friedr. Everything we know about him tells us his great strength is his ability to plan for every eventuality. So, what we must figure out is what contingency he planned for with this strange moat." Edwin yawned. "Zan and I will scout the air tomorrow when we're closer. But for now, I think we should try to get some sleep and let you take your watch as planned. I'm still tired enough to sleep anyway."

"I'm tired too," replied Christoph. "It just seemed so odd to me." He too yawned, and wishing Friedr a good night, he crawled off to his blankets. Edwin too went to his bedroll for a few hours of rest.

Later that morning, they continued moving through the thorn canopy as fast as they could, and by sunset, they were in the hills overlooking the haunted keep. Just as they had done all those years before, they found a rock outcropping where they had a perfect view of the Shadow Castle and the barren ring surrounding it. There, they established their base camp, although they hoped they would only be there for two days at the most.

They were camped high on the hills that formed a half-circle behind the Shadow Castle. The thorn-brake they were camped under was somewhat further back in the canopy and had easy access to a place with a perfect view of the whole of the northern valley. Their aerie was shielded from view by some of the large boulders.

Once they made their camp, Edwin and Zan linked and entered the keep through the water that fed the fountain in the conservatory to begin scouting the interior of the castle.

Christoph searched the soil, unsurprised to find it saturated with the poison affecting the valley. *It'll be a long time before this land is cleansed, unless...but no. I promised I wouldn't try to heal the throne.* While he sailed under the earth, he debated in his mind what was right and what he should do. *I'm an idiot. I'm allowing my strange dreams to affect me.*

Friedr used his little spyglass to observe the guards as they went about their daily tasks, noting where each patrol began and ended and what time the guards changed shifts. They walked along the parapet just as they had before, with the exact same regularity. "Moran was right. Nothing has changed," he told Christoph. "Except different guards walk the parapet."

Linked, Zan and Edwin drifted on the slightest of breezes through the long gallery, looking for windows low enough to the ground they could enter through once they were unlatched. On the far corner of the eastern walls of the keep, just above a barren planter, they found a tall window with a loose bolt. From the outside, it opened about a meter above the planter. The planter lay hidden behind the forest of thorn bushes that ringed the castle, pressing right to the walls.

It was easy to slide to the latch to the unlocked position. Opposite on the western side, they found a long row of windows in the conservatory that were similarly placed. Selecting the window in the corner, they were able to slide the latch open also.

Returning to their bodies they noted the positions of the two unlocked windows on the map of the keep. "This is much easier with you linked to me than it was the last time I was here," Edwin told Zan. They returned to searching the rest of the castle.

Near the kitchen at the northern end of the keep, in the servant's corridor, was a window hidden from the view of the barracks by the forest of thorns with a loose bolt and they pushed it into the unlocked position. Drifting to the southern end of the keep near the inside door to the barracks, they found a low window with a wobbly bolt. They unlocked it and returned to their bodies.

"It's fortunate this keep was never built with the sort of attention to detail Jaxon is applying to Arlen. It's like this place was built for people to enjoy the inside, rather than to keep intruders out," Zan mentioned to Edwin as, with a grease pencil, they marked the map with the unbolted windows. "Now we just have to hope no one notices our work and relocks them."

Smiling grimly, Edwin agreed with Zan. "Neither Jaxon nor his children will ever make mistakes like that in anything they build. I guarantee they'll never let their guard down." He put his grease pencil back in his pocket. "You see, Jaxon's ancestors built the oldest part of this keep *around* the Throne of Stone and Bone over a thousand years ago. They disguised what it is by making it appear as if it was only a vineyard to support the royal family. No cities or towns were allowed anywhere near for a reason. Mal Evol City was on the Lian River twenty leagues to the east, for easy barge transportation of goods and commerce, and they built a flashy castle there, that they referred to as their townhouse. That was where all the business of running the country was done."

"Really? That seems a good diversionary tactic." Zan's love of a good story was legendary. "But someone must have realized the place was important."

"Not for a long time. They never allowed any villages near the Keep of Mal Evol, planting huge vineyards around it and only allowing scattered farms near the keep, so attention was always on Mal Evol City. The wines produced by the royal vineyards were famous and much sought after all over Neveyah, but no one gave this drafty old keep a moment's notice since it was out in the back of beyond. Most folks thought the keep was only the summer house and vineyards of the royal family, thinking they hung on to the old place for sentimental reasons."

"Well, it's certainly not as fancy as a lot of the old picture books portray these sorts of places."

Edwin laughed. "I know. But that anonymity was the family's protection until the day they hired Stefyn Black, as Stefyn D'Mal was known then, to tutor their son. He secretly used his time to learn all he could about the throne. He was a mindbender, and used his skills to make them believe he was just a simple scholar. After a while, once he became unable to hide the buildup of unfocused chi he went back to Serende. When he returned, he had an army at his back, and you know what happened then."

Zan shook his head. "Not exactly. I know the bare history of the war but not all the details."

Edwin said, "Stefyn Black knew very well what the significance of the Keep of Mal Evol was, as he had been specially raised from infancy by the priesthood of Tauron for the sole purpose of taking the Keep of Mal Evol for the Bull God. He's actually the elder brother of King Maxon, Jaxon's father, the child of a casual relationship with a friendly-girl, and whom King Daxyn never knew existed. The priests of Tauron kidnapped his mother before he was born and hid him away.

"They raised him for the purpose of taking Mal Evol and using the valley as a base for conquering the rest of Neveyah. If the old king had known of his son's existence, Stefyn would have been raised in the family as the eldest son and trained to rule the country, and none of this would've happened." Edwin looked down the valley at the Shadow Castle. "This is why the throne accepts him. He's of the blood of D'Mal and is the rightful heir."

"What do you mean, 'the throne accepts him'?" Zan sat on his heels. He understood now why Jaxon had such odd mannerisms and who he really was, but didn't know if he liked him or not. However, he respected him immensely for what he had accomplished in Arlen in so short a time, being only the same age as Edwin.

"Link with me and I'll show you." Edwin and Zan allowed their linked spirits to drift through the water that fed into the conservatory. They drifted into the servants' entrance to D'Mal's private wing. In the vestibule behind the plants under the circular staircase, they found the little door. They went through the keyhole in the door and down the narrow, sharply descending hall to another door. At this one they went under the wide gap at the bottom.

The room was dark, but the amethyst crystal of the throne glowed with a dark purple light, allowing them to see clearly.

The entire throne room was carved into the top of a gigantic spire of marble laced with amethyst crystal, which burst through the marble floor from deep within the earth. As they examined it, Zan realized the top of the spear formed the butte upon which the entire Shadow Castle was built and the foundations of the keep. The gigantic crystal and marble spire was the perfect shape of a spear that pierced deeply into the heart of the earth.

The throne sat atop the haft of the spear and was intricately carved. More than one master had given a lifetime to the carving of it. Their regard drifted up the long flight of steps leading up to the fabled seat of kings, to the arms and back, which were carved in perfect replicas of the branches of oak trees. Indeed, the entire giant throne was formed in the likeness of an immense oak tree when viewed from the base of the steeply rising steps.

Lacy leaves and delicate branches formed the gigantic canopy over the seat, covering the high ceiling and the walls. Embedded in the shaft below the crystal seat was an entire human skeleton, standing and staring upwards through the seat as if looking to heaven. His arms were outstretched as if pleading. In life, the man would easily have been head and shoulders taller than Friedr. Edwin and Zan felt a sense of unhappiness and pain in the room.

After satisfying Zan's curiosity, they returned to their bodies and discussed with Friedr and Christoph what they had seen.

"Well, we won't be going anywhere near it," Friedr reminded them, "although I wouldn't mind tagging along the next time you go to view it with your air-magic. Perhaps we can link and all do it like we do when we heal the soil."

"Let's give it a try." Edwin and Zan fell into the link, and Friedr and Christoph quickly joined them. After only a few moments, Edwin said, "I don't think it'll work, trying to carry both of you piggyback on our air-magic. Let's try to go in under the earth."

They were able to examine the entire throne room and the throne carefully, delving the earth underneath the keep until they reached the very root of the immense, spear-shaped shaft of crystal and marble that was the Throne of Stone and Bone. The poison affecting the land definitely emanated from the shaft itself, and the land cried out to them, but they were unable to help it.

As they returned to their bodies, Friedr sighed despondently, looking at the Shadow Castle that dominated the valley below them. "I'm truly sorry we don't dare attempt to heal the throne. I regret that I asked to see it."

"Don't be sorry, Friedr," Zan told him. "We'll make it as right as we can."

"I could speak now...I could tell them what I've discovered, tell them Ariend lives and what I have to do." Christoph opened his mouth to speak, but Friedr was talking, and Chris's moment of courage passed. He sat back on his heels and said nothing.

"We must seal the throne off from the land when we heal and shield the land, or it'll negate our efforts. Friedr spoke in a low voice. "The man in the throne is taller than me," Friedr's voice was tinged with wonder. "I'm quite tall, but in life, this man would tower over me. How did he end up there? It's amazing."

Christoph started to speak, but Edwin was already speaking. "I don't think he was a man, at least not a human man. Do you recall the epic tale, 'The Fall of Ariend'?" Friedr and Zan nodded, as did Christoph, uncertainly. "Well, I think the skeleton is what remains of the god Ariend, whom Tauron attempted to murder in his effort to steal Aeos and make her his bride. That is what all this misery is about.

"This throne was made to protect what was left of Ariend's world of Cascadia after Tauron took most of it. Aeos claimed all that was left of Ariend's world, including her husband's remains, and chose the D'Mal family as the guardians of Ariend's land. She told them to build a castle over the haft of the spear that contained her husband's bones and make it into a throne they could use to keep the land and people safe from Tauron.

"Think about it. This valley is huge, hundreds of leagues wide, but it's surrounded on all sides by mountains so high our people couldn't live there even if trails could be found to those heights. On the far eastern side of the valley of Mal Evol, the mountains stretch for as many leagues to the east as the land of Neveyah does to the west. The mountains ring the valley with walls so steep there's no way into them from the valley. The valley was cut from them like carving a pumpkin. There's only one way into the valley, which is the pass guarded by the city of Braden, at the Braden Gap.

"This was Ariend's world. I think Benn and Div were right. Rats were once his people, and the madness Tauron afflicted them with drives them to come down to the lowlands. The air is so thick down here compared to what they're accustomed to, they'd soon die even if we didn't kill them. Have you noticed how bluish their lips and fingernails are? They're drowning in our thick air.

"Aeos divided the combined worlds into two and gave one to the Almighty Father, which he called Ariend so his son's name would never be forgotten. This is why the people of my world and the people of Neveyah are the same. The Book of Life isn't an allegory—it's our true history. We're all the children of Aeos, but our original world was divided."

"I think you're right, farm boy," Friedr replied after a moment of contemplation, thinking about what they had seen. "That makes so much sense. But I can see why the Temple has kept that a secret."

I should tell them that Ariend lives in great agony...I should tell them now, exactly what I want to do to heal him.... Again, Christoph tried to speak. Again, he had missed his window of opportunity, as

Friedr was speaking again, giving direction about the foray into the keep.

"...and if Lork finds out we're here, we're all going to meet the same fate as Piers. We must be very careful as we sneak through the keep. We have to use all the stealth and cunning at our disposal. Keep your senses ranging out continuously as far as you can, and when you sense the guards, immediately cast sleep. We must try not to alert the old man and woman since they'll immediately get Lork involved. Once we've taken care of the guards, we'll converge on the kennels. Then, Chris and Edwin can complete their task, and you and I will guard them, casting sleep as often as we must. After we've finished, we'll sneak out through the conservatory window."

"Don't worry, Friedr. I'm certainly not going to draw any unnecessary attention," Zan agreed with Friedr earnestly. "I'm going to sneak in my window, put my minotaurs to sleep, and go straight to the meeting place. I know exactly what's required of me."

"Did you ever find out the reason for the barren ring around the castle, Chris?" Edwin looked at him quizzically.

"Oh! Um...I think they did it to keep folks from sneaking up on the castle after Piers was captured," Christoph replied hurriedly. *Oh no. I never finished checking that out. I wasted too much time thinking about the throne.* Pulling his thoughts together, he said, "They seem to maintain the main swath, but for some reason, they let the thorns grow back near the walls, because those thorns are much younger than the main forest. It's like they can't bear to live without the thorns next to them. If we cross it after the moon sets, after midnight, we'll be least likely to be noticed."

"There'll be the least number of people up and about in the keep then, too," Friedr agreed.

***

Later as Christoph sat his watch, he fully extended his senses through the earth to the throne and the God who suffered within it. As he looked at the suffering god, he came to a decision. *I'm going to help you as soon as I can. Soon the pain will be gone, but I don't know how to free you. I think the Hero Foretold will somehow free you, because he's supposed to 'take back all.' In the meantime, I'll help you as much as I can.*

The only problem would be trying to figure out a way to tell Friedr what he was going to do instead of taking care of the dogs. *Edwin knows what needs doing, and he can do it with Zan and Friedr's help if I don't make it back to them in time. I have to do this. Ariend's pain is unbearable.*

Friedr will be furious if I don't tell him first. If I somehow survive, he'd kill me.

***

The next day, they carefully mapped where each guard was and where the guards in the barracks normally went, while Edwin followed the old woman and old man, who were D'Mal's personal servants, as they went about their tasks.

Lork had a fine set of rooms next to D'Mal's personal apartments in the tower over the Throne of Stone and Bone. The two servants waited on him as if he were their master. He spent part of his day in the dungeon, but Edwin chose not to follow him there. When Lork was not in the dungeon, he drilled his underlings in the small training yard outside the barracks or could be found checking on the dogs and their trainer. The rest of his time he spent napping in his rooms.

The dogs remained confined to the kennel area, and their trainer was careful to keep them safely housed in the specially fenced enclosure. The bitches and pups were in their own enclosed area, and the males were housed separately from each other. The trainer had a pallet opposite the main enclosure.

The guards did not come into the kennel, as the dogs became excited, lunging and barking their strange high-pitched, hoarse bark. They were well aware the dogs viewed them as prey, but every now and then, a guard strayed too close. The only one besides Lork who could go near them was their trainer because he had raised them. The trainer could often be found sleeping on his rather unkempt pallet.

The guards drilled, gambled, quarreled, or slept. It appeared they never left the barracks except to go into New Mal Evol City for a little recreation. Sleeping was the main hobby of the guards at the Shadow Castle.

At the end of the day, the four mages knew where everyone inside the castle would be at a given time. Lork did like to lie in bed until nine or so in the morning, a fact the other guards resented. Each guard would go about his tasks exactly as he was supposed to because D'Mal had set a geas upon him to insure he did his tasks exactly as required with no deviation. Even the two old human servants still performed their tasks exactly the same way at the same time each day.

The companions firmed up their plans. They would approach the castle from the rear as the other sides of the keep were built over the cliff-like walls of the bluff. In the front at the main entrance, the drive was ramped up to the top of the bluff, and the carriage port was there.

Despite several opportunities, Christoph was unable to tell them he would not be meeting them at the kennel. The words simply failed him. Their reaction to his suggestion in Braden had very definitely been "no," and he was not sure how to impress upon them the god was alive and in terrible agony from the poison. *I never win an argument. I always end up agreeing just to make everyone happy. I don't know what to do now, but I must DO something to ease his pain. I can't sleep knowing how he suffers.* As a way to assuage his guilt, he obsessively went over the task of altering the parasite, making sure Edwin could do everything, right down to the smallest manipulation of the life-lights within the tiny creatures.

"Don't worry so much, Chris. We'll be fine," Edwin told him as he finally fell into his bedroll in an attempt to get some sleep before they began the trek down to the moat. "We could do this in our sleep." Christoph nodded, momentarily robbed of his words by his own guilt. Edwin noticed his worry but laid it down to a case of nerves. "I know you hate killing the dogs, but we have to. I'll be quick and painless about it, I promise."

Just before midnight, they packed up and moved out to the edge of the moat. The minute the moon set, they crossed the barren stretch of grass. Crawling under the thorns, they silently approached the keep on the rear side. They stashed their kits deep in the thorns under a large bush outside of the conservatory, and then they moved to their respective windows to double-check that they had remained unlocked.

Edwin and Zan continued scouting with their air-magic, staying in contact with each member of the team, monitoring everyone's position. At last, each of them was in place.

Apparently no one inside the keep ever checked the windows, because they were still unlocked. Making sure the area inside all points of entry was clear, Edwin whispered the signal on the wind. Moving as one to gain entry, they silently climbed in. With their senses extended, they crept up on each guard, casting sleep before the guards even realized intruders had entered the keep. Noiselessly, they prowled the halls and corridors, slowly approaching the kennel and casting sleep as they went.

Chapter 17 ~ Into the Devil's Lair

Upon hearing Edwin's whisper to go ahead, Christoph entered the keep through the conservatory window. Silently he flitted from shadow to shadow, imagining the shadows that haunted the castle moved as if they wished to shelter and hide him. He cast sleep, effectively removing the guards in his area, conserving his chi as much as he could while still eliminating the guards for at least three hours.

Now Christoph crouched in the dense foliage of the lush plants, remaining perfectly still and hiding in the shadows of the conservatory as Friedr passed in the main corridor, looking for him. *I just have to get to the throne. Once I do that...well, I'll worry about it once I get there.*

Friedr looked tight about the eyes, which meant he was worried.

Christoph shivered. *Aaugh! Why didn't I just tell them what I'm going to do? Why do I always try to take the easy way out by lying? It's never easier, but I always do it. Stupid.... Maybe I can do this before they even realize I'm gone and then they won't be upset. It's the only way to avoid Friedr's wrath. I'll have to be quick.* The shadows seemed to rise and swirl around him, concealing him even more. *If Friedr remembered to use his healing-sense he'd know where I am...but he always forgets. I knew I could count on him to forget.*

Peering up and down the corridor, Christoph slipped into the anteroom and entered the wing that housed the Throne of Stone and Bone and D'Mal's personal apartments. Hiding under the curving stairwell behind the multitude of potted plants that concealed the door to the throne room, he remained still while the old man, wearing his pajamas and a silk robe, entered the foyer and carried a tray up the stairs.

Someone's upstairs. It must be Lork. Surely he's not up and about this early.... Oh Goddess. Christoph's stomach lurched. *Maybe I should forget this, just go find the others and get out of here.* Extending his senses to their limit, he saw the tray on the table near the snoring bulk of the minotaur leader, Lork. *Yeesh! He's still drunk. He'll be out for a while. I don't think he'd hear if D'Mal called him just now, judging from the empty wine jugs by his bed.*

After what seemed like forever, the old man came back down the stairs and went into the kitchen, closing the door behind him. Taking a deep breath and gripping his staff, Christoph quietly opened the door and slipped into the passage leading to the secret room concealing the throne. Moving as swiftly as he could, he finally reached the door to the room, only to find it locked.

Pulling Friedr's lock picks out of his pocket, he quickly unlocked the door and entered the room he had only seen when sending his spirit out sailing under the earth. Peering through the ribbons of amethyst crystal, Christoph could clearly see the god, arms outstretched and face turned toward heaven, as if imploring.

He stopped and leaned his ear against the shaft. *Yes! A heartbeat—somehow, he's alive. But of course, he's alive, he's a god. He can't die, but he can suffer for an eternity.* The outstretched hands seemed to beckon to him. Kneeling before the throne, he prayed to Aeos to give him the strength for his task. As he rose, he felt the agony the god suffered. Placing his palms flat against the ribbon of amethyst crystal and speaking aloud to the god, Christoph said, "You've suffered for too long. Somehow I'll take away the pain."

The shadows tugged at him, urging him forward, and Christoph found himself climbing the steps to the seat, his hand caressing the intricately carved stone all the way up. Standing at the top of the steps, he looked down at the upturned face. *How strange to sit upon the face of this god, but this is the only way to heal the crystal and end his pain. I must do this. I must have the courage to do this.* Slowly, the shadows followed him up the steps and revolved about the seat, as if to tell him this was the place they wanted him to be.

Turning and facing down the steps, he calmed and centered himself. Then he sat upon the Throne of Stone and Bone, clearing his mind of all but the task at hand. He set Earthbinder squarely in front of him between his feet, gripping it with both hands and grounding himself. Only then did he open his healing sight to the spear of marble and crystal. Soon, he had completely entered into the healing trance.

Christoph began weaving earth and healing, bleeding the poison away from the throne, turning the crystal clear and pure once more, washing away the amethyst poison of the Bull God, Tauron. A quarter of an hour passed as he attempted to cleanse the crystal of the throne, unaware of the shadows revolving about him, protecting him, and unmindful of anything other than the task he had begun.

Even as he bled it away, the poison kept returning, so that his efforts were in vain. Realizing the source of the poison must be somewhere within the spear itself, he began searching carefully. His senses examined every inch of the haft of the spear, and as he did so, he detected *awareness*, a vague feeling of relief as if the god understood that Christoph was trying to remove the poison from the crystal that held him trapped.

At last, he found the source of the poison, lodged like a knife next to where the heart of the god who was the living skeleton inside the throne must have been. It was a shard of foreign amethyst, and it radiated evil. Pain lanced through Christoph as his senses lightly scanned the poisoned shard. He winced, and the urge to quit washed over him. Grimacing and in terrible pain, he continued examining the poison shard. At last, he saw what he needed to do, and grimly, he set about doing it.

His body trembled with the effort of working through the pain-soaked crystal. The shadows lifted and swirled about him, encouraging him.

Christoph shook with the effort of working through the torturous pain that infused him. A tear formed in the corner of his eye, rolling down his cheek unnoticed. A moan escaped his quivering lips as the pain rose to a crescendo. Stubbornly refusing to give up, Christoph worked despite the poisoned amethyst's will to the contrary.

Gripping Earthbinder even more tightly, Christoph set himself to removing the shard, shuddering and in agony. As he forced it out of the crystal of the throne, he cast earth-magic, bending the amethyst shard to his will, turning it to clear crystal and from crystal to dust scattered on the marble floor.

With the removal of the poisoned shard, the crystal of the throne at last returned to the clear crystal of the throne of legend. Gasping and groaning in relief as the pain faded, he rested, pulling chi through Earthbinder to replenish his strength for the next and most important part of his self-appointed task. After a few moments, he was composed enough to continue, with the clarity of mind necessary to build the shield.

Then Christoph began the shielding of the spear and the throne itself. Using Edwin's special tricks, he layered the shield with multiple layers of spirit barrier, earth shield, and water shield, weaving them as delicately as any lace, more intricately than he had ever before done. *Edwin will see that I do pay attention.* He set the power for it, using the chi of both the earth and the water below the castle, and tied it off, paying special attention to each tie, making sure the ties were secured to each layer and hidden within the combination of water, earth, and spirit.

After he was finished, he meticulously examined the shield for weaknesses, and finding none, he carefully examined the ties.

Satisfied with his work at last, he allowed the healing trance to dissipate. As he returned fully to his body, Christoph groaned, shaking uncontrollably and leaning on his staff for support, too weak to walk. His veins were on fire and his vision distorted. He was so exhausted that for a moment he imagined the god inside the throne was grateful. Gasping, he waited for his strength to return so he could make his escape. *I've really messed up. I don't know which will be worse—facing D'Mal or facing Friedr,* he thought as the dark curtain came down over his vision and the room faded away. *Friedr's going to kill me.*

***

Edwin met up with Friedr in a long, beautiful gallery filled with statues and hung with fine art. Friedr was as close to frantic as Edwin had ever seen him. "What's wrong?"

"Where's Christoph?" Friedr demanded, his eyes full of anger and worry. "He didn't meet up with me. He entered through his window and put his guards to sleep, but now I can't find him." He was upset, fuming, and forcing himself to stay calm. "He'd better not be doing what I think he's doing. I'll kill him when I catch him."

Edwin closed his eyes and sent his spirit out looking for Christoph, looking for his friend everywhere. He was not in any of the places they had agreed to go to. Finally, he found Christoph seated on the throne, with Earthbinder in his hands and fully in the healing trance. Returning to his body, Edwin's eyes opened and met Friedr's, a sick feeling in the pit of his stomach. "He's fully tranced and attempting to heal the throne. He can't hear me."

"He lied to us. He had absolutely no intention of leaving here without trying to get himself killed." Reaching into his pocket for his lock picks, he found them gone. "He picked my pocket." Friedr fired off a string of curses and started off in the direction of the secret door to the Throne of Stone and Bone.

Edwin grabbed his arm in a steely grip, stopping Friedr in his tracks, surprising him with its strength. "Friedr, no! Leave him. He'll succeed or not, but we *must* complete our task and can't let this stop us." He locked eyes with Friedr, holding him until finally Friedr nodded curtly and looked away. "We'll have to do it without him."

"I don't like it. I don't like this at all, and if he survives this stupidity, I'll kill him," Friedr muttered, his face red and angry.

"I won't stop you," Edwin assured him, his eyes betraying his own anger. "I may even help you. But now we have to rendezvous with Zan as we're supposed to. We'll just have to rescue him later."

They peered down the hallway in both directions, and Edwin sent his senses out to see if anyone was in the area. Finding it clear in both directions, they silently passed through the small corridor that led to D'Mal's private entrance to the kennels, pausing just inside where the dogs couldn't see them. Linking with the ease of habit, Friedr and Edwin cast sleep on the dogs, and one by one, the hideous canines lay down, fast asleep. Casting sleep on the trainer, they waited for Zander to find them, letting their chi replenish itself.

"Where's Zan? He'd better not be looking for Chris," Friedr muttered after a few moments.

"Why?" Zan spoke from behind them. "What do you mean? Where is he?" He saw Edwin's tight face. "Oh, don't tell me he's gone off on his own." He looked from Edwin to Friedr, but the look on their faces confirmed his fears. He closed his eyes and sent his spirit out looking for him. He found his fears justified. His eyes flew open. "But I have to go get him. What's he thinking, doing this reckless thing?" Panic was evident in his voice and on his face as he moved to go to the throne room.

"Oh no, you don't!" Friedr and Edwin both grabbed him. Edwin's voice was harsh. "Your duty is to stay and help us rid Mal Evol of this scourge. *His* duty was to do this too, but he's chosen a different path, and now he's committed. Who's to say this is not the will of the Goddess? When we're done, we'll rescue him, but first we'll complete our task." Edwin's grip on Zan was like iron, and his eyes were as cold as ice. The expression on Edwin's face frightened Zan, and he quailed before it. Zan looked to Friedr for support, but Friedr just shook his head, unable to meet Zan's eyes.

Edwin spoke more gently, trying to calm Zan, who sagged in his grasp, despair written starkly on his face. "Zander, listen to me—we'll save him, but we have to do this first. What will happen to Neveyah if we get killed before we destroy the kennel and the dogs?"

Zan just nodded, too overcome to speak.

Edwin said, "My brother, listen to me. I'd still do this if it were *my* father involved. I would continue with my task for the good of Neveyah. My father would expect nothing less from me. *Your* father is counting on you to do this in his stead. Otherwise he'd never have made this choice. He's doing this because he believes it'll save Neveyah. Don't throw away his effort, misguided though he may be. Are you with me? We all vowed to put the good of Neveyah ahead of our own wishes. Are you willing to honor your vows, even if it means we lose Chris?"

Zan saw the anguish in Edwin and Friedr's faces, matching his own. "Yes, of course. You know I am." He shook loose from Edwin, surprised he would question his resolve. "I knew it wouldn't always be easy to be in the service of Aeos, but even so I made the vows with all my heart. Please, let's just do this and get my father out of here alive." He turned to the kennels and was visibly shocked. "Lady in heaven! What demented mind created these things?"

"Tauron created them, Zan. He is demented on a level mere humans can't comprehend." Edwin once again checked the area for guards but only found those already put to sleep. Looking at Friedr, Edwin said, "Friedr, you'll have to guard us by yourself, and Zan will have to support me. Cast sleep as needed, but conserve your chi as much as possible. We're going to need it when we rescue Christoph." Friedr nodded, firmly committed to finishing their task.

Edwin turned to Zan. "You and I will link, and I'll do the task Chris was supposed to do I know exactly what he was planning. He made sure of that. You must link with me and support me in the same way we support each other when we're healing, but right now, I won't be healing. I'm going to stop their hearts. We'll use our swords to increase our strength and range when we seed the parasites in the soil."

Edwin and Zan knelt and faced each other, each drawing their swords, gripping the hilts and resting the points on the floor. Drawing on the power of their swords, they linked and fully entered the healing trance. Edwin then began systematically stopping the heart of each ghastly canine, including the puppies. He made it as quick and painless as he could, disliking every minute of it, but knowing it must be done.

Friedr stood over them, Dragonstorm drawn and at the ready. Drawing on its power he extended his senses, to the limits of his range, down each corridor and around the corners, as he did not want to be caught by surprise. *Why didn't I realize Chris was planning to do this?* Friedr's thoughts ran in circles. *I knew he was lying about something. He had the look he gets when he's hiding something. His willfulness will be the death of us all.*

When the canines were dead, Edwin began searching for the parasite he wanted to encourage. When he found it, he changed it, performing the minute transformations he and Christoph had practiced so many times. Drawing on their air-magic combined with Edwin's healing-sense, they created great quantities of the altered parasite, making copies, each then immediately began making duplicates of themselves.

Then Friedr entered the link, and they spread the altered parasites into the soil as far as they could reach, to a radius of fifty leagues around the keep. Once seeded, the parasite began to spread itself within the soil.

At last, they finished their task. Returning to their bodies they wearily stood, and stretched.

Friedr looked them both over with his healing-sight and cast a healing spell on both of them. "Is it finished?"

"Yes, but there's a problem. I didn't dare take the time to make it specific to bear-dogs. All canines will be unknown here soon. Let's go," Edwin replied. "Is the corridor clear?"

"Yes," said Friedr, through clenched teeth. They begin the long walk back toward the main hall, flitting from door to door.

Edwin replenished his chi, drawing it through Leviathan, and motioned to Zan to do the same. "I fear we're going to need it." The swirling shadows seemed almost to pull at them, as if urging them to hurry.

At last, they arrived at the conservatory and paused there while Friedr checked the area once again, though the kitchen was at the farthest limit of his range. "It's all clear," he said. "The old man is stacking firewood by the stove, and the old woman is preparing what looks like their breakfast. The kitchen door is closed."

Quickly, silently, they slipped down the corridor to the vestibule, through the small door, and down the hall to the throne. It was with great relief they entered the room to find Chris semiconscious and leaning on Earthbinder. The marble and crystal throne had been completely healed, radiating a pure energy they could sense was the true power of the throne.

Placing his hand on the side of the throne, Edwin sensed the land would begin to return to its more normal state now. He ran his senses over the entire throne, and he lightly touched the man inside of it, and could find no fault with the shield. "He did it, Friedr! He's truly healed the throne. I couldn't have set this shield better myself." Awe and disbelief warred in their faces. "Let's get him out of here."

"I did it." Christoph's voice was faint and scratchy. "I did it. It's Ariend." He gasped his words, "Edwin, you were right. It's Ariend in the throne. I had to help him. I had to. He's a god and he was suffering. A god can't be killed, but he can suffer more than you can imagine." Christoph's eyes couldn't focus, and he was trembling and weak, unable to walk. "More than you can imagine...."

"He's delirious—he's nearly burned his gift out." Zan strode up the steps and easily picked Christoph up. Casting a small spell on Christoph for healing and settling him over his shoulder, Zan carried him down the steps. Friedr picked up Earthbinder, and Edwin led the way as they returned up the long, narrow passage.

Pausing to send his senses out, Edwin nodded; the area was clear, and they quietly exited through the small door. Then they went to the conservatory.

"We have to get out of here." Edwin spoke urgently as Zan once again cast heal on Christoph, who was now able to stand on his own but was disoriented and had no chi left. Friedr half-carried him, and Edwin cast strengthen on him as one by one, they climbed out the window. Edwin closed it behind them, and using his air-magic, he locked it.

They collected their packs and crept through the thorns to the northern side of the keep, the one side where the bluff that the castle sat upon gently rolled down to the valley floor.

As they rested in the shadow of the wall, hidden in the thorns, a wave of immense fury rolled over them like a wave crashing on a beach. With their barrier/shields overlapped and sheltering all four of them, they remained as still as the thorns themselves. Even the birds and insects were silent. The rage passed them by. After a few moments, they began quietly moving away from the keep.

At last they came to a place nearly half a league from the Shadow Castle, where they would have to cross the open expanse. "We'll wait here until dark," Friedr whispered. "I'll watch first. Try to rest and rebuild your chi. When we make our move tonight, we won't be alone." He settled himself to stand guard while the others slept. Edwin fell to sleep immediately.

In what felt like no time at all, Friedr nudged Edwin awake. "Something's wrong with Christoph, but I can't figure out what. It's more than simply overextending his gift."

Christoph was shivering, though he was feverish and restless, locked in a nightmare-infested sleep. "We have to heal him. He can't be moved in the condition he's in." Friedr's worried tones woke Zan, and he immediately sat up. Slipping his arms under Chris's shoulders, Zan raised him, supporting him so Edwin could work on him more easily. Anxiety was etched on all three faces as they linked and began the healing work on their friend.

Chapter 18 ~ Poison and Roses

Unaware of his friends' frantic efforts to save him, Christoph was held prisoner in his hellish dreams. *I'll come for you. You belong to me now.* The silken voice was insistent. His dreams were full of horror, and he was frightened. Mad things chased him through the dark and tore at him, pulling him down. *Be ready, mage. I'm coming for you!*

Slipping into the healing trance, Edwin searched Christoph's burning body. "It feels like he's been poisoned," he finally said. Grasping Leviathan and drawing on its strength, Edwin delved deeper into Christoph, searching for the source of the poison. Zan and Friedr followed him, lending support and strength. "His heart's been damaged, and his kidneys. It's not too late. I can still reverse the damage."

"What could've poisoned him? I don't recognize it," Friedr muttered. "It's a poison that feels familiar, and yet it's not." He drew chi through Dragonstorm and channeled it to Edwin.

"It must have been contact with whatever poisoned the throne," Edwin replied. "It's fading but has lingered in his system long enough to damage him." Centering himself, Edwin set about reversing the damage to Christoph's heart and kidneys, delicately rebalancing Christoph's depleted chi. Soon he was sleeping peacefully. "He may have lost some memory of what he did, but he's retained his magic ability," Edwin reassured the others. "He came very near to burning himself out."

"Thank you for saving him. You and Friedr sleep now." Zander's drawn face was full of gratitude. "I'll keep watch for the rest of the afternoon."

As he watched his father sleep, the memories of the many times Christoph's lack of truthfulness brought anguish to their family surfaced, and grimly, he came to a decision. *This is for your own good, Christoph. Dane and I warned you we'd do this if it ever happened again. We love you, and we won't allow you to get yourself killed.* The expression on Zan's face was bleak as he entered the trance and set the geas on his father.

Christoph would never tell a lie again.

***

Brilliant stars sprinkled across the black-velvet sky. The immense full moon, miraculous in its intensity and nearness, illuminated the valley nearly as well as the sun. The four companions sat in the shelter of the thorn canopy, discussing the events of the day in angry whispers, and it had become somewhat uncomfortable for Christoph.

"You lied to me. You picked my pocket." Friedr glared at Christoph. "You jeopardized the mission with your willful disregard of the truth and the task we were charged with accomplishing. You've much to answer for. You will tell the truth now, everything!" His barbarian accent had thickened with his rage.

Christoph looked back at Friedr and met his eyes. "Yes. I did lie to you when I agreed on the meeting place and when I didn't inform you three I had different plans. Yes, I knew I was lying when I did it, and yes, I did steal from you when I took your lock picks. I knew I was making trouble for myself and I kept doing it anyway. I don't know why, but I couldn't tell you." The truth just spilled from Christoph.

"Why did you do it when you were told specifically *not* to?" Friedr's face was red, and his eyes locked with Christoph's. "Why would you do something as irresponsible as to call us to D'Mal's attention like this?"

"I had to, Friedr. I had to make the attempt to heal the Throne of Stone and Bone while we were there because I knew I'd never have another chance. It's Ariend in the throne! He was suffering from the poison. Once I realized who it was, I had to help him, even though Moran warned me off. I knew you wouldn't let me, so I took it upon myself to do it.

"I counted on Edwin to keep you two on track with taking care of the dogs and off my trail until I'd accomplished my task. I knew he could do that part of the job. My plan was to work as fast as I could and then meet up with you, but I wasn't as fast as I hoped. I didn't realize I'd be poisoned in doing it, but if I had known, I would still have done it." His lopsided smile was unrepentant, though he feared the reprisals of his friends.

Christoph's lack of remorse infuriated Edwin. Suddenly, he found himself enraged at being used in so calculating a manner. Edwin's legendary self-control failed under the stress of the day. His tenuous grip on his anger snapped palpably, and as it did so, the others turned to him, uncertain of what would erupt from the seething mass of rage and disappointment.

"You used me." Edwin's shocked accusation hissed, and he looked sharply at Christoph, who flinched. "You know me so well. You manipulated *me* into unwittingly allowing you to jeopardize our mission." Edwin's low voice was as cold as ice and as hot as molten steel. Christoph could not look him in the eye, but Edwin gripped his vest, forcing Chris to look at him.

Holding him so Christoph's face was only inches away from his own, Edwin punctuated each word with a shake. "You must've planned this for days, maybe even weeks. Perhaps you never had any intention of following through with the plan. Possibly Ariend is only your excuse to do what you wanted from the moment you heard we had to come to this accursed place. Maybe you knew you could use me to finish the task with the dogs—oh, so carefully making sure I'd know exactly what to do." Each word dripped like hot lead, and Christoph winced as Edwin's fury boiled over.

"The minute we got inside the Shadow Castle, you did exactly what you've been planning to do since we left Braden with this task. I'd bet you scouted out the throne room for the last three nights while you were standing watch, since you managed to find your way there with no trouble." Edwin's face was white with fury. His blue eyes stabbed at Christoph, looking for some sign of repentance and finding none. "I'm so gullible I even took you along for one of your scouting missions and you never said a word about your plans."

Edwin's wrath terrified Christoph, who blanched, trying to back away from him, but Edwin's grip on his vest held him firmly in place. Even Friedr backed away from Edwin's anger. "And despite all our preparations, I couldn't take the time to make the parasite specific to bear-dogs. I cut it short, Christoph! I've destroyed an entire species in this valley just to save your life.

"Lork and his boys are out here looking for us because *you* tipped them off. All the work we did trying to keep our presence a secret—you just threw it away." Edwin's low voice became even more furious. "Lork will be the vector for D'Mal, just as Brec was six years ago. You wait and see. Now we'll have to fight D'Mal's personal guard to try to get away from here, and the rest of our quest is over. The shields we've already set in Neveyah will just have to be enough to protect her because he won't allow us to finish the job we were tasked with. If we escape from this mess with our lives, it'll be a miracle."

The intensity of his fury shattered Christoph's barriers, and bowed Friedr and Zan's. "I hate to leave a job half-finished, and you bloody well know it." Edwin suddenly let go of Christoph's vest and turned away as his bitterness and seething anger combined with fear into a torrent of myriad emotions that crashed over the other three with the power of a landslide over a cabin. Christoph fell back, momentarily stunned.

None of them had ever seen Edwin in a fury before, and the intensity of his rage shocked his companions, who sat in stunned silence. Christoph shakily rebuilt his barriers, trembling under the impact of Edwin's fury. Zan and Friedr had drawn back from Edwin as far as they could, uncertain of what would happen next.

Finally, Christoph spoke. His face was white and his lips trembled. "I actually expected to hear those angry words from Friedr, Edwin. You have every right to be angry, and *almost* everything you said is true, but not all of it. It was only when Benn and Div reminded me of the old bardic tales that I put two and two together and realized the Throne of Stone and Bone is Ariend's prison. When I scouted it three nights ago, I realized he was suffering on a scale you can't even imagine. He's Aeos's husband and he's alive. I had to help him, Edwin. I had to!" Edwin just stared at him, his gaze as cold as winter.

"I should have told you the truth and simply gone on my own despite your disapproval. I was wrong to lie to you, to make you worry for my safety. I'm a weak person, and I took the easy way out, thinking maybe I could do it quickly and you'd never have to know." Christoph stared into the darkness of the shrubs where they hid. "It's my worst failing. I always lie in an attempt to avoid confrontation, a holdover from my childhood, I guess. It always causes more trouble than if I'd faced it head on.

"I deserve everything you said and more. But I don't regret doing it, in spite of your anger, because I still believe that what I did was the right thing. My shame is that I lied to you. But when I healed Ariend, the spell on the land was broken. Even now I can feel it fading. The god, Ariend, who is the connection to his land, is sealed within the throne. It is he and not the throne itself that is the key to Mal Evol. *Ariend* is the key, and Tauron knows this. It's why Tauron had his high priest poison him—he's a god and can't die. Tauron knew if Ariend was poisoned he wouldn't be able to protect his land any longer. That's why the thorns of Serende could live in Mal Evol. Soon, they won't be able to live here, perhaps within a season.

"It was worth the consequences, and I'll accept them. Indeed I *deserve* them for lying to you. But, you can't imagine the pain Ariend has endured since D'Mal used Tauron's magic to poison and inhibit him." He looked at Edwin's hard face. "I confess I didn't think about how we were going to get out of here once I'd done it. I didn't think D'Mal would notice so soon."

Friedr found himself in the unaccustomed position of trying to be the peacemaker, not sure how to appease Edwin. But even as he tried to think of something positive, he saw his friend's anger fading, to be replaced with resignation. Finally Friedr said, "Well, we can't change what's happened. We must work with what we have now." He turned to Christoph and said, "But if you ever lie to me again over even the smallest of things, I'll set a geas on you so you'll never be able to lie again. Your tiny little sins of omission are just lies waiting to be told, Christoph."

"I set that geas on him while you were all sleeping." Zan gazed out into the clearing they must somehow cross, then turned and met his father's eyes. "I'm sorry, Chris. I had to do it. You know why." Surprised and shocked, Edwin and Friedr looked at each other and then at Zan. Grief and pain had ravaged his face, making him appear much older than his years. "You'll die from your stubbornness, and how will I explain it to Dane? We went through this very thing right after you were augmented. Not telling us your plans when it affects us all is the same as lying to us. Now, we won't have that problem ever again."

Christoph's face was completely stricken. "I deserve the geas. Perhaps it should've been done long ago. I never meant to put you in danger, Zan." His voice shook as he said, "But I never mean it, do I? I just mess things up, and then we deal with the wreckage. Some father I turned out to be."

"Stop it. Just stop it! I don't know anyone whose parents are any better. They all make mistakes. I didn't expect perfection, Chris. All I ever wanted was for you to just be my father and someday be a grandfather to my children," Zan muttered. "You can't if you're dead."

The rage had left Edwin's face, and he took a deep breath, centering himself. "I would make peace with you, my brother," Edwin's voice was rough. "I don't want to have this between us. You're my beloved brother. I don't expect that will ever change." He held his hand out to Chris, who took it with tears in his eyes. "You did an amazing thing, healing the throne. And you set the shield as well as I could, even better maybe."

Christoph looked at him, confused and trying to remember but failing. "I know I must have set the shield, but I don't remember doing it."

"I too would like to put this behind us," Friedr said, clasping Christoph's shoulder. "I've always been your brother. My life would be boring without you. "

Chris nodded, unable to speak.

"Now we must prepare for the battle which is sure to come," Friedr's calm voice belied his worry. "We must play to our strengths."

They began to plan their strategy for when the fight came to them.

***

As the moon set, they gauged each other's health and found it as good as could be expected. They had regained their chi, and were ready to cross the open ground. With the setting of the moon, the field was dark. Moving stealthily, they began crossing the expanse. They moved slowly and deliberately. Suddenly, the silence was shattered as Lork and three minotaur warriors emerged from the brush, calling taunts and charging at them.

The companions drew their weapons and rushed the surprised minotaurs, who had expected them to run. Christoph's staff tripped the leading warrior, and Zan slit his throat, leaving him gurgling on the ground. They turned to the others in time to see Edwin decapitate a guard, pushing his body over and kicking his head out of his way as he charged the leader, Lork.

The last two minotaurs fought desperately, taking many grievous wounds that would have killed a normal person. Lork attacked Edwin, who beat him back toward Zan. Zan attacked him with a vicious rain of blows. Christoph tripped the last of Lork's minions and Friedr finally killed him. They both turned on Lork.

A glowing shield appeared around the minotaur, and his demeanor suddenly changed. The companions felt magic building but were not sure what sort of magic was about to be unleashed. Overlapping their shields, they moved as one to protect Christoph, and Edwin told Zan and Friedr, "Get ready. D'Mal is here now. He'll be testing us, so don't use your best spells against him unless I tell you to."

Suddenly, D'Mal laughed. "I expected to see strong mages, fighting with all their strength, but instead I'm confronted with children sneaking about in the dark." The minotaur's raspy voice had changed, taking on the silken sounds of Stefyn D'Mal. He waved a hand and buried them with an earth spell.

It had no effect on them.

His misshapen minotaur face had a slightly puzzled look, and he tried to drown them with a water spell. It too sheeted off their shields, and Zan diverted the water back upon D'Mal, slipping it under his feet.

D'Mal attempted to get up but skidded in the wet grass. A physical shield of some sort prevented them from getting to him. Quickly, Edwin probed the shield but couldn't see how it was made.

Finally, D'Mal stood and stared at them. "I cannot read you, and yet you've been in my land long enough that I should be able to. You have shields, but I cannot detect them. Are they good enough for this?" Upon feeling D'Mal calling a fire attack every bit as strong as one of Friedr's best hell-fire attacks, Edwin called water, a gully-washer, sending it to Friedr, who used Dragonstorm to snatch both elements and turned them back on Lork/D'Mal in an intense steam attack, shattering his shield. Edwin stepped behind Friedr as D'Mal visibly abandoned Lork, and the huge minotaur squealed, going down writhing under the dreadful attack. Zan quickly decapitated him, putting him out of his misery.

They stood in the silent darkness for a moment, and then they turned to check each other over, making sure no one had suffered any serious injuries. Friedr healed the worst of Christoph and Edwin's lacerations, and Christoph tended to Zan and Friedr.

"We got off too easy," Edwin said. "He was just checking us out to see what we had to offer. He'll come at us with a new vector I guarantee it." He looked over his shoulder as a horn sounded from inside the walls of the keep. "We don't want to face him this close to his home base. He's emptying the barracks now to hunt us down." They turned to leave the open area while they could.

Suddenly, Zander's leg was grasped in an iron grip. Claws pierced his leathers and his calf. The first minotaur whose throat he had slit had survived. Frantically hacking at the arms and stabbing at the minotaur, Zan finally broke free. Friedr knifed the crazed thing to death.

Shaking with fright, Zander roamed around piercing each fallen corpse through the heart. "Die! Die!" His antics made Friedr laugh hysterically and relieved some of the tension they were under. Again, they cleaned their swords while Christoph healed Zan's leg. "This'll have to be looked at again later."

"Let's get out of here while we still have a head start. At least there are only seventy or so of them following us, and they're temporarily without a leader. It could be worse." Friedr took off, crossing the open field and disappearing into the brush. Dropping to their knees, they crawled silently, until they came to a game trail, which they followed until dawn. The sunrise found them many leagues away from the Shadow Castle. They stopped and decided to stay well back in the thorn canopy, resting and regaining chi.

"Well, now we know two new things," Zan ventured as they settled in to rest. The others looked at him. "We know he can't detect our shields." He looked at Edwin. "And we know he can't see well in the dark."

"What tells you that?" Edwin asked.

"He knows you, Edwin. He's had you in his parlor before, so to speak, and he hates you. Yet he didn't know you were here. Minotaurs mustn't be able to see in the dark." Zan's brow wrinkled in thought. "And a third thing. He called us children. He forgot the difference in size between minotaurs and humans."

"Those are valid points," Friedr agreed thoughtfully. "That knowledge could be to our benefit if we must fight him again."

"I wonder…if we must sneak about and hide and he can't spot our shields, why can't we get on with finishing the task? All we have to do is set the shield so the task will go faster. The soil is healed already." Christoph's comment took the others by surprise. "We'll be lurking about in his thorn forest anyway. Let's try to get as much accomplished as we can."

Friedr looked at him and said, "Actually, that's a pretty good idea, Chris—the voice of reason if ever I heard it." They began outlining how they wanted to accomplish the monumental task.

While the others made their plans, Edwin sat back, feeling a sense of uneasiness drop over him. *I just want to get out of here. But thinking logically, we should try to salvage as much of this as we can.*

After a brief rest, they began moving again.

***

They once again camped in a thorn thicket some twenty leagues away from the Shadow Castle. Zan took his turn at watch while the others were sleeping. They had finished setting a cell in the shield, though it was not connected to anything. The cell floated like an island in the center of the land. All was quiet, and Zan stared at the starry sky through the branches of the thorn forest.

As he sat watching, Zan thought of Anna and wondered if she was thinking of him. He felt somehow warmer for thinking of her, smiling in the dark as he listened for any sounds that should not be there, sending his senses out on the wind. Christoph appeared to be dreaming, but Edwin and Friedr were sleeping deeply.

***

Christoph stood in a sunny garden full of lush roses. The fragrance was somehow sensual, though the scent of roses had never had such an effect on him before. A darkly handsome young man was seated on the bench across from him. The eye patch gave him a rakish look and didn't ruin his looks in any way but enhanced them. Chris felt he should know the exceedingly striking man, but he couldn't place him. *A dream. It's only a dream.* He felt better, knowing he was only dreaming.

"I just wanted to meet you," the man said as he smiled persuasively at Christoph. "I wanted to get to know the one I'll have to work with from now on." He looked at Christoph, and a knowing glance passed between them. "We're very much alike, you and I. You're a powerful mage, and I like my friends to be as powerful as I am."

He moved over, inviting Chris to sit beside him. Unsure how he got there, Chris found himself sitting next to the intriguing man.

"Who are you?" Christoph asked. His heart skipped a beat as he looked at the dark-haired man, who was so very charming, and seductive.

"My friends call me Stef," the young man replied ingenuously. "And you are...?"

"Christoph," he replied. His mouth went dry as he looked at Stef, and he recognized this man was also attracted to men.

"We could be good friends." Stef laid his hand on Christoph's knee, sliding it up Chris's thigh.

A wave of intense desire washed over him, and Chris pulled away, knowing the situation was wrong. He suddenly blurted out, "Dane! Dane is waiting for me." The thought of Dane pierced the spell the charismatic man's willing nature and seductive beauty had cast upon him.

Abruptly, Chris stood up, smiling regretfully and saying firmly, "It would be wrong for me to lead you on. I have to go. Someone I love is waiting for me."

"I thought I had a love once, but she betrayed me for a stronger mage. I've had no one since." Stef's hand unwittingly touched his eye patch. A mix of emotions washed over his face when he mentioned his lost love. "I'll be waiting for you. It's good you're honorable to your lovers. When you've settled things in your mind, I'll be here."

Chapter 19 ~ Rats in a Cage

Christoph woke up, burning with desire for the charismatic man he had dreamed of, and was unable to get back to sleep. Calling water, he poured it over his head, enjoying the icy wetness that dispelled the effects of the dream on his errant body. When Zan turned the watch over to him, he gladly took his place and sat staring into the gloom. *Why did I have that sort of dream?* Christoph's thoughts ran in circles. *I must miss Dane even more than I realized, and it's coming out like this. Yet why did I dream of a stranger and not Dane? Dreams are such strange things.*

As he guarded his companions, the details of the dream faded from his consciousness, replaced by a warm, golden reverie of going home. He could see Dane's face so clearly in his mind, and his heart felt lighter. Smiling at a memory of Dane walking in the snow, Christoph watched as his companions slept, at last feeling at peace with himself.

***

The days passed, and they were able to set much of the shield, but it remained a chain of islands, unconnected to anything. Christoph began worrying obsessively, fretting when his companions were tired or uninterested in eating, compulsively checking and re-checking their health.

Awkwardly, a side effect of the geas Zan set on Chris was that he couldn't just say "fine" and leave it at that when his companions asked him how he was feeling. Instead, he had a compulsion to speak the most minute of details, privately telling Friedr, "Gah! It's like I have verbal diarrhea. I just keep spewing information even when silence would be a better choice." He saw the look on Friedr's face and sighed. "I know why he did it. I left him no choice."

"I don't envy you, my brother. Once he forgives you, maybe he'll lift the geas. He's not a vindictive man." Friedr tried to comfort Christoph, saying, "He loves you as a son loves his father."

"No, he won't lift it, Friedr. I've left too many festering wounds from my inability to be honest with Dane." Christoph felt like weeping. "Before we were bonded, I treated Dane very badly, as you know. You took me to task about it more than once. It was terribly hard on Zan, though. The only thing he ever wanted was a normal family, and I was too young and selfish to be a good parent, though I loved them both."

"Christoph, you're a good man, and you're a brother to me. You're too hard on yourself," Friedr replied. "You spent your early life in hell, so it's not surprising you had trouble trusting in your own ability to sustain a relationship. You had to be healed of those scars before you could trust yourself."

Christoph looked sharply at Friedr and then said wryly, "I thought I hid it better. But I could trust nothing in my life until I came to the Temple. The only things I ever knew were abandonment, betrayal, and abuse. I was too small for my age and physically weak. I developed ways of avoiding difficulties, including lying to stay out of trouble. Lying is an easy habit to fall into, but a hard habit to break. I often lied to Dane over the smallest things. I had to learn how to trust myself before I could trust Dane. But in the process, I created a lot of anguish, as you well remember. And once again I made a mess of things earlier this year, so badly Dane nearly left me. It wasn't another man, but I did lie to him over a serious matter."

"Just think about this, my brother—you were sixteen when you fell in love with Dane. It's not unusual for a man to be unable to settle down at that age, although many do. But when you were twenty, you were sure he was the one for you for the rest of your life, and you've been a good and faithful partner to him. Yes, you still sometimes messed up, but you've never strayed from Dane since the day you were bonded." Friedr clasped his shoulder. "You were very young to have the responsibility of a child of Zan's age when you adopted him. *He* thinks you're the best father in Neveyah. He knew very well what your failings were, but he wanted you as his father anyway. Doesn't that tell you something?"

Christoph just nodded, unable to speak for the emotions threatening to overwhelm him. Friedr squeezed his shoulder, lending him strength. "Sometimes, Friedr, you're the wisest of us all," Christoph spoke from his heart. "You always have been."

***

The next day, they ran into several packs of rat-people, which they quickly dispatched. D'Mal and his legions did not make an appearance, but when Edwin and Zan sent their senses out scouting, they found they were being encircled.

"They've figured out where we must be, though how they could do so is beyond me," Friedr said. "They have the numbers to surround us. We'll have to take the mountain trail even though we're not geared up for the cold weather. The weather is fiercely bitter up there." He thought for a moment. "Fortunately, I'm a barbarian. I was raised on how to survive in that sort of climate, so it'll be no problem, but it'll take a week or two to tan the hides we'll need, even with the aid of our magic. Maybe we can hole up somewhere up the trail for a while and then make our escape when the legions have forgotten us. But we must move quickly or be overrun. We won't have time to finish the task after all. We must do what we can and be content."

They set a punishing pace, heading to the northwest. The path they were headed for was a perilous trail, but it offered their only hope of escape. The sheer faces of the escarpment rose in thousand-foot vertical cliffs for hundreds of leagues in a ring around the valley. The sole way into the mountains from the eastern side was a steep, treacherous path. When they'd been in the valley on their quest to rescue Marya years before, the legions had most carefully avoided the trail, so they could only hope the guards would not follow them there.

Pausing only to rest for a short time and create another cell in the patchwork of healed land, they pushed on, as soon as they were able. The shielded and healed land now formed a string of disconnected cells along the Mountains of the Moon, almost to the great barren ring around the Shadow Castle.

Two days later, they arrived again at the southern end of the small line of hills that formed the crescent around the Shadow Castle. This time they turned west until they were heading directly toward the great wall dividing Mal Evol from Neveyah. "The air is too thin to breathe up there in the higher reaches, so I've been told," Friedr spoke as they set out. "The elders of my village were very clear about the dangers in those high passes. They are called the Mountains of the Moon because they're so high you can almost reach out and touch the moon. They're also called the Mountains of No Return because few who venture up there ever return to tell their tales."

But it all ceased to matter when Zan scouted their escape route in the afternoon. He found it had been cut off by a squad of minotaurs. "There's at least one squad of guards not afraid to go a short way up the trail. They're waiting for us." Zan told Friedr it looked to him like they would have to retreat to the general area of the Shadow Castle. "The squad east of us has moved up to the entrance of the pass we're heading to. It looks to me like our only option is to go back and try some other way."

"Well," Friedr mused, "they probably won't expect us to go back since the person we're trying to escape from has his power base there." He was silent for a moment. "We'll just have to take the trade route to Mal Evol City, sneak around the outskirts of the town, and then go southwest to Braden on the old trade road. It'll actually be a faster, more direct route. We need to travel exclusively by night now anyway."

Zan was still not happy with this option, thinking he had missed something that could be in their favor. "Edwin, how does it look to you? There must be a better way. I've no experience, and you do." He was absolutely sure he did not want to go back to the Shadow Castle.

"I'm afraid this is our only option," Edwin agreed after sending his senses out, "although I don't want to go back either. I've a terrible feeling about this."

***

"We're being herded back to the Shadow Castle," Edwin told Friedr on the second night of their retreat. "It's like they know exactly where we are but are holding back. We're going to have to make a stand I'm certain of it. He wants us at the Shadow Castle when we finally do meet him again, but why? He should be able to get at us through a vector anywhere in Mal Evol just as easily as he can near the Shadow Castle. After all, he was able to get to us in Neveyah through Brec because we were so near the border and he had Marya's mind to follow."

"I agree. He gave us Lork with barely a fight, and I can't figure out why, unless he was disposing of him," Friedr replied. "I think he allowed us to kill Lork and make our getaway. But it isn't a getaway, is it—we've been allowed to go where he lets us go and now we're being forced to go back to his doorstep. It's a mystery. What can he do to us there he can't do here?"

"I think you're right, Friedr," agreed Edwin. "D'Mal must've been furious that we got into his keep and killed the dogs. He certainly went mad when Christoph changed the throne back. He knew we must surely have the power to kill his minion, and yet he sent Lork out with minimal backup. He waited to take over until Lork had no one at his back. When D'Mal did take over, he didn't really put up much of a fight, and he let you shatter his shields and kill Lork. He wanted to see who we were, what we were capable of, and he wanted to punish Lork for failing him. He must've gotten what he wanted that day, and now he has something else planned for us."

They spent the next four days retreating to the Shadow Castle, following a winding route that took far longer than it should have. The noose drew tighter around their necks with each day. No one slept well, and they all showed signs of the stress they were under. Christoph was haunted by dreams he could never remember upon waking, but they were disturbing to him. He knew he dreamed of something that was upsetting to him, but it always faded away upon waking. All four suffered from nightmares, so he didn't worry too much about it.

On the evening of the fifth day of their retreat, they arrived back where they started. Just as the sun set, they reached the opposite side of the field where they faced D'Mal less than a month before. Chris and Zan immediately fell into exhausted sleep. The four were standing watch in pairs now.

Toward midnight, Friedr asked, "Edwin, check on the positions of the squads, would you? Who's closest? We'll take them on first. We're going to have to unleash our swords." He smiled at the thought he would be able to fight again, but his smile had a hardness now. His eyes had lost the twinkle they once had.

"You don't have to look like you're enjoying the prospect so much." Edwin laughed at Friedr's expression.

Friedr's momentary glee faded. "To be honest, I'm tired of sneaking around. I just want to finish this and go home to my wife and children," he said, looking toward the west, where the city of Aeoven lay beyond the haunted Mountains and across the verdant midlands of Neveyah.

"Me too, Friedr," Edwin agreed, also looking west, with a longing that hurt like no pain he had ever felt. "I want to be doing that more than anything." Resolutely, he settled himself and sent his senses out to the surrounding area. Returning to his body, he said, "One group is still approaching from the south on the old trade road. They're much closer than the rest. The rest of them are camped and sleeping the sleep of the innocent. They don't even have guards posted. I guess they don't really need them since minotaurs are the top predators in the valley."

"How far away are the lucky bastards?" Friedr asked with a wicked grin.

"They'll arrive tomorrow morning, I think. They're making camp now," Edwin replied. "Well, it's about time to wake up Chris and Zan. We're going to have to fight, and we're tired."

"It's not always possible to have good rest prior to your battles," Friedr agreed. "But we've something on our side they're not going to be expecting at all."

"Oh yeah? What?" Edwin waited to hear Friedr's comment, with the slightly pessimistic expression he had been wearing all too often lately.

"We have three magic swords and an incredible amount of gross stupidity on our side," Friedr replied, smiling grimly. "That's worth something."

***

The day dawned, and the four companions were as rested as could be expected. "We'll alternate spell casting with the swords like we did when we were first starting out on this quest," Friedr said, handing out straws.

Zan pulled the lucky straw and Friedr the second straw.

Friedr reminded Zan, "We have to conserve our chi as much as possible."

"Just leave me some minotaurs to blow up, if you two so kindly will." Edwin's wry comment made Christoph laugh. "We're going to have to bury the dead between battles, or the rats will be all over us. We can't just leave a bunch of dead minotaurs lying around gathering crows."

"Our Friedr is rubbing off on you, Edwin. You used to be so civilized." Christoph's lopsided smile was bleak, but his thoughts were even bleaker. *They're trapped here because of my overweening pride. I was determined to heal a god and have that feather in my cap. Thanks to my inflated ego, they couldn't sneak away after doing the task I was supposed to do. They're going to die ugly, needless deaths because I'm the world's greatest jackass.*

He sat near the front of their copse, feeling terribly alone. *I'll have to help them with this battle. I'm going to have to bring some power to this or they won't prevail. I can strengthen them and heal them, but it won't be enough. Friedr was right all along last winter. I'll need to use my magic as a weapon, and I don't know how because I refused to learn. I have to do something.* He looked back toward Friedr, Zan, and Edwin, who were busy planning the battle. *I got them into this, and I have to get them out of it. I owe it to them.*

Christoph sent his senses out under the earth and found one of the farther squads was camped under a shelf of rock. On the spur of the moment, before he had time to think about it, he dropped the shelf on them. He didn't stay around to see what happened. As he returned to his body, he leaned over and emptied his stomach, shaking and heartsick.

Immediately, the others were there, checking him over, asking him what was wrong. Nothing, he tried to say, but instead he said weakly, "N...n...I think I just killed a squad of minotaurs."

Friedr looked at him, stunned and disbelieving. "How?"

Again, Christoph tried to say, it was nothing, and again, the truth just came out. "N...n...I dropped a shelf of rock on them, while they were camped under it," Christoph's voice shook. *Why can't I just say 'nothing'? Why do I have to keep on spewing the truth?*

On hearing that, Zan looked sick, like he was going to lose his breakfast also.

Christoph's voice broke and despair filled his eyes. "I.... Oh, goddess. I've never killed anyone before and I just killed ten of them!"

Edwin's face registered his shock. "Christoph, you don't have to do this. We can handle it." He felt ill. "We can do this, don't worry." He cast a spell for ease on Christoph, who just shook his head in misery.

"I got you into this. I have to help get you out. I have to." Christoph felt calmer. "I feel better now."

Zan sent his senses out on the wind to see what Christoph had done, and he found what used to be a squad of ten was now seven dead and two dying, with one seriously injured. He told them what he had seen.

"Christoph, when you decide to do something, you do it with a vengeance." Friedr was still uneasy at the thought of the mountain falling on the sleeping minotaurs, although he did not know why it troubled him. "I was planning on killing them anyway, but...."

Abruptly, Friedr realized it was the thought of Christoph of all people resorting to murder that bothered him.

In a an uncharacteristic move, Friedr knelt before Christoph, forcing him to look him in the eye. "Christoph, listen to me. I tried to make you into a warrior all winter. You kept telling me you couldn't do it, but I kept pushing you." Taking a deep breath, Friedr continued. "I was wrong to try to force you to become someone you're not. Forgive me for driving you to do this."

Christoph's eyes filled, and he just nodded mutely. Friedr clasped his shoulder, saying "We must finish gearing up."

"Well, Chris, at least now we're down to only about sixty against us." Zan sent his senses out looking for the squad closing in on them. "We're about to have company," he told the others, his eyes alight with anticipation. "Shall we welcome them properly?"

They met the squad in the field, and before they even clashed, Zan raised Stormbringer, calling "thunder walking." The sky darkened, and nervously, the advancing squad paused to look up. Suddenly from the darkened sky, lightning shot down, looking like a spider's legs, walking, striking, and killing four of the advancing minotaurs, while the others frantically danced and skittered away from the bolts that sought them. The six remaining quickly regrouped. Again, bolts of lightning stabbed down from the darkened sky, and the terrified minotaurs tried to run, only to be struck down. Four more minotaurs fell and only two remained. Friedr and Edwin quickly dispatched the lucky ones, striking them down as they stood gaping at their dead comrades.

"It wasn't even a fight. I counted ten minotaurs, and I only got to kill one," Friedr muttered. "Zander, that was pretty good. I wonder if you could actually control the weather with Stormbringer."

"I suspect not—that took nearly all my chi. Only fifty or so left to go," replied Zan cheerfully as he stabbed each lightning-struck minotaur through the heart. "I think if I try to hold the spell longer and concentrate more, I'll have better accuracy. I missed too many with the first one. With a spell drawing as much chi as this one does, I need to be accurate." He cleaned his blade with his rag and watched as Christoph dug a large hole with his earth magic.

Friedr, Zan, and Edwin rolled the dead into the hole, and Christoph buried them, leaving nothing but a bare spot to show they were ever there.

Then they all sat down and waited for the next group to arrive. "This time, I want to see what Dragonstorm can really do." Friedr's comment was echoed by all.

"You know, today is the fourth day of Scorpius. It should be moon dark tonight, so we'll be able to make our escape as well as possible," Edwin said. "It's hard to believe it's Scorpius already. But now we're heading home."

Chris and Zan napped while they waited for the next group. Too soon, Chris felt Edwin nudging him, waking him from his dream and saying, "Time to get ready, my brother. The next group will be here soon." For a moment, he was disoriented and wondered where he was. Then he woke fully and sat up with the scent of roses still on his mind, though the dream had faded. *What was I dreaming about? I wish I were home with Dane. I miss him terribly. But I've fixed it so it'll never happen without a miracle.* He looked at his companions, cheerfully planning the next battle. *They're miracle workers. Look at what they've done already. Maybe it'll happen. I must help them. I could cast a small earth spell and cause the enemy to stumble....*

Christoph surreptitiously checked everyone's health. Someone had healed him while he slept, and it felt like Friedr. Sitting in the shadows with the hood of his cloak pulled up, he strengthened the other three. Edwin turned to look at him, saying "Don't waste your chi on me right now, my brother. I thank you, but I'm fine, I promise." He smiled, and his eyes thanked Chris, but it was not the unconscious, honest smile he was once so famous for.

That slightly bitter smile had graced Edwin's face since they first left the Shadow Castle trying to make their aborted escape. It tore at Christoph's heart. When he looked at his companions, they all had changed so much from the men they had been. *Friedr no longer looks like a teenager. His face is all grown up now, even without his lamented beard. He's all hard edges and there's no softness there. Worry lines crease his forehead. Edwin still smiles, but his disappointment is clearly written on his face. He looks exactly like his father now. And Zan...oh Goddess! My son is afraid and worried for himself and dreadfully worried about me. Sons shouldn't have to worry over their father's safety. I haven't cared for him as well as I should have. I didn't put his needs ahead of my own when he was growing up. Now he's a man, and I brought him into this danger without planning an escape.* He was startled out of his self-deprecating thoughts by Edwin's hand on his shoulder.

"Talk to me, brother. Tell me what's on your mind." Edwin's blue eyes were full of concern.

Before Chris could answer nothing was wrong, his mouth betrayed him, saying "Everything's wrong and it's my fault." Then he smacked his forehead and added, "And I can't stop telling the truth." A shaft of filtered sunlight found its way through the thorn canopy, clearly displaying the personal guilt and despair on his once mischievous face.

Edwin placed his hands on Christoph's shoulders and leaned his forehead against his. Dropping all his barriers, Edwin laid himself out for Christoph to read. It was a shockingly intimate thing and something he would only do for someone he completely trusted. The action took Christoph completely by surprise.

Tears burned Christoph's eyes as he saw Edwin did trust him completely and loved him as if he were his brother by blood. In the face of Edwin's absolute trust, Christoph unwillingly lowered his own barriers until Edwin could see the pain and suffering he endured because of his actions, and the guilt and sorrow he felt whenever he looked at his companions. And finally, Christoph saw Edwin truly understood what had driven his actions and was terribly proud of his work in healing the god imprisoned in the throne of Mal Evol, believing Chris must have been led by the Goddess in performing such a task.

Edwin held no grudge, only deep friendship and love for him. Indeed, Edwin accepted their predicament as the natural consequence of serving the Goddess and was confident they would win and make good their escape. Raising their barriers, they separated themselves from each other's minds.

Once again casting a spell for ease on Chris, Edwin asked, "Will you be all right now?" His forehead creased with worry for his friend. "You always carry so much guilt, and you don't deserve to. The Goddess led you to the task she had for you, and you managed to do it, though you could've died from the poison. Only you could have achieved it, my brother, only you."

Edwin's concern touched Christoph, and he managed a nod and a lopsided smile. "Thank you, my brother. I'd say I don't deserve you, but you seem to feel I do."

"Christoph, you're too hard on yourself," Edwin replied. "Friedr feels exactly the way I do, but he could never lower his barriers that way for anyone, not even for Aeolyn. And Zan—Zan loves you as a son loves his father. He doesn't expect perfection from you. He just loves the man you are, failings and all. Yes, he feels compelled to protect you, but it's his nature. It's because you and Dane guided him well. Remember, at twenty, you were a very young father to have been given a son twelve years old, but you did your best and he knows it. Most men would've settled for simply being an older brother, but he needed a father, and you stepped up and did it well, though you were certainly not old enough to have been the good and loving father figure you've been to him."

Edwin looked at Christoph, and his face was full of confidence. "Trust me! We'll get out of this mess, you'll see. Our swords will help us immensely. Why else were we given them if not to even things up when we face D'Mal and his legions?" He clasped Christoph's shoulder encouragingly. "Now, we must greet the next wave of guests, as Zander says."

They went out to the center of the open area where Friedr and Zan were stretching and limbering up. "This bunch is about half a league out and running hard," Zan said. He looked much better, as if he had rested during his nap.

Edwin grinned, thinking, *Perhaps with the success of the last battle, he knows we can do this. If everything goes right I think we might survive this.*

Chapter 20 ~ Blood and Tears

"I don't know if I want to call any fire spells in this dry grass," Friedr muttered. "Boiling mud would be okay, I think," Friedr squared himself and began building a combination spell. As the squad of minotaurs raced toward them, he combined water, fire, and earth into a catastrophic, boiling mud, holding it until the last moment and then dumping it on them. Out of the screaming, flailing mass, three survivors struggled toward them, but Friedr followed the boiling mud up with a water attack, and down they went in the slippery grass. He then blasted them with a three-pronged thunder fist. No minotaurs survived.

"Dragonstorm is pretty useful when I need to make combination spells," Friedr noted in a clinical tone of voice as he looked at the last three, twitching corpses. "It did use a lot of chi to kill the ten of them."

"How awfully selfish of you, Friedr," Edwin censured him. "We didn't even get one to play with. Look at poor Zan, venting his bloodlust on the dead." Once again, Zander roamed through the bodies, stabbing each one through the heart.

"Well, I'm not going to have one rise up and surprise me again," Zan told them as he stabbed another corpse. "It wasn't a happy moment for me. I still have the scar."

"It was like watching a game of horseshoes, Friedr. I could sit in a lawn chair and watch you play all day." Christoph's quip elicited a laugh from everyone. He magically excavated another hole to bury the corpses.

The minotaurs were heavy, and rolling them into the hole took some effort. While the others did that, Zan checked on the other squads. Laughing and joking, Chris refilled the hole, covering the bodies and leaving no trace.

Zan returned to his body. "Now we're down to around forty. It looks like they're all going to descend on us at once, probably tonight. They're attempting to surround us." He called water to wash in, while Edwin called water to drink. Christoph shared out rations, and they settled down to clean up and rest before the next and hopefully final battle.

Friedr yawned, and said, "I think ten is about the limit, though, for the swords. It'll take the three of us combined to wreak any real havoc when the rest of them arrive." The others agreed, and they briefly planned their tactics for the next battle.

Christoph and Zan kept watch while Friedr and Edwin slept. They sat, watching the afternoon sky, talking quietly in low voices. "Do you ever think about how wonderful Dane's omelets are to come home to on a winter evening?" Zan asked, as he thought about the warm kitchen in Chris and Dane's home and how, until recently, he had lived there more than in his own apartment.

"I think of Dane and home all the time, Zan," Christoph agreed, with a catch in his voice. "He makes the most wonderful meals. They always look like tiny works of art, the way he arranges the food on the plates." He smiled. "We've been fortunate, you and I."

"I miss that kitchen," Zander said. "I miss the curtains and table linens you made. I miss it because it's home." He looked at Chris. "When I think of home, I think of your kitchen."

"You and Dane are my home," Christoph replied simply. "Wherever you two are will be home for me." He smiled at his son again, and said, "When we get done with this, I'm never leaving Dane again for any reason. He's my heart and my home."

"I think we always had the finest home in Neveyah. That's probably why I never properly left home, even though I technically have my own place." Zan laughed at himself.

"We never wanted you to leave home." Christoph was solemn, telling Zan the truth. "We weren't ready for you to grow up. But I think you'll be leaving us for Anna soon. Her family is much like ours. It's a good match."

Zan smiled broadly, thinking about Anna and what the future might hold for them.

Christoph's heart lightened, thinking about home and seeing Dane again. "I think Winter Solstice is my favorite holiday. Perhaps Anna and her parents will join us for Solstice this year. It would be wonderful having a large family. No one compares to Dane when it comes to preparing the Holy Day feast. And the Feast of Aeos—oh my! Those little sweets Dane makes are divine."

"Do you really think they'll come? I can't stop thinking about her," Zan replied, certain for once in his life about what the future may hold for him. "In her letters, she said she's been visiting Dane every day, and she thinks of me too, perhaps as often as I think of her. I'll ask her to bond with me once I'm sure she wants me as her husband. I'm not going to press her too hard and ruin it. I've finally learned something, I hope."

They sat companionably, reminiscing and enjoying each other's company until midafternoon. Edwin and Friedr woke and took up the sentry task, and Chris and Zan napped until just after sunset, when Edwin found the legions closing in on them from all directions.

They stashed their kits so they could grab them and leave quickly. After drinking some water, they walked out to the center of the open space and stood waiting.

Standing with their backs to each other, they faced out in a circle. "Do we all know what we're going to do?" Friedr asked. Their shields were firm and overlapped, with a spirit barrier tightly woven through, lacing them together, and Edwin had tied it all off.

"A little late to ask, don't you think?" Edwin's wry comment caused the others to chuckle.

"I'm going to call water to make the grass as slick as possible," replied Christoph, as he began building his spell. "A little earth mixed in should make it good and slippery. I'll wait until they're nearly here and then sneak it in under their feet."

"The rest of us are going to link and bring lightning and misery to these nice minotaurs," added Zan. "I, for one, am more than happy to add a little zing to their lives!" His wicked laugh made the others smile.

"Remember, we need to sustain the spell for as long as we can so they're panicked. We'll eliminate as many as possible before we have to resort to hacking away at them." Edwin paused to briefly send his senses out to see where the attackers were and returned. "When D'Mal shows up, we need to use the lightning needles as quickly and effectively as possible. Christoph can call water to put out any accidental brush fires, but we have to end this tonight."

"The pieces of minotaur will be too small to worry about burying," laughed Friedr. "But you'll have what you require in terms of fire and lightning. You won't have to wait for us to give you what you need."

"Zan and I'll maintain the shield/barrier against mental backlash if you have to deal with another D'Mal-controlled minotaur." Christoph shrugged. "Remember, there are forty of them and only four of us. If the pieces are too small, they'll take too long to bury, Friedr."

After a moment of shocked silence, Friedr burst out laughing. "I knew you'd learn to see it my way eventually."

"Now!" Zander snapped back into his body as the legions swarmed them from all directions. "They come now!"

Christoph released his water and earth spell, coating the grass with slick mud. Immediately, minotaurs began slipping and falling. One unfortunate fellow impaled himself with his own sword. Edwin, Zan, and Friedr linked and begin calling thunder walking, standing safely in the eye of the storm.

From the inky black skies, terrifying bolts of lightning lanced down, walking like a dreadful spider, stabbing and seeking victims, chasing and hunting down those panicked soldiers who tried to escape. With each bolt of lightning, another minotaur dropped, twitching on the bloody mud. Straining to maintain the spell as long as they could, they finally had to let it fade. Seven guards broke through to the companions, and they were too close to call magic against.

Keeping their backs together, the companions beat at their assailants, blocking and attacking. Swords flashed, and Christoph's staff whirled, tripping the enemy. He then set Earthbinder on the ground, and the earth shook wildly under the minotaurs in a ring around the companions, causing the enemy to stumble. Friedr gutted first one and then another as they tried to regain their balance. Edwin lopped off the hand of one and then his head and then gutted another one.

Zander raised Stormbringer and a roaring ring of wind expanded from the companions, blowing the enemy stumbling back far enough for Friedr and Edwin to call more lightning.

As the last attacker fell, Zan and Edwin quickly went around stabbing each fallen minotaur through the heart. Then they turned to healing their group.

"Why didn't D'Mal show up?" Friedr asked Edwin, his voice rough with pain. "We're sitting ducks right now. That took nearly all my chi. It doesn't make sense. Why did he force us to come back here if not to settle our differences once and for all?"

"I agree he's missed this golden opportunity, and that's certainly not the D'Mal we know and love," Edwin replied. "He must be planning something to take us by surprise. He's trying to lull us into a false sense of security. We have to hurry and get out of here."

Edwin was covered with blood, much of it his own. Only one laceration was serious, but Christoph had a bleeding head wound. Friedr cradled his left arm. It was broken, and he had multiple lacerations on his legs and arms. Zan was cut badly on his right arm and right thigh.

"We need to fetch a medical kit," Edwin said to Zan. "We'll have to link to do it. I can't reach that far by myself right now. We'll need a kit with a splint in it." Edwin and Zan knelt, drawing chi through their swords, fetching the medical kit to them. Fortunately, Aeolyn had made sure ointments and potions for pain were in each medical kit, along with the leg and arm splints.

The effort left them both drained despite drawing chi through their swords, but they stood up and turned to healing each other, only taking care of the most serious of the slashes and cuts. "We'll have to deal with the minor things later," Friedr said. "We need to hurry with this so we can get out of here."

Christoph set and splinted Friedr's arm, binding it securely to his side. Then he cast the healing spells and gave him a potion of willow for the pain. They looked at each other. "You have no chi," they both said at the same time and then laughed weakly.

"I don't have any chi to use for drawing through Dragonstorm," Friedr said worriedly.

"None of us has any," Edwin replied. "What little we had after the fight, we used for healing each other." He thought for a moment. "We need to get away from here now. The dead are going to attract rats, and we don't have the energy to bury them or fight right now. We need to rest." He looped the medical kit over his shoulder along with his own kit and turned to the others. "Let's just find a dry place as far away from here as we can and camp there." He began walking, stepping carefully in the blood and mud around the corpses.

The others followed him, Christoph bringing up the rear behind Zan. In the moonless night, the darkness was complete. Edwin could see well enough to walk carefully, and the others followed him, picking their way through the corpses littering the battlefield.

Suddenly, the hair on Edwin's neck rose, and the group felt as if an immense magic was being worked very near to them. "Oh, Goddess," muttered Edwin with a sinking feeling in the pit of his stomach. "Not now—I have no chi!"

Abruptly, a doorway opened directly on Christoph's heels. The light spilled out of it, illuminating the carnage they walked amidst. As it opened, they turned and saw a young, dark-haired man with a patch over his right eye silhouetted against brilliant tapestries and gilt furnishings.

Before anyone could move, he seized Christoph and pulled him into the portal, which promptly closed up as if it never was. As one, the companions reached to grab him back, but they were too late.

Christoph's pack lay on the bloody ground where it had fallen. He'd had the presence of mind to toss it toward Zan, knowing full well the quest-diary he carried must never fall into enemy hands.

"Christoph!" shouted Friedr, looking around for signs of the portal, "Christoph!"

"No! No! Where did he take him?" Zan was too frantic to be of any use. "No!"

Edwin gripped Leviathan and forced enough chi from the earth to send his senses to the Shadow Castle. It was empty except for the old man and woman.

"He's taken him to Serende, Tauron's world, I'm sure," Edwin said as he returned. "The keep is empty. There's no place like that there. I know every inch of it, and there's nothing resembling the room we just saw."

They felt the massive energies of another portal opening, but it felt farther away. Though they looked, they couldn't see where it was. "It's still open," Friedr said. "What's he using it for?"

Edwin once again used Leviathan to search the keep. "Oh, Goddess Aeos, he's sending troops directly into the barracks." He went back briefly to count. "Too many...far more than we can deal with now, and I guarantee they'll soon be heading this way."

"What about Chris?" Zan's voice was harsh with tears. "We can't leave him there. We can't." He turned to run to the castle, but Edwin grabbed him and wrestled him down, lying on him to hold him.

"No, Zan. He isn't here. Don't you get it? Christoph is beyond our help now. The portal took him to Tauron's lands. He's a world away from us now, and we can't help him." Zan fought Edwin, but still Edwin held him down. "He's lost to us!"

Struggling and shouting, "How am I going to explain this to Dane?" Zan finally just lay limply in the bloody mud beneath Edwin's body and sobbed. "I let him get kidnapped. I let it happen."

"No! None of us could've stopped it. D'Mal must have a use for him, or he wouldn't have set us up just so he could kidnap him. D'Mal planned it so we'd have no chi left to protect Chris. But now, we have to go. We can't help him."

Once Edwin was sure Zan was not going to try to run off, he helped him up. As Edwin stood and pulled Zan to his feet, a bell tolled, ringing through his every fiber, pure and sweet, yet unbearably sad. The bell rang and rang, and Edwin was consumed with the ringing, lost in the joy and sadness of Aeos's bell.

A distant voice, pure and clear, spoke, "My Beloved Hero has fallen. As has been foretold, he shall sow the poisoned seed, and the garden city will fall to him. Darkness falls upon the shadowed land. Long years of suffering and pain lie before us at his dread hand. Yet, when comes the Hero Foretold, the Beloved will rise up and free the land. On the day of redemption, you will know deliverance is at hand when poison gives way to spring. Seek now the Forbidden Road, lest you be lost also."

Sinking to his knees as the trance left him, Edwin could feel tears flowing down his face. Somehow, he knew the voice was heard in Aeoven. Father Rall had just had the same experience, as had Moran in Braden. "No…Goddess, no." He couldn't believe Christoph had been kidnapped, much less that he was to be broken and turned to evil.

"No." Zander's knees gave out, and he knelt in the bloody mud, stunned. "No, I won't believe it."

Friedr frantically looked for some sign of the portal, refusing to believe what he had just heard. "Christoph! Christoph! Bloody hell, where's the door?"

Horns sounded from behind the walls of the keep, alerting Friedr to the grave situation they were now in. "We have to get out of here." Friedr's urgency penetrated to Edwin. "Where's this Forbidden Road? Do you have any idea?"

"It's not too far from here. But, Friedr, it's a dreadful place." Edwin stood and pulled Zan to his feet. "I don't know if I have the courage to take that road."

"What sort of road is it?" Friedr picked up his kit with his good arm, slinging it over his shoulder. "How do you know of it?" Tears ran down his face, but he refused to acknowledge them.

"I believe it refers to the underground river my father and his companions escaped by when they saved the infant we know as Jaxon Sellsword." Edwin picked up his kit and handed Zan his own. Numbly, Zan took it. "Here now, Zan, let's put this on." He helped Zan put his kit over his unresisting shoulders. "You take Christoph's, and I'll carry the medical kit. I'll take yours too, Friedr. We must get to the east side of the keep. The cave entrance is there at the base of the cliff, below the castle."

"This is not good to hear," Friedr replied, wiping his tears with a bloody sleeve. "As I recall, you scouted it and found it a one-way trap with a waterdrake at the end of it." He chuckled bitterly, his chuckle ending on a sob. "This quest just keeps getting better by the minute." He bit back his sobs, but his shoulders shook. "Why? Why?"

"The prophecy says go, and so we must," Edwin said as he fought down his own tears. "We'll die here tonight if we don't leave now. I've no chi left and no strength for battle. At least we'll regain some chi as we travel." He led the way with Friedr following, while Zan just went where he was told to go, stumbling blindly along behind Friedr.

Going as quickly through the carnage as they could, Edwin led Zan and Friedr back toward the keep. After walking as far along the inner edge of the barren field as Edwin dared, they re-entered the thorn canopy, inching along the very base of the Shadow Castle. "If we enter here, it's the shortest route for you to have to crawl, Friedr."

Once they entered the thorn canopy, Friedr struggled, trying to crawl one-handed. Finally, he stopped and said, "Go on ahead. I'll catch up with you."

"No. We all go together," Edwin replied sharply. "We'll lose no one else."

Edwin took all five kits, and Zan helped Friedr as he struggled along. It was very slow going with Zan supporting him on his weak side and Edwin finding the trail and stopping frequently so Friedr could rest.

The struggle to move through the underbrush with his broken arm bound to his side took a terrible toll on Friedr, and he began to lag further behind, leaning on Zan more and more, hardly able to move. Soon, he became feverish and shaking, periodically disoriented and unsure of where he was.

"Edwin." Zan's tight voice penetrated Edwin's gloom. "Friedr's sick, but I can't tell what it is. It's serious, but it's not his arm." When Edwin checked Friedr, he found something was indeed wrong, but what it could be he had no idea.

"I'm fine. I'm just tired, that's all." Friedr gasped in pain. "I just needed to rest. I can go on now."

Edwin could tell from his voice alone that Friedr was not fine. He pulled as much chi through Leviathan as he dared and healed him as well as was possible, which helped for a while. "We can't stop here. They'll be on us any minute. The entrance to the underground river will be safe and will be a good place for us to hide and heal ourselves. Once we get there, we can stay just inside until we're healed and able to continue. It's only a little farther." Edwin kept telling Friedr, "It's not too far now. We can do this. We're almost there."

The last six hundred feet were hell for Friedr. With each movement, he was in terrible pain. He could barely travel, but somehow, he kept going. Twice more, Edwin cast healing spells on him, but toward the end of the journey, Friedr leaned completely on Zan's back, holding him with his good arm and struggling to keep his knees moving. Delirious, he raved about having to find Christoph.

Just as they reached the brush that concealed the cave entrance, Friedr slipped into unconsciousness.

Edwin left Zan and Friedr in the shelter of the thorn canopy while he checked out the cave. Finding it empty and dry, he returned for them, and together he and Zan half dragged and half carried Friedr into the cave.

As quickly as they could, they laid Friedr's bedroll out on the sandy floor. Edwin drew Leviathan and called a mage-lamp to light the cave so he could work on Friedr, setting the little flame to burn in a shielded corner, keeping the mouth of the cave dark.

Then they gently moved Friedr to his bedroll. Zan immediately began removing Friedr's armor and carefully cut his clothes off to undress him as best as he could, trying to cut along the seams. *I guess we'll have to sew them back together when he needs them again.* His heart was heavy at that thought. Sewing was Christoph's favorite task.

Calling water, Zan and Edwin scrubbed their hands as well as they were able under the circumstances. Finally, Zan laid Friedr's sword in its special scabbard next to him, touching his skin so the spells to enable healing could have the greatest effect.

Again, Edwin drew as much chi as he could from Leviathan. Entering the healing trance, he delved Friedr's body, finding his arm had to be reset and a gash on his left leg that had been deemed too minor to be healed had developed a raging infection.

Edwin's heart sank. "One of them had a poisoned blade, probably bear-dog saliva. I'll have to cleanse his blood and reset his arm." He gently cleaned the wound and purified Friedr's blood of the infection. Then he reset and re-splinted Friedr's arm, once again binding it to his chest. He knit the bone as best he could with his depleted chi. Casting pain-relief and healing spells, he searched Friedr for other wounds, finding several new gashes Friedr had gained from crawling through the thorn canopy. Edwin reached for chi but had none and emerged from the healing trance, lights flashing before his eyes.

Edwin's voice shook as he said, "I've no chi left, and he has three new gashes. With the infection in his system, we dare not leave them unhealed." Edwin looked at Zan for the first time, seeing he was in pain from several new, deep gashes of his own. Fortunately, none were infected. "I must stitch your gashes and apply some ointment first so you can concentrate. I'm sorry, but I'll have to use sutures. We can rest with our scabbards next to our skin, if indeed we can rest at all."

Edwin gently cleaned and sutured Zan's bloody gashes, applying ointment and bandaging them. Zan endured it with no sign he felt anything, thanking him for his care when he was done.

Once he was healed, Zan drew Stormbringer, drawing chi and entering the healing trance. Healing Friedr's gashes, he layered a dampening field over him.

He wove his spells into Edwin's, lacing them together the way Edwin had so often shown him. Finally, he tied them off and withdrew from the healing trance.

Edwin was shaking with fatigue. "Can you set the shields over us? I have no chi." His hands shook so badly he was almost unable to remove his own boots. He lay on his back, holding Leviathan in its sheath across his chest. *Hopefully, the spells wrought for healing will work for me,* he thought wearily as his eyes closed of their own volition. "I can't keep my eyes open, Zan. I just can't do it."

"We thought your immense capacity to store chi meant we'd never be in this sort of situation," Zan said, and his bitter tones grated in his own ears. "How could we have known it meant we'd need it all and still require more? Where would we be now without you, Edwin? You must sleep now. I'll keep watch. I can't sleep anyway." He watched as Edwin fell asleep almost as soon as his eyes closed.

Zan used the last of his chi, layering a barrier/shield over them and tying it off. *He's completely burned out. What will we do?* Zan fretted, looking at his friends, unable to use his sight to delve them and fearing he had missed something serious and one or both would die. *Aeos, Goddess...if you can hear me, we're in trouble.* His eyes filled with tears as the full weight of their situation became clear to him. *We're in big trouble.*

As the little mage-lamp faded away, Zan sat staring into the dark. Tears ran down his face, and he relived the horror of seeing his father taken by Stefyn D'Mal. The look of terror on Christoph's face was burned into his soul. He would never forget that sight for as long as he lived. *I wasn't fast enough. I swore I'd protect him and I failed.*

The still, bloody bodies of his companions were barely breathing. Edwin lay on top of his bedroll, having been too exhausted to crawl into it. Friedr too lay on top of his bedroll. Neither Edwin nor Zan had possessed the strength to put his unconscious form inside it. Both men looked as if they were dead or dying. Zan covered them with their cloaks, tucking Friedr's tightly around him, fearing that, being unclothed, he would catch a chill on top of the infection.

Zan was consumed by his own dark thoughts, and listening to the breathing of his two patients. The reality of their plight was brought home to him. He remembered the look on his father's face as he was pulled into the portal. *I was too slow. I let it happen.... Goddess forgive me, I was too slow!* Tears fell, and then dried on his grief-stricken features.

Chapter 21 ~ The Palace of Dreams, Serende

Christoph's captor dragged him through the portal, which then closed and vanished, pulling him into an ornate bedroom. Surprised, terrified, and exhausted from the battle, Christoph didn't even think to fight back, although he had the presence of mind to fling his pack toward Zan before the portal closed. At last he got a good look at his captor. "No!" his voice registered his shock and horror. "You're Stefyn D'Mal. You sent me those dreams. Oh, Goddess. I actually liked you." He was sick to his stomach with fear.

"I like you too, Christoph, very much. Even though you singlehandedly destroyed decades of my work and turned my father's throne silent to me, I still like you. But now you must be more than my friend." Stefyn's voice was as warm and compelling as it had been in his dreams. "You see, you made it so I can't read the land or people of Mal Evol unless I go there physically and sit on my father's throne. But it's not possible, since I must remain here and be a nursemaid to the children of Tauron. At least when I'm here, I'm sane more often than not. Now you must make right what you've done."

His grip on Christoph's shoulders tightened painfully. "Before anything else happens, you'll need to learn to love me. When I felt you sit on the Throne of Stone and Bone, I knew every part of you, and I loved you. You belong to me now." Stefyn's face betrayed his every emotion—love, lust, and something akin to fear all played across his face. "But even though I love you, you must change the throne back, undo what you've done. There will be pain involved, but it will bring us closer together." He squeezed Christoph's shoulders even more tightly until Chris was gasping from the pain. "Pain and pleasure are so closely related, don't you think?"

Abruptly, Stefyn's voice changed, becoming gentler, more genuine. He sounded concerned and worried as he said, "You must be brought to Tauron as I was. Since we are children of Aeos by birth, there is only one way to do it, and it will be hard on you. You must undergo the Ritual of Remaking. I'll perform the ritual and try to make it easier so it won't be as hard for you as it was for me. Still, there will be pain. I can't change that, though for you, I would if I could."

Using his strange magic, Stefyn shredded and tore Christoph's armor and clothes from his body. His armor was nothing but bits of metal and scraps of leather, and his clothes fell into rags on the floor. Even his boots were nothing but scraps in the pile. "You've no further need of these clothes, my love. Your new life begins here. There are clothes in the closet. I had them made especially for you. These rooms are yours, and mine are through that door." He gestured toward a door hidden in the shadows. "If you wish to wear a robe while you wait for me to return, you may, but you won't be leaving this room tonight. We'll share a meal here later, after I've finished my work."

Stefyn pushed Christoph onto the bed. Chris was stunned and terrified of what would happen next. Earthbinder clattered to the floor as Stefyn kissed Christoph with a lover's kiss. Unwanted, desire roared through Christoph's body, leaving him weak and angry at his own weakness.

"I have to finish my task, but I'll be back very soon, within the hour. You've much to think about, my love. You can make this easy, or you can make it hard." Stefyn released Christoph. "Either way, hard or easy, tonight you begin your new life with me." Turning, he left Chris dazed and deeply in shock. Turning, he exited through the door he had used as the frame for the portal.

The sound of the door locking behind his captor was loud in Christoph's ears.

Tears of rage and helplessness ran down Christoph's face. *I let this happen because of my conceit. I've caused more misery with my arrogant actions than I ever dreamed possible. We walked into the trap I helped to set. But, when he finds out only the four of us working together can undo what's been done in Neveyah, the others will be in danger. He'll break them just as he plans to do to me.*

Abbott Garran's words from so long ago came back to him. Garran had been talking to Edwin, who had repeated them to Christoph and asked him what Garran meant, but it was Christoph who was in dire trouble now. *D'Mal is a master of mental magic. You're a healer and most vulnerable to it. He can break you and turn you to his purposes.* Edwin didn't understand what Garran meant until Christoph explained it graphically to him. *I never thought I'd be facing this ordeal. Aeos, Goddess, help me. I know I'm lost through my own folly, but I must be able to protect them somehow.*

Christoph was sure he was no longer in Neveyah, feeling certain he must be in Tauron's world of Serende. He'd had no chi when he had been brought here, and he could sense it was slowly gathering in his augmentations, but it was different. He could sense his magic and knew he would be able to use it, though it would be diminished in its strength.

He also knew with a sickening sense of finality he had absolutely no hope of ever being rescued from this place. None of the others had been fit for working any magic whatsoever after the battle. Most importantly, none of them had the ability to make a portal like Stefyn had made, even if they had known *where* to make a portal go *to*. This time there would be no escaping his punishment. He was well and truly done for.

Christoph felt alone, so very alone. His captor was going to use his greatest weakness, his sensuality, to break him. If that failed, he would resort to other methods, but Christoph knew with a chilling certainty sooner or later he would be broken and Stefyn D'Mal would have the key to the shield that protected Neveyah.

With dismay, he knew Zan, Friedr and Edwin would soon pay the price for his folly. *They're all healers, and right now, they're sitting ducks. Once I crack and tell him the truth, D'Mal will* have *to kidnap the three of them to take down the shields we've set. By my own fault, I'm under a geas to speak only the truth. He has only to ask, and I'll tell him what we've done and how to undo it. But I can't blame the geas because I would've done so anyway. Oh, I would've struggled a bit, but in the end, I would've given him what he wants. He can make me do anything.*

Christoph's mind ran in circles like a rat in a cage. *I won't leave here until he's made me into his creature. He's made clear his intention to have me either by rape or with my consent. I've regained some chi, but I should be able to draw what I need through Earthbinder. Magic must work differently here. What can I do to stop Stefyn from using me to destroy Neveyah?*

From somewhere, the memory of a day from six years before came to his mind. It was a memory of Marya, frantically begging him to cast a spell of forgetting on her so she couldn't give them away. As he remembered, he knew what he had to do. *It's not impossible. I know we can't heal ourselves, but this isn't healing, and it requires so little chi to cast I'll have plenty for this task. I must simply have courage. I must do this for Dane and for Zan. I just need courage.* The thought of Dane nearly broke him again, but he forced himself to completely focus on what he knew he had to do.

Unfortunately, I can't erase my skills and abilities, so he'll still be able to use me for his purposes. But I can erase the knowledge of who I am and where I've come from. I can erase what I know of what we've done. He bit back a sob. *I'll lose my memories of Dane and Zan, and everyone I know and love.* Christoph's head fell into his hands, and he wept as the full impact of what he had to willingly give up sank in. It was his own fault, all because he had been so intent on healing the throne no matter what the cost to the team and to the quest.

And now he knew what the personal cost to him would be. It was almost more than he could bear. Christoph trembled and tried desperately to firm up his resolve. "O Goddess, Aeos, this is so hard!" His voice was thick. "I'm never going home after all." Tears flowed down his cheeks, but at last, Christoph pulled himself together. Speaking firmly to himself, he said, "This is it, Christoph. This is where you act like a man and protect your family. Friedr and Edwin would do it without a second thought. Just do it."

Resolutely, he picked Earthbinder up from the floor and drew as much chi through it as he could muster. Still speaking aloud, he said, "Edwin always told me many impossible things are possible when you have great need. Aeos, Goddess, if you can hear me in this place, I beg of you to grant me the strength to do this one last thing for you and for Neveyah." Sitting cross-legged in the center of the bed with Earthbinder on his knees, he cleared his mind and formed the spell, a more massive spell of forgetting than he had ever cast.

The spell would completely sweep away his memories, all of them. It was a spell of such magnitude as no healer would ever have a need to cast, and indeed, it might have been the first time such a thing had ever been attempted, but these were not normal circumstances.

Channeling directly through Earthbinder, he built his spell meticulously, layering it with a spirit barrier combined with a water/earth shield, lacing them more intricately than he would ever have thought he could do. Then Christoph reversed the buffer so the spell of forgetting would settle next to his skin and be held in place by the shield and buffering. It would be undetectable by anyone else, and he would never know he was carrying it.

Instead of letting go of the spell, he held it away from himself for just a while longer while he tied the whole combination off. It would remain powered by his ambient chi, the same chi that existed in all living things. Carefully, he gave an extra twist to the ties. Because it was not tied to his magic-chi but was instead tied to his life-chi, the spell would fade only when he was dead.

Finally he cleared his mind of everything except for the mental image of Dane. *I love you, Dane. You were my one true love. I'll always love you.* With the image of Dane as the last thing he saw, Christoph released the spell of forgetting, and it settled over him, unbreakable, undetectable, and fitting like a glove.

His eyes turned blank, and then he was slightly confused.

The man sat on the bed. Absently, he noticed he was naked, but he paid no attention to his state of undress. He'd just become aware of something odd, a thing that took all his attention. He had suddenly realized he didn't know where he was or how he'd come to be there. Even more strangely, he had no idea who he was. He had the suspicion he'd just lost something extremely important, although he couldn't imagine what it could be. He pondered the problem, oblivious to everything around him.

Behind him, a door opened and a young, dark-haired man with a patch over one eye stepped into the room, locking the door behind him.

The man on the bed didn't notice the intruder. He was lost, wondering what it was he'd been thinking about only a moment before. Completely disoriented and suddenly fearful of what it could mean, he sat on the strange bed, trying desperately to find some memory, some clue of who he was and why he was there. He was so utterly engrossed in this problem he didn't even hear the man who spoke so softly to him.

***

In the darkness of the cave, Zander grieved alone, unable to imagine Christoph going to the Dark God Tauron's side willingly. It made him nauseous, knowing the ways a healer could be broken. Every healer knew the risk, but no one ever believed it would happen to him. He was filled with fears and myriad emotions, and frightened Friedr would die because he was terribly ill and most certainly would *not* be well soon, despite their best attempts at healing him. Sitting cross-legged, Zan held Stormbringer in the bespelled scabbard, trying to absorb strength and some chi from it.

He was low on chi, nearly burned out, but Edwin was even worse, and Zan was terrified that he might well be burned out. If Edwin did recover, it would take most of a day to regain his abilities, even with the aid of Leviathan. Despite his inability to fully use his healing empathy, Zan could tell Friedr was not properly healed, and he could only pray that what they had managed to do that night would be enough to contain the damage until Edwin had recovered his abilities.

Miserably, Zan looked at Edwin, who shivered as he slept, holding Leviathan in its scabbard across his chest. He covered Edwin more closely with his cloak and pulled his own cloak around himself. *I don't know what to do to save Friedr, and I don't know how to get Christoph back. I can't even delve Edwin or help him in any way. Goddess, Aeos, I don't know what to do!*

Zan knew he was weeping again, but somehow he didn't care.

***

Edwin stood in the ornately gilded room he had glimpsed briefly through the portal, fully aware he was dreaming. Beautiful tapestries graced the walls. He felt sure it was a room in a palace. His eyes were drawn to a huge, canopied bed in a darkened corner. Unable to move or speak, Edwin saw Christoph, naked and seated cross-legged in the center of the massive bed. Earthbinder lay across his knees, and his augmentations were faded and dull. The pile of rags and bits of metal on the floor bore testament to the violence with which his clothes had been torn from him. His eyes were blank. To Edwin, he appeared stunned and confused, numb to his surroundings.

His slight frame bore many cuts and bruises from the battle, and his ribs were clearly showing. Christoph had always been small, but he looked frailer than ever, clearly appearing in poor health. Edwin was heartsick as he realized he couldn't help him in any way. He could only mutely watch. *Oh, my brother. I didn't realize how thin and tired you'd become. The last few weeks have been so hard on you. Forgive me for my anger. You did the right thing. The Goddess, had her hand on your heart.*

A movement of air beside Edwin freed him to turn his head. A mist formed, and then Christoph stood next to Edwin, looking compassionately at himself on the bed. He wore his old moss-green healer's leathers that they had left behind in Braden. His slender form and elfin features looked exactly the way they had when Edwin first met him so long ago. For some reason, that broke Edwin's heart more than anything. *This is Christoph's ghost, come to comfort me.* Tears rolled down Edwin's cheeks. *I hurt him badly when I was so angry at him. I was unreasonable about the risk he took, when what he did was the will of Aeos, easing Ariend's pain.*

The ghost looked up at Edwin, who still could not speak. "Be easy, my brother. I always knew you didn't want hurt and anger to come between us, though you were right to feel it. I did wrong by not telling you what I was planning. Whatever was wrong between us has long been forgiven." His old mischievous spark was reflected in his face, and Edwin was deeply moved by the familiar elfin features and the impish grin.

Seeing that smile, Edwin's heart was sore, and he was shocked by a realization. *Christoph stopped smiling the day he healed Ariend. We all changed that day.*

"Aeos has granted me this time with you out of her love for us all. I've one last duty that must be accomplished, though it's a bitter charge. When this task is complete, I'll go to sit beside Aeos's Great Hearth. Her love will comfort me, as she comforts all who pass on in her service." The humor faded from the ghost's face, and he became serious. "The task that lies before me is to tell you what this man did to save Neveyah and to protect his son."

Speaking as if he were telling a story of someone else's deeds, the ghost continued. "Be assured Tauron won't gain Neveyah, though you will lose Braden to this unfortunate man. When you return to Neveyah, the Temple must save all they can of the people of Braden, for within two seasons of your return, this man will be on their doorstep with an army behind him. Fully aware of what lies in store for him at the Dark God's hands, he's done what he can to protect Neveyah. He willingly sacrificed himself to ensure the three of you don't share in his terrible fate, because only the four of you working together can undo what's been done. D'Mal kidnapped him for just that purpose, believing Christoph alone is responsible. Do you understand what he's done for you?" Edwin nodded, mutely, sick at the thought of Christoph's sacrifice.

"He has no memory of you or anyone he ever loved. The man he was has died. Tonight this man will be reborn to a new life. This has been written in the heavens and must happen."

Edwin's heart sank upon hearing these words.

"He knew it was only a matter of time until D'Mal would break him. He willingly gave up his most treasured memories so you wouldn't be betrayed and so the shield won't be broken. Tell this to the people he loved. The last memory he held was of his love for Dane.

"Tell Dane and Zander that Christoph is dead, because the man you see there is no longer Christoph Berryman. The only life he will ever know will begin in a few moments. His only memories start here in this room, where he'll be reborn to serve Tauron and Stefyn D'Mal, though not quite as Stefyn had hoped." His grim smile was pleased. "He'll serve D'Mal, but he'll always serve Neveyah, though great evil will come of his perverted service. Still, because of his sacrifice, Neveyah won't fall to Tauron.

"Tell Father Rall that a mage who is a healer can cast a forgetting upon himself, if he's careful to hold it un-released until his barrier/shields are completely built and tied off. You do it this way: you must reverse the buffer and allow the spell to rest against your skin when you let it settle around you. By using your own ambient life-chi, you can power the shields to hold it so you'll never know you're under a spell of your own making. It'll be undetectable. When you tie it off, you must use the special, extra, little twist your father developed, and then it'll last until you die. Unfortunately, it won't erase your powers or abilities, but it *will* erase what you know of your life until that moment. It'll erase who you are, and it's irreversible."

The dream shifted and the door behind them opened. Stefyn D'Mal entered the room. His skin had a dull, grayish tone to it. Perhaps because of the lack of unfocused chi swirling around him, he appeared to Edwin's eyes as if he were at least temporarily sane. He had obviously just finished a great working, most likely the sending of the legions to the Shadow Castle.

The ghost at Edwin's side observed dispassionately, "Truly he is a great mage to work two such massive spells in one evening from so great a distance."

The man on the bed looked at D'Mal incuriously, still too wrapped up in his own confusion to really notice anything. As he undressed, D'Mal spoke to the captive Christoph, but Edwin could not hear his words. Then Stefyn climbed onto the bed. Edwin desperately wanted to look away, to not see what he was about to witness, but he was held there. "One moment, and then you can leave," Christoph's ghost said. "This is what you're here for. Listen...."

Gradually, Edwin could hear the conversation. "...your soldiers are dead. I'm sorry it had to be that way," Stefyn's silky voice told Christoph as he put his arms around him, kissing his shoulders. Christoph shrugged him off, completely uninterested in anything but his own problem. Closing his eye, D'Mal healed Christoph of his injuries. All the old bruises, cuts, and slashes simply vanished, leaving no trace. Still, Christoph did not appear to notice the gesture, and D'Mal kept talking. "They were brave soldiers who served you well. I should be so fortunate as to have soldiers as fierce and loyal to me as they were to you, but they couldn't be allowed to leave the battlefield alive. I'm sure you understand why."

Although he was surprised and awed by the ease with which D'Mal had healed Chris despite his own exhaustion, Edwin was angered by the spell of compulsion D'Mal used so heavily on Chris. He strained to hear the conversation.

"Now you must learn to love me, and then you must rule the land you subverted. *You* must rule in my stead since I can't change it back while I must languish here. I'm unable to restore it until you tell me how you did it. So, my love, how did you do it?" D'Mal kissed the back of his neck, but again, Christoph did not respond.

He turned Christoph to get his attention. "You mustn't ignore me, my love. It's not polite." Chris just looked at him in surprise, yielding, his eyes changing from confused to hurt.

"Christoph? Eh…what is this?" Stefyn looked into Christoph's eyes and said "No! What could have caused this?" He closed his eye, obviously delving Chris's mind. "Someone triggered a forgetting on you, my love. It's very delicately done. Perhaps it was one of your soldiers as I took you? Or, more likely, my spell to unclothe you triggered it. The spell was wrought to keep you from speaking what you know if you were trapped by a mage." D'Mal fell silent, and his face contorted with pain as he attempted to heal Christoph's memory, though he was nearly burned out.

"An adept set this spell. I can't reverse this to regain your memories, though I've many useful skills in this area." His voice was no longer as silky, as it was when he used his voice of compelling. Instead, it was honest and raw with emotion.

Stefyn sat looking at the wall, obviously stunned. His voice was thick with pain and he spoke as if to himself, "I thought I'd found a real companion. I liked your wry wit so much when we met in your dreams. Still, we will be lovers, and now you won't reject me as you did. Your bondmate won't stand between us." His voice caught. "But now it will be much more difficult for you. Now, Tauron himself will have to remake you, and I can't change this. I'd hoped to make it easier for you."

Tears filled Stefyn's one good eye, and he turned, holding Chris close to him. "I wish someone had been so kind to me as to cast a forgetting. Memory is a cruel mistress here in this place—I think I'm so much happier when I'm mad." His face could only be described as haunted as he held Christoph.

"Who are you?" Christoph asked Stefyn. "What's your name?" His eyes now were full of confusion.

A moment of pained silence ensued before the answer followed. "I'm Stefyn. I'm to teach you what it means to become a priest of Tauron," Stefyn replied, emotion raw in his voice, obviously making up his mind as to how he should handle the situation. "You've no history, only a future. You've just been born."

"Where am I?" Anger touched Christoph's confused eyes as he looked at Stefyn, demanding an answer. "I don't know who I am." Fear and confusion warred upon his face. "Why don't I know who I am?" Barely controlled panic combined with his rising anger to color his voice. "Who am I?"

D'Mal was silent, struggling with his emotions. Loss and resignation were written on his beautiful face. "Lourdan. Your name is Lourdan." His face crumpled, and tears flowed down his cheeks. A sob escaped him, but he bit it back. "It means 'lost one.'"

Christoph was silent, and then he repeated the name, "Lourdan. It's true, I'm lost. My name is Lourdan, but I didn't know. Why didn't I know?"

"You offered up your past and your memories to Tauron. Now you are to train as an acolyte."

Silently, Stefyn wept at the loss of the one he had hoped to make his lover, unable to continue.

As he struggled, the ghost spoke to Edwin. "Stefyn visited me in my dreams after I forged a connection with him in the process of healing the throne. The poison itself forged the connection to me. He could find me anywhere. I didn't realize he was manipulating my dreams. I could never remember them upon waking, and what little I did remember…well, I thought I was suffering from missing Dane. When I met him in my dreams, I liked him. We laughed at the same things and had so many common interests. He was witty and charming. I didn't know who he was, though I should have. I suspect he used his skills to encourage me not to recognize him. He even told me he'd lost his former love to a mage who was stronger than he was. We enjoyed each other's company immensely. But though he tried each time to seduce me, I didn't succumb to his temptations because even in my dreams, my heart saw only Dane. Still, he recognized I found him attractive. I was flattered by his desire, and I'm a weak man. With his gifts of empathy, he was fully aware if he could have me just once, I'd be easy to break.

"He had to force me to go back to the keep so he could make a portal to kidnap me, as his ability is limited to the keep. This is why we were herded back there. When he opened the portal on the battlefield, it was at the furthest limit of his ability. It took as much from him as did the second portal that he held open for twenty minutes to send seventy-five guards to the keep.

"His ability to make portals is limited to the Shadow Castle because the power to make one comes from the Throne of Stone and Bone. Only one person may pass though at a time, so all must be ready when he sends his guards through. Thus it's a task he doesn't do lightly. He thoroughly planned every step of this, starting the moment I drew his attention. You'll be relieved to know he can't walk through a gateway of his own making, which is why he had to open it on my heels and snatch me away as he did."

At last recovering himself, Stefyn D'Mal spoke softly, gently holding Christoph. "You have no memories because you've just been born. You're not alone. You're my companion, and I love you," Stefyn told him, as tears rolled down his cheeks, his eye patch damp. "As to where you are—you've been brought to Hell, my poor Lourdan—though I truly wish it were otherwise. Now *He* will have to remake you, and it'll be hard. I regret you must suffer, but it's necessary, to know Tauron's love. You've been born to rule in Mal Evol in my stead since I can read the throne through you. But for tonight, we won't worry about these things. I'm so sorry you're lost and alone, my love. I'll be with you."

"My name is Lourdan. Yes." Lourdan's voice was frightened, though his anger had gone. "Don't leave me alone here. I don't know this place."

"We're never alone. Tauron is always with us. You'll see. All will be explained to you. He will show you the way just as he did with me, and you'll live forever young with me, but...I've done you no favor, Lourdan. I'll teach you what you must know before you undergo the Ritual of Remaking, so we'll have a few weeks before your ordeal, but...oh my poor love, it'll be so very hard. You'll be changed...as I was." Stefyn could no longer speak.

Edwin felt a tugging on his sleeve. The ghost looked up at him, and his dark eyes were unbearably sad. "You must return now, my brother. I won't see you again. Remember what you've seen and tell my son and Father Rall. Tell them I'm truly dead, for I'll see none of you again. Tell Dane he was and will always be my one true love. I set him free to find peace and happiness if he'll allow it into his life. He mustn't grieve for too long."

Then the ghost turned as if hearing a voice, and as he did, peace and a quiet radiance replaced the grief, lending his face an unearthly beauty. "I must go now to her Great Hearth, where Aeos will comfort me until the day of my redemption. On that day I will return to complete the task set before me." His transcendent smile comforted Edwin as nothing else had in the tragedy he had witnessed.

Christoph's ghost shone like an angel, shining so brightly Edwin's eyes were dazzled with his beauty. Then he faded to rainbow motes, leaving Edwin to watch Stefyn D'Mal weeping disconsolately, holding a lost and fearful man whose name was Lourdan.

Chapter 22 ~ Melancholy in the Dark

Edwin was abruptly released from the dream. His eyes opened, and with great difficulty, he sat up.

"Edwin, you need to rest I'm keeping watch. Friedr is a little better, and I'm regaining chi." Zander's voice was raw. "We need you too much. Rest now."

"Zan, I've been sent a true-dream. I spoke to Christoph." Edwin was not sure how to tell Zander what he had to. "I think you'll need to see what I've seen, if you'll allow me to open myself to you." Edwin's face was full of anguish. "It'll be hard to watch."

"I'll gladly open myself to you, if that's what I have to do to learn what's happened to Christoph," Zan replied, fear and hope warring in his heart. "I have to know for my own peace of mind."

"I don't find this knowledge comforting," Edwin told him grimly. "I'm destroyed by it. But it's important for you to see." He knelt before Zan and placed Zan's palm upon his forehead. Lowering his barriers, he opened his mind.

As Zander saw the dream and the message, he trembled under the weight of his grief, but didn't weep. Edwin maintained the contact, letting Zander's grief wash through him, sharing his own sorrow with Zan. Then he shared his love of Christoph with Zan so he might know how beloved his father was to Edwin. Last, he shared his compassion for Lourdan, who would only know misery and who would, in turn, create much suffering before he was done.

At last Zan pulled away but left his barriers down. "Thank you for letting me into your mind to see the truth of what happened to the man who was my father." His voice caught as he said, "It'll bring Dane no comfort though."

"I know, Zan. But at least we know what happened." Edwin tried to find peace and failed. "I don't think I'll be able to sleep now. I'd like to sit with you a while and try to regain some peace of mind."

"I'm glad of your company. 'In the light and warmth of Aeos's love for us all, let us talk of the life now passed to sit beside Her Great Hearth,'" Zan said simply, using the time-honored formula the bereaved in Neveyah had used for generations when sharing the death of a loved one with friends and family. "My father died today. Let us talk of the man he was and how he shaped me." He found something comforting about the formality of the familiar litany.

They sat watching over Friedr in much the same way Christoph and Edwin once sat watching over Marya on a quest long ago. Edwin told Zan of that time, and they shared their memories until the dawn's light filled the entrance of the cave. At last, Edwin slept next to Friedr while Zan kept watch, maintaining the shields over them and bolstering the pain-relief spells they had layered over Friedr.

***

It was sometime around noon, and Zan finally lay dozing fitfully next to Friedr. Edwin sat at the entrance of the cave, scouting the area, using the minimum of chi he could. Edwin now knew just how close they had come to being captured the previous night. He eavesdropped on the squad of minotaurs watching the cave entrance, learning the rest of the squads were ringed about the valley in the hope they would try to escape.

We're committed to walking the Forbidden Road now whether we want to or not, he thought with a sense of gloom. He could see no way to escape through the valley now. They had no choice but to take the fearful path down the underground river. The soldiers were happily camped, laying wagers on how long the three fugitives would survive once they made the decision to go down the long, dark road. Fortunately, none of the squads would enter the cave for any reason. They feared it too much.

Edwin cast a spell of aversion and tied it to the opening of the cave to make sure the squads and every other creature avoided their shelter. It was a simple ward that worked on most large creatures, and was one they frequently used when camping.

He checked the area both inside the cave and down the dark road a long way and found no creatures other than the usual cave denizens. Sending his senses out, he called water from the high clouds, filling the jugs with drinking water. Then he concentrated on calling water for bathing. *Cold water is better than no water at all. But Friedr's wounds need to be bathed, and he won't be able to tolerate icy water, as feverish as he is,* he thought. Gradually the basin began to fill with ice-cold water. *I need to find a way to warm it, but I don't see how we can keep a fire going without tempting the legions to look at us more closely.*

As he called the water and wished for a hot bath, he remembered the first night he met Christoph and Friedr. *We were all so young then,* he thought. In his mind's eye, he could see them laughing as they sat in the men's baths at the Lion's Share Inn in the town of Wister. He suspected every small task would remind him of Christoph in some way.

As he sat contemplating the cold water, it suddenly occurred to him that Friedr's mage-lamp trick might be adaptable to heat water for any number of uses from cooking the dried soup to making hot water for tea and bathing. The little flames didn't give off smoke or flicker, but they did give off heat. Feeling immensely better at having an actual task to do, he looked around the cave until he found enough rocks to make a small fire ring and then set three mage-lamps in the center, tying them off to the ambient chi of the rocks. After looking around a bit more, he found two flat rocks to set the pots on, and with a bit of trial and error, he had the cookpot merrily cooking a nourishing soup made from the dried-soup rations and the teakettle full of hot water. The cold soup hadn't been terrible, but it was so much better when it was hot.

After bathing Friedr, Edwin drew Leviathan. Focusing his will, he built a barrier within Friedr to contain the infection in his leg. It was the best he could do if he was to conserve his chi for the surgery he and Zan would most definitely have to perform that evening.

Edwin bathed himself as well as he could, but he was unable to reach his own wounds. He knew they should have been looked at, but Friedr would need all the healing skill Edwin and Zan could muster, and he would also need the herbs and ointments. Friedr's wounds were terribly serious, and he worried that, despite his efforts to contain the poison, Friedr would lose his leg.

The spells he and Zan had already cast in an effort to keep the infection under control were still working, and would have to do until he had regained enough of his chi to properly rid Friedr's body of the poisons from the bear-dog saliva. The infection still lurked within his system, and much of the tissues of his leg were becoming necrotic. The healing he and Zan would perform was a major surgical procedure, and they would both have to be fully tranced for it. It would be a miracle if they could do it without killing him.

Edwin still had not regained enough chi to properly heal Friedr and wouldn't have the full ability even with the help of Leviathan for at least a few more hours, but he should be wholly able to work by the time Zan was awake and ready to assist him. *I've nearly burned myself out, and now I can't draw chi very well. It's like my ability has been bruised.*

To care for his own wounds, Edwin would just have to rely on the healing power of Leviathan's scabbard, thinking, *It could be worse. I could've been poisoned like Friedr.*

Edwin washed the dirty clothes from their kits and spread them out to dry, then carefully cleaned Friedr's wound again. Friedr's leg was no better, and despite Edwin's efforts to contain the poison, it was gradually getting worse.

Sitting next to Friedr, Edwin held his hand, praying and trying to absorb the events of the previous two days. *I wish...I hope I'll see my son again. I hope I live to hold our new baby.* He found himself daydreaming about Johnny. Thinking of Marya and a home full of children and laughter warmed him and gave him strength. *Friedr has a new baby on the way too. We will make it home. I had the true-dream. Jaxon, Friedr, Zan, and I waited at the door, and we were old men. I know we can do this. I know what I have to do to make it happen.*

Feeling rather like he was invading Friedr's privacy, he retrieved the surgical instruments from Friedr's kit and prepared to make things as ready for the surgery as he could. *I can't make this clean enough. We don't have enough clean bedding, but somehow we'll make this work. We have no choice but to work with what we have.* He washed Friedr's wounds again and checked his heart rate and breathing.

When Zan finally awoke in the early evening, feeling stiff and sore, he was amazed to find a merry fire warming the cave. Though he didn't mention it, he had trouble moving his head, both from seriously pulled muscles and because of the gashes on his neck. Although Edwin had sutured them and put a healing salve on them the night before, they were deep and painful, and his shirt was stained where they had broken open again.

Edwin heated warm water for Zan to bathe in and made hot soup for his breakfast. "This is wonderful, and completely unexpected, Edwin," Zander told him gratefully. "You're always so good at finding practical uses for things." He sighed in relief as Edwin healed him. "Thank you. I appreciate your care, but now we need to save your chi for Friedr."

"I've regained enough chi to enable me to draw on Leviathan to replace the little I just used, though I grant you my ability to draw is limited. But you were bleeding again, and we need your strength and ability since I can't do this alone." Edwin drew chi through his blade. "I don't want your wounds to become septic. We've a serious matter to deal with for our brother. He's not much better than he was last night. In fact, he may be worse. I've bathed his wounds and built a containment barrier around the infection, while trying to conserve my chi for this evening's task. I boiled the surgical kit and prepped him as well as possible under the circumstances, so when you're ready, we'll heal him properly. I'll do the actual surgery, and you'll support me and keep him sedated, using your very unique skills. We have to get rid of the infection completely this time, or we'll lose him."

After Zan had eaten and bathed, he and Edwin knelt and linked with each other to delve Friedr's body, once again cleansing his blood. This time, Edwin had the strength to go to the source of the infection and eradicate it. Once the poison was gone, they turned to removing the dead flesh surgically. The infection was from a slash he had received on his left leg just above his knee. Friedr would lose much of his muscle, but because of the healing they were able to do the previous night and the containment field Edwin had been able to build earlier, the bone was still healthy. He would not lose his leg, though he would be severely crippled and would never be the same. Somehow, they would deal with his debilitation when the time came.

Edwin incised the poisoned flesh and muscle away, using his magic to staunch the bleeding and his surgical skills to cut away the flesh. He then healed what he was able to save and continued removing that which was beyond his skills. Zan maintained the pain-relief spells, closely monitoring the delicate balance that kept Friedr unaware of the surgery, while ensuring his heart did not forget to beat nor his lungs to breathe. Periodically, they drew chi through their swords.

Zan carried most of the spells toward the end, and Edwin lent his support, saving his chi for the final, most important part of the surgery. At the end of the procedure, Edwin had to regenerate Friedr's skin so it covered and sealed the terrible wound. It was a spell Edwin had to carry alone as it was an advanced technique Zan had only observed once before. Edwin had to stop and draw chi through Leviathan three times before they were done.

As they finished the task and looked at their work, it was clear that even with what they'd accomplished Friedr wouldn't be able to move without assistance for many days. His leg was horribly scarred from ankle to thigh. He'd lost much of the flesh and muscle he once had. Although Edwin had tried to make the wound as neat as possible, it was lumpy and ropy. The scars would be fresh-looking for some time.

"This'll be very painful for a while, at least for the first few days when we do therapy on it. I fear it'll never be pretty, and he won't be able to fully use his leg ever again," Edwin told Zan. "We had to remove too much poisoned flesh. But I think I can make a brace to help him get around while we try to make our escape. I had a true-dream long ago in which I saw him as an old man, his leg in a brace and leaning on a staff. I know what I need to do."

"I can help with the pain for the most part. I won't alleviate all of his pain, or he'll do too much and damage himself." Zan's brow's knitted in thought. "The road home will be rough, and he'll have to be careful how he sets his foot. Once we're back on level ground, I'll do more."

Using both the herbal remedies and their healing skills, they repacked the rest of Friedr's wounds and re-bandaged them. Then they rested a while to regain their chi before they checked on his arm and worked on knitting the bones a bit more, replacing the splint so the bones would have the opportunity to strengthen properly. They withdrew from the healing trance and saw he was resting much easier and was no longer fevered. Last, they placed Dragonstorm in its sheath next to his skin.

Drawing chi from their swords again, they rested again and kept watch on Friedr, maintaining the pain-relief spells and then tying them off. Then they both made liberal use of the hot water available to them and were able to really rest, being clean and well fed for the first time in weeks. Zan reset the mage-lamps, and Edwin napped next to Friedr, his senses extended over him, but resting and regaining his chi. It was a technique first-year journeyman healers who had to spend long days and nights watching over gravely ill patients learned.

While Edwin napped, Zan carefully went through his father's kit, setting aside everything they would need, and putting Christoph's spare clothes into a pile. *I don't know what to do with these. They're too small for anyone else to wear but I don't want them to just be abandoned,* he thought. *I guess we can fetch them to the cache nearest Braden.*

Under his spare shirt, Zan found Chris's sewing kit. It was a flat, wooden box with a carved lid. As Zan sat holding it, he was overwhelmed with grief once more, but resolutely, he put it in his pile to keep with them, his hand lingering on the ornate top. *He's always had this kit, since before he came to Aeoven when he was a bard-in-training. Everything he needed was in this little box. He often used it for quick repairs at home.* He paused, looking at the well-stocked kit. *I can't remember one night on this journey that he didn't have to repair some damage to our clothes. Now I'll take up the task and try to make my father proud.*

At the bottom of Christoph's pack he found his father's notebooks and pencils. Leafing through them, his eyes burned, but he continued examining things. Carefully, he tucked the notebooks into his own pack, knowing he was not ready to read them yet.

Later, when Friedr was better, the three of them would read through them, perhaps, but not now. After he had repacked his own kit with everything of his father's that he was going to keep with him and set aside things for the others to carry, he put the rest back in Christoph's kit.

When Edwin woke from his nap, he found Zan seated before the fire, mending Friedr's shirt. He fought down a wave of emotion upon seeing Zan sitting cross-legged in the same pose, performing the familiar task Chris had always done, with the sewing kit open beside him. Zan saw the expression on Edwin's face, but just said, "I'm nearly finished with Friedr's shirt. I was careful when I cut his clothes off. They'll have an interesting style to them, but I've an idea for how to fix his leather trousers so he can put them on by himself when he's stronger." A small pile of mending sat waiting next to him, and he'd already mended Edwin's clothes.

"Thank you for mending my shirt, Zan. This is very well done." Edwin's voice was thick, but he didn't give in to his urge to weep. "You learned a lot from him."

Zan was unable to answer, mutely nodding his head. He had withdrawn into his private world of grief, and Edwin allowed him the time to mourn. Going to his pack and bringing out his diary, Edwin sat opposite Zan and began the arduous task of logging the events of the previous three days. Several times, he had to pause and wipe tears away, but somehow he managed to write everything down.

Some hours later, Friedr stirred, and Edwin immediately went to his side. Zan set his mending down and helped Friedr to sit up, supporting his shoulders, following along while Edwin delved him. It was with relief they found no resurgence of the infection; he was finally healing well. He was conscious but disoriented and very thirsty. He was able to swallow some water and the broth from the soup, but the effort left him exhausted. Edwin bathed him again, and using the skills they learned in the infirmary, they changed his bedding, replacing it with Christoph's now unused bedroll. Zan rebuilt the layered spells, casting heal and ease, along with a light sleep spell. Soon they had him settled back down, sleeping naturally with his pain well dampened.

Chapter 23 ~ Truth and Tears

Edwin cleaned Friedr's blankets and spread them to dry. Then he turned to cleaning and polishing their boots and armor, making small repairs while Zan continued mending Friedr's clothes. "I think it'll be at least two, perhaps even three, weeks before Friedr's well enough to travel, despite our healing. I simply couldn't perform the surgery as well as *he* could've done it, and only time can heal where I lacked the ability."

At Edwin's comment, Zan looked up and nodded, his forehead furrowed. "I know."

Edwin feared they wouldn't have enough time for Friedr to heal properly before they would have to try to make the long, dark journey. "We'll have to scout the road carefully, and we're going to have to use earth-magic to make the road passable for Friedr. At least we won't have to worry about drawing D'Mal's attention. He's going to be occupied elsewhere for much of the next season, and the squads watching us don't seem to have any mages embedded in them. But we won't leave here until Friedr's as strong as we can make him, because we've another serious battle to fight several days' walk down this path."

Zan's grim expression betrayed his resignation. "What do you know about this place? I scouted down it a short way to make sure we were alone, but I didn't want to leave you last night, even with my air-magic," he replied. "I knew you were nearly burned out, but I couldn't do anything to help you either. You're still nowhere near ready to do battle with anyone."

"No, you're right, I'm not up to fighting anyone," Edwin agreed wryly. "It'll be several days before I've recovered enough. But you're no better off, Zan. You can't do anything fancy either, so we'll just hole up here in the cave for as long as we can and try to regain our health." Edwin collected his thoughts, trying to answer Zan's original question. "But you're curious about what sort of mess we've gotten ourselves into."

He looked into the dark depths of the cave and then began his tale. "Do you remember what I told you about Jaxon Sellsword, and how my father, Garran, and Halee rescued him from the pile of bodies that had been his family, and then brought him safely to Braden?"

Zan nodded, his dark eyes somber.

"This is the entrance to the underground river my father found. They escaped to Braden down this river. It travels underground until it emerges only five days' walk days north of there." Edwin was silent again, thinking of his father, but soon continued the tale. "Six years ago, we came to the Shadow Castle to rescue Marya. Once we arrived at the hills above the keep, Aeolyn decided we should have another escape route planned, one D'Mal might not know about, if possible.

"So I scouted it with my air-magic, and I found it was much different from the place Garran had described to me. It wasn't a place where a tired, wounded man could run with a baby strapped to his chest. I soon found out why. D'Mal had discovered it and rearranged it, making it into a one-way trap. He probably found it when he turned the wine cellar into his dungeon and decided to use it as a tease to torment any would-be escapees.

"This is what I found—once a person commits to taking the easy trail, which leads down to the river from this cave, things quickly change for the worse. Perhaps a furlong down the path to the underground river, escapees are forced to scale a fifteen-foot drop with some handholds that might help them down, but which would be terribly difficult to return by quickly, if at all.

"There are now many blind corners and narrow ledges where you have to slide along single-file, pressed to the wall for long, dangerous stretches, and the trail is slick with damp moss and mud. Parts of it have been pulled down and rearranged to force any unwary escapee down the path D'Mal has chosen for them, but we'll be able to restore and improve the original path by the time we leave here. We're going to have to fix the trail so Friedr can make it down the path, because we'll have to leave here long before he gains any strength in his injured leg.

"But the best part of my tale is this—at the end of the narrow, winding path is the den of a waterdrake. From the drake's lair, there's a tiny exit to the old natural road of the river, but you have to get past the waterdrake and then crawl on your belly through the tunnel to the exit. When I last scouted it, the area was littered with bones and rags that must've been clothing at one time, and even a minotaur's breastplate was lying in the mud."

Zan looked at Edwin, consternation written on his face. "Then why are we going this way? We can still leave under cover of dark when Friedr gets better."

"No, Zan, I'm sorry. Friedr will never be able to crawl through the under-canopy again. And there's another reason Aeos told us to remember the Forbidden

Road. All eight squads of the legions are out there, camped in this part of the valley, watching us. They won't come in here because they know what lies waiting, and they're terrified of it. To make sure they stay away, I set a ward of aversion on the entrance.

"You see, this cave is where the guards who 'get up their squad leader's nose' end up. That is, they're brought here if they're not just killed outright in a fit of annoyance. Their good friends usually knock them out and take them further inside, to the first fifteen-foot drop and throw them in. Then, they make sure they don't climb out by shooting arrows at them. There is a squad camped not too far from here, making sure we don't leave by the front door. They're posting a watch on the cave entrance.

"They were on our heels and very nearly caught us last night, but they gave up when we entered this cave. I can promise you they're not going to leave until they know we've gone down the road."

Zan's face fell as he understood what Edwin was telling him. "We're prisoners here, aren't we?"

"Yes, so they believe," Edwin chuckled sardonically. "I eavesdropped on them this afternoon, and they're just like all minotaurs. Fortunately for us, D'Mal is busy with his own problems. This means right now, there's no official leader acting as a vector for him, so they're on their own. They're planning to camp out and make sure we don't leave this cave alive. They're looking at this as a chance for a little rest and relaxation and are hoping for at least two weeks of observing us, maybe three. The squads don't have to do any real work, just post a guard, hunt some of the stranger creatures to fill their pots, and sleep all they want." Edwin smiled grimly. "They're laying wagers that at least one of us will either try to make a break for it out the front door or we'll take the long, dark road before a week has passed. They want us to have a chance to get healthy so if we do decide to make a break for it, we'll provide them with a bit of sport. They're worried the big one will die before they have the chance to kill him."

Zan sat quietly, absorbing everything. "At least I know what we need to do to kill the waterdrake," he finally told Edwin, "depending, of course, on how big the beast is. If it's a really big one, we might be in trouble. Friedr could also tell you this story. He had Feia for a teacher too."

Edwin looked at him quizzically. Seeing Edwin's interest, Zan continued, "I once heard a story about a quest Father Rall went on as a young man. He was traveling with a famous lightning-mage named Wynn Farmer...." He broke off and looked at Edwin in surprise. "Your grandfather! It was your grandfather he was traveling with." The look of consternation on Zan's face was comical.

"Father Rall told me he traveled with my grandfather," Edwin replied, smiling. "I've only a dim memory of him. He died very young, though I thought he was old." Edwin remembered him as an often sad but kindly old man who loved to play games with him as a young child.

"Your grandfather's exploits are taught to every young lightning-mage, often as examples of what not to do, but mostly just as great, fun stories. He was a mage who'd been blessed with more dumb luck than anyone had a right to, according to Feia, who knew him. She told us this story...well, of course she knew him, she was married to Father Rall...but anyway, this is the story as I was told it.

"Wynn Farmer and Rall Ivarsson, along with Jules Brendsson and Devyn D'Mal, all fought against the last of the great rogue-mages. He was named Grakken, which means 'destroyer' in the language of Serende. Grakken was a beastmaster with an affinity for water-elementals. He's rumored to have actually created some of the nastier water-elementals we still occasionally deal with, such as water-wraiths and water-sprites. Feia said he didn't create them but was able to control and use them. As you know, those beasts are all really susceptible to lightning and easy to kill. But the last beast they had to fight to get through to Grakken's keep was a waterdrake.

"They finally came to the cave high in the Mountains of the Moon, at the headwaters of the River Fleet, where the drake had his lair. Once he was faced with the beast, Wynn forgot and did the one thing, which as a lightning-mage, you're always cautioned against doing when fighting a major creature of the element water, like a waterdrake. He called a massive curtain call on it, and of course, the result was predictable. The waterdrake had shielded against lightning, and it cast water at the same time, so the water came back at them fully charged with a colossal amount of voltage.

"Because he was a water-mage, Rall's armor was bespelled to shield him against lightning attacks, and he tossed up a water shield. The backlash washed right over Rall and somehow reflected off Wynn Farmer's shield. It rebounded back on the waterdrake, still fully electrified, and because it was water, the drake didn't shield against it. When it hit the waterdrake, the explosion was so thunderous they were deafened for hours afterward. The drake thrashed about in its death throes, knocking down part of the mountain so the mountain pass was closed behind them, and they were nearly caught by the landslide.

"Waterdrakes aren't really clever, but they're very hard to kill, and usually, they win any battles they're involved in. It's fortunate they're very rare, as most mages won't ever have to face one. In fact, they're so rare, until a few years ago, most people thought they were extinct. This may be the last one. Where D'Mal found this one, I can't imagine."

"They're actually native to Chysat," Edwin supplied. "But the borders have been closed to that world since the god, Ariend, fell, so it must already have been living somewhere in the Mountains of the Moon. They don't like the warmth down here in the lowlands, so this drake would never have chosen this cavern on its own." Edwin saw the incredulous look on Zander's face and laughed. "Father Rall gave me chapter and verse on waterdrakes when he heard about this one."

"He knows a lot about elementals. Well, when you have to fight one, the only thing that works against them is lightning, or poison, if you are lucky enough to have any and stupid enough to get close. But the main trouble is they have excellent shielding abilities. They always cast water on you, randomly interspersed with all of the other elements, and they're able to switch between elements almost with no pause, casting spells as fast as you and Friedr do. As you know, before *you* came along, mages could only protect themselves against one element at a time, so any mage facing a waterdrake had three chances out of four of raising the wrong shield."

Edwin grinned and said, "Actually, that's the main problem we've always faced against any major elemental creature and is why we always sent out groups of four, with good strengths in each element represented."

Zan nodded. "Feia told us Wynn had lightning-quick reflexes and was faster at raising his shields than anyone she'd ever met. She used to laugh and say his strongest magic was his ability to turn a calamity into a windfall by sheer accident. Old Jules swears Wynn panicked and raised both water and lightning shields at the same time, but if he did, no one was ever able to do it again until you came along and showed us how." He paused and looked at Edwin quizzically. "Legend has it Wynn was quite the ladies' man, collecting friendly-girls the way you do, except he'd enjoyed them until he met his wife." Zan's mercurial switches in topic amused Edwin. "Now I think of it, it really is sort of a family curse, isn't it?"

Edwin's face reddened, but he smiled, saying, "My dad always says it's a curse. I do find it hard to picture my old granddad with a bevy of friendly-girls hanging about him, although I suppose it's possible."

Zan shrugged and nodded. "But the point of this epic tale is we need to cast water laced with lightning, and we should be able to prevail. Our shields will be the critical factor." Zan smiled as he finished his tale. "What was it like being raised in a famous family?

Easily half of the bardic repertoire of epic quest-tales is about your family."

"I didn't actually know anything about my family's history other than the fact our farm has been in our family for several generations and we've always raised sheep. We certainly aren't famous where I grew up. Actually, your family is much more famous than mine. We're just like anyone else," Edwin replied, surprised by the question. "We grow apples and raise sheep. Our farm is a good farm, and we usually do pretty well if there is no apple-blight, or a bad year for scrapie, a disease that affects sheep terribly and sometimes goes around our area decimating the flocks. We certainly aren't among the rich in Markett. You know my dad and you know me. We aren't mighty heroes. We're just people who usually manage to get put in the right place to find trouble."

"Well, I didn't mean to sound ignorant, but your family's very important here," Zan replied awkwardly. "Many of the most famous mages come from your family, and they all seem so much bigger than life when you're reading about their adventures."

"Zan, don't you realize novices will read about our adventures and you'll be a hero to them?" Edwin's wry question took Zan by surprise. "All the questers become heroes in stories."

"Well, no, I hadn't really thought about it." He looked away from Edwin, no longer able to meet his eyes. "Well, if this is what it takes to be a famous quester, I'd rather not be famous. I find it hard to believe I was so worried I'd end up teaching novices about other people's quests, never having had an adventure of my own." His deep sadness was palpable.

"I'm glad I didn't know how quickly things could go bad, before we started out on this journey." Zan's dark eyes were bleak, and he struggled to keep his voice light. "I wouldn't have had the courage to come with you. I think I've had enough adventure now." He looked away, grief lending severity to his profile.

"I was bored too, when I was your age. I was terrified of rotting away in Markett, and I admit I'm still not ready to go back there. I may never go back. My life is in Aeoven as a healer right now," Edwin replied, sensing the depth of Zan's depression and wishing he could somehow help him. "Friedr and Christoph were very excited about going on their first quest too. We were all sure we'd be successful with our task and never once thought of possible failures. It never occurred to me I'd find myself trapped in a dream, trussed up like a feast-day goose, and lying on a hearthrug with a knife in my chest. But even if I'd known ahead of time, I would've done it anyway. I meant every word of my vows the same as you did, and so did Christoph. I know for a fact he would've healed the throne anyway, even if he'd known he would be called upon to give up his life to preserve Neveyah."

Zan was silent for a moment, overwhelmed with a sharp feeling of guilt. *I set the geas that made him unable to tell a lie. It's my fault he had to die to save us.* Instead of voicing his thoughts, he said, "I wish I could tell Dane what happened. He still doesn't know. He'll be waiting for Chris, and Chris won't be coming home." Zan's voice was rough. "How am I going to explain what happened? How?"

"I know exactly how you're feeling right now. Believe me I do. I keep thinking about it too. But Father

Rall had the vision, and so did Moran. Somehow I felt them, almost like we were linked. I think Dane has been told by now Chris is gone, but I don't think he knows the full truth. That'll have to wait until we get back to Aeoven." Edwin tried to comfort Zan as best he could.

Edwin clasped Zan's shoulder comfortingly. "If Dane wishes it, I'll do for him what I did for you. I think it'll be the only way he'll be able to accept it. In the meantime, Marya and Dad are taking care of him, and I suspect Anna and her parents are too. You can be sure our entire family is with him, helping him and comforting him. From what my dad wrote, Anna's family has taken to him well and frequently visits him." Edwin tried to send supportive thoughts to Zan, deciding he was grieving normally, and it was good for him to express his emotions. He would not cast any spells to block the natural grief process.

"You're right, Edwin. Thank you. And at least I know Chris is with Aeos," Zan replied, and clamped his teeth shut to keep from crying again.

Friedr began to stir fretfully, and they were soon occupied, caring for him again.

***

It was near dawn, and Zan lay sleeping deeply beside Friedr. Edwin had finally resorted to surreptitiously casting sleep on him, realizing Zan wouldn't rest unless something was done for him. He felt a little guilty, but they needed Zan as well rested as possible.

He sent his senses out to check on their guards and found eight of them sleeping and two standing a bored watch. Other squads dotted the valley, all of them happily camping, feeling as if they were on a holiday.

They were sleeping now, having dutifully combed the valley, but all were fully aware of where the quarry was, and they were just using the hunt as an excuse to stay out in the field. The keep was empty except for the old man and woman and the few cooks who served the guards in their barracks.

After checking on the minotaurs, Edwin again sent his senses out, looking for a good, sturdy stick to make into a staff for Friedr. Each time he found a likely looking stick, he 'fetched' it into the cave. He found several that would help Friedr get around while Edwin worked on finding the 'special one.' He would make as useful, unique, and beautiful a healer's staff as he was able, which would also assist Friedr when he walked. It was a given the man would never again be able to walk without support of some sort.

The sticks he'd found so far were long pieces of wood, spare tent supports for the legions. He didn't recognize the wood and realized they must be from trees in Tauron's world of Serende. It was a good joke, that—Tauron's legions were supplying the basic components for Friedr's brace and his staff. Edwin grinned at the thought. He wondered if they would be resistant to Serende's magic in any way, and then thought probably not, though it would be nice if it did have some special property. Next, he looked for the components to make the brace for Friedr's leg and found several more sturdy pieces of wood in the various camps that dotted the huge valley. Soon, he had several long, strong pieces of wood to choose from.

Humming softly, he planned how to turn them into a brace that would support the weight of the big man when they began to make their escape. He carefully drew the design for what he planned in his journal. He picked each pole and rod up and made notes detailing the way the wood felt to him, noting he was using wood not found in Neveyah. Using all his senses, he examined them closely, finding they were all were good, solid lengths with no inherent weaknesses, would be tough to cut down to size, but would be strong and long-lasting for Friedr. *I can cut these down and make them into a fine brace for him. We'll have to leave long before his leg will have regained any real strength, and these'll do nicely. What I have in mind will act like armor to cushion his leg from bumps and scrapes and will carry his weight fully.*

Next, Edwin snooped about the encampment of the squad watching the cave entrance, looking for a leather garment he could 'borrow' to use in making the brace. Finding a thick leather tunic at the end of a messy bedroll in which a minotaur snored, he fetched it.

Soon it lay waiting to be cleaned and made into the brace that would allow Friedr to walk and perhaps even fight in a limited capacity. He wondered what sort of leather it was—he didn't recognize it at all. It felt almost like it may have been from a thunder-cow, but he'd never heard of anyone using them for anything. Then he laughed softly, thinking that if anyone could, the legions would. Who knew—it was clear they enjoyed hunting and the trick of avoiding the lighting discharge might present a challenge they'd enjoy.

Sometime near dawn, Friedr stirred again, waking completely with no disorientation for the first time since the dreadful trek from the battlefield. Edwin immediately went to his side, casting spells for pain relief, and propping him up on his pack.

Friedr's voice was hoarse from his having been so ill. "Edwin...what...what's wrong with me?" He cleared his throat briefly. "How did I get so sick? Did we get Christoph back yet?" He looked at Zan and noted that only the three of them were there. He shook his head sadly. "We have to get him back. Why are we camped here instead of looking for him?"

Sitting on his pallet next to Friedr, Edwin said, "Just let me check you over and get you taken care of. Then, I've some hot soup for you, and while you're eating, I'll tell you what I know."

"Forgive me, Edwin. I know you would've gotten him back if it were possible." Friedr wiped a tear from his eye, hating his weakness. He attempted to rise and hissed as pain assailed him. "Good grief, what happened to my leg? I can hardly move it." His eyes widened as Edwin uncovered him so he could see the scarred mess that was his left leg. "I'm sure this is looking much better than before you healed it." Shock and disbelief colored his voice. "There must be a story involved, and I'm looking forward to hearing it." He tried again to rise but couldn't do it on his own.

"Oh Goddess...Edwin, I need to get to the privy-pit, wherever you've put it in our lovely cave. I'd appreciate it if you'd help me," Friedr told Edwin, his discomfort overriding his dignity. Even with the help of a stick on his right side and with Edwin half-carrying him on his left, it took everything Friedr had to get from his bedroll to the privy-pit and back again. With his left arm still splinted and his left leg nearly useless, it was an ordeal he dreaded having to repeat.

At last he was back on his bedroll, gasping and sweating and propped up with both his kit and his clean bedroll behind him. "They don't ever mention this sort of misery in the epic tales, do they? Somehow, the hero's massive injuries never seem to inconvenience or embarrass him." Friedr's wry comment belied his discomfiture and mortification at having to rely on his friend for so personal a matter.

"We're healers, Friedr. We really don't make good patients," Edwin replied comfortingly as he checked Friedr's other wounds. Finding him healing as well as he'd hoped, he then layered healing and easing spells within a dampening field and tied it off.

As Friedr leaned against his kit and regained his composure, he watched Edwin get him his tin cup of hot soup and looked around the cave. "Cozy little death trap you have here. You two have made it downright homey." His attempt at humor fell a little flat, but Edwin smiled back at him anyway. "That's a good idea, using the little flames like that, my brother. What were we going to call them? Oh yes, mage-lamps."

"Drink your soup, and then I'll tell you everything that's happened to you and what your prognosis is. Then, if you're still up to it, I'll show you what happened to Chris." Edwin's voice was calm and reassuring, but Friedr was not fooled. His empathy told him Edwin was grieving deeply and not dealing with it well. "You'll have to see what I saw in my true-dream."

"I'll gladly lower my barriers right now, so go ahead and do your worst. I have to know what you know." Friedr's voice was weak and shaky, but he was firm as to what he needed.

"Soup first, and then I'll show you once you have eaten, my brother." Edwin was every bit the healer-in-charge, firm and confident. After a moment, Friedr nodded. He sipped his soup, finding he was hungry. He handed the empty tin cup to Edwin, who refilled it for him.

"We'll keep your arm splinted for a few more days. We were able to knit the bones, but we need to make sure they're strong before you put too much stress on them." Edwin's bedside manner comforted Friedr, who had no desire to be the patient. Still, he knew he should try to be appreciative and indeed was very thankful to his friends for saving his life.

"Thank you and Zan both for healing my sorry carcass." He raised his cup in a toast to Edwin. "And also for the soup. It's filling and very tasty." Friedr's blue eyes reflected the concern he tried to conceal. "I do thank you for saving my life instead of leaving me behind as I told you to do, though you wouldn't be trapped here if you'd done as I said. But what happened to my leg, and why have I been so sick? I remember my arm was broken, and Chris…umm…Christoph healed it." Resolutely, he ignored the tears the mention of Christoph brought to his eyes.

"Well, with all the crawling through the thorn-canopy, we had to reset it. Zan and I did what we could, but your leg is going to take a long time to heal completely, even with our skills. One of the most minor cuts on your leg was from a blade infected with saliva from the bear-dogs."

Shocked understanding dawned on Friedr's face upon hearing the news. "Ah."

Edwin's compassion soothed his patient as he explained the damage Friedr's leg had suffered. "We almost didn't get it in time, and we didn't have the chi to do more than try to contain it and delay the inevitable when we finally got you safely here. But because of the delay in getting you properly treated, the muscle was seriously damaged. Still, because of what we managed to do the first night, the bone was healthy and we were able to avoid amputation." Friedr's eyes widened upon hearing the word "amputation."

"We didn't regain enough chi until yesterday afternoon to properly heal you. Because of this, we had to cut away much of the necrotic, poisoned flesh. It's not going to grow back, my brother, though I was able to regenerate enough skin to close and seal the wound." Friedr slowly nodded, and Edwin continued, "It's too bad it was you who suffered this and not me, because you're far better at surgery and regenerating flesh than I am. But fortunately, I assisted Darlen for a season as a journeyman and learned a lot from him. I did the best I could for you, but I'm afraid the augmentations on your leg have been compromised. I understand they've occasionally been known to return to their proper places when a mage has been seriously injured, so we'll keep an eye on it to see if they reappear." Edwin had his healing-senses extended fully over Friedr, monitoring his reaction to the news he had to hear.

Friedr curtly nodded his head, unable to speak until he absorbed the magnitude of his disability.

"I'm not going to lie to you about this, my brother. You'll never regain the full use of your leg." Edwin's open face was shadowed with his regret for what he had to tell his friend. "I know you, though. You'll make it work for you, though it's an injury that would cripple anyone else. In the meantime, I'm working on an idea to help you get around better on your own and enable you to get down the road we are going to have to travel."

"Ah...ahem...." Friedr's blue eyes were bleak as what Edwin had told him sank in. "Yes, well." He was silent, and then he said, "I'll do whatever I must and work with what I have. I know you'll figure something out to help me. You're the cleverest man I know when it comes to making things we need." Friedr felt numbed by the realization he was crippled, at least for the time being. "I'll build it back up, you'll see. It's just a challenge I have to meet."

Edwin nodded, understanding Friedr's shock and disbelief. "Are you sure you're ready to let me open my mind to you? You'll have to do this to truly understand what has happened to our brother." Edwin's blue eyes searched Friedr's face for some sign of his thoughts.

"I need to know what happened to him." Friedr's voice shook, and he hated the sound of his own weakness. "I'm done with fearing the intimacy of the healing gift, Edwin. I'm done with stupid cowardice. I will use what the Goddess has given me to the fullest extent of my ability."

Accessing his memory of the true-dream and kneeling next to him, Edwin placed Friedr's palm against his forehead. With his barriers completely down, he allowed Friedr to see the whole experience exactly as he had lived it. On feeling Friedr shaking and raising his barriers, Edwin leaned back and raised his own barriers again.

"I'd hoped...but you can't go against the prophecies, no matter how much you want to." For a long moment, Friedr was silent. Squeezing his eyes shut against the anguish that threatened to crush him, he tried to hold back the sobs, struggling to control them, to no avail. They burst from him, and shaking and sobbing in his grief, Friedr clutched at Edwin with his one good arm. Once the storm was past, he simply cried against Edwin's shoulder, unable to accept that Christoph was really gone and there was nothing anyone could do about it. Edwin put his arms around Friedr and just held him until he had cried himself out.

At last feeling Friedr's sobs subsiding, he handed Friedr his clean bandanna to blow his nose. Edwin spoke the words in his heart. "I take comfort in knowing he's gone to the Great Hearth, to be held warm and comforted in Aeos's love. I can accept this loss, though it breaks my heart."

Finally having himself back under control, Friedr quoted from the prayer the children of the Goddess Aeos had said since the beginning of time, "'When our days on earth have come to an end, take us to your Great Hearth and hold us warm until the day we are born again, in the light of your love.' I always feared it'd be him. Somehow, I knew—I had this feeling something bad would happen and it would be Christoph who died. He was my first friend as a novice. He wouldn't stand for anyone picking on me for being a big, stupid, northern barbarian, always leaping to my defense. Life will never be the same without him to keep me laughing."

"Lie back down now, Friedr. Try to rest," Edwin told him and helped him to get settled back down. "We can only work so much magic. The rest of the healing will have to come from you." He cast ease and a light sleep-spell, just enough to help Friedr fall into a dreamless sleep.

Once Friedr was sleeping, Edwin sat in the doorway of the cave, watching as the sky dawned all pink, blue, and golden. The magnitude of what lay before them in trying to get home seemed insurmountable. Trying to travel the underground river for who-knew-how-many leagues and having to fight a waterdrake somewhere in the middle of the journey, with Friedr crippled and unable to swing his sword was almost more than he could comprehend.

Edwin tried to distract himself, trying to sense Marya, but he was unable to feel their connection. He wondered if he had lost ability to sense her because of having nearly burned himself out. They had always had that special, subliminal bond no matter how far apart they were, and its absence worried him. *Or maybe we're just too far apart this time—but I'm sure I felt her this morning.* He was sure he would get it back after he was more rested.

I wonder if this is really just the end, and we're too stubborn to admit it. Calling himself sharply to order, he thought brusquely, *I'm being ridiculous. I'm not giving up! I'll carry Friedr home if I have to. We're going to make it home by winter solstice and Holy Day. We'll surely be home by then.*

Chapter 24 ~ Love thy Neighbor

It was nearing midday, and Friedr and Zan still slept, both under sleep-spells. Edwin knelt by the campfire, shirtless. Soaping himself and washing thoroughly, he once again tried to wash his own back, but his improperly healed wounds restricted his movement.

Zan woke from his sleep, feeling fully rested for the first time in weeks. Kneeling, he checked Friedr, who slept deeply. Finding him on the mend, he looked over and saw Edwin attempting to bathe. His eyes widened as he saw Edwin's right shoulder. Silently reproaching himself for not noticing his injuries before, he went to Edwin, resting his hand upon his shoulder.

"Edwin, let me see to your wounds now." Edwin started to demur, but Zan cut him off. "Don't argue, just let me do it." Zan took the cloth and gently bathed his wounds. "Forgive me for not noticing you were injured, Edwin. I was too wrapped up in my own misery to see anything but Friedr's injuries."

Once Zan was satisfied the wounds were as clean as he could get them, he layered a healing-spell over Edwin. "Why didn't you tell me you were injured? Don't you think you deserve healing? Granted, they weren't infected, but they were hampering your ability to take care of yourself. Now, you'll have some ugly scars and your augmentations could be damaged. I'd have sutured them, at least." Zan sounded exactly like Dane as he fussed over Edwin, who suppressed a laugh. "I've more than enough chi to handle what we need to deal with now, so there's no excuse for this. Now you're going to lie down, and I'm going to cast sleep on you so you'll have enough chi to treat Friedr's arm again later."

A wry smile crossed Edwin's tired face. "Thank you, Zan. I did need healing. And I'd appreciate you helping me fall asleep." He went to his pallet. "Friedr's been up, but he's terribly weak, and it was an ordeal for him. He's eaten and has been shown my true-dream. Also, he knows how seriously injured his leg is. But I'm making a special brace for him so he'll be able to walk unassisted." Edwin settled himself on his bedroll, while Zan cast the spell. Soon he was sleeping a restful, dreamless sleep.

Zan looked at both Friedr and Edwin with his healing-sight once more and checked the pain-relieving spells layered over Friedr, finding them still strong.

Sitting cross-legged, he sent his senses out scouting the area and found the legions camped and preparing to roast various types of fresh-caught game for their afternoon meals. Many of them were dressing out thunder-cows. The great carcasses hung on tripods as the hunters skinned and butchered their kills. "Huh," he muttered to himself as he made notes of what he saw. "I never knew they could be eaten by anything. Certainly, *we* don't eat them."

Thunder-cows didn't usually bother anyone unless they were breeding or protecting a calf. Also, they looked nothing like a cow, so why they were called that, Zan couldn't imagine. When startled, the creatures had a nasty electric discharge that could kill a weak person, but apparently the legions had ways of getting around that little inconvenience.

The squads were in eight camps dotting the wide expanse of the valley in front of the cavern. Each squad was separated by five or more leagues with no mingling with the other squads. *Edwin was right. They know we're here and are hoping one of us will try to escape and provide them with a bit of sport.*

After observing them for a while more, he took up his mending and began repairing Friedr's leather trousers so he would be able to put them on without assistance. He decided the most practical way to make them work would be to make it so his left leg laced up. Friedr would be able to get them on with the laces loosened and then tighten them once they were on.

He noticed that Edwin had borrowed some leather from the 'neighbors' for his project, and decided to do the same to make laces. After some thought he decided to make the repairs look intentional, like the old-style fringed leathers John and Garran favored, only more modern, without the pockets all down the legs. He smiled, thinking, *Friedr will have to wear them no matter how they come out, but it'd be nice if I could make them stylish. He'd certainly like it better.*

Concentrating, Zan sent his senses out again and snooped about the camp nearest to them. He found a bit of an uproar happening there. He eavesdropped just a bit, discovering that Edwin's theft had been discovered and a drama was unfolding. Zan decided to hang about and see what was going on.

The tunic's owner, an unpleasant guard named Yelk, was angry and demanding his fellows return his property immediately. Soon, the whole unit was in an uproar, with Yelk angrily searching everyone's kits for his missing tunic. When he didn't find it, he decided

Berk, a squad-mate he didn't much care for, had hidden it. Predictably, they were soon fighting.

After a rather nasty battle, Berk won. The unfortunate Yelk lay dead, and Berk had the privilege of eating Yelk's heart. With the matter settled, the squad calmed back down, and the squad leader informed Berk that since he had killed Yelk, he could stand watch by himself. "I ain't rearranging the schedule just cuz you had to go and make the numbers uneven."

Berk shrugged and got on with roasting Yelk's heart. "He weren't much good on a watch anyway," Berk replied. "He made too much noise, always yammerin' away about some darn thing." The others just nodded and returned to their tasks.

Laughing softly, Zan scouted several other camps, looking for some unattended item of leather he could borrow to make the laces he needed. He found what he was looking for in a camp halfway to Mal Evol City and fetched it back to the cave. It was a rather dirty leather tunic, but once it was cleaned, he would be able to use it to make all the leather thongs for laces and fringe he would need and many other useful items.

He found himself snickering as he thought about Yelk and Berk. *If the rest of them would just kill each other off with their petty quarrels, we might be able to walk out of the front door after all,* he thought to himself. *But I suppose that'd be too much to ask.* Zan's smile as he set to work was sardonic. The light of the fire illuminated his ever more hawk-like features that remained set and grim, despite the smile.

Toward midafternoon, Friedr woke again, and Zan helped him to the privy-pit, supporting him on his nearly useless left side. Once the big man was again back on his bed, Zan layered the healing-spells into a dampening field, making him more comfortable. Quickly delving him he found Friedr was still healing well, although he was suffering some pain and was terribly weak. As Friedr settled back onto his pallet, Zan served him a cup of soup, and they talked quietly while he continued repairing Friedr's leathers.

Seeing Zan mending his clothes caused Friedr's eyes to burn with unshed tears, but he refused to give in, saying only, "I'll miss that stubborn man. He was my oldest and dearest friend."

"I know, Friedr. He loved you. He often spoke of how you looked out for him when you two were novices." Zan's features softened with a wry smile. "I find working at this task he enjoyed so much brings me closer to him somehow. I may actually have a talent for it—I rather enjoy doing it. I wish I could do something about the bloodstains, though. I hate going about in stained clothes. I need to think about this."

"I know what you mean. Aeolyn always keeps my clothes looking nice." Friedr's heart felt leaden, thinking of Aeolyn, briefly wondering if the ugly appearance of his leg would change anything between them. He couldn't change his situation, so he resolutely put home out of his mind. "I'll have a great deal more sympathy for my patients when I get back to Aeoven." Friedr's voice was still weak but not as shaky as it had been earlier. "It's different being on the receiving end of healing. I'm fortunate to have you and Edwin to care for me." Friedr looked closely at Zan, seeing his grim, worn features, sadly observing how changed Zan was by the loss of Christoph. *He looks like Dane now, full of worry and loss.*

Friedr contemplated the journey that lay ahead of them, attempting to divert himself from his gloomy thoughts. "I confess I'm not looking forward to continuing down the path we must travel, though I suppose I'll be better able to get around by the time we have to go. You'll still have to assist me much of the time, I fear."

"You'd do the same for us, Friedr. It'll be a tough journey, but we'll be together, so it won't be so bad," Zan tried to convey a sense of confidence. "We just need to work as a team when we face the waterdrake, and we'll be fine. We've been planning how we're going to make it to the drake's lair. Edwin will guide us in, rearranging the path before we go so you can make the trek. I know we'll get through this. It's why the Goddess gave us these skills. I know this now."

Edwin woke, yawning and stretching, automatically checking the health of his companions. "Well, you're looking much better, my brother. You almost look like your old self." Edwin stood, served himself a cup of soup, and sat back down by Friedr. "How's the new skin feeling on your leg? Are you itching yet?"

"No, not yet, but it's still tender. I hope Aeolyn put some numbing salve for bug bites in the medical kit. She most likely did. She planned well for every eventuality. Perhaps it'll help some when the itching begins. It's fine right now, though," Friedr smiled wryly. "I'll try not to snivel too much when the healing really begins!" His comment received an answering smile from Edwin.

"I might be able to help you with the itching," offered Zan. "I think it's just like any other sort of sensation, pain or pleasure. I'll think of something if it becomes too bothersome for you, because we won't have the time to let you get over it naturally, and we might need the bug salve when we leave this place."

Edwin spoke. "Which reminds me, Zan, we're running low on some supplies." Edwin looked at Zan closely and then added, "You should get some sleep now. When you wake, we can fetch things."

"You're right. I'm tired enough to fall asleep without your help this time—thank you, by the way." Smiling at Edwin's faint embarrassment, he put his work away, undressed, and got into his bedroll, falling asleep almost immediately.

"I've a task for you, Friedr, one you can do while you recover," Edwin said, smiling encouragingly. "You should take up the task of chronicling for us now, while you build up your strength. You can use my diary entries for the last few days to bring the quest-journal up to date." Edwin handed Friedr the general notebook and pencil Chris had carried for them until his capture. "Zan has agreed to keep his father's private diary safe in his own kit until we can bear reading it."

Friedr nodded and agreed, although journaling was not a task he enjoyed. "I'll bring the diary up to date, although you'll have to tell me some of what happened." His face showed his lack of enthusiasm, but he didn't voice it. "Perhaps writing the whole sorry mess down will help me get it straight in my head."

Sadly nodding, Edwin reassured him. "I've a project of my own to complete. I've an idea to enable you to walk. I fetched several sticks that will make excellent staffs for you, but I'm not yet sure which one will be right. All of them are sturdy enough for you to use while I make the special one. I don't know if I can bespell it for strength or not, but I'll try. I also have an idea for how to make a brace for your leg. I think I have all the necessary items to make what you'll require, and tomorrow I'll begin. I think I know how the armorers go about making the bespelled armor and weapons we've been given. It must be a matter of visualizing the need clearly. I'll open myself to Aeos's will and pray for her guidance as I begin working on your brace and walking stick. At least I hope that's what it takes."

Friedr smiled gratefully at Edwin. "Whether you can accomplish what you're planning or not, I'm sure you'll give me a good stick for support as we travel and a brace that will help me. And you're right—I wasn't looking forward to sitting here doing nothing useful while you and Zan wait for me to heal. I'll try to do as well as Chris did in his chronicling."

"You'll be working hard in regard to your leg, my brother. In the meantime, let's have a look at your arm." Edwin once again began delving his friend's still weak but healing body.

The arm had gained strength and looked good to Edwin's healing-sight. The leg was also healing well. Friedr would rapidly improve with every day that passed.

Keenly feeling Friedr's deep depression over both his disability and the loss of Christoph, Edwin threw a challenge out to him, knowing Friedr could not refuse a dare. "Now begins the toughest fight of your life, Friedr. This's where you must do the work, though I'll guide and help you as much as I can. We have to make your leg useful, and it's a task that will not be painless. Are you ready for this, my brother? Most people fail miserably at this part of the recovery until we find a way that works for them, so if it's too much for you, we'll go easier. I don't want to undo the work we've already done."

The bleak look in Friedr's eyes returned briefly at the thought of having to move his leg, but he nodded and situated himself better for Edwin to begin the physical therapy he knew was necessary if he was to make it home to see his wife and children. "I'm as ready as one can be when facing the unknown. Do your worst. I'll endure it." He smiled grimly. "I'll learn to embrace the pain and make it my friend."

"Lie flat on your back. We must work your hip and ankle. We won't disturb the knee. It'll never bend again." He firmly grasped Friedr's ankle. "The tendons in your ankle are very tight. Your ability to make it down this road will depend upon your being able to move around as well as you can. I can't cast pain-relieving spells during this part because you can harm yourself if you don't have the pain to set limits. I'll feel the pain with you, but still I want you to tell me when it's too much. Be honest."

Friedr worked harder than he ever had before, even though he was lying on his back. Privately, Friedr was worried because the leg was so thin and wasted looking, with only a fine layer of skin and muscle covering the bones. It looked pathetic, and he was wary of moving it. Still, he set aside his fears and grimly did as he was asked despite the pain. Edwin's promise of a brace and walking stick helped, giving him the impetus to endure whatever was necessary so he could use the creations Edwin would make for him.

When the pain became difficult to bear, Friedr reminded himself that he was now forced to rely on Edwin and Zan to help him to the privy-pit and back to his bed, a circumstance he hated. Each time he thought about the embarrassing ordeal, he had even more reason to work for his independence.

Edwin worked Friedr until he sensed his patient was reaching the limits of his endurance. Only then did Edwin cast ease on him, and help him bathe himself, after which Friedr fell asleep from exhaustion.

And so they began a routine of sorts, each with tasks to occupy them while they waited for Friedr to become strong enough to begin the long, hard journey down the underground river. Friedr's physical therapy combined with Edwin and Zan's healing-magic took priority over everything else.

***

Four more days and nights passed. Zan spent his hours sewing and spying on the squads, 'getting to know the neighbors,' as he thought of them. He discovered that watching their daily activity was interesting, and he began to feel rather attached to several of his favorites. Increasingly, their small tragedies and triumphs began to occupy more of Zander's waking moments, diverting him temporarily from the unbearable sense of guilt he suffered each time he thought about his father and the geas he had cast on him. When Zan was not spying on the legions, he was embellishing their own shirts to hide the bloodstains.

Soon they had regained their health, and even Friedr was doing as well as could be hoped. Still, the legions camped on their doorstep, waiting for them to make a move in either direction. They fetched supplies as needed, and Friedr frequently used his talent to scout as well as he could, pushing his limits and attempting to stretch his gift.

Zan finished repairing Friedr's leathers, and the big man was pleased with the look of them, declaring he should have all his clothes made that way from now on. Edwin too admired them, and Zan immediately began changing the style of Friedr's spare trousers so he could put them on by himself.

Edwin had finally fully regained his abilities and was now ready to begin making Friedr's bespelled brace and staff. He knelt in the dawn's light, just inside the cave entrance where he could see the sky. Opening himself to Aeos' will, he humbly prayed for guidance in the making of Friedr's brace. He knelt in a trance for nearly two hours, praying. At last, he arose and gathered his supplies. Though his eyes were open, he was clearly focused on something only he could see.

Zan felt him using his skills to fetch the oily leaves of the thornbushes which dotted the valley, then a large quantity of an inedible berry that stained everything it touched with a deep dark red, and the dark green sprite-weed that choked the creeks. These he set beside the wood and leather he had gathered for the project. His Temple knife was laid out next to his supplies.

Friedr and Zan watched as Edwin at last began his project. To their eyes, his somber features had softened and he appeared to be filled with peace and serenity. He was still fully tranced.

In a reverie different from but similar to a full healing-trance, Edwin created a brace to enable Friedr to stand and walk with minimal pain. Aeos guided him in tooling and dyeing the leather, engraving the designs of dragons and stars with crescent moons, and placing runes for strength, agility, and stealth on the brace, a touch that surprised him when he emerged from the trance.

The engravings perfectly mimicked the augmentations that once adorned Friedr's leg, with the additions of several unusual runes. Runes for ease and grace had been added to those for strength and wisdom. The leather and wood were polished with the oily leaves of the thornbushes and dyed with the berries and sprite-weed, creating a beautifully crafted brace for the Temple's greatest warrior.

"The magic chooses," Friedr declared as he looked at it, smiling broadly. "This is a work of art. I won't be a cripple with this to support me."

The brace was made to be worn on the outside of his leathers and protected his leg almost as if it were armor, though it had no metal in it. "This will greatly assist in protecting my leg until the muscles grow back naturally." Edwin and Zan exchanged a glance, and Edwin faintly shook his head at Zan, both visibly nodding agreement with their patient. Friedr knew their opinion, and it did no good to tell him differently.

Later, when Zan relieved Edwin at the watch, he mentioned Friedr's stubborn faith that he would re-grow the muscle he had lost. "Edwin, the Goddess as much as told us he won't re-grow muscle because she gave you the ability to create that marvelous brace.

Should we let him cling to this stubborn belief? What'll happen to him when he realizes it'll never be?"

"It doesn't hurt him, and it gives him a goal to work toward," Edwin replied gently. "Believe me, Zan, he knows." Shrugging, he reminded Zan, "We both know Friedr should have been the one performing the surgery, because he has better skills at regeneration magic than I ever will. He'll deal with it in his own way."

***

Daily, Friedr became more able to get around with the brace and needed their help less and less. He gained strength, learning how to walk again, leaning heavily on a stout stick and immediately began learning how to fight again. He pushed himself hard, rebuilding his endurance, and developing a new center of balance so he would not easily fall when faced with uneven terrain or a battle. "I must be capable of defending myself and be a working member of this team" became his mantra as he pushed himself to his utmost limits.

The new way of walking and standing put a lot of stress on his good leg and his hips, and he was often in pain from both while he adjusted to his new situation. The strain of living in constant pain began to show on his face. Zan was unable to fully relieve it except when Friedr was at rest. Friedr understood Zan wouldn't be able to set the proper pain loops until he had learned what he needed to about walking. The pain set the limits on what he would press himself to do.

Despite having lost weight from his illness, he still weighed more than Edwin or Zan, and this increased his chances of reinjuring himself if he was not careful.

Nonetheless, he persevered, unwilling to admit how badly he suffered and refusing to appear weaker than he absolutely had to.

While Friedr learned to walk and fight again, Edwin finished creating the special healer's staff he'd long ago envisioned in the true-dream for Friedr, entranced the same way as he was when creating the brace.

The finished staff was two meters tall, and fit Friedr's hand perfectly. The staff was visually divided into thirds—in the central third of the staff, intricately carved dragons identical to the ones on Friedr's arms held pride of place. Vines also wound up the staff from the bottom to the dragons, and from the dragons to the top. Runes for strength, agility, and stealth were placed at various places around the dragons and woven into the vines.

As with the brace, Edwin had dyed the engravings. The natural vegetable stains penetrated deeply into the wood and would never wear off. Lastly, Edwin had polished the staff with the oily leaves, bringing out the colors and the beautiful carvings. The ends of the staff were capped with the tin from Christoph's cup so the bottom would not wear away. To keep the staff from make a clicking sound when Friedr walked, Edwin made a leather sleeve for the bottom.

"I can't believe you made it from a tent pole. I've never seen such an amazing staff, other than Earthbinder," Zan said as they looked at it for the first time. "Truly, Aeos has placed her hand on you in the making of this amazing thing."

"I agree with you, it is Aeos's hand in this. Ordinarily, I'm a fair wood carver. I can make spoons or toys for Jonny and such, but this is way beyond anything I ever thought I could do," Edwin replied, feeling a little awed. "It's the will of Aeos that you should be healed of your injuries and able to walk again, Friedr."

Friedr felt nearly overcome, unused to feeling such confusing emotions, but determination won out. "She's seen fit to empower you to heal me and to allow me to continue on this journey with this brace and staff. All that I am and will ever be I owe to Aeos. I won't fail her."

Chapter 25 ~ Zan and the Neighbors

At last, after two long weeks of healing and trying to regain Friedr's strength, they realized they would soon have to move on down the Forbidden Road. The legions still camped on their doorstep, waiting for them to try to escape by using the front door. Edwin and Zan linked and scouted the length of the underground river together, returning frequently so Friedr could map it out in detail for them. They pored over the map, deciding where they had to smooth the road, trying to figure out how to do this without drawing attention from either the waterdrake or D'Mal.

"I've seen no sign of D'Mal or Lourdan in the keep, but we must keep our work here along this trail as quiet as possible anyway." The mention of Lourdan was difficult for Edwin, but he tried to be dispassionate about it. The pain of losing Christoph was still so raw. Even with his healer's training, he struggled to separate from the despair the mention of Lourdan brought him.

"D'Mal is still creating Lourdan. He won't be done with his task for a while, I think," Friedr too appeared troubled. "It sounded like it's a long and difficult process." He looked faintly ill at the thought of what the mysterious, occult process might entail. Just contemplating it had upset Stefyn D'Mal in the true-dream. "I wish...but never mind. We must work with what we're given. I just don't feel right fighting him."

To Edwin's surprise, it was Zan who cautioned them, speaking calmly but with a strength and assertion at odds with his usually temperate demeanor. "We have to accept that Lourdan exists, Friedr. He's not

Christoph, and we mustn't for a moment think he is. Lourdan will be a terrible enemy when he comes to Mal Evol. The Goddess has shown us that he'll live and reign in Mal Evol for many long years, perhaps for several generations. We've been told that one day in the future, the Hero Foretold will somehow be the catalyst who brings Christoph back to finish his task, on the day she calls 'the day of redemption.'

"It may be *we* won't see that day. I know I'll never see my father again, but our children or our grandchildren may, and on that day, all will be made right. In the meantime, Lourdan is the enemy who must be contained in Mal Evol. That's our task now. We must get to Braden and do what we can there to help Moran. We've been told Braden will be the western wall of Tauron's kingdom in Neveyah, and Lourdan will 'sow the poisoned seed' there, whatever that means. There's a great deal we can do to keep him contained in Braden and the Valley of Mal Evol." Zan's somber face was stern as he spoke of what he had thought long and hard about since the first days after Christoph fell to darkness. "There's a way we can protect our southern lands and keep his poison from encroaching on the rest of Neveyah. I dream of it so vividly and so often I now believe it must be a true-dream."

"Why haven't you mentioned this before now? You must have a plan. I can see it in your eyes." Friedr's sharp blue eyes took in the man Zan was now, seeing no trace of the raw young journeyman he had been only five months before. "Share it with us, please."

"I haven't shared it because I was afraid it might just be me wanting to look important. At first, I wasn't sure it really was a true-dream. Also, I didn't want to add my being an idiot to the list of problems we're dealing with here," Zan replied wryly. His drawn features momentarily dissolved into the old familiar grin he had once worn so regularly, but which faded as he spoke. "I've thought a lot about this, and now I believe now I'm being told what we're to do next. This task has figured so largely in my dreams since we came here, I can only think it's a sign from the Goddess."

"What must we do?" asked Edwin. "Whatever it is, we'll do it." His unconditional support eased Zan's mind, as did Friedr's nod of agreement.

"We must ask another strong battle-mage, perhaps Moran or Jase, to act as the fourth and help us build a shield-wall that nothing can cross. This wall must be built across the Braden Gap from where the Cascadia Escarpment becomes the Horn of the Moon all the way to the Horn of Misery. In my dream, it's both a ward, only much more painful, and a physical, visible wall raised from the earth."

Friedr sat back, trying to comprehend what Zan was proposing, and Edwin looked at Zan in surprise.

"Edwin, you can devise a way to do this. I *know* you can because I've seen the wall in my dreams. *You* shaped the parasite to keep the bear-dogs out of Mal Evol and Neveyah. Christoph trained you well in every aspect of healing the land. No one knows more about shielding and wards than you. In regard to the fourth element, I know Moran has strength in water as does Jase, though it's not their main strength. But they're strong enough to help with this. Father Rall could, if he's available to help us. I've seen blue, so I know the fourth mage must supply water, and other than John Farmer, Father Rall is the strongest water-mage currently active in the Temple."

He paused, thinking about the situation. "But with any one of these mages in the link, Lourdan won't be able to sense what we've done. Even though we know he has healing, earth, and water magic, he'll be unable to sense our familiar resonance and see what to do to enter the heart of Neveyah. The other mage's vibration will confuse his senses."

Friedr nodded, seeing the wisdom in what he had proposed. "I don't know if it's possible, but we can't take chances that he could follow our resonance. The only problem is neither Moran nor Jase is a healer." Friedr was reluctant to speak against the plan, but it could only work if they were all linked. "They can't link with us. And, John and Father Rall are both in Aeoven, and too far away."

"A water-mage would be best, I think," said Edwin, considering Zan's proposal. *Does this speak to Jaxon's prophecy regarding the wall? It must.*

Zan said, "Well, there must be at least one water-mage in Braden, attached to the militia there, and *we* can link with whichever mage will do this. The three of us together can 'drag' the mage into the link, and once he's in, he can provide the element needed." His grin was wry as he said, "We can't force a mage to let us pull him or her into our link—they must be willing to do it. We have to be prepared to find another mage who will allow us to use him if our first choice won't.

"But even though it'd be best to have four mages who're each the strongest in their element, all we really need is one mage who has moderate strength in any one element and who's willing to allow us to link with him, and then we can do this. Edwin and I are strong in all the elements, and so are you, Friedr.

"With a mage of strength in any element, we can provide the four elements with the power that will be needed. Then the three of us will weave the spirit in, with Edwin guiding us.

"We can do this in such a way that Lourdan can never unravel it because each small cell we build on the southern border will be slightly different from its neighbor. The slight differences will give the shield stability and make it very uncomfortable for any creature to remain in contact with it for any length of time."

Zan sat on his heels, completely sure of the successful outcome of his plan. "When each cell is done, we'll raise the physical wall that will be the visible denial of passage to Lourdan and Tauron's hordes. In my dream, it's black, as smooth, as ice and stands as tall as the walls of Arlen. The magic of the barrier will repel them from the wall, and the wall will be the visible sign they are penned up in the Valley of Sorrows."

"You're right, Zan. We can do this." Friedr agreed and then shrugged, "Of course, we have to survive the waterdrake to get there, but we could do it. You really have been thinking about this. I wouldn't have considered 'dragging' another mage into the link, but if he'll consent, then it wouldn't be a 'rape' of his magic. That was one of the dangers of being caught by a rogue-mage in the old days, you know."

Edwin nodded as Friedr spoke, agreeing with him. "We'll also bear your words in mind, Zan, if we're ever faced with Lourdan, though I rather doubt our paths will cross. In the meantime, we must do what we can here so we can get to Braden." Edwin's respect for Zan had increased immensely since the loss of Christoph. "Your idea about the barrier and the wall is exactly what must be done."

"And we must hurry now to make this road passable for us," Friedr added, his own face grim but determined. "The sooner we get to Braden, the sooner we can get this barrier/wall up."

"Besides, you're looking forward to adding a waterdrake to your list of 'Unusual Things Friedr Has Killed,'" right?" Zan's sly comment drew a moment of surprised silence from Friedr. Edwin burst out laughing while Zan snickered at Friedr, who also laughed uproariously, before admitting Zan was right.

"The difficult thing will be convincing the Temple to abandon Braden," said Edwin, when they had settled back down. "Moran definitely won't be amenable to this idea at all. But the city will be overrun, and the people will be given to Tauron. The ghost was very clear that Lourdan will arrive with the legions at his back."

"Aeos will provide a way to convince Moran," replied Friedr, feeling certain. "She's given us the tools we needed all along, and she won't fail us in this, I'm sure. After all, this is her will."

Later the same day, the three sailed under the earth as they once did with Christoph, making small adjustments to the path, leveling it in some places, widening and firming it in others. They worked as quietly and carefully as they could, but even so, their activities stirred up the waterdrake, whom Friedr named Aggie.

When Edwin asked him why he'd given it that name, Friedr said the creature's behavior reminded him of the quick-tempered, old herb-woman who'd lived on the edge of his village when he was growing up. "She had a short temper and no great love of company. You only went to her if you were really sick because she'd threaten to set a curse on you if you bothered her over something trivial."

Aggie paced back and forth in his cavern, sniffing the air, hoping to smell out the source of the movements in the earth. "The poor old thing is far too big to leave his cavern. His wings are atrophied," Edwin noted when they compared notes and rested up. "It looks like he gets fed fairly regularly, at least on fish. But there's a lot more minotaur armor in the general muck of his cavern than when I checked his cavern with Aeolyn."

"And here I was so worried he might be too weak from hunger to justify all the work we're putting into preparing to kill him," Friedr replied, rolling his eyes. "I suppose it'd be too much to ask for him to be a bit underfed."

"I'm sure he'll be happy to see us," Zan commented. "We'll make his day, I'm sure. At least we'll be properly dressed for the party." He held up the shirt he was embellishing.

"I'm amazed at how you've prettied up our clothes while we've been holed up here," Friedr said. "Your style of embellishment is a lot different than Christoph's was, but it's really good. I'd wear these to any feast-day celebration. We're the best-dressed vagrants in Mal Evol."

Zan laughed. "I'm just trying to cover up the bloodstains. You know how fond I am of my finery, and it gives me something useful to do while we wait for your leg to become strong enough for travel."

"You know, Zan, I've been wondering where you've gotten the colored thread to do all these nice embellishments," Edwin ventured. "I don't recall Chris having a lot of colored thread in his kit."

"Oh! Ah...." Zan suddenly turned red, and he mumbled, "Don't get too mad at me, please?" He looked at Edwin and Friedr's inscrutable faces. "I borrowed it from the neighbors."

Friedr looked him, completely dumbstruck. "The legions do needle work in their free time?"

Zan didn't talk very often anymore, but when he did, it tended to get a little convoluted, as if he had too much to say and had to spill it all at once. Friedr and Edwin both looked at him, waiting for the torrent of words that normally would have followed, but Zan appeared reluctant to talk about it. Finally, he said, "Well, their women apparently do rather fine needlework."

"And?" Friedr prompted.

"Um...I was thinking about the stains on our clothes, and I was bored. I was watching the neighbors as usual because they're so entertaining. I could watch them all day. There is always some drama or another going on." Zan warmed to his subject, despite his trepidation. "Anyway, you know they're very careless with their possessions."

Friedr and Edwin nodded.

"Edwin, you gave me the idea. You borrowed Yelk's tunic, which led to him getting killed by Berk, who was unhappy at being falsely accused of theft. But really, Berk wanted to take Yelk's woman when he gets back to Serende, so their love triangle is short one leg. Berk will be a much better mate to her, trust me." This was almost the old Zan speaking, with his words tumbling over each other.

Edwin sat back on his heels, astonished at hearing the news. "I had no idea. You're very familiar with them. Continue with your tale. You have my interest now."

"I spend a lot of time watching them. They're extremely entertaining, and we'll never have a better opportunity. Well anyway, I needed leather to repair Friedr's clothes, so I borrowed what I needed, only from a different camp than you borrowed from." Zan told his tale truthfully, unconsciously assuming the stance Christoph had always assumed when telling an epic tale around the campfire. "The different squads don't talk to each other except with their swords, so they each think they're the only ones with thievery in the ranks, and they certainly won't tell any other squad about it because they'd lose face. But while I was looking for leather, I noticed they really like bright colors in their knit hats and socks." Zan waited to see their reactions, but they were both looking at him with unreadable expressions.

"I don't think these guards had time to get the usual tan socks and such from their commissary in Serende before they started looking for us, because the socks they all have on are totally unsuitable colors for hiding in the brush. They really stand out. Of course, it's partly because their feet and heads are so much bigger than ours, so it's a lot of color to be flashing around out there, you know." Zan's earnest expression was the one he'd always wore when trying to justify a major prank of some sort. "Qark's hat was as large as a sweater for an older novice might be, and he's actually somewhat small for a minotaur." He fell silent and began working again.

"Yes? Go on. Tell Uncle Friedr the rest of your story." Friedr eyes had the flat look he often had when he was about to take apart an impertinent opponent. "Finish explaining how you got the pretty thread for the new flowers on my shirt."

Zan's heart sank as he looked at Friedr's expression. "Oh, dear, I've put my foot in it, haven't I?" Taking a deep breath, Zan continued his story apologetically. "Well, I noticed they're very careless with their nice socks and hats. They just leave them lying around drying after they wash them. Anybody could steal them, so I decided to…um…take a few of the prettier ones into protective custody."

He noticed Edwin's face growing expressionless, hurriedly continued his tale. "All I had to do was give them a better wash than their original owners did, unravel them, and then split the yarn into individual strands. Once I did that, the yarn was perfect for what I needed, and now I've more than enough for anything I want to do." He took the lid off the sewing box and showed them the neat balls of colorful thread. "We can stay clean looking, no matter how bloody we get between here and Braden."

Trying to avoid his friends' eyes, Zan looked down at the shirt he wore, which now had bright flowers on the shoulder and collar. He'd completely disguised the stains with tiny flowers, even on the cuffs. Just like Friedr and Edwin's shirts, every stain had a bunch of tiny flowers perfectly camouflaging it. "I did yours first because I was worried I was being too much of a dandy in wanting mine done so badly. But now, all our clothes are looking good. And I've enough yarn so when we're done killing Aggie, I can fix us up again."

"So what you're saying is you stole *their* clothes to use to decorate *our* clothes so we won't have to wear *stained* clothes when we go to fight a waterdrake, which will be rather messy." Edwin looked at Zan expectantly. "Have I got it right?" His expression was unreadable.

"Yes," Zan admitted. "I guess so." Utterly embarrassed, he burst out, "It just seemed so wasteful to me to let those nice socks get stolen by passing strangers when I needed the yarn and we're part of the family, so to speak. I mean we *have* been neighbors now for quite a while."

"Has anyone else died over this 'borrowing'?" Friedr's voice shook with trying not to laugh.

"No, they're all still healthy, I swear. But, there are a few bloody noses and black eyes, and some of them have gotten blisters from not wearing socks in their boots. Qark, in the camp near the river, often had an earache at first from not wearing a hat when on guard duty at night." To Zan, it appeared Friedr was angered. His eyes had gone flat, and it was evident he was holding his tongue.

Desperately hoping to stave off Friedr's wrath, Zan quickly added, "But it's not my fault, Friedr. They're supposed to be professionals. They should have more than one pair of socks in their kit, don't you see? It's very poor planning on their part."

His voice took on a tone of superiority as he said, "I've three pairs of socks in my kit. They should too." On seeing Friedr's eyes glaze over, Zan hastened to say, "I swear I only took one sock from each campfire, I promise. So each guard I borrowed from still has one sock, and he can alternate which foot to wear it on. About the green hat...I do feel a little bad, but Qark should've kept a better watch on it. Yark was planning on stealing it too, you know, so I took it to make sure it was nice and safe. Besides, I needed green for leaves and such. And Qark is a smart minotaur. He brought spare underwear. He's been wearing it on his head to keep his ears warm when he stands guard at night, so he'll be fine. He'll get over them taunting him and be stronger for it.

"Yark isn't very smart. In fact, when they get back to Mal Evol City, I bet Yark's woman, Nal, changes huts and becomes Zirik's woman. He's really a much smarter minotaur, and she should've picked him originally. But Yark's family is well-placed, so there you go."

Finally, Edwin managed to say, "Well, I knew they were all stirred up about some interpersonal issues in several of the camps, but I'd no idea you were the culprit." He snapped his mouth shut, as he was very close to giving in to a fit of hysterical laughter.

Friedr agreed. "I did notice they've been dealing with each other rather more harshly than usual."

Zander tried to look remorseful and failed. "I suppose I shouldn't have done it. It wasn't very neighborly of me," he muttered as he observed Edwin's and Friedr's red faces and bulging eyes, assuming they were angry with him. Sighing and not feeling as sorry as he should, he shrugged and grudgingly added, "I won't do it anymore. Besides, I've enough yarn now to keep myself busy for a long while unless we really get bloody. Anyway, they've all settled down now. They're back to being as happy as their sorts of folk ever are."

He suddenly grinned. "But I didn't know you two liked watching them too. I thought I was the only one who liked to spy on the neighbors. I've never come across people as interesting as them and this may be the only chance we have to get to know them and how they think. I've been keeping a journal of what they do and all their dramas. It's just like a romance novel, only much more violent."

Edwin and Friedr couldn't stand it any longer. They burst out laughing, howling until they were gasping for air. "Oh, Zan! What a madman you are, stealing their laundry to embellish our clothes." Edwin laughed hysterically. "Every time I think you've completely grown up on me and I'll never again see the mad, merry lightning-mage I loved so much, you do something like this." He howled with laughter, tears running down his face, while Zan sat nonplussed, wondering what he said that was so funny.

"Zander Christophson, it's rude to borrow with the intention of keeping, but you're forgiven." Friedr finally got himself under control. "Zan, you're a treasure. What would we do without you? And I do like the way you embellished away the bloodstains on our shirts."

Chapter 26 ~ Traveling down the Road

It was around noon of the seventeenth day they had been camping in the cave entrance. Linked, the three of them smoothed and widened the path as much as they could up to the lair. There they stopped, and Aggie had a chance to calm down, sinking back into his usual somnolent state. Even with all the work they were doing, they would need to refine the path more as they traveled.

No matter how smooth they were able to make it, the journey would be difficult for Friedr.

Despite his occasional bursts of conversation about the neighbors, Zan became more withdrawn each day, slowly becoming consumed with his own guilt over having set the geas on his father. Nevertheless, he pretended he was fine, and though Friedr and Edwin knew he was hiding something, they agreed not to force him to talk unless it became a problem.

Friedr made great strides in devising ways to get things done for himself, developing his independence as rapidly as he was able. "I'm getting stronger every day," Friedr remarked as he walked in circles in their cave. He made two turns around the cave one way and then reversed, going the other way for two turns. "I'll be able to walk for most of a day soon, even over rutted ground, I think."

"Your new fighting skills are coming along well too," Edwin told him. "You'll still be able to kick Dario's butt all over the practice yard just like the old days."

"Hmmm...maybe this lame leg will fool him into letting me heal him each time I knock his ass across the yard until he actually does manage to kick my butt," Friedr mused. "I'd like to see how many times I can do it, for my own personal knowledge."

Edwin just smiled and shook his head ruefully. "Well then, we should work some more on your center of gravity when sword fighting." He handed Friedr his sword, well-padded with the leather left over from making Friedr's brace. "You don't have the agility you once had. I think I can take advantage of you being crippled, so I will be lunging at you, and you need to block and 'kill' me."

Friedr's expression was inscrutable. He took his sword and limped to the opposite side of the cave, preparing himself to do battle. *I'm tired, and I ache everywhere. But if I don't do this, I'll never see Aeolyn again or get to see Freylin and Rynne grow up. I won't even get to see our new baby. I must keep at it.* Friedr was unused to having self-defeating thoughts. He said to Edwin, "The enemy won't always wait until I'm rested to attack, so do your worst, farm boy. I've a few tricks that will surprise even you!"

Pulling himself together, Friedr met Edwin's attack and successfully fended him off, pressing his own attack. Grimly determined to beat his infirmity, Friedr endured what he had to in preparation to make the long trek home.

Later, when they had cleaned themselves up and were seated on their bedrolls having a refreshing cup of cool water and a ration biscuit, Edwin sensed Friedr's mood. Trying to find something to divert him and cheer him up, he suggested they play a game of stones while

Zan scouted the valley and eavesdropped on the squads still watching their cave entrance. Friedr and Edwin frequently joined him in eavesdropping on the neighbors too and agreed with Zan they were a never-ending source of entertainment.

Absorbed in their game, they looked up as Zan dropped down to sit next to them, a worried look on his face. "I hate to interrupt you, but something's going on out there, and I think you should see for yourself, Edwin."

Edwin closed his eyes and linked with Zan. Surprised, he felt Friedr enter into the link unasked, and together they drifted over the camps, listening and discovering what had Zan so upset. A messenger was circulating between the camps. Half of the squads had been recalled to the keep. The others now moved closer to the cave entrance, setting up camp in a wide half-circle.

"We couldn't have gone that way anyway, Zan. Friedr can't crawl through the thorn forest anymore. That's why we were told to remember the Forbidden Road. But it does appear they've decided we have rested and healed for long enough." Edwin looked at his companions. "I say we get a good night's sleep and begin to pack up tomorrow. We can move out at dawn the day after. Agreed?"

Friedr and Zan nodded their heads in agreement. Zan said, "I should share out what we need to keep and use from Christoph's possessions, and then we can fetch what we don't need back to the furthest cache. Once we're nearer the southern end of the valley, we can forward them on to Braden with a note to Moran, letting him know we are on our way."

"You know, that's a good idea. We should go through our kits and fetch everything we don't absolutely need back to the cache. It means we won't be struggling along down here with a lot of excess baggage like we were the night we came here." Edwin gazed into the dark, organizing their move in his mind. "If we start fetching things back to the cache this afternoon, we won't burn ourselves out and we'll still be able to leave the day after tomorrow as we planned, with our chi fully regained."

Friedr shifted, trying unsuccessfully to get comfortable, and Zan surreptitiously cast a spell for pain relief on him, layering it in a dampening field and tying it off. "Thank you, Zan. I do feel better now." He smiled at Zan and then changed the subject. "That was the first time I've been able to tag along with you uninvited when you use your air-magic to spy on the neighbors," Friedr remarked. "I wonder why I can do it now when I haven't been able to tag along before, though I've tried many times."

"It could be you've had to practice to join in. Or maybe it's a compensation for the handicap, like the sense of hearing in a newly blind person. Your other skills and senses may be stronger now. We should test you," Edwin replied. "You'll need every skill you can muster on this trek."

The rest of the afternoon and evening, Edwin and Zan spent their chi fetching things they didn't need back to the cache and restocking the medical kit and food supplies.

That night, Zan sat in the doorway to the cave just out of sight of the watching neighbors, but where he had a view of the valley. Watching the stars shining in the skies over Mal Evol, he thought about Christoph. He missed him and wished he was able to talk to Dane about the whole thing. His mind, as always, turned around the problem of the geas he set on Chris, compelling him to speak only the truth, and the terrible consequences the act had brought upon his father. *Oh, why did I do it? Dane's going to hate me for what I did. Maybe Anna will too. But I did it, and now I have to live with it.*

As he looked out, seeing the campfires dotting the valley before him, he thought in some ways he would be sorry to leave this place. They'd been fairly safe there, despite being completely housebound. With a pang, he realized he would actually miss the neighbors. He spent the rest of his watch spying on the minotaurs, completely diverted by their simple triumphs and tragedies.

Edwin woke up, and after talking to Zan about the legions and catching up on the gossip, he suddenly realized they would need a way to carry the mage-light safely. "I'm going to have to find a lantern," he told Zan. "But I'll be horribly unwell after I've brought it here, if I can even move something like it."

"Don't worry, I'll heal you. We do need to have some form of light," Zan replied. "Your father used the fungi, but Friedr will need better light to travel by."

Edwin found a lantern in the tent of a squad leader. Focusing his will on it, he visualized the lantern on the sandy floor of their cave in front of him. Knives lanced through his head, and the world gave a peculiar lurch. He doubled over, throwing up. Immediately, Zan was at his side, soothing away the pain.

Friedr woke up from his nap. "What's wrong with Edwin?" he asked Zan groggily. "What happened?"

"He just borrowed a lantern from the neighbors. He's having a reaction to fetching the metal. I've healed his headache, and he's not throwing up anymore. We can put a mage-lamp inside it, and then we'll have light while we walk," Zan replied. "He can see straight now, so he'll be better soon."

"Good idea, Edwin," Friedr replied. "The neighbors don't read much anyway." He rose, stretched, and stood looking out of the entrance, seeing the campfires sparsely scattered across the valley before him. With a shock, Friedr realized once the waterdrake was gone, the legions would have a clear road to the border of southern Neveyah.

They could move troops down it, and no one would see them.

"Edwin, we need to seal this road up at both ends," Friedr told his companions. "We'll be removing the only obstacle that prevents them from using this road now. Without Aggie, they'll have a straight shot to Braden if we can't convince Moran to abandon the city. We wouldn't have any warning—they'd have the element of surprise on their side. Besides, we need to keep this road secret for the Hero Foretold, and who knows how long it'll be before he comes."

Chagrined that he hadn't thought about either problem, Edwin immediately agreed. "I'll seal it up before we go, and also leave a message so the next person through here will know what to do to reopen it."

"The next person through here will be the Hero Foretold," replied Zan with certainty. "No one will come this way ever again until he takes this path."

***

At dawn, Zan stood at the entrance, and using his air-magic, he projected his voice to each of the neighbors' campfires where they were all gathering to eat breakfasts of some sort of porridge. Speaking to the surprised minotaurs, who each thought he was in their camp somewhere, he said, "Virk, I meant to tell you—your missing book of poetry is in Squad Leader Bort's tent. He should be just about done reading it now. And Gort, I think you should know Miruk has been coveting your woman since before you came here. He plans to eat your heart before you get back to Serende and take her. I don't think he would treat her well, so…now you know. Goodbye and good luck." He stepped back and turned to securing the straps on his kit.

Surprised, Friedr looked at Zan and said "Minotaurs read poetry?"

"Yes, but in my opinion, it's rather awful. It seems to consist of rather simple rhymes about fighting and such, like, 'I bash his nose and down he goes' or 'the warrior dread with the shield of red,'" Zan replied. "But they seem to like it. They consider it very romantic, and their women adore it, the bloodier the better."

"That sounds right," Friedr chuckled. He was eager to get started but dreaded the physical strain of the journey. A pall of cheerlessness settled over him as he looked down the valley, seeing the sun and the blue sky for what might well be the last time.

Resolutely, Friedr turned his back on it and limped toward the rear of the cave where the long, dark, Forbidden Road waited for him. *What doesn't actually kill me can only make me stronger. I'm sure I'll be stronger for this.* His eyes had become hooded, his face grim and set with his thought. It was an expression that had become his habit. Friedr no longer had a baby-face, and no one who saw him now would call him cute. In its place was the face of a man who had seen too much, all hard planes and grim features.

At the entrance to the underground road, Friedr and Zan watched as Edwin collapsed the entrance to the cave, sealing it completely from the outside, working his earth magic as if in a trance. Even if the legions were to come right up to it, they would be unable to see it as it now perfectly blended into the base of the cliffs below the keep. Then Edwin smoothed the inside of the cave entrance, engraving the image of an arched doorway on it. Over the archway, he engraved the words "Seek through magic the door that lies herein. Earth moves and the Sky appears."

Zan and Friedr looked at what he had done and then at each other. "That's something a hero in a book would have to solve," murmured Zan.

"It'll be his grandson or great-grandson who'll have to solve it," replied Friedr, also speaking quietly. "Aeos had her hand in the message, I'm sure."

Certainly, Edwin appeared surprised as he held the lantern up and saw what he had done. Extinguishing the campfire and looking around, they started down the path to the cave of the waterdrake, with Edwin leading the way and carrying the lantern with the cheery little flame.

Chapter 27 ~ Aggie

The first steps of the dark path were fairly easy for Friedr to travel, with the sound of running water growing progressively louder as they walked down the narrow tunnel. Although they had done a great deal of smoothing of the way, a lot remained for Edwin to do to make it easier for Friedr to walk the long, dark road.

Once away from the cave mouth and the small glimmer of sky they'd enjoyed there, time seemed to stretch, and the darkness closed in. Friedr limped painfully but with dogged determination, while Zan maintained as many pain-relief spells layered over him as they dared to use. It might be months before he would be able to walk without a certain amount of pain.

After what seemed a long time of walking, they came to the first drop, though in reality they knew they weren't too far down the path—in truth it was very near the entrance. Edwin had created broad steps for Friedr to walk down, one step at a time, and he refined them as they went along. Each time they came to a place that was too rough or required even a small leap, Edwin and Zan smoothed and bridged the way. Now they neared the river. Once they reached the place that overlooked it, they stopped to rest and scouted the path ahead.

Abbess Halee had originally created, smoothed, and improved the path. She had made places they would be able to rest, though they would not be able to reach the nearest resting place the first day because Friedr couldn't walk even half that far. Edwin would take care of making a place to camp when they had gone as far as they could that day. Much of Halee's work had been destroyed by D'Mal when he rearranged the path and made it a deadly and dangerous place to be. Occasional flash floods had also done their damage.

The path high above the river had been slippery, but it was now safe for Friedr. The walls were dank, and in some places, they wept groundwater, but Edwin diverted it to drain away harmlessly. Many strange growths and tiny creatures were revealed by the light of the lantern, clinging to the walls in groups and clusters. Obviously, they were not suited to life in the light of day, as the rare creatures were a pale pinkish-white and many of them had no eyes. It was hard to know if any of the denizens of the cave were poisonous. They would simply have to avoid disturbing them, if it was at all possible.

Luminescent fungi occasionally dotted the walls, glowing with a pale, greenish light. In some places, one could walk by their light, but more commonly, it was completely dark. The lantern cast a comforting glow, though the pool of light was rather smaller than they'd have preferred.

The cold and damp settled into Friedr's bones, but Zan and Edwin alternated casting ease, layering it into a dampening field and tying it off. Even with their frequent assistance, Friedr limped more slowly as the day stretched on and he tired. Still, they were taking a much more direct route than they would have done had they returned to Braden the way they came. The first day they were able to travel only a short distance, only two leagues, but it was all Friedr could do. Despite that, they were pleased with their progress. The two leagues they traveled underground brought them the equivalent of a day's travel south, had they been above ground.

They camped in a niche Edwin enlarged, high above the river and sheltered from the breeze, which seemed to blow through the cavern continuously. Soon they were cooking soup over a little fire. The warmth of the fire was welcome and so was the hot soup. Edwin broke jerky into it and added barley to make a thick, nourishing, and surprisingly tasty stew. Though the variety of their meals was somewhat limited, they were much healthier than when they arrived in the cave.

That night, they took turns telling tales they remembered Christoph regaling them with, and Friedr took the first watch. When Zan relieved him, he wasn't able to get comfortable enough to sleep. After debating with himself, he finally asked Zan to cast a small sleep spell on him, feeling embarrassed. "If I can't sleep well, I won't be fit to travel," he said wryly. "I'd be upset if Edwin didn't ask for help, so now I must follow my own rules."

"Don't worry about Edwin, Friedr. He'll never change. He'll always think he should suffer in silence," replied Zan. "I'm mixing ease with this, so you won't wake up too stiff and sore."

The next four days passed in the same way as the first, each with varying degrees of difficulty and discomfort for them. Each day was a test of endurance and determination for Friedr. Despite the cheery fire they set each time they rested, they all began to feel the cold and damp.

Friedr had fully regained his abilities as a healer. Edwin and Zan both suspected he had actually gained in strength, as it took very little chi for him to heal any wounds they incurred on their journey. Certainly, his elemental magic had increased, compensating well for his physical handicap.

As they approached the lair of the waterdrake, each man wished nothing more than to have the battle over with and be on their way to Braden.

On what they thought might be the fifth evening, they were camped two hours' walk from the waterdrake's lair. Now they finalized their plans to remove Aggie. Once he was taken care of, they would either have to return to this site or rest in Aggie's lair, because the tiny exit to the rest of the underground road would have to be enlarged. As it was right now, Edwin and Zan could crawl on their bellies through the low exit tunnel, but Friedr was unable to. Regardless, they were all sure they would much rather not slither through the filth that lay in that part of the cavern.

"I think we're in for a tough go of it," Friedr told them while they sat warming themselves by the fire. "Aggie's a canny old thing. He's more than likely seen his share of smart mages come through his caverns long before D'Mal ever brought him here. Shields will be the critical factor in this fight. We must come at him from three angles to keep him distracted and unable to concentrate on only one of us.

"I'll cast spells while you two hack away at him, keeping him busy since my sword skills won't be running to this sort of battle yet. His eyes are set in his head like a bird's eyes, so the safest place for me to stand will be directly in front of him where he can't see me. You two being on either side of him will keep his eyes occupied, I can only hope. Full shields, everyone, and reflect everything he tosses at us right back at him. Conserve your chi as much as possible, and don't forget to draw chi through your sword as you go so we don't end up like we did back at the Shadow Castle."

Friedr looked almost like his old self, planning the battle. "Edwin, use your special trick at your first opportunity, and we'll try to copy it as well as we can. We have to use the power of our swords to magnify the rebounding magic as intensely as we can because Aggie will have shields of his own, and I promise you they'll be far better than ours or D'Mal's. Your lightning needle might be the thing that wins this battle for us, Edwin."

"I rather doubt it from what I've read, Friedr," replied Edwin. "He's a rare beast, but the battles with his sort have been well documented, and most ended up being endurance tests, with one rather famous exception. You just hack and slash until you manage to win."

"Well, your grandfather and Father Rall survived their battle, and magic *did* do the trick," said Zan, "but Feia always said it was just Wynn's dumb luck that they lived."

"Our 'dumb luck' has been rather minimal of late," Edwin replied with a rather grim smile. "I'd prefer to rely on a sharp sword and a good plan, both of which we're fortunate to have."

The next morning after breakfast, the three mages put their armor on, feeling strange as they did so. They hadn't worn it since they had taken refuge in the cave. Once they were completely geared up, they broke camp and began walking toward Aggie's lair. Edwin and Zan had sculpted the trail so they approached the cavern without Aggie seeing them, though he would most likely know they were there, as his senses of hearing and smell were excellent. Moving as silently as they were able, they neared the waterdrake's lair. Once they came to the last corner, they left their gear in the niche they had prepared for just that purpose.

Drawing their swords, they entered the lair of the agitated waterdrake. Zan quickly moved to the left, and Edwin moved to the right, spreading their group out as much as possible and trying to divert Aggie's attention from Friedr, who was less able to maneuver. Their tactic worked. As long as Friedr remained still, Aggie ignored him.

Aggie himself was both dreadful and amazing to look at. His skin was clear and almost jelly-like in appearance. Tiny eyes glared from either side of his gigantic head. He relied upon his acute sense of smell to guide him to his prey. A spiked crest ran from the center of his massive head to between his huge shoulders. Aggie was three times Friedr's height at the shoulder, and the length of his body was easily five times that. At the rear of the beast was a deadly, whip-like tail fully as long as his entire body. It lashed back and forth, not unlike a cat's tail. His huge head and gaping maw were attached to a long, sinuous neck that swung back and forth as he waited for whoever it was he scented coming down the path to his nest.

The lair itself was above the river on a huge, mounded area, sloping down to the cavern walls. The area closest to the cave wall was obviously Aggie's privy, and the stench was indescribable. Huge scrapes on the walls showed where he had occasionally pulled down parts of the walls to bury his leavings. Large clusters of luminous fungus clung to the walls and the roof, lighting the cavern with a greenish glow, lending an eerie quality to the scene.

With relief, Edwin noted the huge creature had not fouled the river. In a way, it was no surprise, since Aggie had to drink from it too. *Most creatures don't foul their own nests if they can avoid it. Thanks to D'Mal marooning him here, poor old Aggie has no choice but to use his cavern as his privy but he's done his best to keep his lair clean,* thought Edwin as he got his first view of the awesome and formidable creature. *At least if we survive this, we can clean up in the river.*

Aggie paced back and forth, sniffing the air. Now his long tail lashed much faster and far more sinuously than any cat's tail possibly could, slicing through the air as quickly as living lightning. Edwin and Zan were careful not to come too close. The tail was as deadly as the rest of him, and a blow from it could knock them out or even kill them.

Suddenly, Aggie raised his head and bellowed, a thunderous sound that shook the cavern. A deluge of water sheeted over them, their shields holding firm under the onslaught. Zan fired a big bolt of lightning off at Edwin, who mixed it with the water and sent it back at Aggie.

The lightning went through Aggie's shields along with the water, and he roared his pain. Immediately, his shields went back up. Fire now sheeted over them and was immediately followed by ice. The companions' shields held strong, and they began returning his magic in various and sundry combinations, whittling away at Aggie's shields. Periodically, they were able to pierce his shields and wound him, but his ability to withstand the worst of their assaults was astonishing.

Fortunately, Aggie did not seem to realize they were using his own magic against him and only rarely using their own. He cast spell after spell, all of which they returned laced with water. Unfortunately, Aggie was an elemental creature who was born of magic and would only run out of the ability to cast spells when he was dead.

It was a long and grinding battle. Each time they thought he was just about done for, he came back at them. Zan had been working his way around to where he was very close to Aggie, who had been concentrating on Edwin. Taking his sword in both hands, he began slashing at Aggie's exposed haunch, ducking behind a large stalagmite between attacks. Edwin had moved to the other side of him and was doing the same.

Roaring his defiance, Aggie lashed wildly with his tail. As the tip of Aggie's tail whipped past Zan, Stormbringer flashed in the greenish light and a good four feet of the tail lay twitching on the cave floor. At the same time, Friedr returned a ball of fire at Aggie's head.

Screaming in pain and rage, Aggie thrashed and his shields faltered. Enraged, he slashed at Edwin with his right claw. Ducking and dodging, Edwin evaded the massive beast's attempts to squash him like a bug. Leviathan flickered and the claw fell, twitching and bleeding on the ground. A high-pitched keening sound erupted from Aggie, and Zan fell to his knees, cowering behind his stalagmite with his hands clutched over his ears, as did Edwin.

Unable to stand on all four legs now, Aggie fell to his right side, thrashing and narrowly missing Zan, who leapt to his feet and began hacking at the flailing beast, as did Edwin.

At last regaining his footing on three legs, Aggie attacked with his water magic. Water sheeted off their shields, but it was not delivered with the punch Aggie's attacks had once had. Still, the two swordsmen's footing was now tremendously precarious in the slippery muck of Aggie's lair. Struggling for balance with every step, they pressed their attacks.

Aggie was confused, swinging his massive head first toward Zan and then toward Edwin, still ignoring Friedr completely, snapping and snarling with his huge maw. The shrieking noise the wounded beast emitted nearly deafened them, and the cavern shook with each stomp of his gigantic feet.

"Back, both of you. Step back!" Friedr shouted. Immediately, Edwin and Zan both retreated as far as they were able. A massive flash of lighting blinded them. Aggie convulsed, his head rearing back. He screeched another ear-shredding shriek. Covering their ears, Edwin and Zan cowered behind their stone pillars. Aggie's shields went down and did not come back up.

Friedr drew chi through Dragonstorm and immediately cast a second massive bolt that transfixed the beast, holding him jerking and twitching. Quickly, Friedr drew chi through Dragonstorm again, being sure to keep his chi level as high as he could.

"Swords up! All together now," shouted Friedr. "One…two…three!" On three, they each unleashed a massive bolt through their swords, and Aggie convulsed mightily. His stump of a tail whizzed past Edwin, spewing blood as it whipped by him, narrowly missing his head, and then lashed back at Zan, knocking him to the ground. Suddenly, the cavern was silent except for the sound of the river. The silence was so unexpected, it too was nearly deafening.

"Is he dead?" asked Zan, struggling to stand up in the bloody muck. "Aaugh…I hit my head. I can't tell if he is dead or not." Spots flashed before his eyes, and he was nearly blinded by a headache. The cavern reeled, and he felt nauseated. He leaned against a stalagmite, clutching his head, then fell to his knees and threw up.

Zan pitched forward as darkness softly claimed him.

Chapter 28 ~ The Forbidden Road

As their hearing adjusted to the silence, Edwin and Friedr both delved the body of the huge beast. "Don't worry, Zan, he's dead. Thank you, Aeos, thank you for the swords that made the difference in this battle." Friedr's fervent prayer was echoed by Edwin. Hearing no answer from Zan, Friedr paused, sending his senses out. "Zan?" Sensing he was alive but unconscious, he said, "He's been knocked out. A concussion, I think." He tried to move through the muck, but his footing was precarious at best. "He's down, lying in the worst part of the mess. I don't think I can get to him."

"You stay there, Friedr. I've enough chi to handle Zan's injury. We didn't use much of our own magic until the end, and believe me, it's too slippery here for you." Edwin quickly waded through the bloody morass, around the gigantic carcass, to Zan's side, moving as quickly as he was able. At last he found him, face down in the muck. As he climbed over the dead beast's massive neck, he delved Zan, finding many contusions and bruises, along with a serious head injury. Just as he arrived at Zan's side, the mage began coming around, rolling on to his back, groaning.

"Don't worry, Zan. I have you." Edwin raised him to a sitting position, leaning against the stalagmite. "Oh. This isn't good...I can fix it. Hold still." Placing his hands on either side of Zan's head, Edwin sent his spirit deep into his body, healing the fractured skull.

When he'd healed the worst of the suffering mage's injuries, he said, "Let's try to find a spot to rest and get bathed. Then we can decide what to do next."

He healed all the rest of Zan's injuries, mostly minor abrasions.

Down by the river was a wide sandy area, obviously where Aggie had spent a great deal of time lounging. Friedr was able to negotiate his way down to the small beach on his own, meeting the other two there. It was dry and clear of muck, and they made camp. Edwin was exhausted and aching all over. Wearily, they began to strip, desperate to clean themselves up and wash their leathers and armor as well as they could.

After a moment of watching Edwin unsuccessfully attempting to move his left shoulder well enough to get his leathers off, Friedr grabbed Edwin and delved him, finding his shoulder not quite dislocated but seriously wrenched. Forcing him to stand still, Friedr healed his multiple cuts and abrasions. Friedr himself was completely unscathed, having been kept out of the physical battle. "Edwin, why do you always refuse to ask for healing? You're a fool when you choose to suffer rather than to ask for help." Edwin looked startled at Friedr's comment.

Zan nodded in agreement, looking rather like Dane as he did so. "I said the same thing to him not too long ago. But at least this time, he didn't have huge gashes lying open for so long they couldn't be healed properly." He glared at Edwin. "Thankfully, your augmentations came back over those."

"I didn't realize I was injured," Edwin said sheepishly. "I guess I just don't feel it. I'm so tired right now."

"Well, it affects your performance and, trust me, you really don't want anything to get infected," Friedr replied dryly, as he tied his spells off. "There. Now we can all rest, even you."

"Yeesh, but this place stinks," Zan said, once he had recovered somewhat from the battle. "Let's do what we have to and get out of here. I can't eat in this place. I've enough chi to help widen the exit, if you two do."

"We're going to do something even better. We're going to bury Aggie and the upper part of his lair," Edwin told them. "I don't want anything big able to nest down here ever again. Something tells me we must make this into a passable and safe road for the future. Now that we're down here, I know what I have to do."

"You may have a good idea, Edwin," Friedr replied, trying vainly to get comfortable on the hard ground. "I think it'll take a very fine touch, though, to do it the way you want."

Edwin layered pain-relieving spells over Friedr, winking at him.

"Thank you, my brother. I needed that." Friedr felt like sighing with relief but restrained himself.

"I think the three of us can do it and make it safe. You two will use your earth magic to bury Aggie, and I will keep it from burying us. I'll make this place into as neatly built a tunnel as you could ask for, with the path high enough to stay dry even during floods. It won't take much effort or chi." Edwin's confidence was reassuring, and Zan and Friedr both agreed to his plan.

"We know from our true-dreams that the Hero Foretold will need to use this road," Zan replied. "The campsites we've made already will help him, as will the path we've smoothed. Edwin can do the same for the rest of the length of this river, but we're under a time constraint. We must do what we can and quickly move on. I have this feeling of urgency I can't be rid of."

Edwin and Friedr looked at Zan, wondering what he meant.

Zan said, "It's been three weeks since Christoph died. I don't know how long it takes to get prepared for it, but Lourdan might be ready to undergo the ritual that had D'Mal so upset, this remaking process. Once it's done, he'll be ready to return to Mal Evol and be at our doorstep within two seasons. Christoph's ghost was very specific there."

Zan exhaled heavily, looking off into the darker corners of Aggie's lair. "We know Lourdan has earth magic, so we must assume he will able to sense what we're doing if we're not finished before he comes to Mal Evol. It's vital we don't alert him to what we've done here or he'll ruin all our work. So we must set a ward on this place that will keep it from his sight." He paused and then added, "Also, we need as much time as possible to build the shield/wall. We absolutely must seal off Neveyah at the Gap if we do nothing else, or we will have failed and Lourdan will win."

"Once again, you're correct, Zan. You have sliced right to the meat of the matter." Friedr's deep voice conveyed his respect for Zan's thinking. "Sometimes, you skitter around from topic to topic like a fart in a skillet until my head spins trying to keep up with you. But somehow, you've had a one-track mind through it all and have remained fixated on your goal. You haven't once stopped thinking about it, have you, no matter what silly thing you bring up to entertain us?"

"You're right, Friedr. I only care about this one thing—finishing the job as well as we can under the circumstances and getting home alive." Zan's face showed no trace of the silly façade he'd once habitually cultivated. Then he broke into a wide smile. "I guess I *am* like 'a fart in a skillet' though, now you mention it. So many things go through my head even I can't keep up with them."

The three men laughed, with a great deal of banter back and forth as they rested and recovered their chi until finally, Edwin said, "Well, if you two are feeling up to it, then let's get the poor old thing decently buried." Edwin stood and stretched. Friedr also rose with the peculiarly graceful way he had developed, using his walking stick and his good leg to lever himself up, standing at Edwin's right side. Zan took his place at Edwin's left side.

Facing the reeking lair and the gargantuan bulk of Aggie's carcass, they linked and raised their shields, overlapping them. "Okay, you two loosen the roof over Aggie. I'll guide and form it as it comes down," Edwin instructed them. As the roof began to fall over Aggie, Edwin contained the soil and rock, forming a smooth wall that completely sealed Aggie's tomb off from the new underground road. The rumblings ceased and the dust settled.

On the center of the wall, which was formed as neatly as any mason could have made it, Edwin deeply engraved the words, "Here lies Aggie's tomb. He was the last waterdrake in Neveyah. We did not wish to kill him but had no choice. Stefyn D'Mal kidnapped him and imprisoned him here to devour unwary travelers. He died alone and friendless and far from his home. Though Aggie was born in the world of Chysat, may Aeos comfort his soul. He was only trying to live as well as he was able." Edwin also listed their names and what he thought the date might be.

Zan and Friedr stood looking at the engraving and then looked at Edwin. Zander's left eyebrow was raised, giving him the questioning look he often had when he was unsure if he should ask or not.

"The next person who comes through here should know he's not alone, that others have been down this path." Edwin shrugged. "Also, I fear if we don't make the rest of this road as fine as we can, Friedr won't make this journey as quickly as we need to go."

The place they first entered the old lair now led directly to the wide, sandy place they were standing on. Turning their attention to the tiny exit tunnel, Edwin began guiding them in enlarging it, making an arched tunnel tall enough for Friedr and wide enough to walk four abreast. Using the earth Edwin removed from the tunnel, they built the path up so it was high above the river and wouldn't be washed away in one of the infrequent floods, leaving access to the river for getting water and bathing at the sandy beach. Edwin then moved a few samples of the luminescent fungi to the new walls so that, eventually, they would light the way.

After they had finished the new tunnel, they rested and regained their chi. "It's amazing how much better this place smells already," Friedr stated, as he shared out the dry ration bars and cups of tea. "The wall and tunnel both look as good as the work of the best stonemasons," he told Edwin. "Your control of earth-magic is something else, my brother."

"I can't help but be amazed at the inscription you put there for the Hero Foretold." Zan said. "It'll be a comfort for him to know others were here before him, and they survived their ordeals. He'll feel he can go on when things are at their darkest."

"This may be why I was given such large augmentations for earth magic. I confess I've wondered about it, as I've not really used my full earth magic abilities on this journey. I still haven't," Edwin replied, shrugging. "Still, Aeos foresaw we'd find ourselves down here, and she knew I'd need to rebuild the long, dark road. I've been thinking about the wall you said we need to build. *That* is what she gave me this ability for, I am sure—she wants me to build the visible wall."

Friedr agreed. "So much of what we were given was for this part of the journey, though we didn't know it. The swords, the extra augmentations, the skills—they made the difference in our other battles, no doubt. But it was here in the battle with Aggie and in the reforming of the Forbidden Road, as well as for our next great task of sealing off the Gap, where the swords and skills really come into play. When we arrive in Braden, we'll find out what they really do. But she gave me something for later, for when the quest is done and I've returned to my home and my family." His voice was certain. "She made me a healer so when I go home, even though I'm lamed, I'll have a life-work before me that I can feel passionate about. She gave it to me to reward me for serving her faithfully."

They ate, warmed by the little campfire they now sat around. As they rested, they noted fresh air seemed to follow the river as it carved its way under Mal Evol toward Braden. "The stench began to disperse as soon as you buried the poor old thing," remarked Zan. "I feel sort of bad we had to kill him."

"Very true," Edwin agreed. "I suspect Aggie wasn't very healthy because he wasn't made to live in such a warm environment."

"Well, I'd prefer never to see one that's healthy then," Friedr averred wholeheartedly. "I confess he scared the liver out of me when I first laid eyes on him."

"You aren't alone in that sentiment, my brother," replied Edwin. His face broke into his rare smile as he said, "We did something today I once promised I'd never do. In fact, when I first discovered this place and Aggie, I told Aeolyn flat out I'd never take on something as foolish as this. I told her at the time the four of us didn't have a chance against him, and she agreed with me."

"You were right," Zan laughed. "Only three desperate idiots would even believe they'd a chance against a fully grown waterdrake, but somehow we did it. Friedr, you've a lot more lightning ability than you think you do. Now, we just have to get the rest of the way home to Braden."

"It's Dragonstorm, my brother," Friedr replied, trying to be honest with himself as well as with Zan. "With Dragonstorm, I can call all of the elements with strength. I'm fairly good with lightning when I'm not using my sword, though I had to work hard at it as a journeyman. Lightning is the weakest of my magic, but sadly, I find myself using it regularly, so I've had to cultivate it."

They sat and talked a while longer and then rode the wind to scout the rest of the long road before them.

They spent the night as they always did now they were on the road again. Friedr cooked the soup, Zan and Edwin did their laundry in the river and spread it out by the fire to dry.

As they sat around the fire enjoying their meal, the conversation turned to their homes and family, as it so often did. "I hope our new baby is a daughter, although I'll be just as happy for another boy," said Edwin. "But girls—we haven't had any daughters in my family that I know of for several generations. I've always wanted a big family."

"I'm fortunate I've a daughter and a son," agreed Friedr. "I'm hoping for a sweet, quiet child like your Jonny is. The noise in our house is something else at times." He rolled his eyes, and Edwin laughed.

"Jonny's been an amazingly easy baby to raise so far." Edwin tried to hide his sudden pang of longing. "As an only child, I was the sole source of noise in our home, and I was lonely. I'm glad Jonny will have a brother or sister."

"I was so much older than my little brother that we didn't have the chance to become close. I was sent to the Temple when he was only six," replied Friedr. "Mohr has done well with his life, despite having no father and a brother who was absent for most of his childhood. He has four daughters and despairs of ever having a son. They rule his life, and he loves it."

"I just hope to get bonded," said Zan, fearing his dark secret would make it impossible. "If I can just do that, I will feel blessed." Later, in an attempt to appear normal, Zan challenged them to a game of stones, although he was, in truth, depressed and torn between dreading going home and wanting to be there more than anything. Desperately, he tried to keep his unhappiness and guilt from Edwin and Friedr. He had first watch that night, and as always, Zan mended their clothes and fretted over the new bloodstains. *At least I've enough thread to have us looking good again by the time we get to Braden. But why do I care? I'll still have to tell Dane what I did. He'll hate me forever, and why not? I hate myself.*

The darkness seemed to increase his morbid obsession with the horrible decision he'd made in setting the truth geas on his father. Trying to put it out of his mind, his thoughts drifted as they always did to memories of Anna. He had a hard time picturing her face, which upset him. At last, he woke Friedr and fell into his bedroll gratefully.

During his watch, Friedr brought the quest journal up to date. He'd found, since taking on the task, writing in the journal made everything clearer in his mind. He was careful to note he was unsure of the exact date, and then he detailed the fight and the work Edwin had done in making the road passable. Friedr carefully wrote down the conversations pertinent to Temple business, making sure Zan's plan for the wall and shield was detailed and credited to him. He thought, *He has a fine career ahead of him. I think someday he'll be an Abbott. He's really grown into his armor on this journey.*

When Edwin took his place at watch, he spent his time cleaning their boots and armor, washing the last of the muck off and polishing them. When he finished, he called water for drinking and began preparing a packet of one of their favorite porridges, one containing dried fruit and nuts, and brewed the tea for their breakfast. Scouting the road both ahead and behind, he found no one and no creatures other than the small cave denizens.

They were completely alone on the Forbidden Road. Even so, they would post a guard each night.

As soon as they had eaten, they broke camp and began the march down the road, moving as fast as Friedr could go without injuring himself. This was the routine they fell into for the rest of the journey under the ground.

Each day, they traveled a little further than the previous one. By the evening of their sixth day, two days after their battle, they were making good time. The underground road made straight for Braden, allowing them to cover the distance quickly, whereas the old road and trails wound through the valley. Friedr developed an odd, but fluid gait with the assistance of his staff, and he gained in strength and endurance every day, although he was struggling by the end of it.

Early in the morning of the third day after they left Aggie's tomb, Zan and Edwin fetched more supplies. They cleaned out the cache closest to the Shadow Castle and transferred all the goods to the southernmost cache. They were nearly halfway to their goal. Privately, they each wondered what was happening to Lourdan, knowing he would soon be undergoing the remaking, though they didn't know exactly when. None of them would discuss the arcane and mysterious ritual, as each man believed the others were still too raw to talk about it.

All three yearned to get to Braden, even though they dreaded the questioning they would have to endure at Moran's hands. But, more than anything, none of them wanted to spend any more time on the Forbidden Road, locked away from the sunlight, unable to see the sky at all. At least they'd been able to see the sky from the cave entrance.

The melancholy they now felt went deeper than simple grief at the loss of Christoph. The darkness and eternal damp had begun to take a toll on them. Each man now sought to find a talisman to hold on to, some precious seed of light and warmth to keep the darkness at bay.

For Friedr, the knowledge of his children's trust and faith in him spurred him on. He couldn't give up when he had another baby on the way. Three children needed a father, he was alive, and he had to get home to them. The remembrance of the way Aeolyn's hair felt as it fell across his bare chest and the earthy passion she aroused in him gave Friedr the strength and courage to continue when the darkness and pain were too much to bear.

For Zan, it was his memory of Anna and the way he had nearly been moved to tears by the way the candlelight shone on her hair as it spread across his pillow. It had happened on waking together in his room their last morning. The sparkle in her eyes, the sound of her laughter, the passion that lit up the night—all these things were combined in the one golden memory that strengthened and sustained him. The claustrophobic feeling of the road diminished and became bearable when he dared to daydream of the moment that had changed him so profoundly.

Edwin consoled himself with the memory of the day Jonny was born. The memory of the delight in Marya's eyes as she first held their son sustained him. She was born to be a mother, and her joy in the birth of her son was nothing short of a miracle to Edwin. It had been the happiest day of his life and the knowledge they would share that joy again drove him to persevere no matter how the walls of the underground road closed in on him.

He daydreamed of his family constantly. He had felt disconnected from Marya since the days after he nearly burned himself out trying to save Friedr, and he hoped it would return once he was back on the soil of Neveyah. But he could picture the scene at home so clearly in his mind's eye. *How Johnny will love having a sister or brother to play with*, he thought, resolutely placing one foot in front of the other, making the slow journey toward home. *We're going home to our children. We're almost there.* The words formed a mantra, and his feet marched to the beat.

And so they struggled on, each trying to sustain their flagging spirits with their dreams of home, whilst encouraging the others. Zan sang silly songs, Edwin told stories he'd heard as a boy in Markett, and Friedr practiced juggling in the evenings around the campfire. He found that juggling brought him closer to his memory of Christoph and also helped immensely with his balance. Edwin would juggle again one day, but he couldn't bring himself to do it yet.

They each maintained a cheerful façade and buried their melancholy under firm barriers so the others couldn't sense it. Each was sure he was the only one suffering from depression, and they individually made a concerted effort to keep a cheerful attitude.

At last, on what they believed might be the twelfth day underground, they reached the place where the road began the climb to the southern exit from the underground river. The last thing Edwin and Zan did before leaving the Forbidden Road was to empty the southernmost cache, moving everything to the guest-study in Braden, along with a note they placed on Moran's desk, saying they were five days away and had been given a task to complete once they reached Braden, and it was a task that would take several weeks.

They emerged into the twilight of a late harvest evening in southern Mal Evol. The twilight seemed well lit to them after the darkness of the underground road as they camped in the shelter of the cave entrance. As darkness fell, Edwin sealed the entrance, finishing it so it resembled an arched entrance to a Temple that had been bricked up and plastered over. Above the arch he engraved the words "Shadows lie waiting at the end of the Forbidden Road. Let the Hero walk it at need. Earth moves, darkness awaits. Seek ye the truth that lies shrouded beneath the throne."

"You're getting really good at that, Edwin. But why did you write such a mysterious thing?" Zan asked. "It looks like a door to a Temple or something."

"What?" Edwin looked at what he had created and written. He shrugged, an expression of surprise on his face. He had no idea how the words got there, as he couldn't remember writing them. "I don't know," he said, feeling confused and somewhat dismayed. Zan and Friedr just looked at each other.

Edwin was silent for the rest of the night. *It's the door I saw in my dream, the one before which we will all be waiting on a particular day, long years from now. I didn't know...I didn't realize I'd made that door.*

The next morning, they shaded their eyes with their bandannas as they traveled in the bright daylight of southern Mal Evol, until they had grown used to the sunlight. The river had emerged on the Neveyah side of the border. At last, they were behind the shield John Farmer, Garran Andreson, and Halee Randsdottir had erected against the mind-magic of Stefyn D'Mal and the throne of Mal Evol, but even so, they didn't really feel safe. The first day they were above ground, they were attacked by a group of rat-people. Quickly dispatching them, they moved on, driven by their desire to get to Braden.

Chapter 29 ~ Braden

For five days, the three walked down the rough, abandoned road toward Braden, an easy walk for the most part. The rat-people made their presence known, and Zan suffered several annoying encounters with water-sprites as he washed their clothes in the River Morte. Finally, the walls of Braden loomed in the distance. Knowing they would arrive in Braden by noon, Zan made sure they all looked as well turned-out as guests at a bonding ceremony.

Moran was waiting at the gate for them, with John Farmer and Abbott Garran wearing new leathers done in the old style that they favored, their shock clear as they took in the stunning changes in the three questers. The surprise of seeing Friedr so horribly crippled was clearly evident on each face. John was grey and fatigued from his travels. Garran didn't look much better. Both had their swords strapped at their sides, two men whose demeanor said trouble loomed on the horizon.

Edwin's heart sank on seeing his father and Garran looking so grim, overcome with foreboding. After embracing his father, Edwin said, "I think you have news for me, and perhaps it's not good." He looked at his father, who nodded briefly, his eyes unable to meet Edwin's. "You wouldn't have been sent here to meet me otherwise."

"I do have bad news. I'll tell you now or we can wait until you're settled, whichever you prefer," replied John, clearly wishing he did not have to tell him whatever it was.

"Tell me now, and I'll try to absorb it while we walk to the Temple." Terror struck his heart. "It's not.... Is Jonny...is he well?" It was all he could do to ask the question.

At his father's nod, Edwin's heart sank. "Marya...."

"She...the baby came too early, Edwin. You had a daughter, who lived less than a day. It happened right after we got the news about Christoph. Marya is physically healed, as well as they could." John met Edwin's eyes. "Coming on top of the news about Christoph as it did, she suffered a complete breakdown. I won't lie to you—she's in a bad way. Dane's with her, and when he's not there, Anna or Halee is. The three of them have been caring for her around the clock, and the one blessing in all of this is that it's been the catalyst to pull Dane out of his own well of misery. With Christoph gone, no one had the skills to help her, so Beryl called in a mind-healer from Farmington for her. Do you know of Lorana?"

At Edwin's mute nod, John continued. "She arrived three days before we left, and Marya's already showing signs of improvement. Aeolyn still had Jonny with her when I left, but I'm sure he'll come home soon." A worried smile crossed his father's face. "Halee and I went ahead and registered our bonding when Marya became so ill. We can have a big ceremony later if everyone wants, but we had to decide quickly. As her mother-in-law, Halee can legally act as both Jonny and Marya's guardian until you or I return."

Edwin nodded, but it was hard to tell if he was listening.

John continued. "Halee and Dane will stay with her for every minute until we return. Aeolyn is handling Halee's job rather well, actually." He paused, then said, "We all agree Dane shouldn't be alone right now either, so our arrangement works out well."

At a touch on his arm, John turned to meet Zan's worried eyes. "It's that bad?" Zan's eyes probed John's, full of unspoken questions, seeing the answers in John's expression. "If they sent for Lorana, she's suffering from more than simple postpartum depression. It's not good news." He said nothing more but regarded Edwin, gauging his reaction to the news.

John nodded and his face was grim. It had been terribly difficult to keep Marya safe from herself, even with all three of them watching her around the clock. It would be difficult to explain what had really happened in Aeoven and how it had changed everything. He would have to explain it all in detail to Edwin later and dreaded it more than he'd ever dreaded anything.

Numbly, Edwin tried to understand what his father had just told him. Tears stung his eyes as his inability to do anything about the situation came home to him.

Nervously, John looked at his son, seeing a multitude of emotions crossing his face. He spoke to the others, all the while watching Edwin from the corner of his eye. "We know you three have a new quest, although we don't know what Aeos has given you to do. Father Rall said only the true task for which you three were called has been set before you now and that Christoph had completed his task. Garran and I too have been called to use our talents on behalf of the Goddess." John's smile was self-deprecating. "You may remember that Halee encouraged me to get back into practice with my magic somewhat."

"She kicked your butt all over the practice yard until you used it out of self-defense, you mean." Garran wouldn't let him off so easily. "A novice could have wiped the floor with you, you were so pathetic."

In what was obviously a lifetime of habit, John grinned and replied, "If you say so, Garran." He turned back to Friedr. "I've built my sword arm back up to his standard," he said with an ironic smile for Garran, "and my ability to plan a campaign is still what it was. The omens are unclear, but Rall thinks our skills in leading a military campaign are probably needed here, so we've been preparing for war since just after you left Aeoven. I can't imagine what else Aeos would call me away for, when Marya needed me so badly."

"I know you had no intention of going questing ever again, John, especially under the circumstances. We do know what is needed, and we'll talk about it later," ventured Friedr, his eyes full of worry for Edwin, who had remained silent though all of the revelations. "But the Goddess calls us and we must answer, no matter what the cost." Friedr placed his hand on Edwin's shoulder and said, "Lorana was the finest mind-healer of her generation, and she taught both Beryl and Christoph. She's a close friend of Father Rall, so I'm sure Marya will have the support she needs until we're able to go home."

"Yes. Rall is there as often as he can be. She has a family who won't let her fall back into the terrible place she was in those first few days." John looked at his son, and roughly hugged him, trying to comfort him as well as he could. "Are you okay, son?"

Edwin stood still in the road, unable to speak. Dimly, he felt Friedr casting ease on him, but the anger building inside him completely negated it. His voice, when he spoke, was harsh. "No. How could I possibly be okay? I could've stopped it. I have the skills that could have saved my daughter's life! I let Marya down by not being there when she needed me. Jonny needs me, and I'm not there." His stomach was a ball of lead and his fists clenched and unclenched as if searching for something to smash. "How she must hate me. All those years ago, I promised her I'd always be there for her, and I wasn't there when our baby died. I wasn't there when *I* could have saved my daughter's life."

Rage and helplessness overwhelmed him. "When I got Marya away from D'Mal, I promised her I'd always be there to take care of her." With each word, his voice had risen, and now he was shouting. "I failed my wife, Dad. Do you understand? I failed her!" Suddenly, he was consumed by the desire to just drop everything and run, to just go anywhere. "I could have prevented it. I could have saved the baby. I have the skills!" He tore himself away from John's grasp and turned to run to Braden.

John grabbed his arms, forcing Edwin to stay. "No, son! You couldn't have changed anything. Marya was consumed by guilt, thinking *she'd* let *you* down in some obscure way by this unavoidable tragedy. We finally convinced her you'd never think so of her."

"No, no, no!" Abruptly, Edwin burst into tears, sobbing in frustration, releasing all of the grief and misery of the last month in a torrent of tears. The ordeal in Mal Evol, Christoph's death, the baby's death, and Marya's breakdown—it was all too much for him. As if a dam had burst, he howled, sobbing and holding on to his father for comfort, not caring he stood in the road wailing like a child. All the anger, frustration, and misery of the last weeks combined with his gut-wrenching guilt for abandoning Marya when she needed him, and he broke under the weight of it.

John held his son, reassuring him. "You'll have time to write her a letter, and she knows you'll be home soon. Lorana's there. She'll help her if anyone can. The omens all point to our return the week before Winter Solstice and Holy Day. I've letters for you from Halee, Dane, and Beryl, and Marya herself has written one, but…I warn you she was distraught when she wrote it. There'll also be many other letters from before we learned of Christoph's death."

Edwin's emotional storm had finally subsided, and he wiped his tears away with the back of his hand. His voice was still thick as he said, "This all seems unreal." Numbly, Edwin began walking toward the Temple again, feeling like he was in a nightmare. His thoughts had ground to a halt, and he was unable to think of anything except their baby had died, Marya needed him, and he wasn't there to support her. His voice caught as he asked, "How bad is it? Was it a simple miscarriage, or were there complications?"

This was the one question John didn't want to answer. "No, son, she came very near to dying. She had serious complications, but the finest healers cared for her and they pulled her through it. Dane's written you a letter explaining what happened, but now she's physically healed as well as can be expected under the circumstances, and her mental state is improving too." He caught Garran's slight headshake, and John hoped against hope he was telling the truth. "She makes progress every day. Everyone's completely focused on keeping Marya from slipping back."

Edwin's legs threatened to give out on him as he heard his worst fears confirmed, but somehow he held himself together. "Zan—it has to be Zan. He's the only one who can help her now. We have to finish up and get back home so Zan can heal her." He resumed walking toward the Temple, blindly putting one foot in front of the other. Friedr and Zan moved up to each side of him. Linked and working together, they cast the healing spells. Zan then layered a dampening field with several of the unique spells he had developed on his healing journey.

For a moment, Edwin was distracted, the spells were so gently done. He was unaware of the magic that now took effect, thanking Friedr and Zan for their support.

No one else was sure just what the two had done, though the three older mages suspected Friedr and Zan of working some sort of healing magic, on their brother. Edwin's change of demeanor was too marked to be natural under the circumstances. "They're changed," murmured Moran. "I've seen many go into Mal Evol and return changed, but these aren't the same men they were two months ago. Friedr's changed in the most obvious way, but Zan.... Those two just did something so Edwin isn't rendered incapable of doing whatever it is he must do. They didn't even discuss it. They just did it."

Moran, John, and Garran walked behind them, noting how the three were almost one person, working together as if they knew each other's thoughts. *At least my son won't suffer from his own guilt as I did for so long,* thought John, as he saw Edwin accepting their support. He looked up at Garran, who smiled wryly. His old friend was obviously thinking the same thing.

By the time they arrived at the Temple, Edwin was over the initial shock, intent on reading his letters from Dane and Beryl, and appearing outwardly normal. The loops Zan had placed were set to fade with time, allowing him to mourn and yet still get his task done.

Zan badly wanted to get to Aeoven to see for himself what had happened to break Marya's mind in such a way that they had called in Lorana, but he knew they couldn't go back for at least six weeks, possibly more. They most certainly couldn't go back until Edwin had completed sealing off the Braden Gap. It worried him though, because Lorana specialized in mind-healing Stefyn D'Mal's victims. There could be no other reason for her to be called back to Aeoven.

Moran ushered them into their quarters, still trying to absorb the magnitude of the changes in them. Each man had been marked by the journey, in both the physical and other intangible ways. Although Friedr had suffered the most obvious physical changes, Zan was the most changed by far. Moran helped them put their kits in their rooms, talking quietly to John. "Zan's definitely not the crazy lightning-mage he used to be. I don't know what's changed exactly, but he's a force of nature. I wouldn't stand in his way if he was set on something." John just nodded.

When they finally relaxed in the men's baths, the three older mages were stunned into silence by Friedr's pitifully scarred leg, which resembled nothing so much as a bone thinly disguised by the red welts of ropy, scarred skin. They were impressed by his strength of will, amazed he could even walk at all. The fact he had traveled all those leagues on that leg was mind-boggling. Trying to hide their shock, they greatly admired Edwin's handiwork in creating the brace and the walking stick for Friedr. The difference in his ability to walk while wearing it was miraculous. Without the brace, he needed help getting in and out of the bathing pool, being unable to support his weight on it for any length of time.

In what was obviously their habit, Edwin and Zan assisted him out of his leg-armor and carried him down into the bathing pool. In John's eyes, it was a measure of how the experience had changed Friedr. He simply accepted Edwin and Zan's help with no complaint. Once they had finally lifted him down into the pool, he sighed, soaking the aches away and thanking them for their assistance.

Moran frankly admitted to being shocked by the sight of Friedr limping so painfully as he walked the last league to Braden. "How will you kill every beast in Mal Evol as you once planned?"

"I just wait until they come to me now. Edwin is usually kind enough to act as bait to attract them." He smirked at Edwin, who rolled his eyes. "But even lame, I can still kick your butt, Moran." Friedr's remark was not a taunt. He simply spoke the truth. "I've relearned what I had to in order to survive. Perhaps we'll work out when the task that brought us here is done, and I'll school you. You've been getting lazy without Garran here to force you to work out with him."

"Jase works my sword arm daily, so I'm not as slack as you think," Moran replied, rising to the bait despite his sadness, "I must say you're looking rather proficient with the fine staff, old man."

"That's quite true, so be careful I don't thump you with it," Friedr replied, with his blue eyes twinkling. "I've spent much of my time lately learning to work with what I have and not worrying about what I don't have any longer. I'm an adept with the staff, as all know. Who do you think trains healers in the art of the staff?"

"I somehow forgot that," Moran replied ruefully. It wounded Moran to see the Temple's greatest warrior so uninterested in the battle arts when every aspect of battle had once consumed his waking hours.

John asked Friedr about the strategies they had used in their battles with D'Mal's legions and then with the waterdrake. As he listened to their talk, Moran couldn't shake his depression. He looked up and saw Zan's keen eyes watching him.

"Friedr's still a warrior. Now he's fighting a different war, Moran, and this war consumes his mind," Zan said softly.

Moran was a bit dismayed his thoughts were so easy to read but then realized that only Zan had picked up on his melancholy. The others were still talking about the battle with Aggie.

Zan continued speaking in low tones. "Friedr now desires to battle death in every patient he sees, and he'll use his scalpel and healing abilities to win each battle as often as he can. He's truly an adept at surgery. It should have been him performing it, you see, not us."

Moran raised his eyebrows, a querying look upon his face.

Zan said, "Edwin is a most capable surgeon, and he saved Friedr's life, but if it had been Friedr performing the surgery on me or Edwin, the outcome would have been much better. He would have been able to regrow much more of the muscle than we could. Friedr has the ability, but he was the patient, so the result wasn't as good." His face grew somber as he added, "We didn't have enough chi to do a proper job of it. Edwin was nearly burned out when we got to the cave, and I was barely able to draw chi through Stormbringer. We couldn't wait long enough. We were forced to do it before Edwin was fully recovered."

"The Goddess gave you and Edwin the ability to save Friedr's life. She knew this task would require each member to be a healer, not just for the original task, but for the aftermath of the battle. She saw to it Edwin had the knowledge to create the brace and staff to allow Friedr to walk unassisted," replied Moran.

As they all dressed, Edwin remarked he had forgotten what true luxury was. "It feels so good to wear these nice, soft trousers and shirts," he said, shaking his head ruefully. "It'll be hard to go back to our leathers."

The three older mages had laughed uproariously on hearing why the questers' shirts were as highly embellished and elaborate as feast-day clothes. "Only you, Zan! Only you would think of doing something so outrageous just so you wouldn't have to wear stained clothes." John laughed for the first time in days over the tale.

"I've been very happy to wear the clothes he's made for me," said Friedr. "I can't think of when I've liked my leathers so well. He's promised to design my clothes from now on."

"His love of finery has kept our spirits up during the darkest days." Edwin's grin was strained, but he made the effort. "I admit I'm becoming as bad a clotheshorse as they are." Everyone laughed, and then John and Garran brought them up to date on their children's lives and accomplishments.

"There's a lot you have to tell us, but we'll meet for dinner here in the dining hall tonight and you can tell us what your task is," Garran told them as they took their soiled clothes to the laundry. "John and I only arrived this morning on the mail coach."

"We know why you and John were sent here, and it's not for the reasons you believe," replied Zan, with certainty. "We have two immense tasks in front of us and only one season in which to complete them. There's a great deal to discuss, and little enough time to rest before we're back to work. But we'll go into the details after dinner."

Garran's eyebrows rose and he nodded. The others left them in peace, and the weary questers then turned to reading their mail.

"I don't know which amazes me more," Garran said later to John, "the fact Edwin and Zan were able to save Friedr's leg while they were holed up in a cave, or the fact he fought and killed a waterdrake and then walked all the way here on the underground road. I suspect we've not even heard the half of what went on in Mal Evol."

"We never will," replied John. "We were never able to explain fully what happened to us either."

Chapter 30 ~ Letters from Home

As they expected, the three found many letters waiting for each of them, and they spent the rest of the afternoon reading their mail and answering it, sensing spikes in anxiety from each other as they read. The three men were subdued, as the letters were full of worry and heartache, but in their own replies, they promised to be home by the solstice and they would explain everything then. They all agreed that as far as Christoph's healing of the Throne of Stone and Bone went, they would imply he had done it with their knowledge and not discuss the dissension his act had caused within their group.

Confirming Edwin's fears, Dane wrote Marya would never conceive another child. At first, it looked as if Marya would recover normally, but it had soon become clear she had suffered a mental breakdown, which they could trace back to her experience as Stetyn D'Mal's captive.

The letter from Halee proved even more difficult than Dane's had been for him to read. "I fear the madness may be caused by something from her ordeal in Mal Evol that was never healed, and which has been triggered by the miscarriage,' wrote Halee. 'Lorana is here now and already things are improving—I'm better able to keep Marya from hurting herself. She'll be able to tell us what, if anything, can be done. In the meantime, she is beginning to take an interest in Jonny again and I hope to bring him home from Aeolyn's soon. He misses you terribly, but he's doing well there."

In her letter, Halee said that when the miscarriage happened, things had seemed to go well until the third night afterward. John woke to a strange sound in the house. Halee followed him downstairs, where they found Marya in the kitchen, which was ablaze. Immediately casting water, he was able to douse the fire while Halee cast a sleep-spell on her. They sent for help.

Marya's state of mind was precarious. She was lucid on occasion, but most of the time, she made no sense whatsoever and was suicidal. The decision was made to keep her condition a secret, since Edwin was known to be on a healing-journey, one that had already suffered a loss. Halee and John had registered their bonding immediately.

Halee's letter read, "If you agree, your father and I will most likely remain here with you until Marya is fully able to care for Jonny. I will be honest and tell you that Lorana says it will be a long while before that is possible, if ever.

Aeolyn has proven she is most capable in filling in for me in my absence. I feel sure she will make a fine Abbess when the time comes."

Edwin had a few moments of private tears as he read Halee's letter and contemplated how alone and helpless his wife had been though the whole ordeal of losing the baby, wondering if Marya knew the bitter truth and thought it must be the root cause of her breakdown. He didn't want to consider anything else. It was too much for him. Stuck in Braden as he was, he could do nothing, especially if it was a vestige of her time as Stefyn D'Mal's captive that had broken her mind.

But it did occur to him that the day he had noticed the severing of their special, subliminal bond had been the day of the miscarriage.

He wrote to Halee, telling her how right it felt to know she was now his stepmother and how much he was comforted by knowing she was caring for Marya and Jonny. "Dad and I will be home as soon as we are able, and we will all be happy again. I have to believe it. We have our task to complete, and then we will come home, never to leave again."

Last of all, he read the letter from Marya, and this time he shed more than a few tears as he tried to make sense of the incoherent, rambling apology she'd written. It was almost as if the girl he'd first rescued in Mal Evol was back, full of nameless fears and insecurity, but with the addition of something akin to paranoia. At last, he was able to compose himself enough to write her a letter that expressed all his love for her.

Edwin's letter to Marya was the most difficult one he had ever had to write. He found himself with no idea of where to start or how best to give his wife comfort. As he prayed to Aeos for guidance, the words to tell his wife how much he loved her and how desperately he wished he had been there for her began to come to him. His own pain and longing to be with her again were expressed in one of the more beautiful love letters he had ever written.

Through writing the letters home and having the time to pray, Edwin found his center of balance again.

Since he could do nothing about the situation at home other than writing letters, he mentally shelved the pain and turned his attention back to trying to think of a way to convince Garran of the need to abandon the city of Braden.

Before anything else, he had to get Garran and Moran to understand what had really happened to Christoph and why it was imperative they immediately evacuate the populace. *Lourdan will be a fearsome master when he comes to Braden,* Edwin thought, as he tried to think of ways to convey what he knew in his heart was true. *He'll be a full priest of Tauron and will be as formidable an enemy as D'Mal.*

At last, he thought he had a good plan to put forth, although he knew Zan would have the real task of convincing them. *But if I offer to build the visible wall along the entire Mal Evol side of the river myself...it's not a hard task, and it's one I can do with very little effort while we build the new shield.*

After dinner, which they shared in the dining hall with Moran, John, and Garran, they talked about the events that led up to Christoph's getting kidnapped and then explained Edwin's true-dream and his instructions from Christoph's ghost.

"I don't understand what you're telling me," Garran said, plainly in shock. "He lives? How could Lourdan not be Christoph?" Finally, Edwin offered to let him see the true-dream, explaining what was involved. After a moment's hesitation, Garran agreed. "I have to see this to understand what you're telling me, I think."

In the end, Edwin shared his true-dream with each of the three, who were all stunned, horrified, and desperately saddened to think their beloved Christoph had come to such an end, when they had all believed he had died a clean death.

Moran too was silent, staring at the darkness outside the windows, pushing his food around his plate. Finally, he said, "We lost so many good people this last year to the mad priest. Ivar Kalensson...my own Piers...and now Christoph. Now your quest hangs in the balance. What can you do to stop Lourdan that he can't undo? He'll have all of Christoph's magic, along with the magic of the Dark God. Now you must tell a great many people what really happened."

"No," Zan immediately disagreed. "Except for Dane and a few others, we'll only say Christoph is dead, taken by D'Mal. The truth is too confusing to keep trying to explain. It will have to remain a close Temple secret only the highest ever need to know."

Edwin agreed. "People must never confuse Lourdan with Christoph, which is what would happen. We don't them to think Christoph went to D'Mal willingly as a traitor." His companions each nodded their agreement. Smiling the rather sardonic smile he now wore all too often, he added, "I can't let every person in Neveyah into my mind to see the truth." They all laughed, agreeing with him.

At last, Zan spoke. "Now though, we have been given a new quest, and by necessity, it's a short one. We thought Moran would be the one to help us, but Aeos has called John Farmer to be here on this day to meet us. Now I know why in my true-dream I see blue represented as the fourth element. Your veterinary healing gifts and your strength of water, combined with your legendary sword—these things confirm that what we've planned is exactly what Aeos wants of us." The authority in Zan's voice surprised the older mages.

John looked questioningly at Zan, not understanding what he was being asked to do.

Zan continued, "We will add you into the link. You're a veterinarian—you have strong healing empathy. It's different than ours, but you're able to link. We can easily do this, but only if it's your will to give Edwin control of your magic. We are to build a spirit barrier to seal off the western wall of Braden. The spells will require four mages, linked and weaving each of the four elements into one shield laced with spirit. Edwin will lead us and guide and shape it, with our swords focusing the magic."

He was met with blank looks from the three older mages. "There *must* be four elements or Lourdan and D'Mal will be able to link and break the barrier."

John nodded. "That's why the barrier we built that ended the war doesn't work as well as it should. It lacks lightning."

"We need *you*, John. You must provide the fourth element. You must help us seal off southern Neveyah while Garran handles the evacuation of the people of Braden to Aeoven. With the use of a horse and cart so Friedr doesn't have to walk, two weeks should be enough time for us to build the barrier from Braden south to the Horn of Misery, then two weeks more to the Horn of the Moon. On our way back to Aeoven, we'll go north along the Escarpment, restructuring the shield we've already built there, making it deadly to cross. The visible wall across the Gap will be our additional special project. Because of his strength in earth magic and our swords, raising the visible wall will take very little extra effort on his part."

Stunned silence reigned around the table.

Sensing disagreement, Edwin said, "We will raise shield and the wall on the Mal Evol side of the River Fleet, stretching across the narrowest part of the Gap from the Horn of the Moon to the Horn of Misery. That way we can use the river as we always have to transport our goods up the River Fleet to the towns in the shadow of the Escarpment, and the Barbarian lands. My earth-magic is more than adequate for this task and with all of us linked and working together, it won't take much more chi than erecting the barrier alone would. The wall will be the visible border. There will be no doubt they're denied entrance into our land."

The three older mages all spoke at once, objecting strenuously, but John's voice prevailed. "Absolutely not. *Rall* said we are to *protect* Braden. We've been stockpiling and preparing for this since the end of Lunne. We've spent months on this." He thumped the table. "We've moved the entire militia to the area surrounding this city. They're fully trained, stationed perfectly, and ready to move as soon as we give the word."

"Don't argue with us. We've been told to evacuate Braden. Didn't you hear the ghost?" Friedr surprised John with his lack of deference. "Lourdan will take Braden regardless of your preparations. We must abandon Braden or needlessly lose people. There's no point in defending this city when it will fall no matter what we do. We'll lose more than just people, John—we'll lose their knowledge and skills, and for what? We have been given clear instructions as to what we are to do."

The disagreement escalated, with Garran and Moran siding with John. Edwin and Zan sat, wondering whether to speak or remain silent. Still Friedr refused to bend. "This is exactly what happened in Mal Evol City. The histories are clear it was doomed, but we struggled against what we knew must happen. We must not repeat this with Braden. We must learn from our mistakes."

Garran's breath hissed angrily, and John spoke in heated tones. "What do you know about Mal Evol City? You were a babe. We were there, Friedr. *We* were there!"

In the distance, a bell tolled, and the disagreement dwindled away as they listened to the familiar tone that resounded through the ears and souls of Aeos's children. All eyes turned to Edwin, but this time it was not Edwin who was the voice of Aeos.

The bell rang, tolling through Zander's body, in every pore, and every fiber of his being, resonating in his soul. The glorious sound was exquisite to the highest degree. Lost in the beauty of the bell, he heard a voice saying, "The end days are upon us! As has been written in the stars, the Garden City must fall. Let your heart be eased, Dark Knight. Your beloved rests at my Hearth. He has earned his place in heaven. Now must the Companions aid the Father and the Son in building the wall which cannot be breached, from Horn to Horn.

"The Elder Warrior and the Dark Knight must gather my people and lead them to the Holy City where all lies ready for them. In less than two seasons, the Lost One will lead the hordes of Tauron to the gates of the Garden City. He stands on the walls, unable to enter the golden land, and the broken children of Mal Evol stand behind him. In his grief, he sows the poisoned seed, a vain effort to recreate the verdant land.

"This must happen before the Throne of Stone and Bone lies broken and the Mountain God is free of his prison. The One Who Takes Back All shall right the balance of the worlds."

Gradually, the bell let go of Zander, and tears of joy and sadness filled his eyes. Everyone at the table stared at him, stunned, while Zan sat confused, and unsure of what just happened.

"She has spoken directly to us." John breathed the words. "She gives me a task, a duty of her choosing. The Goddess speaks, and I must obey. I will do as you wish, Zan."

Garran was also dumbfounded at the turn of events. "This monumental duty is indeed why Halee was told we had to be here today. We guess and guess, and we're always wrong," His mind was already focusing on the enormous task before him. "We must act now to plan the evacuation." He too was overcome that Aeos had chosen him personally for this task. "I've never heard of her speaking directly to anyone in such clear terms."

Zan remained silent as the echoes of the bell ringing still within his heart and soul faded, unable to speak a word. Edwin clasped Zander's shoulder in sympathy. "It's not easy being the voice of the Goddess, my brother, but it's a great honor. Your father's great task will be complete, Ariend will one day be free, and you prophesied it. The Goddess spoke through you tonight."

"You're right, Garran. I've never heard of her being so specific." Friedr's pen scratched as he frantically wrote everything down exactly as the Goddess had spoken the words through Zan. "This is also the first prophecy to speak directly to the problem of Ariend," he told the others. "Now we know Ariend's imprisonment is soon to end. Christoph healed the throne, and one day the Mountain God will be free of his prison. The Goddess has spoken."

A quiet sob had escaped Moran. Normally impassive and stoic, he sat trembling with his head in his hands, momentarily completely overcome. "She chose to comfort me, telling me what I so badly needed to hear." He raised his eyes to the others, and both his joy and intense sorrow were laid bare for all to see. "The Dark God may have murdered Piers, but he didn't deny him his reward. He rests with Aeos." Brushing the tears from his eyes and pulling himself together, Moran abruptly stood up. "Jase must be in on this meeting. We have to plan the evacuation. We must prepare the people for the long march to Aeoven. Tomorrow, you four will leave on your quest. We will do what we're tasked with, so you can concentrate upon your work."

While Moran attended to sending a message to Jase, Friedr and Edwin moved to sit on either side of Zan. He was obviously disturbed, and Friedr found himself casting ease on Zan, making him smile faintly. "Zan, Lourdan isn't your father."

"I know. Believe me, Friedr, I know. I just feel so desperately sorry for this man whose name means 'lost one,' a person even the Goddess refers to as lost," Zan replied. "Nevertheless, we must limit the damage he can do to the heart of Neveyah."

At last John spoke. "I'll have my kit ready to go when you three are. You must have some notion of what's required, and I'll do whatever you need me to." He was silent, feeling completely adrift and out of his element. He was now in the position of being the raw journeyman on the team, the one who knew nothing, not even what his own strengths were. He wondered what he had to offer that the others really needed.

Even his father's masterpiece, his supposedly magic sword, had never been what he wanted and had failed him when he needed it most. He felt a pang of remorse at his doubt about the sword, because it was a finer sword than any he'd ever seen. Also, to be honest, he'd always been able to draw chi through it, and it had enhanced his water-magic more than a few times. He simply was never able to make it work the way he wanted when he needed it to. Realizing his mind had wandered, John turned his attention to the conversations around him.

Zan was speaking. "John, your strength in your element is as strong as Father Rall's. Now we'll have all four elements equally represented the way it must be to make the ward. All of the pieces have fallen into place. You told me you've no memory of building the barrier that has protected Neveyah from D'Mal's mind-magic for the last twenty-five years, but your son has the knowledge we need. He'll guide us."

"I'm not arguing with you. I'm just trying to absorb this." Feeling as if he were dreaming, John nodded. "Don't worry. I'll do as I'm asked with all my heart and ability. I swear it upon my vows to Aeos."

When Jase arrived, he was bowled over by the changes in the three he had last seen only a season before. "I'm sorry your father who was the gentlest of men was killed," he told Zan sadly. "He was a good man and a dear companion. D'Mal has much to answer for. So many good and dear people have died at his hands."

"Thank you for your kind words," Zan replied. "I miss him more than I can say, but it comforts us to know he's resting at Aeos's Great Hearth."

The rest of the evening was spent on the task of outlining what they would need in planning the evacuation of Braden. John Farmer's greatest strength had always been his ability to lead the military forces, and now he was severed from the task that he'd mentally prepared himself to assume once again.

Still, the others looked to him for guidance, as he had supervised the evacuation of several cities during the war, and knew exactly how to organize such an undertaking. He rapidly wrote out lists and instructions, counseling Garran, Moran, and Jase, who listened carefully. "It's essential we notify Father Rall straightaway. Now we know why Halee and Father Rall were sent dreams telling us to station the militia around this city. It was not a war—they are needed to protect our people as they make this long journey north. We have to send messages to the squads nearest us and get them here as quickly as possible. They and the mages posted with each company will be required to help you maintain order when you tell the people what they must do."

Garran agreed. "Perhaps Edwin and Zan could wind-speak or send messages to those they can reach. The people aren't as used to walking as we mages are, but the road is smooth, and we've many carts at our disposal. Even so, it'll take the full two weeks of the first leg of your task to prepare the people for the long journey to Aeoven."

John nodded. "We have to assume it will take a bit longer—we don't know what will happen once the powers-that-be in Mal Evol City realize we are cutting them off. When you begin moving them out of here, take them up the trade road through the Midlands. Many farms all through the Midlands have been untenanted since the war, so all the displaced farmers now living in the city who wish to return to that task will have plenty of good homesteads to choose from. Some won't, but I know that the Temple has plenty of livestock and can spare a few animals to help rebuild the flocks they lost."

Edwin and Zan moved to a table away from the others so Moran and Jase could continue their discussion, while they fetched the letters to the squads they could find. When they had finished the task and the messages were all sent, they returned to the table where John was still speaking to the group.

"Now we know why so many homes and shops are untenanted in Aeoven that even if every person in Braden relocates, there will still be empty houses." John's calm exterior hid his inner turmoil from all but Zan. "When you move them out, tell each person to take only items dearest to them, and begin organizing groups roughly the size of a company. The Temple army will be better able to protect them in groups of that size.

"Don't allow anyone to remain behind. Take them out by force if necessary. Tell them this is the sign that the end-times of Tauron's dominion are upon us. Within the next three generations, the Hero Foretold will walk among us and we'll see the land of Mal Evol bloom as it did in the time of our forefathers."

Jaxon was right, thought Edwin as he listened to his father speaking, overwhelmed by a sense of disbelief. *The end-times are upon us. My son or my son's son will be the one whose task it is to free the Mountain God.* It was a thought that boggled his mind. *We've always discussed it as if we believed it. Now we know it's true. Perhaps I'll see that day after all!*

.... To Be Continued in *'Valley of Sorrows'* ...

APPENDICES

EXCERPT FROM THE BOOK OF LIFE

In the beginning, there was only the void, and the void was barren of life. Nor did any element exist there no fire, no lightning, no earth, and no water. All was as it should be, and the void waited.

Two spheres from beyond the void approached each other, as gently as bubbles blown in the breeze. When they touched, a new sphere was born. And in the void, new spheres appeared until ten new worlds had been born.

The Father and Mother were pleased and admired their work. Then began the great unraveling, and they surrounded the spheres of their children in a protective cocoon that they called the universe.

In the center of the universe, a star flared into existence. The day glowed with the light of the star, the physical manifestation of the Almighty Father. The ten worlds revolved around Him, one touching the other, and all was well in the universe.

The universe grew strong. In the night sky, the Mother cast a myriad of stars and set the moon to illuminate the dark. The moon was the physical manifestation of the Mother of All.

No longer did the spheres create new worlds when they touched. Instead, where they touched, gods were born. Upon awakening, each god made the choice to be male or female, and in this way, the spheres were divided, five worlds for the gods and five worlds for the goddesses.

For the long time of their childhoods, the gods and goddesses shaped their worlds, creating the lands and waters. Each world was different and yet similar, as were the deities who formed them, and each admired the handiwork of the others.

As they grew to adulthood, the deities began to populate their worlds with diverse peoples, whom they considered to be their children, and all were content to live in their worlds, and the universe was at peace.

And the gods and goddesses were five each, and these were their names in the order in which they came into existence:

Meren, god of the Water World Aquas, and his wife Grete, goddess of the Woodland World Alrunne.

Olod, god of the Sky World Geminis, and his wife Oriane, goddess of the River World Danus.

Priscis, god of the Winter World Morovi, and his wife Delhine, goddess of the Summer World Erendi.

Berrin, god of the Grasslands World Sanuvyr, and his wife Feylyn, goddess of the Ice World Chysat.

Ariend, god of the Mountain World Cascadia, and his wife Aeos, goddess of the Verdant World Neveyah.

All was as it should be. Eons passed in harmony until once again, a sphere appeared. From whence came this sphere, none of the deities knew, nor did the universe. Nonetheless, they welcomed this new world, and when the new god was born, he chose to be male. They called him Tauron, and in his childhood, he created the Arid World of Serende. All was well until Tauron grew into his adulthood and realized he alone of the gods had no mate.

At first, all the deities agreed if he had come into existence, then surely another goddess would come to be his wife. Tauron listened to their counsel and was patient. But as the eons passed and no new goddess was born for him, he became miserable in his loneliness.

"Why did you create me only to leave me alone?" Tauron often asked of the universe, but he received no answer, for the universe had not created him. Yet he was beloved, and the other deities made much effort to ease his loneliness, to no avail.

And the eons passed.

With the passage of time, Tauron became ever stranger, jealous, and cruel. The other deities began to fear and avoid him. He became even lonelier, and eventually, he descended into madness. He demanded abject worship from his people to ease his pain. As the eons passed, he realized he was alone and would always be so unless he could find a wife worthy of him.

In his obsession, he decided Aeos should be his wife. "She is the youngest of the gods other than me. She should have been mine."

Thus, it was in the guise of seeking counsel, he went to Ariend's mountain home of Cascadia and sought him out. During the feast Ariend set before him, Tauron took him by stealth and surprise. Tauron sealed Ariend alive into the haft of a spear carved from Ariend's own mountains and thrust the spear deep into the earth of the world of Cascadia.

Aeos, seeking her husband, could find him nowhere. She was distraught and sought the help of the other deities. The other gods and goddesses did not know where Ariend could be and knew something had happened to him, for he would never have abandoned his wife or his world and his children. They searched for a thousand years but did not find him.

Though all the deities came to Aeos's aid, one only pretended to search. Tauron was occupied in a different way. He added league after league of Cascadia to his own world and at last took Ariend's own beloved people, subverting them and making them into creatures lower than beasts. What once had been a gentle, clever, and scholarly people now were voracious and filled with an unquenchable hunger, mindless and violent. Tauron was filled with joy as he looked at his improvements to Ariend's people. "They were too full of pride before. Now they are as they should have been."

When Aeos saw what Tauron had done to Ariend's people, she knew he was responsible for the disappearance of her husband, and she searched the land. At last, she came upon the crystal and marble spear that had been thrust into the ground, creating an immense crater. There she found the skeleton of her husband Ariend embedded in the haft, arms outstretched and face raised to the heavens. Upon touching the crystal, she felt his heart beating and knew him to be alive. "Mother, Father, see what Tauron has done to my husband! Help me to save him, I beg of you!"

The Mother of All wept to see her son in so terrible a place. "My daughter, I must remain to hold up the sky, but the Almighty Father hastens to your side. Though many long years will pass, this evil deed will be made right. I have foreseen it."

Her father came to her side and wept upon seeing Ariend. "My daughter, it pains me, but I cannot interfere in this, though I wish it were not so. This tragedy must play itself out."

The other deities counseled Aeos to take the valley for her world and thus protect her husband until she could find a way to free him from his prison. The oldest brother, Meren, said, "Ariend still lives. There must be eleven worlds and one God for each. Tauron has added half of Cascadia to Serende and still attempts to take it all. He has subverted Ariend's people and made them into less than beasts. We must seal our worlds so none can cross the barriers, else Tauron will be the only god in the universe and our people will be abused in the same, cruel way." And the eight gods and goddesses sealed away their worlds.

Aeos did take all of Cascadia that Tauron had not yet gained and sealed the world of Neveyah from him. Then she ceded half of the combined worlds to her Father to ensure the balance would not be disturbed, and he guarded the land and people most carefully, for there must be eleven worlds, one for each of the eleven deities. Together, they nurtured the two worlds, weeping with sorrow over the fate of Ariend's people at the hands of Tauron. Each did what they could to mitigate the peoples' suffering, though they were not able to completely undo Tauron's work.

Aeos named the crater Mal Evol, which means Valley of Sorrow. For three thousand years, she guarded her husband and the spear that entombed him, ruling Neveyah and Mal Evol with love and a gentle hand. Aeos bequeathed great magic to a few of her people so they could withstand Tauron's hordes. She also gave the valley to one of her most trusted servants and instructed him to build a castle around the haft of the spear, saying, "When the blood of your blood sits upon the throne, you will have knowledge of everything that lives in the land of Mal Evol. Ariend will accept you and the blood of your blood to guard the remains of his world."

Thus, the trusted servant and his sons gave their lives to the carving of the throne.

Once more, Tauron began pressing Aeos, saying her husband was surely dead, and she must wed him and cede the other half of Cascadia to him to right the balance, as there must be one god for each world. She refused saying, "My husband lives. The Almighty Father is a god and worthy of the care and keeping of the eleventh world until my husband can be freed from the prison of your making." Tauron at last went away, weeping and descending ever deeper into madness.

Thus was born the enmity between Neveyah and Serende, the land of Tauron, the Bull God.

And in the world that he named Ariend, the Almighty Father planted the seed of the vine from whose line will come the Hero Foretold, the One Who Takes Back All.

Time and Calendar of Neveyah

Each year consists of 365 days and is divided into four seasons: Winter, Spring, Summer, Harvest, and one Holy Month.

Each season consists of three months, making twelve months that equal 28 days each, plus a Holy Month. Harvest (Autumn) and Winter are separated by the Holy Month of 29 days. The actual winter solstice falls on the first day of the month following (on the first day of Caprica). This is a month sacred to the Goddess Aeos, Goddess of Harvest, Hearth, and Home. It is a time when people travel to visit family and simply take time off for a small vacation, often taking two weeks to do it. On the day that falls between last day of the Holy Month and the first day of Caprica (called Holy Day,) each family holds a ritual feast in their home. It is a feast of thanksgiving and prayers for the New Year. Every four years, an extra Holy Day is added to the calendar and the day is a festival day all across Neveyah. Such a year is called a Long Year, though it is really only one day longer.

The months and seasons are as follows:

Caprica, Aquas, Piscus	(Winter) Begins on actual day of Winter Solstice
Arese, Taura, Geminis	(Spring)
Lunne, Leonid, Virga	(Summer)
Libre, Scorpius, Saggitus	(Harvest)

Holy Month   thirteenth month, stands alone on calendar, ends day before the winter solstice
Holy Day   Bridge between old year and new, belongs to no month, a day of celebration

Days of the Week -

1. Sunnaday—Minimal business is conducted; each family's tasks for the Temple as a whole are completed, such as chopping firewood, quilting, making clothes, and preserving food. The members of the temple clergy assemble in work gangs to accomplish these tasks from which they all benefit.
2. Lunaday
3. Tyrsday
4. Odensday
5. Torsday
6. Frosday
7. Restday – no business is conducted, and only minimal work is done on farms and other places where some work must be done seven days a week. This is a day for people to spend with their families or to pursue their personal interests.

Prominent members of Edwin Farmer's Family Tree

Aelfrid Firesword, founder of College of Warcraft and Magic

Biann D'Braden – 1st abbess and founder of Braden Temple

Iain Farmer

Liam Farmer

Wynn Farmer - *Mountains of the Moon*

John Farmer – *Forbidden Road,*

Edwin Farmer–*Tower of Bones, Forbidden Road*
Son – Jon Farmer

The Prophecies of Neveyah

Abbot Devyn D'Mal to the assembled clergy at Mal Evol Temple in the year 3215

"Keeper, you must save the remnant of my children, for when the end-times are upon you, you shall be barred from the valley of poison and beauty. The wall shall stretch from Horn to Horn and shall be the sign that none from the Valley of Shadows can enter the golden land. The eternal youth, the Lost One, will take the City of Gloom and those of my children left behind will suffer unto the third generation. He stands on the wall and gazes on the golden land, unable to enter."

Mother Lera to the assembled Clergy at Aeoven in the year 3229

"Hark now! The advent of the Bull God is upon us - he comes to claim his bride. She rejects him, and his mad desire is thwarted. Still he claims the dowry as was promised. The verdant lands shall fall to the Bull God and shall become a wilderness of thorns. Seek the hero who will hold safe the Heart of Neveyah. Take the Heir down the Forbidden Road and shroud him with the light of truth. Now comes the Hero from the lands of the Almighty Father; from his line shall come the one who

will take back all. From him shall come the Hero Foretold who will triumph on the day of redemption."

Father Rall to the assembled clergy at Aeoven in the year 3254

"The storm rises in the lands of Neveyah, though it does not bring its wrath fully for yet awhile...when falls the Beloved Hero into darkness, then will the storm's wrath fall upon Neveyah. The children of the Bull-God answer the call that rides on the wind. The light of truth remains shrouded beneath the Throne of Stone and Bone. The cradle of the rightful heir lies obscured by the truth. Let the Hero go to the Shadow Castle to seek the hand of her whom darkness has claimed. The moon is dark - In stealth seeks the hero for the window to the Tower of Roses; in stealth he unbars the door to the forbidden room. Four heroes depart and five return; yet the battle is not won, but only the first skirmish. The Beloved must fall to darkness ere the light of truth is restored to the Shadow Castle! Blood and tears reign in the Shadow Castle until the Hero Foretold comes to restore the scion to the throne."

Edwin Farmer to his companions on the Holy Quest in the year 3254

"The verdant springtime lies coiled beneath the surface of the shattered lands, waiting for the call of the Beloved, to set it free. The Beloved Hero falls to darkness; he sows the poisoned seed across the shadowed land, yet will he rise up to set free the land of

Mal Evol on the day the land takes him home. All will see the fruiting of the land of the Living Shades. This will be the sign; the day of redemption is at hand."

Father Rall to the assembled Clergy in the year 3259

"The Dark God laments his betrothed, she chooses him not. The hordes of the broken lands despoil verdant Mal Evol. Now send the heroes four into the land ruled by the Throne of Stone and Bone. Should the treasured one be lost to darkness, those left to walk in the light must flee down the Forbidden Road. Treasured and Beloved, beware the voice of reason. Long days of darkness shadow the realm. The poisoned land flowers, but death walks amidst poison and thorn. When blooms the land again, the day of redemption is at hand. Four heroes journey to bring forth the spring, but balanced on the edge of reason is the outcome.

Edwin Farmer to the assembled Clergy in the year 3260

"Now begins the quest in earnest. Send now the heroes four to the Shadowed Land. Beware! Beloved, the true task for which you were born begins. The storm rages, the door opens upon the field of battle, in grief recall the Forbidden Road. The Beloved Hero will rise on the day of redemption. Mist and shadows shroud the truth, but the Hero Foretold shall one day set them free."

Edwin Farmer to the assembled on the battlefield in Mal Evol in the year 3260

"My Beloved Hero has fallen. As has been foretold, he shall sow the poisoned seed, and the garden city will fall to him. Darkness falls upon the shadowed land. Long years of suffering and pain lie before us at his dread hand. Yet, when comes the Hero Foretold, the Beloved will rise up and free the land. On the day of redemption, you will know deliverance is at hand when poison gives way to spring. Seek now the Forbidden Road, lest you be lost also."

Zander Christophson to the assembled at Braden Temple in the year 3260

"The end days are upon us. As has been written in the stars the Garden City must fall. Let your heart be eased, Dark Knight. Your beloved rests at my Hearth. He has earned his place in heaven. Now must the Companions aid the Father and the Son in building the wall which cannot be breached from Horn to Horn. The Elder Warrior and the Dark Knight must gather my people and lead them to the Holy City, all lies ready for them there. In less than two seasons the Lost One will lead the hordes of Tauron to the gates of the Garden City. He stands on the walls unable to enter the golden land, and the broken children of Mal Evol stand behind him. In his grief he sows the poisoned seed, a vain effort to recreate the verdant land. This must happen before the Throne of Stone and Bone lies broken and the Mountain God is free of his prison. The One Who Takes Back All shall right the balance of the worlds."

Connie J. Jasperson lives in Olympia, Washington. A vegan, she and her husband share five children, a love of good food and great music. She is active in local writing groups, an editor for Myrddin Publishing Group, and is a writing coach. She is an active member of the both the Northwest Independent Writers Association and Pacific Northwest Writers Association, and is a founding member of Myrddin Publishing Group. Music and food dominate her waking moments.

When not writing or blogging, she can be found with her Kindle, reading avidly.

You can find her blogging on her writing life at:
Life in the Realm of Fantasy
http://conniejjasperson.wordpress.com

Myrddin Publishing Group
www.myrddinpublishing.com
~~~

More great books from every genre await your reading pleasure!

~~~

MYRDDIN PUBLISHING GROUP BOOK LIST

WWW.MYRDDINPUBLISHING.COM

URBAN FANTASY ~ PARANORMAL ~ ROMANCE
YUM by Nicole Antonia Carson (YA)
Can Jim and his great-granddaughter Emily stop the carnage?

Brawn Stroker's Dragula: The Journal of Dee Flaytable by Nicole Antonia Carro (Mature Readers)
When the Vampire Queens battle, who will win?
Dragula is pure smut. Enjoy!

HEART SEARCH SERIES by Carlie M.A. Cullen (New Adult)
HEART SEARCH, book one: Lost, HEART SEARCH, book two: Found
One bite starts it all...Fate toys with mortals and immortals alike, as two hearts torn apart by darkness face ordeals which test them to their limits.

THE GUARDIAN SERIES by Joan Hazel (New Adult)
Book I THE LAST GUARDIAN, Book II BURDENS OF A SAINT
Delta Pack is an elite force of shape-shifters charged with maintaining order in both the shifter and human communities. High adventure and sizzling romance!

HIRED BY A DEMON by Gypsy Madden (YA)
A simple babysitting position goes terribly awry for Vara…Urban fantasy at its best!

GIRLS CAN'T BE KNIGHTS by Lee French (YA urban paranormal)

~~~

SCIENCE FICTION
LAND OF NOD SERIES by Gary Hoover (Appropriate for all ages)
Book I—The Artifact,
Book II - The Prophet
Jeff Browning has been haunted by terrifying dreams since the mysterious disappearance of his father (a renowned physicist). But when he finds a portal in his father's office, he must overcome his fears in an attempt to find him.

THE DREAM LAND Series BY Stephen Swartz
Book I Long Distance Voyager,
The Dream Land 2 - Dreams of Futures Past,

The Dream Land 3 - Diaspora
An epic of interdimensional intrigue, alien romance, and world domination by a couple of high school nerds mashed with psychological thriller and time travel.

MAZE BESET TRILOGY by Lee French (Superhero science fiction)
Dragons In Pieces
Dragons In Chains
Dragons In Flight
Superheroes in denim.

~~~

STEAMPUNK
THE CROWN PHOENIX SERIES by Alison DeLuca (Teen)
The Night Watchman Express
Devil's Kitchen
The Lamplighter's Special
The South Sea Bubble
A magic typewriter, time-travel, a mysterious train— high adventure written with Edwardian flair!

The Infinity Bridge (The Nu-Knights) by Ross M. Kitson (Teen)
Three teenagers are propelled into an action-packed race against time, involving alternate realities, airships, clockwork killers.... and Merlin.

~~~

LITERARY FICTION
AFTER ILIUM by Stephen Swartz (Mature readers)
Seduction and betrayal on the road to Ilium. An epic of interdimensional intrigue, alien romance, and world domination by a couple of high school nerds mashed with psychological thriller and time travel.

TALES FROM THE DREAMTIME by Connie J. Jasperson (Literary Fantasy, Mature Readers)
Three grownup Tales from the Dreamtime in one novella....A conversation with Galahad, a prince on a quest and a goddess in mourning, a stolen kingdom and the Fractal Mirror. Three tales of wonder and great deeds, three tales of heroes and villains.

HUW THE BARD by Connie J. Jasperson (Medieval Fantasy, Mature Readers)
Fleeing a burning city, everything he ever loved in ashes behind him, penniless and hunted, no place is safe. Abandoned and alone, Huw the Bard must somehow survive.

~~~

EPIC FANTASY

TOWER OF BONES SERIES by Connie J Jasperson (Epic Fantasy, Mature Readers)
Book I, Tower of Bones
Book II Forbidden Road
The Gods are at war, and Neveyah is the battleground.

DAMSEL IN DISTRESS by Lee French under Tangled Sky Press (Dark fantasy)
Even cut flowers can bloom.

PRISM SERIES by Ross M. Kitson (Epic Fantasy, Mature Readers)
Darkness Rising 1 – Chained
Darkness Rising 2 – Quest
Darkness Rising 3 – Secrets
Darkness Rising 4 – Loss
Darkness Rising 5 - Broken
Bravery is measured in moments. The forces of darkness are rising—and tragedy awaits even the most heroic.

THE GREATEST SIN SERIES by Lee French and Erik Kort under Tangled Sky Press (Epic fantasy)
    The Fallen
    Harbinger
    Moon Shades
Prophecy. Secrets. Lies. It's all an illusion

Made in the USA
Charleston, SC
30 May 2015